The Secrets of Wilder

–

A Story of
Inner Silence, Ecstasy and Enlightenment

Yogani

Cover photo: Sunrise at Fort George Inlet, Florida, circa 1972

AYP Publishing

For ordering information go to:

www.secretsofwilder.com

Library of Congress Control Number: 2005904455

Published simultaneously in:

Nashville, Tennessee, U.S.A.
and
London, England, U.K.

This title is also available in eBook format – ISBN 0-9764655-3-1 (for Adobe Reader)

ISBN 0-9764655-1-5 (Paperback)

"Blessed are they which do hunger and thirst after righteousness:
for they shall be filled."

Mathew 5:6

Table of Contents

Chapter 1 – The Question

Why not me?

John Wilder brushed the sun-bleached hair away from his eyes. The firm autumn wind blew it back again, but he didn't notice. Neither did he notice the steady roar of the surf coming over his shoulder. He sat high on the dune, his elbows resting on his bare raised knees and his head propped on his hands. He was transfixed by the miracle unfolding before him.

It came slithering out.

John fell on his side in the warm sand, intently watching the quivering creature perched uncertainly on the dead empty shell that clutched the strand of wind-wavering sea oats. It slowly, painstakingly, opened and dried itself in the morning sun. After a while it went up. He rolled on his back, smiling into the blue northeast Florida sky and its living texture of magic sparkling specks. And there, there it went, the butterfly, fluttering away on great golden wings. His eyes were wide with joy as it flew up, going gradually out of sight...

He didn't find a caterpillar changing into a delicate creature of the air very often. But when he did, he'd stop to witness the excruciating beauty of nature unfolding, feeling the fantastic mystery. He wanted to become a butterfly too. So strong was his longing to be transmuted that he made a vow that in this life he would find a way to become much more than a mere human being bound to the earth by this body and these thoughts.

He lay face-up in the sand pondering his eighteen years of humanity.

How will I get beyond this?

He gazed into the great breathing blue. A deep silence overtook him, enveloped him. His eyes closed slowly. He disappeared from the world. He didn't know where he was. Then he heard the woman's voice.

Come to me.

His eyes snapped open. He shot to his feet and looked around.

No one in sight.

"Who are you?" he called out nervously, looking around the great white mounds guarding the shore.

No one was there.

He'd been hearing the voice for a few weeks. It came when his longing settled deep inside where he was quiet. The voice seemed to come from inside him. Familiar, but he couldn't place it. Now it was gone again.

He sank back onto the sand and into the spiritual hunger that never left him.

After a while he got up, gazing at the massive shuttered Coquina Dame Hotel decaying behind the shelter of the dunes. He turned toward the sea and swooshed playfully down the great sand slope, his feet pointed inward like a slowing skier. He navigated between the clumps of tall blowing grass, looking past the huge surf and endless white caps to the rippling horizon.

A hurricane was whirling two hundred miles offshore, making its way from the Caribbean to the Carolina Outer Banks, yet another raging beauty passing by the concave coastline of the Jacksonville area. It was clear and sunny here, but the wind gushed in over the horizon, bringing the huge and chaotic sea with it. Its sweet salty mist beckoned him. It heaved rhythmically, tossing its waves on the wide beach, taunting him.

John gazed at the sea. "Is it you calling me?"

Nothing but the roar replied.

He threw off his T-shirt and ran into the warm seductive water, diving under a large wave as it curled over him hungrily. Then another, and another. He swam through the first line of waves heading for the outer break where they were three times the size. He dove under the walls of foam that came roaring down on him. A dozen dives later he reached the outer break. Tired, he treaded water as he bobbed over swells as big as two story houses, on the edge of breaking into boiling oblivion. The shore seemed miles away.

His adrenaline pumped with anticipation each time a wave lifted him high into the air.

I'll catch one. I know I can.

With a sideways snap of his head he whipped the hair and seawater from his eyes. The salty taste filled him. Then he smiled inwardly like a skydiver about to jump out of a plane with an untested parachute. The impending encounter produced a resonance in him. It was something deeply quiet, yet intensely pleasurable. He lived to become that. Sometimes he felt it in cross-country, when he was dashing for the finish line, on the verge of passing out, fighting to win again. He'd lose track of everything, even his body, yet, be more alive inside than at any other time – it was a dying that filled him with life. He was here challenging the sea to send him there.

When the next towering swell approached, he swam like mad to catch it. Catch it he did, a second too late. The tip of the wave licked the sky, on the edge of climax, and he was still on top instead of long gone down the slope heading for a survivable ride out front. It would have been better if he had been a few more seconds late. Then he'd only have to contend with the turbulent backwash behind the wave. No, he'd caught this one just wrong. He knew it as soon as he hadn't made the slope, finding himself on top with no place to go but into the abyss with tons of churning water falling in behind him.

He'd never been in this situation on a wave this big. He knew to curl up in a ball with his head between his knees and arms wrapped around his shins. He hoped he wouldn't hit the bottom too hard. When a wave crests it gets shallow in front, even this far out, and that is where he would land. He took his last breath and balled up as he and the water plummeted together. It was like going over Niagara Falls, minus the barrel.

Thunk ... whoosh... He hit bottom on his back. Half his air got away. He tumbled wildly. He kept his head tucked and hugged his shins in a death grip. He hung on to his remaining air. He'd need it until the wave left him behind, and maybe for the next one that could hit him when he came up.

It seemed like the thrashing currents went on for hours. His lungs were burning for air. Somehow he drew strength from the urgent sensation. It was a phenomenon he discovered in running, how a shortage of air could bring a mysterious energy from deep within him. But no pondering it now, except to be thankful that it was saving him from drowning. When he came up in the trail of light foam behind the departed wave, he was staring at another monster coming over him like a hungry predator. He gulped air and went down, back into the ball, splattering on the bottom as the whole Atlantic Ocean crashed down on him. His ball came apart. The air was smashed out of him.

He was dazed, disoriented, on the verge of blacking out. Would this be it? Should he breathe in the great sea and become one with all of life? He saw a light and instinctively swam toward it. He broke the surface into the air, gasping an in-breath. If another wave had hit him then, he'd have been gone for sure. He took a few desperate breaths and then looked around. He was in a lull – nothing but a thin trail of foam between him and the safety of shore. He could make it if he went now.

He turned back out. He could see the mountainous swells coming at him from far out. It was an easy decision – he went straight out toward them. He fought his way under a string of giant waves to get back to the outer break. He was aching, raw, exhausted. But finally he got there and was being lifted high over the tops of the huge walls of water again, ready to try again. This was all that mattered.

He summoned all his breath. "I'm going to ride one of you if it kills me!" he cried, waving his fist at the endless procession of mammoths rolling in toward him from the hurricane over the horizon.

One arrived soon enough. His arms and legs felt like rubber as he flailed to catch it. This time he managed to get in front of it, but not too far. He hit it just right and came down the giant slope head first, arms trailing on his sides, screaming all the way.

"Yeeeehaaaa!"

The wave exploded, burying him in white behind the leading edge of the roaring water. He maintained his board-like posture. He knew he had it. He could feel himself skidding down the hill under the foam. Then his head and shoulders popped out, established in front of the white conflagration and flying toward the beach. When he and the wave approached the inside break, the wave slowed and he started swimming again, catching it as it broke for the second time, much smaller by now. He rode it all the way to the beach, stopping short on the firm sand like a fighter jet landing on an aircraft carrier.

He rolled on his back, exhausted, as the remnants of the great wave receded past his beaten body, sucked back into the sea. He spread his arms and legs out wide in the wet sand and started to laugh, shaking all over.

"Wheweeee!"

Still laughing, John got up and staggered toward his shirt.

Six middle-aged walkers were gathered there. They'd been watching the crazy kid getting pounded by the wild surf a hundred yards out. Their apparent leader, a man in Bermuda shorts with a large sunburned belly and Panama hat, came up to him.

"Are you all right, son? We were about to go for help."

John grinned. "Oh yeah, I'm okay." He turned toward the sea, squinting with a slight cock of his head, and then slowly back to the man. "Some surf, huh?"

"Looks dangerous out there. Did you know what you were doing?"

John shook his head hard, blubbering his lips and slinging water on the man's reddish feet. "Just barely." He wiped his face with his shirt. Then he started jumping up and down on one foot with his head tipped to get the water out of his ear. Drops of salty sea fell to the sand from his shaggy hair.

"The ride ... was it worth the risk?" the man asked.

"For me? Yeah. There's something in it besides the ride."

"Like what?" The man took off his hat, scratched his bald head, and quickly covered it again.

John looked up at the blazing sun and then into the man's sunglassed eyes. "It's hard to explain, sir. It's a kind of inner opening. A going beyond."

"Going beyond? Beyond what?"

"Don't you think there could be more than what we are seeing here?" As the words came out, John made a slow wide gesture with an outstretched arm, encompassing the land and the sea.

The man followed John's hand. "Well, no ... I don't think so, son."

John's arm hung in the air for a second, like and unfinished sentence, and then dropped to his side. It splatted against his soggy cutoffs. His facial expression also hung in the air a few more seconds... "Anyway, that's why I was out there."

He pulled on his shirt, gave the man, the woman behind him and the two other touristy-looking couples a wet salty salute, and took off trotting north along the waterline in his pigeon-toed way. As he sped up, his hands opened loosely, and his fingers began flicking downward conspicuously with each accelerating step. He sure didn't look like a high school state champion cross-country runner. But that's what he was, two years in a row.

The walkers watched him go, that short wiry teenager who gave himself to the raging sea, came out laughing, spouted a few mystic bits and trotted off like that. After a minute, he was but a dot on the shore as he sped away.

The house was three miles up the beach, near the north end of Coquina Island. The sun was high in the sky. Morning had yielded to mid day. The wild surf and steady northeast wind clothed the shoreline in a thin luminous mist. John ran through the white sun-drenched moisture, his slender legs slicing through the mounds of foam that were scattered on the beach. The exhilaration of the surf and the exertion of running made him feel bigger inside.

Never mind the pain. Maybe if I run hard enough I can burst from this body that confines me. I'll try.

He ran faster on the hard wet sand ... and faster.

After all, if a caterpillar can do it...

By the time he got home he was breathing hard and shining with sweat. As he came up the long wooden walkway over the dunes, he heard a shout.

"Hey, squirt, where you been?"

"Kurt? You back from Florida State already?" John called. "You just left last week,"

Kurt Wilder stood among the palms at the top of the faded wooden steps leading up the big dune to the veranda in front of the house. He had one hand on each rail, blocking John's path.

"Not again," John said as he trudged up the stairs.

"Just like old times," Kurt said. "It'll cost you a buck to get through."

"I don't have a buck. Do I look like I have a buck?" John held out his arms, revealing all he had on him was one pair of wet cutoffs and one sweaty gray T-shirt with a fading *Duval High Cross-Country* on the front. "Even if I had a buck, what makes you think I'd give it to a moron like you?"

"Hey, screw you." Kurt stood his ground. He was four years older and six feet tall, nearly half a foot taller than his younger brother.

John went up the stairs toward Kurt. *Seems every time I come up these steps, he's waiting for me.*

When he got to the top, he stopped.

Kurt had a big grin on his acne-scarred face. "Hi, dreamer."

John tried to press through and Kurt gave him a knee, sending him half way back down the stairs. John came right back up.

Kurt released one hand just as he arrived. "Whatcha been doing out there?"

John knew Kurt didn't care for the beach or the sea, usually referring to them collectively as, *out there.* Kurt's taste was more for games of conquest, which included chess, Risk, and student politics.

"Not much. Thanks for the free pass," John said as he went by, limping slightly on the knee he banged on the way down the stairs.

There was no way he could tell Kurt about the butterfly. He wasn't sure himself why he had such strong and giddy feelings about it. So how was he going to explain it to his pain-in-the-ass big brother? Kurt would just as soon squash the bug, so what would be the point? But to John, it meant everything – the changing ... the changing. It filled him with wonder.

As John headed to the house, and the solitude of his room, he wondered why he got so worked up about something as simple as a butterfly. Why did such things attract him so strongly? His life seemed to be about breaking through to something. But what? He was more concerned about himself than the butterfly, or Kurt. His strongest interests were limited to what even he considered dubious. He loved pondering his nebulous inner possibilities, and indulged himself freely in that. He knew his parents were concerned. So was he. It was his senior year and he had no plans. *What's wrong with me? And that voice, that woman calling inside me. Who is she?*

By the time he crossed the lawn between the house and the pool, Kurt had caught up. "Wanna go swimming?"

"No thanks." Kurt's idea of swimming was wallowing in the pool like a manatee, vomiting business and politics.

"Gotta go. See ya later." John was in the side door of the sprawling weather beaten cedar shingled house and heading up the creaking back stairs three at a time. He traversed the long musty hall on the third floor, went into his room and shut the door. The skeleton-key lock clicked.

It was here that he had his most exciting adventures.

Chapter 2 – Plans and Secrets

The twin engine Cessna roared off the runway at North Atlanta Municipal Airport. Harry Wilder watched the city spread out under them as he took the plane up. Straight and winding roads penetrated the green neighborhoods. Most were clogged with cars, spurting occasionally like blood cells through narrow arteries.

"Here we go, Sam," Harry yelled over the loud drone of the engines. "Glad you could make the trip."

Sam looked down uncertainly as the urban sprawl passed under them. They banked south, headed for the Big Bend of Florida, the huge elbow that hugs the Gulf of Mexico, a sparsely populated region known for its inhospitable cypress swamps and meticulously cultivated southern pine timberland.

"I've heard great things about the mill you built for Big Bend Paper down there," Sam shouted back. "Appreciate the offer for the tour."

"My pleasure." Harry checked the instruments. *Sam is going to love this mill. It's the perfect prototype for Southeastern's Alabama Project.*

"You know," Harry said. "In the fifteen years Wilder Corp's been at it, the Big Bend job is by far the slickest mill we've done. It's state of the art. Highly automated. A real moneymaker."

"How'd you get into mill design?" Sam said.

"What?" Harry yelled.

"How'd you get started."

"Oh, when Stella and I came down from New York, we had nothing. I just wanted to design and build. It's in the blood, you know."

Sam nodded through the noise.

Harry continued, "We started small with mill rehabs around Jacksonville. Then we got into the Delta joint venture."

"Oh, yeah, I remember those mills," Sam yelled. "You worked on those? Great projects. All on time and in budget weren't they?"

"Yep. Then we got the Carolina jobs. And then Big Bend."

"Some fifteen years you've had," Sam said.

"We got into other markets too."

"Yeah?"

Civil especially – bridges and office buildings. Now we're bidding on Interstate highway upgrade work all over Florida."

"No kidding?"

"We've got good people in Jacksonville. Great leadership, great project teams."

"Sounds like Florida's been good to you."

"It's great," Harry said. "We've got a place on the beach on Coquina Island. Stella and the boys love it."

"You've got sons?"

"Yeah, Kurt's the oldest. He's a business major at Florida State. John's a senior in high school. He's ... ahhh, a runner. But enough about us. How are those pretty daughters of yours doing? Is it true you've got one headed for Harvard?"

By the time they got to the Big Bend area, it was mid-afternoon and the sky was thickening with showers. The closer they got, the less visibility they had. The rural airstrip they were headed for had no instruments, and Harry had to bring the plane down low to see the ground – too low. He found the Gulf coast and was heading south, picking his way along, looking for something familiar.

"Hey, there's the mill!" Sam shouted, pointing to the east as it came into view through the rain. The pungent odor of wood pulp processing filled the plane and their nostrils. "It smells like money, doesn't it?"

"Sure does," Harry said. "But we're too far south. The strip's a few miles north of here." He banked the plane inland around the pulp mill and they headed north. The rain thickened. By now, they were just a few hundred feet above the ground. Harry figured they'd see the strip and be landing in a minute.

"Now, somewhere around here…"

"Look out!" Sam yelled.

"Oh shit!" Harry turned hard right. The aircraft banked away, whining like a dive-bomber as it peeled right in the severe turn. They missed the microwave tower by a few feet.

Harry got the plane leveled just as they skimmed the tops of the pines. He pulled hard on the yoke and brought them up. Finally, he turned to Sam. "That was close."

"You're not kidding." Sam was white, and the sweat was running down his temples. "Let's get this damn thing on the ground."

The airstrip came into view through the rain and Harry touched down as smooth as he could on the weed-infested asphalt.

Despite the rough start, the pulp mill visit was a success, and Wilder Corp got the Alabama project. But Sam flew commercial from then on.

Harry and Stella were moving into the upper echelon of Jacksonville society. The big hundred-year-old cedar shingled house on the wooded dune overlooking the ocean suited them well. It was a far cry from their first little hole-in-the-wall in Brooklyn, New York all those years ago. The five-acre property was covered with live oaks and palms. A long driveway wound up the hill from Beach Road.

They were proud of their boys. Harry wanted them both to join Wilder Corp after college, and eventually take over. Both had worked part time summer jobs there since they were sixteen.

It all seemed too perfect.

"Dinner!" Stella called as she put the food on the big oak table in the kitchen.

"Pot roast. My favorite," Kurt came in and took his seat. He was home from school for the weekend and was enjoying the nostalgic meal even before he dug in. He'd long since gotten his weight under control, and could afford it now.

Harry came in from the study. "Where's our athlete?"

"Oh, runner boy is locked in his room again," Kurt said.

"That boy. Will you get him, Kurt?" Stella said. She was admiring the symmetry of the table she had set.

"Mom!" Kurt complained.

"Go on. The climb'll do you good," Harry said as he stabbed a slab of pot roast.

Kurt went into the foyer and hollered up to the third floor through the center of the spiraling banisters. "John!"

He listened – no answer.

"John!"

Still no answer.

"Shit." Kurt began to climb, hollering "John!" every few steps on the way up. By the time he was about to start up the last flight leading to the third floor, John appeared on the landing. He looked otherworldly. His eyes were glazed.

"I'm coming," he said in a voice that was barely present.

"Thanks," Kurt said.

"Thanks for what?"

"Thanks for not waiting until I was on the third floor before you came out."

John laughed. He was coming back to life, and in good spirits too.

"I knew I messed up somehow –" He bounded down the stairs four at a time with his funny gimp, leaving Kurt far behind.

"Jeeesus," Kurt muttered as he ambled back downstairs. His jack-rabbit brother had always been a mystery to him, and to a lot of people. How could such a weirdo be so fast?

During the meal, Harry was quiet. Kurt wasn't sure, but it looked like he had some news or something. Finally he spoke.

"How are things at school, John? Did you get all the classes you wanted?"

"Yeah, it's not too bad."

"How does the cross country team look this year?"

"I've got a challenger. There's a new guy, Jimmy Marco. Man, he can run. I have to fight to keep ahead of him. He is going to do the mile in spring track too. Coach Johnson tried to get me for the mile last year, but I said no. I'm much better in a long race. Jimmy can do both. He's amazing."

"A challenge never hurts, does it?" Harry said.

"No, not at all." John put his head down closer to his plate as he ate, like he knew what was coming next. By now, Kurt knew too.

"Have you given any more thought to college?"

"Well, I don't know exactly what to do, Dad."

To Kurt it looked like John was talking to his mashed potatoes.

"How do you mean? You're going to keep your grades up this year, aren't you?

"Yeah, but I'm not sure I want to go to college."

"No? How will you make a living?"

"I don't know, but I feel there is something else for me, and wrapping myself up in college seems like it will be a distraction."

"A distraction? A distraction from what?"

"I don't know."

Kurt was enjoying this. He could see their father was getting wound up. He watched as Harry took a deep breath.

"Well, if I understand correctly you don't want to go to college because you feel it will distract you from you don't know what. Does that make any sense to you, Stella?"

Stella winced. "Well, he just doesn't know what he wants to do yet…" Her fearful eyes wanted to leave the room. It looked like she was clutching the chair under her to keep from running.

Kurt watched his mother's face writhing with discomfort. Her aversion to conflict disgusted him. She'd do almost anything to avoid it. He'd never let himself be like her. It was her spineless vulnerability that drove him to fight for dominance over whomever he was around.

"Exactly," Harry said, his voice getting louder. "That's why people go to college, so they can find out what they want to do, and be progressing with at least a general education while they are finding out. I don't know what you are going find out hanging around here, John."

"Something," John said softly but firmly. Kurt saw he was looking straight at their father now.

"Something?"

"Yeah, something."

"Okay," Harry said in an exasperated tone. "I'll have to take your word for it, because I don't have an inkling what you're talking about."

"I know it isn't easy, Dad. Just give me some time. That's what I need right now. Some time to figure things out. I know I need to keep myself available for something. When I know what it is, I will let you know."

"Okay, son." Harry speared half a dozen string beans and shoved them in his mouth.

Stella seemed to shrink. Her perfectly fixed hair and crisp patterned blouse were not protecting her. Her life was based on appearances, and appearances meant nothing at this table.

There was a long silence while they ate.

"Way to go, John," Kurt finally said. "You just promised to make something out of nothing. When will you tell us what that something will be?"

"I'm going to be making something leftover for tomorrow if you three don't eat all this." Stella looked proud as she mounted her counterattack on the disharmony that invaded her pristine kitchen.

They all took another helping, but Kurt could see the tension between John and their father remained. He knew his mother's extreme fear of disorder, and everyone's awareness of it, was all that was preventing a good knock-down, drag-out at the dinner table. He, on the other hand, thrived on it. "Come on, Mom, don't change the subject. I really want to know how to make something out of nothing."

Stella started to shrink again.

"That's enough, Kurt," Harry said.

"But, Dad, aren't you curious how he –"

"Eat your dinner, Kurt," Harry said, dodging Stella's burgeoning fear, the tyranny that ruled her life, and gnawed insidiously at the three Wilder men as well.

All that was left was the clinking of the silverware on the plates as they ate.

Kurt knew that John had a special gift, and that it was somehow spiritual. He knew John was much smarter than he was too, and resented it. He sensed John would do great things. Whatever his *something* turned out to be, he knew it would be big. He did not have John's spiritual ambitions, if that's what they were, but he was ambitious. He had been one of those students in high school who didn't stand out very much. Back then, his pudginess and acne assured that no one who was anyone wanted to be seen with him.

But Kurt was smart enough, and he worked hard. He got good grades and harbored dreams of wealth and power. He was aggressive, enterprising ... and ruthless. He had the traits necessary for a successful adulthood in the material world, and he knew it. College had been his coming out, and he was ready to do whatever was necessary to get ahead.

But none of this hidden strength made it any easier for him in his awkward youth, and he carried the scars of it. He grew up being teased or ignored, which only strengthened his resolve to control the lives of others. That, and his fear of being a spineless weakling like his mother...

Of everyone Kurt knew, John was most decent, the most sincere. He wondered why John put up with him. He was the one person Kurt could pick on while growing up, without fear of retribution. And he was still in the habit, even though they were both grown. John had determination, grace and humor, an incredible combination that could open doors. It was in his eyes. Even so, Kurt could not resist the temptation to exploit him any way he could, being the enterprising person that he was. It was how he treated everyone.

John's room was his cave, his sanctum, the place where he conducted his deepest thinking and self-discovery. He explored himself fully there, delving into the strange and powerful forces churning in his loins, filling himself with the mysterious energy, exploding into the great all-consuming releases to nothingness. He wasn't sure what these experiences were about except that they were sex. But that hardly explained it. Hardly explained it at all. The feelings seemed bigger and more far-reaching than the simple act of reproduction. At times he felt he was floating off the bed in the midst of his persistent reveries. He was determined to get to the bottom of it. He knew if he continued to explore himself he would eventually find the answer.

Since his explorations began to go noticeably deeper the year before, John began to write about his experiences in a big three-ring notebook that he kept stashed under his bed amidst the rubble of old running shoes, books and a long-forgotten Tonka truck. The first blue-lined page in the notebook read simply, *"The Secrets of Wilder."* A hundred pages followed, covered with his distinctive scrawl. Little did he know that the hundred pages would turn into thousands, or that the world would be changed by his life and writings.

Orgasm, while all consuming and instinctively mandatory, was not John's favorite thing. It ended the journey within him, at least temporarily. He knew there was more. It was the long pleasuring in front of orgasm that produced the most lasting effect. When he could stay in front for an hour, and then stop, he would find himself filled with peace and an enjoyable luminous sensation for hours afterwards. In such a state, he would practically float out of his room to wherever he was going. He could run like lightning in that state. The trophies on the bookcase were a testament to the secret energy he cultivated. But it wasn't about that kind of winning.

When engaged in his *practice*, as he called it, his eyes would drift upward, coaxing a strange pleasurable current up through him like a golden breath. His tongue would be drawn back on the roof of his mouth. Sometimes his head would shake rapidly from side to side. Often he would become completely lost in the experience, forgetting he had a body at all, losing awareness of his surroundings. He would become thoughtless, nearly breathless, needing nothing, and fully awake inside. He tried to recreate the sensations without physically stimulating himself, in his mind, with his feelings. He reasoned that there might be more ways into it. Whatever would take him into that expanded zone of immortal well-being.

He craved these experiences. His heart became deeply attached to them. He devoted more and more time to his explorations. The quest consumed him. It was why he ran cross-country so fearlessly, often to the edge of collapse. He took risks that others would not consider. The expansive inner experience was to be found on the edge where everything let go. Why? He didn't know. He wanted to find out. He wanted to have more control over his daily routine so he could experiment on himself. He knew he would lose it if he went off to college.

John was addicted to a powerful drug ... his own ecstasy. Each day he worked to extend his bliss states.

Is this right? Am I out of control?

He felt guilt about what he was doing. But he could not stop. The silent power it gave him was too great, and the pleasure too consuming. He was aware that people could notice a presence emerging in him. He sensed he was on a journey.

Is it wrong to seek the source of all that I am?

He didn't feel he had a choice. He had to find the way inward. He would learn the secrets of himself, or die trying. He had to know the truth.

His need to find the hidden truth in his sexuality overshadowed the longings for a mate that bubbled up in him. Would he ever have a lover? What woman could ever understand his compulsion? His friends were interested in girls, in *getting laid*, as they put it. He was interested in God.

This was the *something* of John Wilder. But he could tell no one. Not yet. Not until he could put more of the pieces together.

Chapter 3 – Those Eyes

She had on the frumpiest dress she could find. Her hair was pinned up in a bun, and her face was adorned with the thick-rimmed plastic glasses she'd bought at the drug store a long time ago.

Devi Duran imagined herself to be invisible. At five feet two, she felt like she could disappear if she tried hard enough. She wanted to. She held her breath as she entered Duval High, holding her books close to her bosom and praying that she'd somehow be able to conceal the terrible secret that everyone knew; that her mother and brother had been brutally murdered two years before. The illusion had succeeded for many months. For the most part, everyone left her alone. They looked on curiously, sometimes sympathetically, and gave her the space she needed. Even so, certain boys looked at her hungrily, for under her disguise an incredible beauty was bound up, and they could see it. They could feel it. She turned her eyes and body away from them.

No. All they want is to exploit me.

At home, in her room, Devi tried to let herself breathe. First, she let her hair down. It fell off her shoulders in waves of shimmering black. She removed her clothes slowly as she stood in front of the mirror on the closet door. She looked at her exquisite proportions, and the sultry energy buried in her eyes. She ran a hand down her hip. Her light brown skin was soft, on the edge of moist. She remembered what her mother told her shortly before she died:

"Enjoy yourself fully in private, my dear. Your beauty and your light are God-given gifts. Accept no man into your heart but he who will love you until the end of time. When you find him, give to him your soul. In doing so you will save his, and your own."

Devi clung to these words. Her mother had been filled with love and compassion, the great granddaughter of a temple courtesan in India, and skilled in the arts of love. She gave herself to a handsome American merchant marine, Charles Duran, and came to this strange land of contradictions where great promise and deep darkness seem to mingle on every street corner, and in every heart.

Charles went into the tug boat business on the great St. Johns River, and they made their home on Coquina Island. Joe and Devi were born here. When Devi reached puberty, her mother shared with her the secrets of cultivating inner pleasure.

But none of it mattered anymore. Mama was gone, Joe was gone, and Devi was a young woman alone, left with this consuming longing for completeness, and this fear of the world – a world conspiring to destroy all beautiful things. Would she be next to be murdered by the insane, racist Lashers? Their sordid family history went back generations to the earliest days of the Ku Klux Klan – their fixation was on projecting hate and violence toward the mixing of the races, including white and East Indian. The threat hung over Devi like a guillotine. She knew not when it would fall again. But she couldn't give up completely. More than anything she wanted love. She wanted it more than life. Somehow love would lead her to freedom. *Does my lover wait for me? Oh God, please help me find him.*

A wave of desperate sorrow welled up in her. She began to weep in front the mirror. She wept for her dead mother. She wept for her dead brother. She wept for her father who was left alone too, and had taken to drink. But, most of all, she wept for herself. The tears dripped down her cheeks onto her body. She needed to be consoled. Her sorrow mingled with her passion. She couldn't prevent her hands from gliding up her hips. She lightly spread the tears across her breasts. She held the sacred talisman hanging around her neck tenderly for a moment. Her mother gave it to her the week before she died. Her hands slid down over her firm belly and then lower. She began a long stirring of the fire that smoldered deep within her. Her eyes went up in lonesome ecstasy. Here she found some comfort.

It was the second week of school. John Wilder closed his locker in the noisy corridor at Duval High. He worked his way through the throng of students on his way to his first class, English literature. He went through the chicken-wire windowed door and found a seat near the back of the packed classroom. The teacher had not arrived yet, and he sat quietly observing the din.

A pen fell on the floor and rolled against his sneaker. As he leaned to pick it up, something hit him hard on the side of his head.

Bonk...

"Oww!" a sweetly irate feminine voice cried.

Halfway bent over, with his hand on his head, he turned and there was Devi Duran, a few inches away, her hand on the side of her head too.

"I'm sorry," he said as he rubbed his head. "Are you all right?"

"What do you think?"

Her dark eyes flashed through her glasses. He was transfixed for a second.

He picked up the pen. "I think this is yours." He placed it carefully on the writing board of her chair. "I was only trying to help."

"I know." Her eyes darted away. She was straightening her glasses and still rubbing her head. She looked flustered. "I didn't mean to scold you."

"You didn't scold me. I should've looked before I leaned over. My fault." He peered at her through the noise of the classroom. Her eyes came back, and he got that feeling again. They were like magnets pulling him in.

"What?" she said.

He didn't say anything.

"What?" She opened her eyes wide, mocking his gaze.

He blinked. "Sorry. I do that sometimes."

"Do what?"

"Stare. Well, not stare, really. Get lost is probably more like it."

"Oh?"

"You are Devi?"

"Yes, and you are John?"

He smiled. "We meet at last."

"At last?"

"Yeah, we've been going to this place for years, and we meet at last. And so gracefully too."

She smiled.

"I'm forgiven?"

"For now."

"Thank God," he said.

Their eyes reconnected and he was getting lost again. He wanted to go deeper. But something in her scared him, something unfathomable. He could tell she feared him too, though she now met his gaze with determination. Her eyes reached deep into his soul, seeming to inquire, *Are you the one*?

His inclination had always been to go straight into the jaws of his fear. Invariably he ended up better off, though usually for a price. *What is she about, this plainly dressed girl in the bun with those eyes behind the glasses that make me want to dive in?* Like everyone, he'd heard the story of the death of her mother and brother, and that explained something about her. He wanted to find out more.

John watched Mr. Culpepper, tall, tan and disheveled, walk into the chaotic classroom and begin waving his arms.

"Hello, hello, hello, everyone!"

When the final rustling faded he put on a look of deep discontent. "Now, will someone please tell me, what are we doing here in August? Doesn't the school board know that summer isn't over yet? Wouldn't you rather be on the beach?"

"Yeaaah!" the class cried in unison.

"Me too. Well, like it or not, here we are. We shall try and make the best of it." He took a small brown book out of his battered briefcase and wrote three lines on the blackboard:

...Two roads diverged in a wood, and I –
I took the one less traveled by,
And that has made all the difference...

"Does anyone know what this is from?" Mr. Culpepper said, pointing to it over his shoulder with a chalky hand.

A studious-looking Filipino girl in front said, "It's from *The Road Not Taken*, by Robert Frost,"

John didn't hear it. He was absorbed in the three lines.

"That's right, Wendy. Would anyone like to comment on what these words mean?"

John raised his hand. He rarely did.

"Yes, John Wilder, in the back."

"It means that going your own way instead of everyone else's can make all the difference."

"That's a pretty good answer," Mr. Culpepper said. "And that's pretty good advice for all of us. Now maybe, just maybe, this class can be a road less traveled, and maybe it will make all the difference. Whether you walk it or not is for each of you to decide."

Yep. John understood that. He knew it applied to every choice in life, to do what others expected or to do what one must, regardless of the consequences.

The discussion continued, and John's mind went quiet. He heard and absorbed all that Mr. Culpepper was saying. He liked him, because he cared and tried to inspire the students. From time to time, he'd look over and get caught in Devi's eyes again. She seemed to know what he was feeling as she gave him looks that reached deep into him, moving him inexplicably. *Whew...*

But more than anything, he was in his silence, the place from where he watched all things, the place from where he directed his unconventional fledgling life. He did not know exactly what this place in him was, but he knew he could not be touched there, and this is what enabled him to walk through his fear. Whatever it was that gave him this separateness, this independence, even from those beautiful eyes sitting next to him, he wanted more of it. He didn't mind appearing to be a bit detached at times. He didn't expect to be in two places at once, at least not yet.

Before John knew it, class was over and he was gathering up his notes and getting ready to leave. He turned to Devi.

"Are you going upstairs?"

"Yes, I'm in your history class too, remember?" She gave him a *What, are you a dope?* look.

"May I walk with you?" he said.

"Only if you promise not to whack me in the head again."

"Cross my heart," he said, making the gesture.

They went out through the mob of milling students and up the well-worn stairs at the end of the corridor.

When Devi got home that afternoon the first thing she did was dive into her closet. The uninteresting clothes came flying out over her shoulder scattering onto the bedroom floor behind her. She was looking for something she could wear the next day – something nice, not too inviting, but definitely not unflattering. As she rummaged, she began to hum a tune to a song she and her mother used to sing together on the back porch as they watched boats pass by on the Intracoastal Waterway. They called them *snowbird boats*, because they were northerners cruising south for the winters and north for the summers.

Then she let out a laugh ... she realized she was happy, actually happy, for the first time since that fateful day two years ago.

Am I finally coming back to life? She found two outfits that would be acceptable until she could get to the store for more, and moved them to the front of the rung in the closet. She gathered the rest off the floor and threw them all toward the small trashcan in the corner of her room. They buried it under nondescript floral patterns. *Good riddance.*

She turned away from the heap. *This John Wilder, he is so kind, so smart, and so mysterious. And now he is interested in me.*

She had known of him for some time. Everyone knew about his accomplishments in cross-country. His endurance and dramatic finishes were legendary. He even crawled to win a race once after collapsing a few feet from the finish line. But no one knew him really. When he wasn't running, he practically disappeared. He was kind of a loner. Not like the other boys at all, and this is what attracted her.

The icky dress fell to the floor for the last time, and joined the pile in the corner. She changed into jeans and a halter, and sat in front of the vanity, brushing her hair as she hummed. It felt so good running the stiff bristles over her scalp and down through her long black shining mane. It sent prickly waves of pleasure all through her. Her flesh stood up as she reveled in the radiant surging energy running up and down her body. She filled her hands with her hair and put her face in it, breathing in the sweet smell. She let it go. It cascaded down over her breasts. She shook her head and looked into in the mirror.

Should I wear it down tomorrow? Yes, it's time.

Lately, she'd become more concerned about her withdrawn condition than about the tragedy that had caused it. *That knock on the head from John Wilder must have been fate. It's time for me to get on with my –*

Suddenly there was a crash and the whole house shook.

Devi jumped up and ran out through the living room and out the front door. In the yard, wedged between the big live oak tree and the corner of the house, was her father's Bronco. Charles Duran was slumped over the wheel.

"Oh my God!"

She ran over, hair flying, and yanked open the door. "Papa! Papa! Are you all right?"

She pulled him carefully off the wheel and leaned him back against the seat.

He began to move, turning his head slowly toward her.

"Well, hello, darlin'. Did you hear me park?" His breath was strong with whisky.

"Papa! Don't you know you shouldn't drive when you've been drinking?"

"But how'll I get home to you, darlin'?"

"I'll come and get you. Just have someone call."

"Whatever you say, dear."

"Papa, that's what you said last time when you nearly drove into the waterway. What am I going to do with you?"

"I'm sorry. I'm sorry. You deserve better than me."

"Now quit that. You know I love you and will always take care of you. But you have to help."

She hauled him down out of the truck and held him up as she navigated crookedly across the yard. Charles Duran was a burly tug boat captain, and twice his daughter's size. She nearly collapsed under his weight as they staggered through the front door. They made it to his recliner in the living room and she unrolled him into it like a rug. In half a minute he was sound asleep.

Early the next morning, Charles Duran sat at the breakfast table with a headache, sipping hot coffee and looking ashamed. Devi came in, all ready for school. She had on an attractive skirt and blouse. Her hair danced down her shoulders like black rain. The glasses were gone, replaced by a modest amount of makeup. She didn't need much.

"You are beautiful, darlin'," he said. "You're always beautiful, but especially today."

"Thank you, Papa," she said. "I need some clothes. Do you mind if I drive to the mall after school and charge a few things?"

He paused, looking into the brown mug. "Yeah, go. I'm so happy to see you dressing up again. You haven't done that since your mother and brother went out that night –" He stopped himself, putting the cup back up to his mouth.

"It's okay, Papa," she said. "I just think it's time to get on with our lives, don't you?"

"I do, but it's hard, you know."

"Yeah," she said. "It's hard."

She wished she could give him what he needed to go on. But it had to come from inside him. She knew that now. There was no way she'd be wanting to get to know John Wilder if there wasn't something in her that wanted to live, pulling her out of her grief and depression. Her father hadn't found it yet. She hoped he would.

"I'll be here for you, Papa. Please don't drink after you get back to dock today. Promise me."

"I'll try," he said, visibly trying to shake off his hangover. "We've got a big cruise ship comin' in and they'll be needin' an extra tug. I may be late."

Devi prayed he'd come home sober.

"I'll have dinner on the stove for you," she said.

She got up, kissed him, and went out. As she drove to school she was tingling with anticipation.

I wonder if John will recognize me?

Chapter 4 – Initiation

It was Tuesday afternoon and John was cruising up A1A with the top down on his way home. He wasn't thinking about much. He was in his silence. The sun beat down on him from the clear blue sky.

Then he heard her inside again.

Come to me.

He slammed on the brakes. The dusty red 1972 Buick convertible skidded to the side of the road. He jumped up and stood on the driver's seat, looking around in all directions.

"Where are you?"

The traffic hummed up and down along A1A, the palm-lined backbone of Coquina Island. The row of old wooden houses that lined the once-sleepy boulevard looked back at him sadly in their gaudy commercial clothes.

Then it hit him. *Of course – it's not far from here.* He dropped back into the hot vinyl bucket seat and floored it, screeching back out into the traffic. Three blocks later he took a sharp left down Tropical Lane. He wound back until there were no houses and the road turned into packed sand. *Maybe this is it. Lord knows I've looked everywhere else.*

John drove into the empty lime-rock graveled parking lot of the Island Christian Church. The wheels crunched to a stop at the edge of the uncut grass. He got out and took the path through the palm grove. The breeze coming off the ocean a mile away rustled through the thick palm fronds above. Soon he came to the large white wood frame church with its adjoining fellowship hall.

When he got to the fellowship hall he went up the steps he'd climbed so many Sundays as a child. It had been years since he had been here. There had always been something magic about this place, and he could feel it again now. His heart surged with emotion as he pulled open the double doors with both hands and went in.

It looked the same. First he noticed the long rafters high above. Under them, the cavernous hall was divided into multiple classrooms on both sides by big child-art-decorated bulletin boards on wheels. The center of the room was set up with neat rows of folding chairs for the services that were held for the children before Sunday school class each week. There was an aisle down the middle. He walked slowly to the front, to the white draped table under the plain wooden cross hanging on the wall. There was a stand on the table with a large Bible on it, open, waiting for his eyes. He looked down at it and read the first words he saw:

...his delight is in the law of the Lord;
and in his law doth he meditate day and night.

It was the first Psalm. He felt a spark of recognition, something, but what did it mean? He looked up at the old brown cross that had been hanging there on the wall for as long as he could remember. And what did that mean? Sacrifice? It looked so static.

No, this can't be it. He walked back up the aisle toward the door. He was about to leave, but stopped. Something moved him to call the one name that might help him. He turned.

"Mrs. Jensen!" His words echoed among the old wood rafters above. "Mrs. Jensen! Are you here?"

To his surprise, he heard a muffled voice. It seemed to come from behind the cross.

"Who is it?"

"It's John ... John Wilder," he called across the large room, doubting for a second that he'd heard anyone.

An old woman appeared at the side door in front of the hall. They walked slowly toward each other.

Christi Jensen was stooped over. She had a bad limp and a black cane with a smooth white ivory handle on top in her gnarled hand. Her curly white hair framed a face withered by a life of ambitious seeking. She wore wire Ben Franklin glasses and a plain blue dress. Over many years, she'd become an expert on the scriptures looking through those glasses, and on people looking over them, especially young people. Her penetrating green-rimmed blue eyes shone as bright as ever.

"John? Oh my goodness, it's you," she said. They met in the center of the hall and embraced. "How you've grown, my boy."

John stepped back shyly. "You look just as good as ever," he said softly.

"Flattery will get you everywhere," she said, taking his arm. He felt a prickly sensation going up from where she touched him. "We have missed you these past few years. I've read about your running in the paper. I'm so proud of you."

"Thanks."

She gestured to the nearest row of folding chairs, and they sat down.

"And how is your relationship with God these days?"

He knew she'd get right to the point. She always did. It is what he admired most in her when he was a child.

"I'm struggling," he said. "Something is happening, but I'm not sure what."

"Something is happening? Ah..." She stroked her wrinkled chin.

"Something is calling from inside me. I want to get to it more than anything, but I just can't seem to break through."

"And how are you trying to break through?"

John hesitated. "I'm not sure how to explain it. With my feelings, with my body, with my thoughts. It seems everything I do is a way to try and break through."

"Blessed are those who hunger and thirst after righteousness, for they shall be filled," she said. "Remember that?"

"Yes, very well."

"That's good. Remember the lessons you learned here, and you will be all right." She placed a misshapen hand gently on his chest. "Everything you need is in here, always be listening here."

He felt a strange thrill surge through him.

She took her hand away. "It will be all right," she said. "Believe me."

"Sometimes I regret not coming back here," he said. His voice was beginning to tremble from the vibrations still reverberating in his chest.

"You did the right thing."

"I did?"

"Absolutely. A person shouldn't stay one minute in a situation that compromises the living spirit in their heart."

"But I walked away, even after accepting Jesus as my personal lord and savior in front of everyone at the confirmation service. It didn't stick."

"It doesn't matter," she said. "You knew what you needed to do, and acting on that was much more important than what the church wanted. I suspect you still know what you want. You always have had it in you."

"Jesus was my role model," he said. "Still is. The problem was I never saw him as different from anyone, except that he chose to join with God, to become God, and worked hard at it until he succeeded. Like Abraham, Joseph, Job, Moses and all those tough people in the Old Testament. They'd crawl through glass for God. That is what I always have wanted."

Her eyebrows went up. "To crawl through glass?"

"To find God, somehow, some way in myself," he said. "It has never appealed to me to use anyone else as a middleman."

"Seeking first the kingdom of heaven within is a good thing," she said. "By whatever means … You are blessed."

"I don't know about that. I think I'm doing it the hard way. But the other way doesn't make sense to me. If we put Jesus way up on a pedestal, there isn't room for anyone else up there." John ran his fingers along the smooth edge of the metal folding chair in front of him. "If Jesus is just like us, then there is no reason we can't be just like him. The separation can be gone much quicker, can't it?"

"But how can that separation end without the help of God?" she said.

"I don't know. I want to be like Jesus so much. I don't think it can work for me to put it all in the hands of him or any another person. I feel irresponsible doing that. Like I'm waiting for someone else to do something. I can't give it over like that. I have to be doing something."

"Like what, John?"

"I don't know. I want to give it all to God. The only way I know is to put myself on the edge, where I have something to lose. Everything to lose. Then something moves in me. That's what you've read about me in the paper, between the lines, behind the running."

"I see ... do you do these things in God's name?"

"In God's name? You mean in the name of Jesus?"

"Not exactly ... you see, Jesus is a given name. Even God is a given name – man-made. The power is in the ungiven name of God, the real name of Jesus, who is one with the Father. That name is not given, and is not man-made. That name has always been and will always be. That name is very important. It is the original vibration – the *word* that lives in us."

John's eyes lit up. "So what's the name?"

"Can you surrender to it?" she said. "Can you let go?"

"I don't know. Isn't it in our hands to do more than just surrender? Most people try really hard to surrender and don't get what they want. Me too. There has got to be more to it than that. Why should we expect God to do all the work? What about the struggles we read about over and over again in the Bible? No one in the Bible ever said it would be easy. The church tells us all will be fine if we accept Jesus. Just sign up for the program and it isn't our problem anymore. I think that's a trap. It is convenient for busy people, and maybe for the church too."

"You think finding God is a struggle?"

"Well, yeah. Hunger and thirst, remember?" he said. "It's got struggle written all over it."

"Oh, I see your point," she said. "We all have a tendency to drift along. There is no question we have to be actively wanting God, actively pursuing God in every minute. Perhaps it is a matter of finesse."

"Finesse?"

"Yes, being smart about it, a little cagey," she said. "Developing the skill of active surrender. Hungering and thirsting, but surrendering too, learning how to dive into God."

John's inner antenna shot up. "How do I do that?"

"I can't tell you."

"Why not?"

"It's something you have to work out yourself with God," she said.

"What's that supposed to mean?" he said. "If there's something more I can do, I need to be doing it right now. Please tell me." His hands began to squeeze the back of the chair in front of him.

"I don't think I've ever seen any child in Sunday school as intense for God as you were..." Christi Jensen gazed off into space.

"I'm much worse now," He practically leaped out of the folding chair at her. *What does she want from me? Do I have to beg?*

She turned back to him. "My goodness."

"And no one knows it. Am I praying in my closet instead of on the street corner, or what?" he said.

"It seems so ... John, why did you come here today?"

"I need something, a good swift kick maybe. I graduate this year and the pressure is on me to make plans. I don't want to make plans, not the kind others want for me. All I want is to break through. What should I do?"

She became silent. She opened her mouth slightly and something moved deep inside. Her eyes went to the center and up as she closed them. She sat motionless. Her old hands were hunched on the handle of her cane. She didn't seem to be breathing. He sat with her, not knowing what to do. He closed his eyes too, trying to find his quietness.

Finally she stirred in her chair. He opened his eyes to find her looking at him intently.

She reached out with a crooked index finger and tapped his breastbone. The air whooshed out of his lungs until he was completely empty. A few seconds went by, and he gasped in a deep breath. As he did, pleasure surged up through him from his loins.

"Ohhh God, what was that?"

"*i am,*" she said

"I AM?"

"No, *i am.*"

"I AM?"

"No, *i am.*"

"What's the difference?" He could hardly breathe.

"Intention," she said. "I AM has an outward intention. *i am* has an inward intention. It makes all the difference. Can you say it?"

He tried to point the thought inward as he said it. "*i am?*"

"Good. Like that. Always remember, less is more." Her hands moved down through the air with palms down, like she was quieting the whole cosmos.

"Meditate on *i am,*" she said. "*i am* is God of the Old Testament, and God of the New Testament. The only God there is. *i am* is the secret name of God, the true name of God, the only consciousness in the universe. All things are reflected rays of *i am*."

He was bewildered by her words. Could it be that simple? "Meditate on *i am*?"

"Yes, for as long as it takes until you have all the answers you seek. Remember, *i am* is God, the kingdom, the power, the glory. *i am* is also Jesus in all of us, for he and God are one. Outward I AM is not much, just a human sound, a noise, a dim shadow of the inner truth. Sound has little substance until we turn it inward in ever-quieting vibrations to our silent depths. 'Be still and know *i am* God.' This is the greatest secret of the scriptures – the most ancient, sacred wisdom. Follow *i am*. Everything else flows from that."

"Everything else?"

"Yes, much will happen. *i am* will open many doors for you. That is all."

"Is that it?" he said.

"Isn't it enough?"

"I don't know."

"One more thing," she said.

"Yes?"

"Pass it on," she said.

"Pass it on? Pass what on?"

"You will know. I'm so glad you came today. It will make all the difference."

John hesitated. His gaze was down on the wooden floor worn by thousands of small eager feet. Then he looked at her. "Are you the one who has been calling me inside?"

Christi Jensen shrugged her stooped shoulders. She looked up at him. Her green-rimmed blue eyes pierced his soul. "There is only one who calls. It is *i am*. There is only one who hungers and thirsts. It is *i am*. You hunger and thirst. I respond. It is all *i am*. And now it is time for you to go, my dear."

She got up painfully, and limped with him slowly through the double doors of the fellowship hall, out into the sunlight. It illuminated her weary face in a way he did not remember, like her being was going up into the bright light.

"Thank you," he said as he went hesitantly down the wooden steps. She stood on the small porch in front of the fellowship hall. He was dazed and quivering inside. *Have I forgotten something?*

She put up her right hand as though blessing him for some great purpose.

"I will come to you," she said. "Now go. There is much for you to do."

He didn't know what she meant. "What?"

She shook her head slowly. Her God-like eyes sent him away.

He went back through the palm grove to his car. He looked over his shoulder several times. She was still standing in the sunlight watching him go. Something important had just happened ... but what?

While driving home, John pondered all that he had ever heard or read in the Bible about I AM. He remembered it was I AM who addressed Moses. He remembered Jesus referring to himself as I AM several times. He remembered him saying:

Before Abraham I AM.

He remembered the famous words Jesus spoke that penetrated his being when he was only six years old, attending Sunday school for the first time:

I AM the way, and the truth, and the life. No
one comes to the Father except though Me.

Why had the focus in the church been on Jesus the person, and not on Jesus the I AM? Or the *i am*? He repeated the sound, *i am,* inwardly in thought and he was filled with new understanding. A strange pleasurable thrill rose through him, the same feeling he got when Christi Jensen touched his chest. He looked in the rear view mirror and saw a trail of glistening white light behind the car extending all the way back to the Island Christian Church. It was made of billions of sparkling white specks, following him as he drove.

His skin crawled with an intense desire for God. He could barely stand it. He had to do something about it right away. He pressed hard on the accelerator. The red convertible roared home.

Locked in his room, John sat cross-legged, leaning against a pillow propped at the head of the four-poster double bed. He heard the soft rumble of the ocean coming through the dormer window.

He'd sat here many times before, exploring his thoughts and feelings. Usually he'd end up pleasuring himself, hoping to find an answer in the intense feelings that were so hard to control. Instead of an answer, he often found temporary relief from his longing. A small consolation.

Now he had I AM to explore. Would this be different? He began by posing a question in his thoughts.

I AM, what is the truth?

He repeated it half a dozen times inside, and waited. There was no response. Then he tried something else.

I AM, who am I?

This time he repeated it a dozen times, and then waited – still no response.

Then he tried a more direct approach.

I AM the way, and the truth and the life.

Over and over again...

Again, there was nothing.

He tried different combinations, putting all the meaning he could find into his solicitations. He aimed for precision of purpose and mental enunciation.

Still nothing.

After a half-hour of trying, he was getting irritated.

I AM, where are you? Why don't you answer?

And a while later...

I AM, you bastard! If you are there, show me now. God damn-it!

Only the waves of his rising anger remained when he stopped his increasingly chaotic incantations. He threw his pillow at the bookcase across the room, knocking the trophies off. They clattered to the floor.

He jumped up and down on the bed yelling,

"I AM! I AM! I AM!"

In his fury he missed the bed with one foot and went tumbling to the floor onto the hooked rug. A stream of obscenities came out of him.

He lay heaving in emotion on the floor. Desperate longing swept over him again and again, and he began to weep. He pulled himself up on his knees, into a prostrate position with his forehead on the rug. His arms lay on the rug wrapped around his head. He rocked forward and back.

I AM, I AM, I AM...

He let go ... his intention slipped inward.

The meaning was gone. The mental sound faded and he entered a completely different quality of thought.

i am, i am, i am...

It was subtle, silent, yet luminous and alive inside him. He became filled with its presence.

i am, i am, i am ... iii-aaammm ... iii-aaammm...

His body began to pulsate with a living silence. Each *i am* reverberated through him as if he were hollowed out empty space inside. Then the vibration was gone, and he was far bigger than his body, far bigger than the house, than the earth, than the solar system. He became infinite blissful awareness ... Then he was back in his body with a thought. *Oh, what was that?*

He began again, letting go, giving up his need to hold on to the meaning, or even the thought itself.

i am, i am, i am...

Gradually he became infinite again. It was a uniquely pleasurable journey inward, this letting go. A few minutes later he was back in his surface thoughts. With determination to stay infinite, he began with a more enunciated thought.

I AM, I AM, I AM...

It didn't fade as long as he held on to the clarity of the sound and the meaning. So he let go. He watched as *i am* went from a clearly enunciated thought to a fuzzy thought, then to a feeling, then to a faint feeling, and finally having lost all its boundaries of thought, meaning and feeling, expanding infinitely within him, and his awareness with it. Every atom in him quivered deliciously as he went beyond the concrete levels of *i am* to the unboundedness of it. The less he held on, the more there was, and the more he experienced a pure pleasure that bordered on erotic.

Huddled on his knees on the hooked rug, he did it over and over again, giving himself to the cycles of gently embracing *i am* and losing it in the glorious expansion of inner silence. After a while, he crawled back onto the bed, resuming his cross-legged sitting position with the pillow at his back. Then he did it some more. He was filled with awe and gratitude to have *i am* caressing him deep within.

It was only the beginning.

That night John awoke with a start. He looked at the clock. It was two-thirty. He was upset. He didn't know why. He sat up in bed. He felt the brush of a luminous feminine hand on his cheek. The curtains rustled in the quiet night breeze. Then she was gone. Immediately he knew what had happened. Christi Jensen had just died. She touched him tenderly as she went. He didn't understand how she could be gone. He felt alone. He tried to meditate with *i am*. He couldn't. His heart broke as he lay back down, sobbing into his pillow.

You gave me the greatest secret. It won't be wasted. I promise you, Christi Jensen, it won't be wasted. I will grow in i am, and I will pass it on.

He slowly faded off to sleep, filled with a new determination, a new hunger for God that would carry him rapidly along his road home. The new hunger was Christi's gift to him. With her last breath and final touch, she quickened *i am* in him.

Chapter 5 – The Big Angel

Several weeks had passed.

The young couple walked down the school corridor. It was past recess and few people were around. John was deep within himself.

Devi gave him an inquiring look. "What's going on with you?"

"Huh?" he said.

"See? You aren't paying attention."

"Yes, I am."

"You seem like you've been somewhere else lately. Is it the loss of your friend Mrs. Jensen?"

"No, it's not that. Sorry, I'll do better."

They went out the back door of the school and started the hike across the deserted soccer field toward the parking lot. They didn't notice the four hulking figures stalking them with their gaze from within the cluster of parked cars.

Her eyes penetrated him again. "What's going on?"

"Uh, I've been doing a new positive thinking method." He figured he'd better tell her something. "It is taking some getting used to."

"Positive thinking? You mean like affirmations?"

"Yeah, something like that."

"Well, okay," she said. "Is it working? It seems to be spacing you out so far."

"That should pass." He really had no idea what would happen, whether it would pass or not, only that it had to happen.

He was much in the radiant silence of his meditations on *i am* in the weeks since he discovered his ability to go deep into himself with it. He was doing it for at least a half-hour before and after school each day, and more on the weekends. It had not adversely affected his schoolwork or cross-country so far. He felt clearer and more effective than ever. But what is this with Devi? *Do I really seem detached to her? Maybe –*

"John, would you like to come over to the house for a while this afternoon? Papa won't be home until later." She wasn't looking at him when she said it.

"Um ... Well, yeah, sure. But I have to run first." He didn't look at her as he said it.

"Can't it wait?"

They stopped in the middle of the soccer field. He turned to her as she turned to him. Her gaze was one of deep longing that instantly turned him inside out. He had to go with her.

"Well, I could run later, and eat late," he said. He was thinking of his meditation, how to squeeze it in. But he didn't want to tell her about it yet.

"So you can come?"

"Yes."

Her face blossomed into a smile and she took his hand. "Wonderful. There's something I want to show you."

They started walking again. The four pairs of eyes were still on them – watching … waiting.

They crossed the field and were among the cars that were left in the yellow gravel lot. Most belonging to the football players working out on the practice field behind the stadium across the street. They went between a big black pickup truck and a station wagon.

A large form moved in front of them, blocking the way. It spoke in a menacing squeaky southern tone. "Hey, lovey doves, where you goin'?"

Devi froze next to John. He looked behind and saw that three big young men had come around the truck, blocking the way back. He turned back to the front. "What do you want, Jake?"

He knew of Jake Lasher and his buddies. They'd been in trouble with the law before. It was Jake's father who had killed Devi's mother and brother, and he now sat on death row. Jake had been eyeing Devi with lustful hatred off and on ever since his father had been taken away.

Jake was bulging out of a short-sleeved dungaree jacket and black pants. He had long, greasy, slicked-back hair, tattooed arms, and pork loins for hands. The other three were big too, much bigger than John.

"Why, we want to try out the merchandise," Jake said, eyeing Devi with a half-toothed smile. They moved closer to John and Devi from both front and back.

Devi looked scared stiff. Then, suddenly, her eyes turned to anger. "Oh, is that all you want, you dumb shit! Let me help you out."

To John's amazement she strode toward Jake, looking straight up into his eyes. He was stunned and he didn't see her foot come sharply up into his crotch.

"Owwwww!" Jake nearly crumpled. He managed to stay on his feet and grab Devi by her long hair with one hand.

"You Hindu bitch!" he yelled. "My daddy's on death row 'cause of your whore mother and pimp brother."

"Your sick father murdered them!" Devi screamed. She was swinging and kicking at him in a blind rage, held back by her hair held firmly in Jake's grip. "Murderers! Murderers! Murderers!"

He gave her the back of his free hand, not letting go of her hair. Her head spun around from the blow.

John saw the blood fly from her mouth. He sprang forward, but the other three grabbed him and threw him against the side of the station wagon with a crash. Two held him while the third planted body blows, and then a hook to the side of his head. The world started to disappear.

Devi could see what was happening to John. "Stop! Stop!" She cried, struggling under Jake's hair-grip. She turned back to attack him. Jake's arms were so long that she couldn't reach his face with her nails. So she went for the arm that held her, making long bloody trails through the skull tattoo.

Jake hit her again, opening a cut over her eye. John was nearly unconscious. The thug kept hitting him while the other two held him. He wanted to break free, but he couldn't. They were too strong. *Oh God, help Devi, please help her.* He fell into himself, seeming lifeless, but awake inside. His spirit went outward, calling ... calling.

Devi was bleeding from the cut over her eye and from her mouth and nose, and crying. Seeing John being beaten visibly weakened her.

"Please don't hit him anymore," she begged. "Please…"

Jake shook her whole body by her hair. "You ready to do for me, bitch?" She was rag doll in his hand now, visibly surrendering to his dark intentions.

"Yes, yes, anything. Please stop them," she pleaded. She had both her hands on the thick arm that clenched her by the hair. She no longer was digging bloody gashes in it with her nails. She began caressing the arm, stroking it with the blood she'd drawn.

Jake jerked his head, and the three let John fall to the ground. One gave him a kick in the ribs. He didn't feel it. He was awake inside, but could not move his body. He felt an energy coming, a great lumbering energy moving toward them from across the soccer field. He sensed it deep inside. *Yes, over here. Over here...*

Jake pushed Devi against the sun-baked blackness of the pickup.

"Hold her," he said.

Two came over and one took each of her arms, holding her tight against the hot truck. The third stayed by John. He was vaguely aware of the boot the thug propped on his neck as he lay broken in the gravel.

Jake let go of Devi's hair and took her by the throat with his bloody hand.

"Let's see what you got here," he said. With his other hand he ripped the front of her blouse open. She was breathing hard. Her chest was heaving over her bra. There was something else there, something hanging between her breasts on a silver chain.

The sun hit it, and a bright white beam shot into Jake's eyes. For a split second he was blinded. Jake and the two that were holding Devi looked to see what it was.

"What is that?" said Jake.

"It's a little glass cross," one of the thugs said. "A little glass – "

The third man, the one who had his boot on John's neck, hit the ground with a thud. Jake turned his head just in time meet the huge brown fist coming at him with high velocity, flattening his face, knocking him instantly unconscious and onto the ground. Half a second later, one of the thugs holding Devi had the elbow that went with the massive fist in his face, and he was out. The other thug holding Devi let go and started to take a swing at the six-foot-ten all-American offensive lineman in front of him. The other huge fist knocked him out before he could bring his arm around. There was silence…

"Hello, Miss. My name is Luke ... Luke Smith. Looks like y'all had some trouble here."

Devi squinted up through her blood at the big man who spoke with the deep gentle voice. The sun was behind his head. He looked like a divine being, an angel of salvation. Then she looked over toward John lying unconscious on the ground. "John … John…" she cried weakly, reaching toward where he lay in the gravel. She went to take a step and fainted into Luke's big brown arms. By then, others were arriving at the scene.

Later, John vaguely remembered huge Luke Smith, the crowd of people, Luke putting his flannel shirt on Devi, the police, and the ambulance that took Devi and him away. But he didn't remember feeling the pain. Somehow it had all washed over him, leaving no trace.

By the time they got to the emergency room, John started to feel his body again, and it didn't feel good. Luke, in his white sleeveless undershirt, followed the ambulance over. He stayed with John, still on a gurney with his shirt off, while they waited for the test results to come back. Devi had gotten nine stitches above her eye in another room, and joined them.

"Man, it's a good thing you were by my truck," Luke said.

"Your truck?" Devi said through the ice pack she held on her swollen lip. Luke's shirt was so big on her that she was nearly lost in it. Half the sleeves hung loose over her tiny hands, reaching for the floor.

"The big black pickup," he said. "It's mine. Ya know, somethin' inside told me I'd better cut out there…"

"Yeah, it's a good thing," John said. He winced and shifted to favor the pain in his side.

Luke and John's eyes met, finding a deep inner recognition. It was then that John knew their coming together in this way was no accident.

Stella Wilder rushed in. She looked like she had been crying.

"I got a call from school. They told me you were here in the emergency room. Are you all right, John? Are you all right?"

"I'm okay, Mom, but I don't know about this body. They took some X-rays, and we're waiting to hear."

"Oh, dear," Stella said. "This can't be happening."

"Mom," John said painfully. "This is Devi ... and Luke, who saved us."

Stella barely acknowledged them. "God, what happened? Don't be hurt. Don't be hurt." The tears were streaming down her face.

They told her what happened in the parking lot.

"That's terrible, just terrible." Stella was unable to keep her hands still. They flailed back and forth through the air.

The doctor came in with the results of the tests, and it wasn't as bad as it could have been. John suffered a minor concussion and two cracked ribs. There was no internal bleeding.

"How awful. Life is so unfair," Stella said. "How could this ever happen to us?"

"It could be worse," John strained. "We are going to be okay. We're lucky Devi only needed a few stitches, thanks to Luke. It was about to get a lot worse."

"I just don't see how people can do things like this. Your father is going to be furious."

"Those four boys are in jail now," Luke said. "The police say they are facin' charges for assault and attempted rape, and will be tried as adults. They are bad ones."

"When can we leave?" Stella looked away, fidgeting nervously in front of big Luke. "I want to get you home, John."

"Not for a while," Devi said. They have to bandage those ribs. She pointed to the ugly black and blue marks coming up on John's side.

"Oh, it's so horrible." Stella shrunk. "I have to go."

"I'll bring him home, Mrs. Wilder," Luke said. "He'll be okay." He tried to soothe her. No one ever could.

"Good. Thank you," she said without looking at Luke. "John, dear, I'll go home and fix you something good for dinner. I know that will make you feel better." She leaned over stiffly and pecked him on the cheek, and was gone.

An hour later, they were in the front seat of Luke's truck, heading back up the island toward the school, where John and Devi's cars were.

"You sure you can drive?" Luke said.

"I'll be okay," John said. He had a long elastic bandage wrapped around his torso. "You know, Luke, our meeting today was not by chance.

Luke smiled. "I know it, brother John. I know it."

No one spoke for a few minutes. Devi pulled the little crystal cross that hung from her neck out from Luke's massive plaid flannel shirt she was wrapped in, and kissed it softly.

"Thank you Jesus," she said. "Thank you Luke."

"Amen, Lord Jesus," Luke said.

"Amennnn," John said. He leaned over and kissed the crystal cross too. Then he kissed Devi gently, careful not to too hurt her swollen lip. She responded, running her fingers through the hair on the back of his head as she kissed him back. He put his head on her shoulder, favoring the pain in his side when he moved. She took his hand.

"I'm sorry we never made it to your house today," he said.

She caressed his hand. "We'll get there."

He quietly slipped into the undulating bliss of *i am*. Soon he'd tell her about this treasure inside. She was part of it. Eventually he'd tell everyone, for all were part of it.

With his cracked ribs, John was out of cross-country. It hurt to breathe deeply. The season was ending soon, and it looked like he'd miss the state championships too. It was a blow, more for others than for him. He was off a few days from school, and he took the opportunity to do extra meditation in his room. He would sit an hour or more at a time on the bed, and lie down to rest in-between. Sometimes he would fall asleep during or in-between. At least, he thought it was sleep. It felt like sleep physically and mentally when he woke up. But he never lost consciousness. In fact, he wasn't sure he ever completely lost consciousness anymore since beginning to meditate. More and more, he was watching life from a separate place behind everything, behind what he saw in the outside world, behind his thoughts, behind his feelings, behind his dreams, and even behind his dreamless sleep. He was always present as this unmoving blissful awareness. He had the experience to some degree before beginning to meditate, but nothing like this. He really noticed it when he was getting beaten up. What a contrast. He witnessed all that chaos from a place in himself that wasn't touched. Maybe this is what Devi was complaining about? It was true he felt a kind of aloofness. Yet, at the same time, he was experiencing what was happening to others around him like it was somehow happening to him. Happening to him, but not touching him. Was he going mad? He kept on with meditation. It was usually so pleasurable that he didn't want to stop ... but not always.

The day after the attack, he came out of a long meditation angry and upset. It got uncomfortable about half way through. Then he got extremely irritable. His skin crawled with unpleasant sensations. He wanted to fly out of his body. The world seemed wrong, like everything would fly apart. What was happening? All he could do was stay in bed and watch the strange struggling nightmares, as he lay awake for hours after meditation. He even skipped dinner, which disturbed his mother especially. He stopped meditating for half a day and he felt better.

He realized that he could meditate too much, so he learned to regulate his practice, limiting himself to half-hour sessions before breakfast and before dinner. He found out the hard way that *i am* did not like to compete with a full stomach. Sometimes he'd ratchet up the time or increase the number of meditations he'd do in a day, but only if he had nothing else going on that day. He realized that he needed to allow time of quietly doing nothing after each session. Lying down seemed best. This reduced the risk of carrying irritability into whatever he was doing afterwards.

John developed a theory that meditation was somehow cleaning him out, making him a better window for the *i am* within, and that it was his joining with the deep silence of *i am* within repeatedly that gave him the sense of silent separateness. In the joining with *i am*, the window of this body, mind and emotions was being cleaned. He imagined there to be many layers of dirt on the window. If there was too much cleaning at once, too much dirt would come loose, creating a mess that took time to clear up and wash away. This was his theory about the irritability – too much pile-up of dirt, creating discomfort. Better to take out the garbage a little at a time ... less mess. It seemed to work that way.

It was a lot like running. He'd learned long ago that building up distance and speed gradually in workouts was the best way to condition his body. Whenever he got hurt, it was because he tried to do too much too soon. He had come to realize that practicing meditation was much the same. He'd have to gradually build up over time, condition himself every day, but not too much. He realized he was training to become a spiritual athlete. For the first time, his mission in life was becoming clear. He was beginning to grasp what his *something* was.

Two days later, John sat on his bed enjoying a deeply blissful meditation. He let the thought vibration of *i am* fade again and again. He was getting better at picking up the vibration at the faintest level of feeling inside and letting it refine into the vast expanded awareness – bliss, pure bliss. His whole body tingled with it. He felt like the universe was tingling with him.

In the midst of his experience, he began to move slightly, instinctively, from side to side in his cross-legged position. His head also moved from side to side slightly in coordination with his body, like a snake would move from left to right as it slithered across the ground. The tingling increased. Then, to his surprise, he felt a wave of erotic pleasure rise through his center from the base of his spine to the top of his head. He swayed a little more, and it continued. He was covered with goose bumps, his nipples became erect, and he became sexually aroused. His body quivered with desire.

What is this? Something moving in my spine?

He swayed a little more, and the sensations increased. Then, distracted by his arousal, which became a strong erection, he was not deep in *i am* anymore. The sensations subsided, though the erection didn't. He restarted with *i am*, ignoring his erection, letting go, and settling back in. Then it happened again. The slightest physical movement created an erotic energy movement inside him.

In the midst of it all, his anal sphincter muscle began to flex gently, slowly, rhythmically. This seemed to be caused by the energy moving up in him, and directly amplified it as well. His tongue pulled back pleasurably on the roof of his mouth, seeking something, hungering for a connection – but what?

The experience took him by surprise. He was overwhelmed with both joy and fear. He couldn't stop it. It had him. He couldn't stand the tension as he was being erotically engulfed from within. He rose out of the silent expansiveness of *i am,* and pleasured himself frantically on the bed, finding relief in orgasm.

"Ohhhhhhhhh!"

Later, when he recovered, he was ashamed. He felt he had cheated himself, and *i am*. It was unmistakable. He was entering a new phase. He was beginning to make love with *i am*. And *i am* was beginning to make love with him. And he had ruined it. External orgasm was not the right direction for this lovemaking. It drained the experience, stopped it in its tracks. To what end was this happening? He desperately needed to know. Wherever this was going, he would have to go inward and upward to find out.

He resolved to follow the pleasurable energy rising in him, to follow it home, no matter what. He would do better.

But what about Devi? He loved her. He wanted to fill her with his essence, with everything that he was. He craved her touch. He knew she wanted him too. He longed to hold her, to dive into her unfathomable depths of love again and again. He was confused, conflicted.

Chapter 6 – God Quest

The bridge was perfectly proportioned, the finest structure ever built across the Hudson River. And who would have been a more appropriate person to name it after than George Washington? It was two feet long and sat on the mantel in Devi's living room. It was a scale model, painstakingly made with matchsticks, and much in need of repair. Devi's brother, Joe, had made it the year before he died. Now, here it sat, an aging testament to his lost wish of becoming an engineer.

"It's beautiful," John said as he got in close, imagining himself driving across the matchstick road held up by the matchstick cables that were connected to the matchstick towers.

"Yeah, but it's falling apart," Devi said. "See the pieces coming loose along the side there? And that cable is about to fall."

"May I fix it?"

"You want to?" she said.

"I do. And I can make a glass case for it," he said. "I have time now that I'm out of running."

"That would be really special," she said. "It's all we have left of Joe."

"I'm so sorry," he said. He had not brought up the subject of the murders with Devi at all, even since the attack on them six weeks before by Jake, the murderer's son. The grisly double murder just over two years ago was the worst crime ever recorded on Coquina Island.

She came and put her arms around his waist, and her head on his chest. He put his arms around her.

"It's been a long time," she said, "But it still seems like last night Joe drove Mama to the convenience store for a loaf of bread. Only that crumbling matchstick bridge can measure the time. I can't."

"You're moving on," John said. "I admire you for that."

"I have to," she said. "We all have to."

"Yeah, we have to keep going, no matter what tries to stop us. But you've had it tougher than any of us."

She looked up into his eyes. "And where are you going, Mr. John Wilder? As much time as we've spent together, I still feel I don't know you."

He shrugged, and then he kissed her.

A few minutes later, they were sitting on the couch. They were aroused and eagerly touching each other through their clothes. They both had on jeans and T-shirts, Devi was braless, and they were barefoot. Then they were lying down on the couch. He was on top of her.

"Wait," he said. "Wait ... I ... I ..."

"I want you," she whispered in his ear. He could feel her moving under him, rhythmically massaging him through their clothes with coaxing motions of her hips. Her legs were spreading to let him in closer. She was moaning into his neck.

"Devi..." He was pleading now.

His tone stopped her. She looked into his eyes.

"Is something wrong?"

"I want to talk," he said. "You asked me where I was going."

"Yes, and you kissed me," she said. "And now we're here on the couch. Isn't this where you wanted to go?"

He thought of telling her how complicated it was. But that would not be fair. He had to tell her now, especially since sex had become involved in his meditations. He did his best to settle into *i am* for a minute.

She waited.

Then it came out of him. "I'm on a God quest."

"A God quest?" she said. "Oh, I think I get it. No sex, right?"

"Not exactly," he said. "Actually, it looks like it will be more sex, a lot more sex. But not like this." He gestured with his eyes to their hurried posture. He was still lying on her, his crotch jammed between her spread legs.

She brushed the hair from his eyes softly and kissed him on the cheek. "Well then, what? I'm not following you."

He pushed himself up with his arms and sat on the couch between her legs with one behind him and the other draped across his lap.

She propped herself part way up with a pillow. She locked her ankles together in a scissors around his waist and gave him a squeeze.

"Ow!"

"Oops, sorry," she said. "I forgot about your ribs."

"They were getting better until now," he said, feigning a grimace.

"Okay, so what's the deal?" she said. "Do we go off to a monastery together and have sex every hour on the hour for the rest of our lives?"

"Something like that." He slid his hand under her shirt and rested it on her firm belly, beginning to run his thumb slowly around her navel.

"Yeah, right. I wish." She was starting to quiver under his touch.

He felt her warmth against his side, penetrating like hot steam through her jeans. *Oh, how I long to be inside her.* He put his other hand on the bulge in his jeans. She saw him do it. For some reason he wasn't shy about it.

"It's not simple," he said.

"So tell me. Maybe I can help." Slowly, with her eyes in his, she moved both her hands to her crotch, reached under, and pulled up, like she was gripping a saddle horn. She moaned softly. "Is this what your God quest is about?"

Suddenly, through the heat of his arousal, John realized that it was, for he was being filled with delicious energy as he and Devi were sharing their arousal. For the moment, he was well in front of climax, even as he was being filled with the beauty of the one he loved. He knew he could go on like this for hours. But was she being filled too? He wanted so much for her to be.

"Yes, it is about this, at least in this moment," he said. "Do you remember the positive thinking I told you about the day we got beat up by Jake Lasher and his buddies?"

"The affirmations?"

"Yeah, well, it is much more than that. Christi Jensen gave me a way of going deep within myself meditating deeply on the sacred name of God – *i am*."

"The name of God in the Bible?" she said.

"Yes. But I found out going within is not about the outer meaning or pronunciation of it. It is about letting it disappear inside the mind again and again, and doing it every day. Then something wonderful happens."

"Letting it disappear? What happens?"

"Yeah, letting it become less and less clear. Letting go of it while still being with it. It makes me infinitely huge inside. And blissful, real blissful."

Devi closed her eyes. He saw her lips barely moving, silently, repeating I AM. Then her eyes popped open, jolting his essences deep inside.

"It doesn't work for me," she said. "Nothing happened."

John pulled his hand out from under her shirt and tapped her on the breastbone with the tips of his fingers. She got a strange flushed look on her face.

"What ... what was that?" she said. "What did you do?"

"I just passed on what Christi Jensen gave me – *i am* meditation. It takes time and practice," he said. "And not giving up. Learning how to let go in the beginning is tricky, because our habit is to go out, with everything. Remember, less is more. That's the key. Once you go in and feel it take you, you'll know. Then it's easy letting yourself fall into *i am*. The trick is to practice it every day like clockwork, getting good at it. Like an athlete working out. Doing it like that is changing me."

"And this is what made you spaced out? You seem better now."

"Yeah, the effects of it take some getting used to. It is making me feel more and more quiet inside, not just when I do it – it's changing how I see things all the time."

She moved herself against him. "What's this got to do with sex?"

"I didn't think anything until a few weeks ago. But something started moving inside."

"What?"

"Like this," he said. He slid his hand under her shirt again and lightly up her belly, nearly to her untethered breasts, and then slowly back down. She shivered with pleasure and began pulling up on her mound again. He saw her nipples bloom through the thin white cotton, among the letters that spelled, *COQUINA ISLAND*.

"Ooooh," she said. "Do that again, only a little higher."

"That's what it's like," he said. "My meditations have become like that."

"My God," she said.

"...Unless I can't stand it, and give myself an orgasm. Then it stops. Poof, the bliss is gone."

"You give yourself orgasms?" she said.

"Yeah," he said. "Now you know. Is that the end for us?" He gave her a vulnerable look.

"I guess that makes two jerk-offs on this couch," she said.

"Jerk-offs anonymous, huh?" he said.

"Yup," she said. "I think I'm starting to get it."

"I'm so glad. I didn't know if I should tell you all this."

"I'm glad you did," she said. "So, where do we go from here?"

"I dunno."

They were silent for a moment, basking in their mingled arousal.

Finally, she spoke. "Mama told me before she died, 'Always fill your man. It isn't just about filling you. Don't rush your man. Help him go as slow as he wants.' That's what was passed down to her by my grandma in India, and to her by my great grandma before that. Now I'm starting to know what it means. Maybe you are just the kind of man they were talking about."

Devi sat up straight. She moved her warm hands from her mound and placed them on John's bulge. He moved his hand away, surrendering himself to her touch. He closed his eyes and was filled with a surge of energy, a mixture of carnal pleasure and divine ecstasy. This kind of sharing with Devi seemed to mirror the internal loving he was beginning to experience in his meditations. Was this tender touching a reflection of what had begun inside him?

After a few minutes, John moved his hand out from under her shirt and placed it gently on her where her hands had been. She felt warm through her jeans. She closed her eyes as her face drifted into pure pleasure. Her mound pressed up into his hand.

"So where do we go from here?" he said.

"We go slow. We go as slow as the God quest needs," she said.

"Is that going to work for you?" he said through his passion.

"Slow is good for me. I want to be where you are." She moved one of her hands to where his was resting on her, and began guiding him closer to her secrets underneath –

The sound of a car pulling in the driveway invaded the house. Devi emerged through her deep moistened eyes. "Papa's home."

The engine stopped, and, with difficulty, they began to untwine from each other.

"It sounds like he had a good day," she said.

"How can you tell?"

"He didn't crash into the house."

"That's wonderful news," he said.

They stood up and faced each other. Their bodies went together again like magnets.

"There's something I should tell you," she said. She was slowly moving her belly from side to side against his jeans as she ran her nails lightly up his spine.

"...What?"

"My name ... Devi. Do you know what it means?"

"No, I don't." He had joined her in her belly dance.

"Divine Goddess," she said

He looked into her loving eyes as she coaxed his energies upward. "Boy, am I in trouble."

Chapter 7 – The Mountain

Devi cleared the table after she and her father had dinner.

"You know, Papa, you look terrific tonight."

"And you too." Charles Duran gave her daughter a big smile.

It was the best smile she had seen on him in a long time. He seemed to be inspired by her growing zest for life. That made her happy.

She felt herself beaming. She was born today into a new life. She wanted to reach out and hug the world. She'd have to settle for hugging Papa as he made his way from the kitchen to his recliner in the living room for some TV.

"I'm going to study," she said, bouncing off to her bedroom.

She was deeply in love. But more than that, she was in love with a man who resonated with the long unthought of lessons Mama had passed on to her. She wanted to give John everything. His desire to hold back made her want to give it even more.

She wanted to try the *i am* meditation he told her about. Mama told her something about meditation, describing it as a secret inner art of the ancients in India, long obscured by external rituals, guarded and dispensed judiciously by gurus, but more often reduced to the chanting of *OM* out load in public places. That was all Mama had said.

Devi took off her jeans and sat cross-legged on the quilt in the middle of her bed. She was in her T-shirt and panties, resting her hands on her knees. She shook her hair out of her face and closed her eyes.

I AM, I Am, *i am* ... she continued repeating the thought deliberately inside for some time. Nothing much happened, or so she thought. She wandered off it, fantasizing about what she and John might have done that afternoon had Papa not come home when he did. Then she went back to repeating *i am* for a while ... then off somewhere vague, and reemerging into another stream of unrelated thoughts.

She noticed that when she realized she was off *i am*, she was backtracking to a clear mental pronunciation of I AM, and pulling herself out of whatever level of fuzziness she had fallen into. She remembered what John said about letting *i am* become less and less clear, letting it go, while still being with it. She also remembered she had her legs wrapped around him when he told her this. *Well, never mind that for now.*

She began again.

I AM, I Am, *i am*, *i am* ... she soon lost it. It was gone. This time when she became aware of her thought process, she allowed herself to stay on the edge of the goneness, and she picked up a faint unclear seed of *i am*.

i am, i am, i am ... Then it had her.

Everything disappeared but her awareness, and she expanded out in all directions inside. Silence, deep unfathomable silence. In that first introduction to the depths of *i am*, she knew herself as she never did before. The inner pleasure was beyond anything she imagined. With that realization, she was back in her thoughts, evaluating, and struggling to reclaim the inner expansion. Soon she realized it could not be had that way. She could not possess it. She'd have to let go, following *i am* as it faded into infinity. So she did, spreading out in cosmic delight within herself over and over again. Less was more, just like John said.

Devi was a natural born meditator, and she was hooked.

John carefully glued the loose matchsticks back in place on the George Washington Bridge. He had made a plan for the wood and glass case he would soon make for Joe's model. He worked with a deep reverence. In his hands was what would have been a soul's life work. He hoped that his life work would someday be as significant.

The window to the shop in back of the garage was open and he could hear the murmur of the surf quietly caressing the shore. This was often its mode in the crisp winter months. It could be as peaceful as a lake.

He had every reason to be happy. His relationship with Devi couldn't be better. She understood him far better than he dreamed possible. He sensed she would be his lover and companion forever. Yet he was feeling exhausted, drained. A huge force in him wanted to leave and go into her. It was his whole life, his total essence that cried continuously to go to her. While the silent part of him watched with seeming amusement, the rest of him was overwhelmed and desperate.

Wouldn't it have been better if he had just done it with her? Then he would have fulfilled the life and death mission of his seed. No. He was following his deeper instincts, and they hadn't failed him so far. *My seed has another purpose. I'm sure of it.*

He realized that men seeking God might become celibate and go off to monasteries to avoid the powerful forces of passion that the love of a woman stimulated. But how could that protect them from the relentless energies within that must have their way? Didn't the monks meditate? He could feel himself being rearranged inside by the unquenchable love springing out of *i am*. Being on the edge of falling into the depths of Devi magnified the love currents in him. *She is changing me inside. My precious divine goddess is changing me. Isn't it a good thing, this glorious love agony?*

He pondered how the line was becoming blurred between Devi in the flesh and Devi moving inside him. He could feel her moving in him during his meditations, licking every nerve in him erotically. He realized his love for her was his love for God's divine will coming alive in him, God coming alive in him as the seductive *i am*. He dared to think it – God is seductive and passionate when aroused in the human form. And his passion for Devi magnified the God passion a hundred times. No, a thousand times. *It's the death spiral I have secretly craved. Now I'm in it.* It was almost too much.

As John wandered into the house from the workshop in his overwhelmed love state, his mother handed him the phone.

"It's Luke," she said in an irritated tone.

He took the phone.

"Hey, Luke."

"Hello, brother John. You interested in going up to the Georgia mountains for a few days? My uncle's got a cabin way out, and I'm goin' up for the weekend to ponder life."

John thought for a second. This could be the break he needed, Providence offering him a short change in the outer scenery, and maybe the inner scenery too.

"Sounds like just what I need. Yeah, count me in," he said. "Anyone else coming?"

"Not unless you got somebody," Luke said. "You want to bring sweet Miss Devi?"

"Not this time," He felt Devi would understand, in the spirit of taking things slow. *Slow? Ha!*

"How about my brother? Do you know Kurt?"

"No, but bring him along."

"He's home from Florida State on break, just hanging around. I'll ask him."

"College guy, huh?" Luke said. "Can he make us smarter?"

"I doubt it."

"How about I pick you up around nine in the morning. That'll get us up there by dinner."

"Great."

"Bring warm clothes and a sleeping bag."

John hung up. His mother came out of the kitchen. He could tell she had been listening to his end of the conversation.

"Are you going somewhere with that Luke?" Stella said.

"Up to the Georgia mountains. His uncle has a cabin up there. I'm inviting Kurt too. Nothing much going on here this weekend."

"I wish you wouldn't go off with him, that black boy. He's so ... big."

"Mom, he saved my life. Devi's too. He's a great guy. If it helps you, he's Duval's top offensive lineman, and headed for the University of Georgia on a full scholarship next year."

"Oh, I didn't know that," she said. "Well, still, he's not our kind, is he?"

"I don't know what our kind is. Whatever it is, I'm not sure I am either. Anyway, Luke is my friend. He's more than that."

"Well, be careful. There are still people in this part of the country who think the Civil War isn't over yet."

"Okay, Mom. I promise I'll try and stay out of trouble."

He knew she insisted on a guarantee from him, always. But there was no such thing. Demanding that external appearances be controlled down to the smallest detail kept her in a constant state of anxiety. Any unexpected thing could put her in a panic. He felt sad for her. But no matter how hard she tried to pull him into her terrifying world, he could not go there. He just wasn't wired that way.

The big black pickup roared along the winding road that snaked up the side of Moccasin Mountain. Luke knew the road, but he hadn't done it in snow before. When they started out in Florida that morning it was fifty degrees and sunny. Now it was thirty, with three inches on the ground, and more was coming down fast.

Kurt was in the front passenger seat. John was in the skinny back seat. He watched with amazement as the landscape gradually changed throughout the day on the way up, going from nearly all horizontal to nearly all vertical. There was a steep white slope covered with naked trees going up one side of the road, and it continued down the other side.

"Hey, where does this road end up?" John said as the truck made a hairpin in four-wheel drive, sending gravel and snow flying over the edge into nowhere.

"We're getting close," Luke said. "Isn't it pretty?" he pointed out into the blinding blizzard in front of the windshield.

"Yeah, but where's the road?" Kurt said.

"Ahhh, don't you worry," Luke said. "I can do this drive with my eyes closed." Another sliding hairpin ... "Won't be long and we'll be pulling off for Uncle Kemo's cabin."

"I can't wait," Kurt said, nervously staring down the steep slope outside his window.

"It's beautiful," John said, rubbing his eyes. He pulled his legs up cross-legged on the narrow back seat, thinking he might be able to squeeze in a short meditation. His body swayed with the truck, and he dipped quickly into the sweet silence of his inner spaces. Moccasin Mountain had a special feel to it. He could tell as soon as he closed his eyes. The air was thick with *i am*. Something was waiting here for him.

After a few more flirtations with the edge of the abyss, the truck pulled off onto a narrow lane through the woods. They were no longer climbing as steeply, just barreling through the gray and white woods. A couple of miles later, they slid to a stop in front of a log cabin with a porch facing the valley they drove up from. All they could see out there was flying snow. Luke assured them there was a big valley there. Behind the cabin was a creek gurgling down the mountain and heading off into the woods away from them. It was getting dark.

"Let's get our stuff in and light a fire," Luke said, slapping his sides as soon as the cold hit him.

"All right," John said, jumping out, grabbing his backpack and sleeping bag off the floor.

"Jesus, it's cold up here," Kurt said, stamping through the snow. "I should've stayed in Florida."

Luke reached under the porch by the steps and got the key from its hiding place and they went in.

The cabin was cold and quiet inside. It smelled of musty wood and all the fires that had come and gone in the big stone fireplace that was barely visible in the fading light. Luke tried the switch box on the wall by the door and the light hanging over the table came on.

"Glory be! We have power." He went and turned on the electric heater along the wall. Then he plugged in the refrigerator, and flipped the switch by the sink marked *pump*. Something whirred under the cabin.

"What's that," Kurt said.

"It's the well." Luke said. "We got all the comforts of home. No phone, but who needs that? Let's get some wood off the pile out back."

Soon they had a roaring fire going.

The front of the cabin was one big room, including the living room and kitchen area. There was a sofa and two easy chairs around the big low square table in front of the fire. It had old magazines and a dog-eared deck of cards on it. John looked out the windows on either side of the fireplace. The porch extended all the way across outside. It looked pretty bleak out there. But maybe it would clear up by tomorrow. In back there were two small bedrooms and a bathroom.

They made some dinner and were eating in front of the fire.

"Ah, now this is the life," Kurt said as he finished and leaned back in the big stuffed chair, putting his feet up on the table. "Your Uncle Kemo had the right idea getting this place up here. I bet it's nice in the summer."

"Oh yeah, it is." Luke said. "He doesn't come here much anymore though. He got arthritis pretty bad and he stays up in Blue Ridge Hollow with O'Pa and O'Ma."

"O'Pa and O'Ma?" John said.

"His parents ... my grandparents. That's what we always called them. That way of calling grandparents goes all the way back to slave days, at least in our family. O'Pa's been a preacher up there in the Hollow forever. The whole community's built around that church. It's in the middle of nowhere. You think this place is remote? That's where my Daddy came from before he went in the Navy."

"That's how you got to Jacksonville?" John said.

"Yep, been there since I was nine." Luke said. "Norfolk before that."

"We've been in the same house since we were younger than that," Kurt said. "Seems like forever."

"Sure does," John said.

"How you likin' Florida State?" Luke said.

"It's okay," Kurt said. "I'm just paying my dues, you know."

"Oh yeah, you're gonna get out there and make them big bucks, I bet." "Oh yeah," Kurt said. "And you're going into the NFL, right?"

"Gotta survive Georgia ball first," Luke said. "Then, who knows? How about you, John? What mountain you gonna climb?"

John was lying on the couch. The other two were in the stuffed easy chairs. He sat up cross-legged and looked into the fire, then at Luke.

"I'm on a God quest." He said. "No college for me. Not yet."

"No kiddin'," Luke said. "I wanna hear more about that. With your running, you could go anywhere, but you're not goin' to?"

"Nope." John put his hand on his chest. "Just in here."

"We're all hoping he will come to his senses," Kurt said.

"I think I have," John said. "And it's what I'm going to do."

"What bullshit!" Kurt's voice raised as he came out of the pillows. "Dad needs us in the business."

"Well, it's not for me," John said. "Sorry."

"Don't be too hard on little brother," Luke said. "Goin' the God way ain't an easy life. O'Pa had lots of tough years, and raising a family too. What crazy stories they tell about him."

"It's all beyond me." Kurt sank back down again.

The fire cracked, spitting a spark out on the floor by Luke. He stepped on it with his size fourteen boot. "So, what's this all about, this God quest?"

"For starters, meditation," John said.

"Meditation?"

"Yeah, going inside where God is. Using the most sacred name of God in a special way."

"Tell me," Luke said.

"I'm outta here," Kurt said. "Which room can I have?"

"Either one in the back," Luke said. "I'll take the other, and John, you can have the couch, okay?"

John nodded.

Luke had an expectant look. "Sure you don't' want to stick around for this?"

"No way," said Kurt.

"C'mon, Kurt, whatcha got to lose?" Luke said. "Here we are, in the middle of nowhere in a blizzard. Where's that Wilder spirit of adventure?"

"What's in it for me?" Kurt said. He'd grabbed his bag off the kitchen table and was about to take off.

John shrugged. "Not much. Only your peace of mind beyond the things that can't last."

"What things?"

"Oh, your wallet, your health, your life," John said. "Your loved ones too. It all goes away eventually, you know. Then what have you got?"

"You think you know what's best for me?" Kurt said.

"Nah," John said. "Only you can decide that. Meditation is just something useful, that's all. It's up to you."

"Okay," Kurt put the bag back down. "I'll stay. Maybe it's better than freezing my ass off in the back room."

"Way to go," Luke said. "When in doubt, do what ya gotta do to keep warm." He got up and made like he was blocking Kurt on a run play.

"All right, all right!" Kurt hung on to Luke's shirt to keep from going down.

Luke flopped down in the chair by the fire. Kurt sat down again too.

"So, tell us about meditation and the sacred name," Luke said.

"If you're both willing to hear it, I'm willing to tell it."

"Have at it, brother John," Luke said.

Kurt stared into the fire.

John got up, came over and tapped Luke on the breastbone. Then he went over and tapped Kurt. They both got strange disoriented looks on their faces. He sat down and closed his eyes. After a minute he said, "*i am.*"

He explained to them the difference between I AM and *i am*, the outward versus the inward intention.

They meditated together in front of the fire. John and Luke went deep into silent bliss. Kurt fidgeted through the whole thing. He couldn't let go, couldn't find the less that was more. His heart just wasn't in it. His hunger was elsewhere.

That night on Moccasin Mountain, in front of the fire, Luke got hooked on meditation. Kurt didn't, but *i am* was awakened invisibly in the depths of him all the same. New futures were created that night. It would take time for the three young men to realize the meaning of the inner life. Each would do so in their own way in the years to come.

Chapter 8 – Ecstatic Radiance

John found himself naked, flat on his back in a tall teepee. There was a bright white light at the top where the walls came together. His arms and legs were tied spread eagle to stakes in the ground. *How did I get here?*

A beautiful young Native American woman came in through the folds of the entrance, closing them behind her. She was glowing bronze. She had on nothing but a thin strand of rawhide around her waist with a small fan of feathers hanging from it in front, covering what he could see clearly in her eyes – her intense green-rimmed blue eyes. *What the…?*

She closed her eyes and shook her head. Her hair moved in waves. It was full and long, flowing down her front and off her generous breasts. She kneeled and leaned over him, smiling, and began to arouse him skillfully with her hands.

Then she was straddling him and coming down. He disappeared behind the feathers where she devoured him. She cried out with delight as she coaxed him out relentlessly, moving up and down while shaking her head in a reverie. Her hands went up under her hair, lifting her breasts high underneath. They were about to come through. Her laughter turned to short moans as she went faster. He was about to climax. Then she came fully down and stopped, pulsating on him, reaching behind her with her hand, tracing the line of his perineum and his manhood to its source where it came out of him just in front of his anus. She pressed into his soft flesh with two fingers and pulled up firmly as he exploded, blocking the exit of his essence. His diaphragm pulled his abdomen up rhythmically in automatic response to the quivering waves of ecstasy that spasmed repeatedly upward into his body. Her cries of passion went up with the waves, filling him to the top of his head, and overflowing. His ties were gone and they floated up in their long climaxing union to the narrowing peak inside the teepee, disappearing into the bright white light. Then she was gone, and he drifted slowly down through soft white light into a luminous sleep.

A beam entered John's eye as he cracked it open. It was the full moon shining in through the window of Uncle Kemo's cabin. His hand was down in his briefs resting on his perineum underneath. Except for a small amount of lubrication that had come out of him, he was dry. He had a lingering arousal and a sense of quiet fullness. *What had happened? Was it a dream? Was it a vision? What was the meaning?*

He got up and went to the window. The snow had stopped and he could see the moonlight shining down the hill into the valley. He looked at his watch and could make out that it was four AM. He sat back on the couch. The fire was still smoldering, with a few tiny flames licking out at him now and then. He decided to meditate.

As he sat cross-legged on the couch with his sleeping bag wrapped around him in a mound, he thought of the exploration of his perineum in the dream. He lifted up on his knees and felt underneath through his briefs. It was soft in the area where his organ came out from behind the pubic structure. He found how the strangely familiar native woman had blocked it by pushing in and forward against the bone. As he probed the area with his fingers, he felt a pleasant current go up through him. Instinctively, he pulled his right leg under and laid his foot, top down on the soft couch and slowly came down onto his heel. It fit naturally into the soft part of the perineum he had just been exploring with his fingers. He let the sole of his other foot rest against the shin of the leg that was under him, tucked under a little, so he was still in a cross-legged position, only resting on one of his heels.

There, how does that feel?

He felt a continuous stimulation, a pleasant current rising up. He felt it as much in his chest and head as in his groin. It was warm and delicious all over. He felt excited energy coming to give him an erection, but no erection came. It was blocked. Instead, the energy also went up into him. He was tempted to squirm on his heel, and did. He couldn't resist. It was so exciting.

After a while, he settled down to meditate. It was distracting having the constant pressure of his heel stimulating him underneath, but he managed to let go into the expansiveness of *i am*. Once he was deep inside, the distraction faded to silence, and the silence had a radiant quality he had not experienced before, a palpable presence. It was as though the essence rising in him was providing a vehicle for the silent bliss of *i am* to flow in him. The meditation tingled from beginning to end through every nerve in his body.

A half-hour later, he lay down into a feeling of wonderment, realizing he had been shown a great secret that night on Moccasin Mountain. Was it Christi Jensen again sharing secret wisdom with him? It seemed so. He'd been given the ability to release his orgasm outwardly or inwardly in any sexual situation, and the means to remain in constant arousal inwardly if he chose to. The possibilities filled him like sweet nectar. Soon he dozed off, cradled in a cocoon of gentle luminous pleasure.

The pillow landed on John's face with a swat.
"Hey, Sleeping Beauty. Wake up!" Kurt said.
"Huh?"
"Wake up. It's time to go play in the snow."

"What time is it?" John said groggily.

"Eight-thirty."

"Awww..." John rolled over in the sleeping bag and buried his face in the back of the couch.

"Okay, but you're missing it." Kurt said. "Look out there."

John forced himself to sit up and look out the window. The crystal clear snowy valley stretched out below them for twenty miles.

"Wow."

"Man, you've been dead to the world." Kurt said. "Luke went out already. He's got breakfast on the stove."

John could smell apple cinnamon oatmeal wafting over him.

They heard stamping feet on the porch. The whole cabin shook. Then Luke came in. "Good morning, brother John. Got about five inches out there. Not too bad for walking. You two want to do the creek trail up to the point?"

"Sure," said John. He was awake now and getting out of his bag.

After breakfast they bundled up and headed up the trail. The bubbling creek and the muffled silence of the snowy woods made for a magical journey up to Lookout Point, a craggy peninsula that hung off the side of Moccasin Mountain like a partially cut off arm. They could just barely see the rocky ledge up through the bare trees as they took the long circle up the ridge leading to the point.

How'd you like to take a swan dive off there?" Luke said, pointing up toward the high ledge.

"No thanks," Kurt said. "Is it safe up there this time of year?

Luke rubbed his big gloves together to warm his hands. "Oh sure. It's a little slippery on those rocks, but the view is somethin' else."

John looked up through the cloud of his breath. "Well, if there's a mountain, we ought to climb it, right?"

"You bet," Luke bellowed in his deep bass voice.

Kurt stepped on a slippery rock on the steep trail and ended up on his face in the snow. The other two laughed and helped him up. "I think I'd rather climb a mountain of money than this."

"Come on, you won't regret it when we get to the top," Luke said.

The air was crisp and their heavy breathing made the only clouds in sight. After twenty minutes of tramping uphill through the ankle-deep snow, they came to the top from the back side. As they walked out onto the slippery rock point, it was like the edge of the world, falling off into nothingness on three sides. They could see forever out across the white rolling peaks in the distance. Below them, off through the woods, they could see a wisp of smoke coming up from the cabin way below.

Luke went out close to the edge. John felt something quiver inside, like the rock was giving way under him.

"Up that way about a hundred and fifty miles is Blue Ridge Hollow," Luke said, pointing to the right. Then he pointed to the left. "And down that way the same distance is Alabama. Three hundred miles in these arms." He held his arms out wide hanging over empty space.

"It's incredible," John said.

Luke grinned. "Sure is. I always come up to the point when we are here. Reminds me that there are things much bigger than me. And now you've shown me a bigger place inside too. I love wide open places…"

"It's a damn cold wide open place." Kurt had his arms wrapped around his chest and his shoulders held high inside his heavy coat. "I'm ready to go."

They stood for a few more minutes. Kurt began stamping his feet. Luke turned away from the edge of the cliff. He had his back to the vast open space. "You ready to get back to the fire?"

"Y-y-yeah," Kurt said.

"Okay, let's go." Luke went to take a step toward them. As he did, a snow-covered rock underneath gave way behind his rear foot. In an instant he was on his belly and sliding over the edge. Luke slid away, legs first. It all happened in slow motion. John jumped inside himself to grab Luke's arms before they were gone, but his body could not move fast enough. Time had stopped for the three young men, but motion did not. He was gone.

"Ahhiiieee!"

John heard him hit the rocks on the way down and then the tree tops fifty feet below with a series of loud cracks of cold wood breaking, a whoosh of light branches he fell through, and finally a muted thud. It was all over in less than five seconds.

"Jesus," Kurt said. "He went over. I can't believe it!"

"Oh God! Luke! Luke!" John cried. There was no response from the woods below. "We have to get down there!"

John rushed along the cliff looking for a direct way down. He found a narrow notch between the rocks on the left side and slid down on his rear end through the snow that had drifted there. Kurt stayed up top, looking over, trying to see Luke.

After sliding down the notch and rushing down a series of ledges leading around the point toward the back, John got down to the woods and began running around to the front of the point to where Luke had fallen. He found him lying face down at the base of a tree. His leg was twisted at a grotesque angle, broken badly above the knee. John fell on his knees by the big body in the snow, putting his hand gently on Luke's back.

"Luke, Luke, can you hear me?"

There was nothing.

"Luke –"

There was a moan. John's heart leaped. "Can you hear me, Luke?"

Silence…

"Y-yeah ... y-yeah… It, it hurts all over," Luke finally groaned.

John got down with his head in the snow right next to Luke's. Their eyes met. "Don't worry, brother Luke. We'll get you out of here. Can you move your head?"

"Yeah, I think so." Luke turned his head a little from side to side. There was frozen blood in the snow underneath that had run down from a gash on Luke's forehead. That was the least of it.

"Can you move your hands?"

Luke opened and closed both fists in the snow.

"You're right leg's busted really bad. Don't try and move it. Can you move your left foot?"

Luke did.

"I'm no doctor, but maybe your back is okay. I don't know. But you can't stay here. You'll freeze before we can get help up here. We're going to have to move you down to the truck, all right?"

"W-whatever you say," Luke managed. Then he passed out.

"Luke, Luke, we're going to have to straighten that leg before we move you," John said. *Damn.* "Kurt! Come on down here. I found him and he is alive."

"Where are you?" Kurt yelled from above.

"Straight below. Come down the pass I went down, and around from the back side."

It didn't take long for Kurt to follow John's improvised trail down from the point. Soon he came lumbering through the snow around the base of the cliff. "Oh, he's a mess. Look at that leg."

"Yeah, we're going to straighten it and drag him back to the truck. It's down there." John pointed down the hill. The roof of the cabin was visible through the trees a few hundred yards down the wooded snow-covered hill. A trail of smoke rose from the stone chimney.

"How are we going to do that?"

"We need rope," John said. "And something we can put him on and drag. We have to do it fast. It must be fifteen degrees out here. You stay here." He looked around at the many dead limbs laying around. "Get as many strong limbs together as you can and lay them here next to Luke. I'm going down there to find some rope." He took off down the hill, bounding through the snow like a jack rabbit. Near the bottom, he jumped the creek that creased the snow and sprinted for the cabin.

He burst into the cabin and looked everywhere for rope. Nothing. He grabbed a pocketknife out of the kitchen drawer and ran out. He found a large coil of rope in the shed behind the cabin and a couple of two-by-fours. He took off back up the hill. By the time he got back to Luke and Kurt, he felt like he was back in cross-country, on the verge of passing out. His breath filled the air like white smoke. He collected some air and looked down at Luke, sprawled in the snow.

"He's out," Kurt said. He had gathered ten long limbs and lined them up like a raft next to Luke.

"Here take this knife and cut three pieces of rope for a splint, and start lashing the rest on both ends of those limbs." He panted as he straddled the crooked leg. "Okay ... okay Luke, this is going to hurt,"

John counted to three slowly and gave the leg a big jerk with both hands. *Crack!* Luke screamed as it went straight, and John fell over backwards.

He crawled next to the big man in the snow, clasping his hand. "Sorry, Luke. It worked. The leg is straight now. We're going to get you out of here. I promise."

Luke squeezed John's hand weakly and groaned.

While Kurt lashed the branches together, John tied the two-by-fours together on both sides of Luke's broken leg with the three pieces of rope that Kurt had cut. Then he helped Kurt with the lashing. In ten minutes they rolled him on it, face up. He roared in pain again when they moved him.

"Sorry, Luke," John said. "We can move you now. Hang in there."

Luke groaned incoherently.

They got on the head end of the drag they'd built and lifted.

"Man, this is heavy," Kurt said. "He must weigh three hundred pounds."

"NFL-sized lineman," John said. "Let's go."

They struggled as they pulled the makeshift gurney down the steep hill, getting stuck a few times on rocks and limbs under the snow along the way. When they finally got to the truck, gasping in the cold air, they managed to lift one end onto the tailgate, then lift the other end and slide the drag into the back bed. They grabbed every blanket and sleeping bag in the cabin and piled them on Luke. There was no way they could get him in the cab of the truck.

"You drive," John said. "I'm staying back here. Open the back window, and blow it all back. That way we might get a little heat."

John got under the pile of blankets with Luke to try and keep him warm, and they headed down the mountain. He kept talking to him, though

Luke was unconscious most of the way. Kurt took the truck down the winding mountain road they had come up the night before.

An hour later, they were in the emergency room in Hagarville.

"Besides the leg," the gray-haired elderly doctor said, "he's got a broken pelvis and a serious concussion. We have him stabilized and we're sending him to Atlanta this afternoon for surgery. He's going to be laid up a good while, but he should make it. Looks like you boys saved his life."

John's cold-reddened face looked away, off into another realm. Then he bent over, put his hands on his knees, and broke down crying.

Kurt stood with his hands in his pockets looking somewhat disoriented. *What did it mean to save a life?*

The next morning in Atlanta, when Luke was coming out of recovery after the surgery, John was there with Luke's parents.

"Brother John," Luke whispered when he saw him. "Looks like I was the one in trouble this time, huh?"

"Yeah," John said. "No more walking off cliffs, okay? Not until you learn to fly."

"I promise."

Luke reached out and took John's hand. They held on to each other for a while, the huge brown hand and the small white one, joined in sacred brotherhood. Then Luke spoke softly:

"I'm so glad you taught me to meditate."

With Luke's words, John felt a wave of ecstatic energy surging up inside him. So much happened on Moccasin Mountain that weekend – Luke and Kurt learning meditation. The gift of inner ecstatic radiance John received in the dream. Luke's near-fatal fall. Nothing would ever be the same.

Chapter 9 – Fastest Man Alive

Thoump...

John took a blow to the hip that knocked him two feet off course in the busy school corridor. Devi gave him a wicked smile as he came back to walk next to her, only to fall prey to her swinging hips again when he least expected it. He'd give one back to her every now and then, but he acknowledged her as the undisputed queen of hip thoumps. *Ah, those beautiful hips.*

The pair had become recognized as inseparable at Duval High. Their ongoing flirtations were visible for all to see. Most thought they were engaging in riotous sex all those afternoons that John's car could be seen parked in front of her house. If only they knew.

"More jelly?" Devi said.

"Oh yeah," John said. "Smear it right out to the edge."

"Mmmmm, how's that?" she said.

"A little more."

"Fussy, aren't we?"

"Well, if you are going to be my wife some day, you've got to know how to make a peanut butter and jelly sandwich."

"I feel like your wife already,' she said, "the way you're ordering me around this slice of bread."

He came close behind her, reached around, and took her hand with the knife in it, helping her smear the purple and brown concoction. "Ah, much better."

"Yeah," she said snuggling against him with her backside. "You know, they're talking about us."

"They are? Who's 'they?'"

"THEM."

"Oh, THEM," he said. "What are they saying?"

"That we aren't meditating and eating peanut butter and jelly sandwiches together over here. That we are doing something else."

"Something else?" he said, nibbling her ear. "Like what?"

"You know, dummy."

"Ohhhhhh ... thaaat." He wrapped his arms around her midriff, right under her breasts, and began a suggestive swaying dance. She responded with her dangerous hips, in unison with his. "Well, let them talk."

"Yeah, let them," she said.

"I'd be happy to stay with you like this until the end of time," he said.

"I'll be there with you," she said, and they danced across the shiny linoleum floor.

John hadn't told Devi yet about his discovery on Moccasin Mountain. Luke's accident and recovery were more than enough to absorb. Besides, he wanted to refine his perineum-root explorations first. There were other things emerging in relation to it. He still wasn't sure what he had. In the weeks since he began sitting on his heel during meditation, his sexual energy was going up more and more, even outside meditation. It was giving him a new freedom to engage in passionate flirtations with Devi without having to succumb to the pressure of outward flowing biology. Their love was becoming a glorious dance to him, a never-ending celestial waltz, whether they were together or apart. This constant loving was coaxing him into new realms of sensation. He was so grateful. When he and Devi were alone, he would sometimes be overwhelmed with love and fall on the floor in front of her, kissing her tiny bare feet. She would lean over and softly stroke his hair. He knew that she understood his journey. Behind their constant flirting and funmaking, she was everything, inside and outside him.

As John continued his practices, he noticed a thin silver thread of pleasure going up the center of his spine. It was clearly visible in his mind's eye. Or was he feeling it? It had an intense cold heat to it, like a highly concentrated muscle liniment flowing up a tiny tube in his spine from his loins. The distinction between seeing and feeling was blurred. Still sitting on his heel at the end of meditation, the silence of *i am* reverberating through his depths, he experienced the intensely pleasurable thread-like nerve rising from his root, extending up the center of his spine all the way to the top of his head. When he squeezed his anal sphincter muscle while lifting inside his pelvis, waves of ecstatic current flowed up, swirling around the nerve, traveling outward in widening orbits around it.

He sat on his bed observing the embryonic spectacle. He knew it was the beginning of something fantastic, because he could easily amplify it with his anal sphincter, by lifting his abdomen with his diaphragm, by lifting his eyes, and by letting go deep into *i am*. He found that the experience was greatly enlivened by holding his breath inside. He began experimenting with his breath in a separate session before his regular meditation.

Why did suspending breath have this effect? He didn't know. But restraining breath clearly had a central role, and he knew he must pursue it. As he held his breath inside for longer periods before his meditation sessions, he sweated profusely. He could feel his nervous system being purged of restrictions to the infant ecstatic energy flows. Breath had been an area of exploration of his for years, an important factor in his running.

He was familiar with pressing breath to its limits. Now he was deliberately stopping his breath to start something else inside him. That something was beginning to swirl around its central silver thread in him like a newborn hurricane.

Where am I going with this?

He began to put the pieces together. He called his heel sitting the "root seat." The lifting of his diaphragm he called the "abdominal lift." The squeezing of his anal sphincter and lifting inside his pelvis he called the "root lift." It created blooming flower-like waves of pleasurable energy in him. *Yowee!...* Raising his eyes he called the "eye lift." Raising the eyes had an ecstatic connection to his loins. He called all the connections of pleasure happening throughout his body the rise of *ecstatic conductivity*. He tried coordinating all the moves together while holding his breath in. It was confusing and chaotic at first, but he didn't give up. Over the course of weeks of daily practice, it began to come together. It even began to feel natural. The sweating during breath retention became less as his nerves slowly got cleared out and were conducting more and more ecstatic energy rising up from his pelvis. He noticed during his breath suspensions that his chin would be drawn down onto his breastbone. It stretched the silver thread, making it conduct energy upward more rapidly. The pleasure of it pulled his chin down naturally. He called it the "chin lock." His tongue was drawn back on the roof of his mouth, reaching for a pleasurable connection that was located at the point on the roof of his mouth where his hard and soft palates met. This one he called the "palate lift," because it sent energy up into his head.

He found that stretching the silver thread beforehand benefited his practice later on during meditation, making it deeper and more blissful. He experimented with stretching exercises before beginning breath suspensions. He found that if he stood with both his arms wrapped around his torso in one direction, twisting his spine in that direction, and then wrapping his arms the other direction and twisting that way, it felt extremely good. He didn't know why. The invitation to pleasure was enough for him. He got similar ecstatic feelings when he put his hands over his head and leaned back as far as he could, and then leaned over forward and touched his toes. He'd hold each of these positions for fifteen seconds or so.

Then there was the "abdominal twirl," something he discovered quite by accident one day as he was standing in his room with his hands on his knees, experimenting with his diaphragm and abdominal muscles. He let all his air all the way out and was pulling his stomach in and up with his diaphragm. It felt good. Ecstatic energy bubbled up through him when he did it. He noticed he could tense his abdominal muscles while standing in this position by doing a sit up against the force of his hands resting on his knees. If he did this repeatedly while he had his air out his diaphragm sucked up, pleasurable energy came up through him like a fountain. Flexing the abdominals in this way created a kind of ecstasy pump. Then he hit the jackpot. He found that he could isolate the left abdominal muscle from the right one by flexing against the hand braced on one knee, and then the other. If he alternated back and fourth he could twirl his abdominal muscles in a large undulating spiral, first one way, and then the other. The energy flows this induced nearly knocked him off his feet. He'd do twenty twirls in each direction, usually all of them on one big out-breath. What a way to start out before sitting for practices. Of course he knew the pleasure was contingent on having the ecstatic conductivity awakened in the first place, and that was a function of meditation, root seat, breath suspension, and the combined effect of all his practices. Once he got in the habit of separating control of his left and right abdominal muscles, the abdominal twirls could be performed subtly at any time and in any position. They became barely perceptible twirls occurring naturally during breathing practices, meditation, and any time ecstasy was on the move in him. It was his body accommodating the rise of the divine energies in him.

He would do the standing stretches and abdominal twirls before he sat on the bed in root seat. All of these together he called his spiritual stretching exercises. Then, before he started his sitting practices, he'd stretch one leg straight out from root seat, take a deep in-breath, lean over, and hold his big toe while doing the chin lock, abdominal lift and root lift, going toward his knee with his head without straining. He'd hold this as long as he comfortably could, and then do two more breaths on the same leg. Then he'd switch, putting the other leg out in a switched-foot root seat and do the same thing again three times. By then, his silver thread, and the rest of him, would be opened and lit up for breath suspensions, and for meditation after breathing practice. Spiritual stretching was a wonderful way to start practices.

Most of the things he did were driven by the pleasurable feelings he followed inside. It was an extension and refinement of his erotic feelings, and natural enough. He came to realize that all he had to do was follow the ecstatic currents in his body, mind and heart. His purpose was clear. More answers came each step along the way.

But he did have a tendency to overdo…

The weeks turned into months, and John gradually settled into his routine of practices. First he did spiritual stretching exercises. Then he would do breath suspensions with the lifts and other maneuvers. After that he would meditate on *i am* while continuing in root seat, not focusing on anything else. The *i am* meditation remained at the center of his practices. He had not forgotten what Christi Jensen said about everything flowing from *i am.*

His never-ending love for *i am* and Devi drove everything else. Somehow, these two great loves were aspects of the same thing. He longed to understand why.

Many times while he sat in meditation, he was consumed in the expanding swirling energies that surrounded the silver thread. Often he could not see the thread clearly anymore. It was obscured by the increasingly chaotic multi-colored energy swirling around it. Only during the deepest quiet of *i am* meditation did he find himself in the unfathomable silence of the microscopic thread of his inner being that traversed his body. It was so thin, yet so full inside. It was the manifestation of galaxies within him. He thought the entire universe might be contained between his tailbone and the top of his head. He pressed ahead aggressively with his practices. He was on a roll. He wanted more.

He carried the growing experience around with him, appearing more or less normal. But he was far from normal. While he tolerated the growing storm inside him, he could tell something was out of balance. The more the energy rose in him, the more it became clear that it needed someplace to go. But where?

He felt like a volcano gradually building up pressure inside, until finally –

But he couldn't stop his practices. There was no turning back. *I must go forward and find where this leads. There's too much pleasure to stop. It feels so good that it hurts, but I don't care. I want it all.*

One thing that helped John dissipate his runaway inner energies was exercise, especially running. He missed cross-country season due to his cracked ribs, but, as soon as he was able, he started his daily morning exercises and running on the beach again.

Since early in John's cross-country days, he had done calisthenics and isometric exercises in his room before going downstairs each morning. He called it his "gym time." There were seven exercises he would do:

✓ Fifty half pushups between two chairs.
✓ Fifty hard isometric curls upward on each bicep with the heel of one hand pressed firmly down on the other.
✓ Twenty-five flexes of his neck in each of four different directions against stiff isometric pressure from his hands on his head: front, back, left, and right.

✓ Fifty half squats with his hands on his waist, pushing his chest out.
✓ Fifty calf flexes, standing on his toes on the edge of the chair against the wall.
✓ Fifty sit-ups on the bed, with his feet under the cross-bar of the four-poster.
✓ Fifty straight leg lifts on the bed, his fingers gripped under the headboard.

The whole routine took ten or fifteen minutes, and kept him in good tone for long distance running, and life in general. When he took up spiritual practices, he did his exercises right after the rest period at the end of morning meditation.

He resumed his barefoot running on the beach. He started out slow as his ribs finished healing, and worked gradually up to full speed. The energies surging through him collected in ecstatic fiery balls in his feet, making his feet and legs tingle and itch like they had ants creeping around inside them. Running felt extremely good, like having orgasms in his feet. Barefoot running deliciously released the overflowing prickly currents. He ran like the wind, hardly noticing his body, barely breathing. It was as though he was being carried on the currents spurting out of his feet.

One evening, while running, he noticed Coach Johnson with a stopwatch up on a big dune as he flew by.

On his way back, with a bright pink twilight setting in, Coach flagged him down out of his running reverie. He was a short stocky black man with a torso like a cement column.

"Hello, son. You sure can run. Either that, or this old stopwatch is slowing down." He banged it in the palm of his hand and looked at it strangely. "Anyway, how'd you like to run the mile for the track team at the state finals next week?"

John was bouncing up and down on his bare toes with his arms dangling and hands flicking at his sides. He looked like he was ready to blast off the planet. "I dunno, Coach. You know I've never done the mile. Never wanted to. Why me now?"

"Jimmy Marco's just gone out with a hamstring."

John stopped bouncing. "Oh, sorry to hear that. He's a great runner."

"He said you're the one to replace him. We've got a shot at team state championship this year if we can make the mile work. Can you help us out?"

John stroked the sunset-hued sand lightly with the bottoms of his bare feet. It shot bliss currents up to the top of his head. *Do I need this? They obviously do.*

"Okay, I'll do it."

"Terrific," Coach Johnson said. "It'll be your last race before graduation. You can go out in style."

"I suppose…" John was trotting in place now. His feet were on fire. "I'll give it my best shot."

"That's all we ask," Coach Johnson said.

"Gotta go, Coach. See ya later." John took off running again. It felt much better to be running than to be standing still. The restless ecstatic energy needed to move.

As he raced along the water's edge, he glanced over his shoulder and saw Coach Johnson trudging back up the dune, stopping to look at his stopwatch again and shaking his head. Then he went over the top of the dune and out of sight into the fading pink sky. John pointed himself back up the beach and streaked home. It was pure ecstasy to run like the wind.

It was a hot sunny Saturday in Orlando at International Stadium. The base of the huge bowl was alive with the bright colored uniforms of high schools from Key West to Pensacola. The stands weren't full, but the showing was reasonable, mostly parents and friends coming to see their young men on this field of competition that symbolized so much in life. There were high-jumpers, long-jumpers, pole-vaulters, shot-put and javelin throwers, and, of course, the runners – all those runners ready to dash from one hundred yards to a mile.

John was meandering around the center of the grassy field by himself in the new violet track shorts and shirt. They felt like shimmering silk on him. He was tingling with energy coming from within. Anything that touched him felt sensually good – the uniform, the new track shoes, the air wafting through his hair. He imagined he might look distracted, but he wasn't. He was ready to run, floating in quiet anticipation, his feet ready to explode.

Finally the call came: "One mile event! Runners to the starting line!"

John went over to the starting area and found a spot on the line with the twenty, or so, runners crammed across the track. They were all bigger than him. It would be a free for all. No qualifying heats for this race. It was too long to do more than once. He looked up and down the line. All of Florida was here. A few of the faces were familiar. *Okay…*

When the gun went off, John immediately fell to the back of the pack. He saw this was no cross-country start, as everyone took off at a near-sprint. *These guys are hot. I better just sprint this thing and get it over with.*

He took off like a bolt of lightning, his hands rhythmically flicking energy toward his fast-moving feet as he started passing runners: red, blue, green, yellow, black … he vaguely noticed the uniforms and legs flailing in slow motion as he passed them on the outside of the first curve. He heard their strained breathing, their fading curses, and distant competitive chides. He could not feel his own breath. All he felt was lightness and the pleasure of the air caressing him. Then there was silence...

Faster!

One lap; now he was in front, and pulling away ... accelerating...

Two laps, half done, and running; all eyes were watching the violet streak, and the big digital clock at the end of the field ... 1:58 ... 1:59 ... 2:00 ... Time seemed to grind to a halt as they watched John fly around the track.

Faster!

Three laps; cheers erupted from the crowd as the lad with the quiet smile, strange flicking hands, and flashing pigeon-toed feet accelerated into the climax. His shoes barely kissed the ground, making a light whisking sound as he passed effortlessly over the cinder track. The other runners were desperately pounding it three quarters of a lap behind.

When he broke the tape at the finish line, he was in silence, in *i am*. As he watched himself slow to a walk on the track, everything was moving on the periphery of his awareness, coming toward him. There was no sound at all. He felt a single bead of sweat run down his temple. It fell in slow motion ... and finally he heard it land on his shoulder with a crash. Then, suddenly, the roar of the crowd invaded him like an atomic explosion. Members from all the teams surrounded him and lifted him up, carrying him across the field on a sea of colors shouting: "Wilder! Wilder! Wilder!"...

I don't get it. I ran. I won. So what?

"Wilder! Wilder! Wilder! ..."

Finally, they let him down and watched him as he walked away, expressionless, and sat down on the grass near the other Duval High athletes. A small crowd followed him. Several reporters elbowed their way through and stood over him, eagerly asking questions, but he didn't hear what they said. He closed his eyes and went into *i am*. A smile emerged on his face and the roar faded. He was out of their reach.

A while later, he felt a large gentle hand on his arm.

"Luke!" John said as he opened his eyes.

"Hello, brother John." Luke sank down onto the grass next to him.

"Look at you. No crutches."

"Yep. I might be able to play ball again in a year, but we'll have to see."

"Well, I hope you can. It's sure good to see you." John connected with someone for the first time since the race. "These people are crazy around here. I win a race and they all go nuts. You'd think I broke the world record or something."

"You did break the world record by more than fifteen seconds," Luke said. "Three minutes, twenty-nine seconds. Didn't you see?"

"No. What? Three minutes what?"

"Three minutes, twenty-nine seconds."

"That's impossible."

"That's what they're saying," Luke said. "That the official clock busted during the race or somethin'. But they got half a dozen watches on it too. All those clocks putting you in that neighborhood. They don't know what to do."

"What's to do?" John said. "I won. The team needed the points. That's it. I'm done. Back to the beach for me."

"They'll want you to do it again," Luke said. "They'll want you for the Olympics. They'll want to dissect you."

"Oh shit," John said.

"You ain't kiddin'."

"Let's get out of here."

"Okay, your parents and Devi are out yonder." He pointed over the top of the stadium toward the parking lot.

They got up and began to walk, trailed by a few hangers-on.

"Hey, you are hardly limping." John said.

"Yeah, the docs and physical therapy folks can't believe it … fastest recovery they ever saw. I think it must be the meditation."

"Most likely," John quipped. "Makes my running look like nothing."

When they got clear of the field they entered the dark breezeway of the stadium.

Luke took John by the arm and they stopped. "How'd you do it? They said you weren't even breathin' hard."

"I don't know," John said. "I wasn't really doing it. I was in *i am*."

"Lord have mercy."

"I guess so." John felt a wave of ecstasy rushing up through him, stretching him inside. His eyes began to turn up in their sockets. He started bouncing up and down lightly on his toes. The energy had nowhere else to go. There was a strange lurching up and down in his spine. He felt like he had insects crawling all over his body. Every pore of his skin felt like it was about to have an orgasm. He started shaking his head from side to side as he bounced. Anything to let the energy out.

"You all right?" Luke said. "You're lookin' ready to fly again."

John forced himself to settle down, though inside he remained lit up like a Christmas tree. His eyes came back. "Let's go home, brother Luke."

Chapter 10 – Rising Tide

"So, now what?" Harry Wilder stood over John, sprawled on the couch in trunks and a T-shirt..

"Now what?"

"Yes, now what? Now that you've graduated."

John gazed out the big bay window at the smooth blue horizon. It was in contrast with his hurricane-like inner condition. He did not look up. "Do you want me to move out?"

Harry stopped short. "Of course not. I just would like to have an idea about your plans."

"Can't we be happy about John's graduation?" John's mother stood framed by the archway to the foyer. "It's supposed to be a happy time –"

Harry turned to her "Oh, Stella, don't you see John has no inkling what he is going to do?"

Stella was beginning to raise her finger. "Well, I just –"

"Maybe junior college in town?" Harry turned back. "How does that grab you, John? It isn't much, but it's a start."

"Let me think about it, okay, Dad?" John was stalling, putting off the inevitable.

"Think about it?" Harry said. "It's only a couple of months away."

John didn't know how to tell his parents what he was experiencing. He hadn't told anyone about the volcano of pleasure building up inside him. *What am I going to do with this?*

Stella turned, sighing. "I'm going to the kitchen."

John watched her disappear around the corner of the dark wood molding. He remembered she once told him that the kitchen is the safest place in any house, and how, as a small child she'd hide under the kitchen table because she felt safe there … protected. John wondered what was protecting him as he hung his ass out the infinite inner window he had opened. Somehow, in his silence, beyond the raging love currents, he knew it would be okay. He was on a divine mission, right? People on divine missions were always protected, weren't they?

"Dad, I know you don't see much going on with me, but there is."

"You mean your God quest? You still not over that?"

"I'll never be over it."

"Then why not go to Bible college, or seminary?"

"I'm in school right here."

"Here?" Harry looked around the living room. "And all the time you spend over at the Duran's? You'd better be careful, son, or you'll find yourself as guest of honor at a shotgun wedding."

"It's not like that."

Harry rolled his eyes. "You think I was born yesterday? She is a beautiful young lady. What are you doing, playing Parcheesi over there?"

"Devi understands what I'm doing."

"I bet she does."

"I'm not telling you much, am I?"

"No, you're not," Harry said. "Do you understand my concern?"

"Yes,"

"And?"

"Hang in there with me, Dad. I need your support."

Harry sighed. "I'll try, son. I'll try. But you've got to come clean with me somewhere along the line."

"I hope it will become clear in time," John said. "I want to know too."

"I have a lot of faith in you," Harry said. "You are capable of great things. You've already shown that. But you haven't given me much to hang on to. They've dubbed you *the fastest man alive who won't run*. They keep playing the damn tape of you on TV, the so-called miracle race. They keep calling – agents, coaches, sponsors, media ... add my name to the long list of people who don't know what makes you tick."

"I know," John said. "I'm sorry. Would it be all right if I work part-time in the drafting room at the company?"

"You mean like you've been doing summers? Operating a blueprint machine and running errands?"

"Yeah, that's all I need for now. Enough to cover my expenses. I want to pay you some rent here too."

"Oh, that's not –"

"I want to. I'll pay my own way. That way I can do my spiritual work without being a freeloader."

Harry shrugged and sat in the recliner. "It's not much of a life you are choosing."

"We'll see, Dad." John's eyes wandered off to the horizon again.

John was running back up the five-mile stretch of Coquina Island beach toward home. It was late afternoon and the beach had emptied of most sunbathers. He had on a black nylon brief swimsuit. He'd run naked if he could. The July sun felt good on his tan back. The hard wet sand fit his feet perfectly. The salt air caressed every cell in his lungs as they expanded and contracted slowly, in contrast to the devilish pace of his legs. Off in the distance, he could see parts of the house up on the dune, buried in the palms and live oaks. He could make out Devi walking down the wooden stairs toward the beach. She waved at him. *I must look like a wiggling speck on the beach to her at this distance.* He waved both arms over his head and stepped up his pace, hands flicking faster as he accelerated. By the time he finished racing to her, he was slick with sweat.

"Whoa, it's Rocket Man in tights," she cried as he ran up to her. "Look at you. You're as tan as me."

She had on a patterned orange and yellow cover-up, a big straw hat, and big-rimmed sunglasses. Her hair was bundled under the hat.

He picked her up by the waist and spun her around as they laughed. The hat flew off, and her shining black hair came down all over them. The sweet scent of her coconut suntan lotion enveloped him as he put her down.

"Oh, now look what you've done." She dropped her sunglasses into the hat and was gathering her hair into a ponytail. He loved to watch her when her arms were up in her hair. She pulled an elastic out of her pocket and bound it. "Okay, you ready for the big show?" She was lifting her cover-up slowly up her thighs with a teasing look in her eyes.

John fell down sideways like a tree, landing with his chest puffed out, legs gracefully crossed, and elbow in the sand with his head comfortably propped in his hand. He looked like a body-builder posing for a foldout. Well, not quite.

"I'm ready," he said. "I have to be lying down so when I pass out I won't fall.

"Silly boy." She eyed him seductively.

Up came the dress in a slow rotating Devi dance, revealing her in a pale yellow bikini that blended naturally into her light brown skin and lovely curves.

"You're beautiful," he said. He let his head fall off his hand into the sand.

She laughed, and took off running for the water. "Last one in's a rotten egg!" she cried over her shoulder. "Fastest man alive can't catch me!"

John lifted his head and watched her go, a perfect divine goddess running into the sea. He sprang up and went after her, catching her knee deep and went under the first small wave with her. They came up together. Her dark eyes blinked wide and her mouth opened for air as the seawater ran down her face. With her ponytail and wet hair, she looked like she had short hair from the front. He picked her up and carried her out across the rippled bottom to the calm chest-deep water where only an occasional gentle swell rolled in toward the small shore break. She turned in front of him and wrapped her legs around him beneath the surface of the warm clear water.

"Now I've got you." She gave him a blissful look, floating somewhere between complete possession and total liberation.

She tilted her head, as though trying to read his quiet mind. The crystal cross drifted in the gentle current flowing between her breasts. It glinted as the sun hit it under the water. They came slowly closer, gazing into each other's eyes. She kissed him. Her tongue lightly darted between his lips, coaxing him out. He joined her in the tongue dance, first in her mouth, then in his. She held him with her arms and legs, and he held her close as he stood on the ocean floor. He was stretching his thin nylon swimsuit into her softness underneath. She sighed softly in his ear. They held each other like everything depended on it. Such intimate embraces were not uncommon for them. It had never gone further than that. It had been their arrangement for their whole senior year.

She leaned back in the water with her arms around his neck. Her legs were still wrapped around him. "I've decided to stay here. The university can wait."

"Are you sure?" he said.

"Yes, I want to stay close to you. I'll get a job, take some classes. Is that okay?"

"Yeah, sure," he said.

"Where are we going with this?" She came off him, and stood on the bottom in front of him. She placed her hand lightly on his swollen member under the water, and ran her fingers along its length through the nylon.

"I'm not sure," he said.

"I'm on the pill. It's safe."

"I know."

"You know?"

"Yes, I saw the pills on your bureau a few weeks ago," he said

"And that wasn't enough?" she said.

"I'm not ready."

"I am," she said as she began to slide her hand down into his briefs. She touched the flesh of his manhood for the first time. Her eyes melted in his. He stopped her, gently lifting her out.

"I'm sorry," he said.

"Is something wrong?"

"You are perfect. Our time is coming. We will do a great thing." John's eyes drifted out across the surface of the warm summer sea that clothed them.

She looked at him in disbelief.

"What great thing?"

It had come from within him in that moment of their embrace, as everything in him craved to be inside her.

He looked back into her eyes. "Our child. She is waiting."

"Our child?" she said. "I'm not ready for a child."

"No one is yet. But the time is coming."

"How do you know?"

"I just know," he said.

Devi was stunned...

They walked toward shore, the spell of their arousal broken. A different kind of spell held Devi. *A child? What does he mean?*

His words stirred something deep in her womb. She felt it glowing pleasurably like a golden pear deep in her belly. She longed to have him inside her, filling her full with his precious seed. She realized that it was more than having him inside, much more.

Yes, I want his child. I want to bring our baby into the world. Why can't it be now ... today? Oh, the damn pills. I never should have started them. I'm done with them. When he's ready, I'll be ready. Mama showed me how to get ready when I was fourteen. She gave me the dildo. I've practiced with it ever since, everything she told me. Now I'm ready. I want our baby. I want –

"Are you okay?" John said. "Sorry if I upset you."

"No, you didn't." She managed with a shy look. "It's just that I hadn't thought about –"

"Our baby?" he said. "Me neither."

"So, where did it come from?"

"It came to me when I saw myself coming into you out there. Our love is so sacred, something so important. And then she came to me, touched me tenderly inside. She's waiting for us to be ready."

They sat silently on the wet sand by the water's edge. The only sound was the small gentle waves wandering in.

The revelation of the purpose of their union had a sobering effect on Devi. Womanhood and her coming motherhood surged within her. She looked down at her body. The thin yellow material didn't conceal much when it was wet. Her dark nipples revealed themselves prominently as the sea breeze cooled her moist skin. *Someday our child will be nourished from these breasts.*

The soft mat of her mound slightly darkened the thin wet yellow that covered it. She could feel the breeze cooling the cloth clinging to her sensitive folds, the entrance to her waiting womb. *Someday our child will emerge from this sacred opening.*

She looked into John's eyes, inviting him to view her womanhood. She leaned back on her elbows. Her breasts came up. She let her knees drift apart until they rested on the sand so he could see her.

"I'm to have our child," she said. "Your words turned me into a woman today, your woman. Together we'll turn this divine goddess into a divine mother."

He leaned forward in his cross-legged position, placing his hands on the insides of her knees, caressing slowly down her thighs. "I feel different too." He gazed lovingly at her contours. Then his eyes rose up high in a look of pleasure she could not comprehend.

She looked at him. His shape was well defined in his black nylon brief. His erection was much smaller than it had been in the water, and it stayed down even as he admired her. She knew he could be much bigger. He always was when he admired her. She had often brushed him with her body to feel him underneath. She'd never made herself visible to him like this before. *What's going on?*

She noticed he was sitting with his foot tucked under him in the sand. She lifted herself off her elbows and came closer. She ran the fingers of one hand softly down the center of his chest, down his hard stomach, and lower until she was touching him again. He didn't stop her as she began to stroke his member through the thin nylon. It stayed the same. His eyes were drawn up again, seemingly by her touching. She didn't understand.

"I want to share something," he said. "I've been doing more practices since I came back from Moccasin Mountain last winter. It's part of what is changing me."

"Please tell me. I feel like I'm losing my touch." She looked around to see if anyone was nearby. Seeing the coast was clear, she began to fondle him with both hands – still no change.

His eyes went up in the blissful expression again. This time he pulled his stomach up as though lifting something inside.

What the...? Devi was baffled.

"You're not losing your touch," he said softly. "It's just going up in me instead of out."

Then she understood. Since beginning meditation, sexual energy often rose in her deliciously. "But how? How do you do that?"

"It's in the heel. Watch." He leaned back slightly and his nyloned member began to grow in her hands. "See? Now it isn't blocked as much."

Her eyes went wide in amazement as he expanded in her hands. He was almost to full size. She made long gentle strokes with one hand while the other cradled the two great sources of his seed. "Do you make it small again the same way?" *Pleeease don't*, she thought.

"No. Not unless you stop that," he said, smiling. "But I can block whatever may come out."

"Oh?"

"Yeah, it's pretty simple," he said. "It can be blocked with the fingers too."

"Why are you telling me this? Do you want me to keep going?" She wrapped her hand firmly around his member now, longing to guide it toward her womb.

"No." He took her hands up in his and kissed them. "I thought it could work for you too."

"Blocking?" she said. "Blocking what?"

"The other part of it might help you in meditation."

"The other part?"

"The stimulation," he said.

"I see," she said. "Okay, where do I put my heel?"

"Where it is soft, right behind the bone underneath. Try it and see."

She backed up from him a little, put one heel under her and came down on it. "Mmmmm ... it feels good."

"It may not be exactly the same for you," he said. "You will have to experiment. I always sit this way in meditation now."

She was moving around on her heel with passion rising in her eyes. "How can I meditate like this? It's sooo ... stimulating."

"It started like that for me," he said. "I couldn't keep still. It gradually settled down. Now it blends with the depths of *i am* in meditation. It's wonderful. Try it with meditation. You'll see."

"Okay, I'll try," she said through her arousal. Can I masturbate if I need to?" Her hands were desperate to join in the ravishing of her opening.

"If you need to," he said. "I do sometimes. I can block everything from escaping now. It's much better, an evolution. It gets easier all the time. It's worth the trouble. The effects are huge."

"Effects? Like what?" She felt her voice oozing out of her.

"I'm the fastest man alive, remember?"

"You mean —"

"Yeah, and that's the least of it. There is huge energy in us that has many mysterious purposes." He looked down toward his crotch. "This kind of sitting is a big part of stimulating it. And there are more things that can be done in the body, and with the breath. If you want, I can show you."

"Yes! Yes!" she cried as though he were making love to her. She didn't know what else to do with the stimulation lighting her up inside. Their laughter danced across the rising waters.

"All I have is yours, my divine goddess."

He told her about the visionary dream on Moccasin Mountain and the developments in his practice since then. He showed her the moves that had become second nature to him over the months. He demonstrated the suspension of the inward breath for her and the way the body embraced these suspensions, drawing the freed living essence upward into the evolving new biology. He shared with her his experience of the silver thread, and his concern about the ever-growing storm of energy swirling up around it inside. He told her of his efforts to dissipate the surges, how it led to his restless jitters and endless running.

"Take it slow until you get familiar with the love waves rising," he said, "and how you will deal with them. Something is missing, something that will balance all this, and accelerate it. I'm sure of it. I don't know what it is yet, but I'll find it. The hunger will bring me to it."

After that, they meditated in root seat by the water's edge. Devi was distracted by the arousal. She couldn't resist the urge for gentle squeezing of her anal sphincter and the opening of her womanhood. It started the instant John mentioned it to her. The lessons of loving Mama had given her were so similar, and took on new meaning – the squeezing, and the coaxing upward. As the waves of pleasure rose in her, she lifted up through her pelvis and abdomen, lighting up her chest and head. It was all connected with the natural pulsations of her love flower resting on her heel. She managed to let go deep into meditation after a while, filling up with the expansive bliss of *i am* mixing with the constant energy rising up from her loins. She melted into it there on the shore, lost to everything around her. Something quivered ecstatically deep in her throat, causing her head to move from side to side slightly. Tears welled up and escaped from her closed eyes as they were drawn upward into a mysterious all-consuming passion that engulfed her body and soul. *Oh God, It's so beautiful...*

Thirty minutes passed, and they slowly came out of their ecstatic meditation. Their gazes embraced in a union beyond carnal grasping. The sky was becoming a soft pink. The tide was up to where they were sitting, flowing quietly around their root seats. The shallow surges of pink-hued seawater came and went, each one craving to reach higher up the beach. When the water withdrew, millions of tiny coquina bi-valves rose out of the wet sand up and down the shoreline, each a galaxy of blue, yellow and red. When the water came up, the coquinas were carried with it to its highest point, where they all dug in before it receded. Then they'd come up out of the sand again before the next surge of the sea came to carry them still higher up the beach. In this way the coquinas followed the water's edge as the tides rose and fell.

"Here come the coquinas." Devi watched as they flowed past them.

"The tide is rising," John said. "And so is the human race."

"Much slower, don't you think?"

"Yeah, but it's accelerating. I can feel it. The gap between human awareness and *i am* is shrinking. Many will be coming in. The hunger is rising. When the tide is coming in, neither the coquinas nor we have a choice. We must rise too."

"And just what will you have to do with this great event, John Wilder?" she said, eyeing him conspicuously.

He shrugged with a slight smile. She gave him a knowing look. As she sat in root seat, divine bliss welled up inside her like a fountain. The sexual frustration was gone and she was filled with divine light. She spread her arms dramatically to embrace all of the shoreline in both directions, like Moses about to part the waters.

"Behold! The ascension of the human race!" she cried out. Just then, the coquinas surged out of the pink-shadowed sand in a wave for miles in both directions. She turned and grinned at him. "See? It works."

"Pretty impressive," he said. "Whatever I may do, you will definitely be the one in charge."

They rose and walked slowly up the beach toward the house.

Thoump...

The hip got him.

"Hey, what was that for?" he said.

Devi cocked her head and gave him a sly look. "So when are we going to get completely naked?"

His gaze drifted to the third floor dormer of his sanctum, on the dune high above where they walked. She followed his gaze. They stopped in the twilight and embraced. Her womb was moaning for him again.

Chapter 11 – Two Brothers

When Kurt went off to college, he was clear about what he wanted to do. He majored in business and took a minor in political science. He wanted to take over his father's company and grow it into a huge conglomerate. He knew that in order to do this he would not only need business connections, but he also would have to influence politicians at all levels in government. His father had done so in growing Wilder Corp into a regional powerhouse in engineering and construction. Kurt wanted to take it to the national level, and beyond. It was his greatest craving.

His youthful awkwardness wore off as he progressed through Florida State. He had gotten his weight down to something reasonable and worked out several times a week at the university gym. He ran too. Not like John. No one ran like John. *Damn him...*

Gradually, he became the person he always wanted to be, appearance-wise. Inside he was just the same, insecure, aggressive and hungry to succeed at any cost in the things that he felt mattered: money and power. These two would add up to what he wanted most of all: respect. Or so he thought. It was the simple formula he lived by.

Kurt became involved in student political affairs and ran for class president in his junior year, winning in a close, dirty campaign. He learned to bend the rules to get the things he wanted. It was rumored that he once received an *"A"* in one of his political science courses by casually mentioning to the professor that he had seen him in a crowded restaurant with a young co-ed one evening during finals week. It was said he even showed the professor a picture. He never said that he knew the professor was both cheating on his wife and going to bed with one of his students, but the professor got the message and Kurt's *"C"* miraculously transformed into an *"A."*

He was similarly influential among his peers in student government. He had a way of getting what he wanted. He seemed to have something on everyone. By the time he was ready to graduate with honors, he was feared by many, and most felt he would go far in the business world.

Kurt worked summers at Wilder Corp. He quickly picked up the ins and outs of the business. Harry planned on him coming into the company after graduation. Due to his lack of engineering skills, he thought to put him in finance, leading ultimately to senior management via that path. Kurt had other ideas.

Kurt was home for the weekend and he had a proposal for his father. They sat on the spacious living room sofa in front of the fireplace.

"Dad, I think we should open an office in Tallahassee."

"Why?" Harry said. "We've always handled State business just fine from Jacksonville."

"All through school over there, I've been watching how things happen in State Government. It's where the power is. We have to be there. I want to be there."

"What? All by yourself in an office? How will you learn anything about the business?"

"I'll spend time here," Kurt said. "And I won't be alone, not if you buy into my plan."

"You have a plan?"

"Absolutely. Ever hear of Darren McKenzie?"

"Isn't he the guy swinging the big bat in Washington for International Design and Construction Corp? Man, they do billions in Federal work."

"That's him," Kurt said. "I've met him, and he wants to come to work for us in Tallahassee."

Harry's eyes lit up. "Really? Can we afford him?"

"I think so. He wants to move to Florida, get out of the rat race in Washington, have an office to hang his hat in, keep swinging that bat on the State level here, and point us at some big Federal work. He's agreed to be my mentor if I can sell you on the idea."

"When can we meet him?"

"Next week."

"I'm interested," Harry said. "You set it up and we'll see where it leads." He got up from the sofa. "By the way, how's that cute little girl you've been seeing at school. Mary? Is that her name?"

"Yeah, she's all right," Kurt said. "But I don't think it will last."

"Why not? She seemed very charming when she was here with you last Thanksgiving. Smart too. We can always use a lawyer in the family."

"She's just not ambitious enough for me. I need somebody with me who is willing to go the distance. Do you know what I mean?"

"I guess I do, son," Harry said. "But remember, a mate doesn't have to be a business partner, though sometimes it happens that way. Your mother has not been very involved in my career, except socially. But she has run the house and taken the lead in raising you boys all these years while I've been building the business."

Kurt shrugged. He didn't have much respect for his mother. He felt she was too soft, too accommodating, cowardly, and had not encouraged him or his brother to be aggressive in pursuing their goals. He thought this was why John was so passive in his attitudes about school and career. It was her fault.

"Well whatever, Dad. Mom is okay, but I'd like to marry someone strong."

Harry looked at Kurt for a second like he didn't understand, though Kurt knew he did. His mother was his father's cross to bear. They all had to bear her weakness. He would not make the same mistake in choosing a mate.

Within two months Wilder Corp opened their new office in Tallahassee. It had three employees.

Darren McKenzie was ready to slow down, but he wasn't finished yet. The wily old lobbyist had made his employers plenty rich over the decades on government contract awards he managed to finagle one way or another.

Kurt was happy to be Darren's understudy for the time being, and was ready to do just about anything to penetrate the hallowed halls of government for the big contracts.

Mable Butkus manned the front desk, kept the office organized, and twisted more than a few arms in the Capitol on their behalf. The voluptuous gum-chewing frizzy blond used to ride herd on everyone working in the Governor's office during the previous administration. Some said she'd been the power behind him. A few joked she was the power under him. Everyone knew she was much smarter than she looked, and paid close attention to the words coming out of her pouty red-lipped mouth that were periodically punctuated by popping pink bubbles.

It wasn't long before they were bringing in small State business contracts for Wilder Corp, earning their keep. Kurt wanted much more. He always wanted to chase the biggest projects coming out and wouldn't settle for anything less. He became notorious in the Jacksonville office for the tantrums he'd throw when he didn't get the support he wanted to pursue multiple large projects. Many thought the young man was a lunatic. He was constantly pressing the company's business development and financial resources to the limit. But Harry supported Kurt, and Wilder Corp slowly strained into a higher orbit. It was never enough. Kurt's aspirations reached beyond Tallahassee to the greatest power center in the world, Washington, D.C.

John deliberately kept a low profile at Wilder Corp, and elsewhere. His world record celebrity followed him around, though he did nothing to perpetuate it. For the most part he ignored it. He put in his time at work and increased his time of spiritual practices early in the mornings and late in the afternoons. He spent his evenings either running on the beach or with Devi. Often they'd meditate together. It was their lovemaking, diving into the gluey bliss of the inner realms with *i am* hungrily transforming the essences rising within them as they sat wearing loose-fitting clothes in deep meditation.

They invited Luke to join them for a session. Soon others came. It became a weekly event. The quality of inner experience was magnified in the group meditations. The whole was somehow greater than the sum of the parts. Thursday night became meeting night, rotating between the houses of several of the participants on Coquina Island.

The spread of *i am* meditation had occurred quietly as breastbones were tapped in the inevitable moments of sharing. It became an unspoken maxim that, if you were once tapped by *i am*, you were free to pass it on.

John had tapped Jimmy Marco and Coach Johnson a few weeks after the State track meet in an attempt to explain to them how he had managed to run a world record mile. They, in turn, tapped others. Dwane Culpepper, John and Devi's former English teacher, was one tapped by Coach Johnson. They both became regulars at the Thursday meetings. Before graduation, John had tapped intense bespeckled Ted Warner, the class Magna Cum Laude, who kept badgering John for his secret before he went off to Harvard.

Luke tapped most of his friends on the Duval High football team. Hal Hunter, the quarterback, tapped his girlfriend, Melony Crighten, before he went off to the University of Southern California on a scholarship. Melony became one of the Coquina Island group's most enthusiastic meditators. She'd sometimes moan softly as she dove into *i am*, taking everyone deeper. Luke also tapped a quiet lathe operator, George Talbot, who worked in his father's machine shop. George proved to be a man of exceptional spiritual intuition.

Devi also tapped a few friends. Carol Frasier was one who took to *i am* naturally, as did Wendy Pinto.

The strong ones could be in the weekly gatherings, or go off for months, even years, and keep up their daily practices. Some needed the support of the group to keep going, at least in the beginning. It all had to do with hunger and thirst.

And so the knowledge of *i am* meditation spread through the intimate tapping by one soul upon another's breast. It didn't always stick, or get passed on. There were many tapped, like Kurt Wilder, who chose a totally outward approach to living, shunning meditation. But *i am* worked in them also, behind the scenes. Through *i am*, each person was shown the truth within them, and each person made their own choice whether to pursue it or not.

The Thursday night group routine was simple. There'd be discussion on the principles and practices of *i am*, along with light snacks, and the meditation. Then there would be more discussion on practices. Some people would leave, while others stayed to discuss advanced practices. Everyone had their own level of hunger. John shared his growing knowledge and experiences freely. He was not in favor of much formal structure in the group. He felt each person should fly on the wings of their own desire to unfold their inner experience. No free rides. He was constantly coaxing the others to be self-sufficient in their practice.

Some wanted to expand the group by more actively promoting the special knowledge that was emerging. John resisted, feeling too embryonic for such a huge responsibility. It was the beginning of a rocky road leading to wide dissemination of what would come to be known as *The Secrets of Wilder*. It would be the rockiest for John. There was still much for him to uncover.

As he practiced each day on his bed, John's breath suspensions grew longer. The hunger to clear the channels in his body exceeded his hunger for air. Over the months, more clarity of purpose had come to his routine. The stilling of breath, accompanied by the bodily manipulations was opening thousands of nerves in him. His sexual essence was awakened by the restraint of breath, and traveled up, facilitating increasing illumination of the enlivened nerves by *i am* both during and outside his meditations. The expanding manifestation of *i am* accentuated his desire to fully realize the divine presence, elevating his motivation to practice more intensely. Rising light, rising desire, rising practice, more rising light, more rising desire, more practice ... like a spiral it went up.

There were physical activities going on inside, beyond his voluntary movements. Even the voluntary movements were becoming reflexive, at times very subtle in him as he coaxed the delicious energies upward with tiny muscular movements in his perineum, pelvis, abdomen and eyes.

The eyes, how they caress me inside!

As he raised them toward the point between his eyebrows, he felt the thrill in his loins as though he was being fondled inside.

He experienced a strange new chemistry in his digestion. His intestines filled with air from somewhere and glowed pleasantly to his inner sensation, so he could inspect the full length of them easily. Sometimes there would be semen-like emissions from his anus. He theorized that alchemy was going on in his GI tract, a mysterious mixing of food, air and sexual essences. The product was a substance radiating pure light inside him. At times he could see all his organs permeated and illuminated by the welcomed invasion of living spirit-juice flowing out in all directions from the walls of his intestines.

The ravishing that was going on made his tongue pull back hard on the roof of his mouth. There was a point where the hard and soft palates met that connected with the pleasure circuits awakening in him. The more he meditated the more his tongue pulled back. The more his eyes went up, the more it pulled back. Every surge of living light in him pulled his tongue back. But why? The constant pulling back of his tongue began to strain his jaw. After weeks of ecstatic nagging from the inner currents, he began to look for a way to let it happen more comfortably. Something had to give.

Late one Saturday night, John finished an extra meditation. He got up and walked to the large dormer window and sat on the windowsill. It was near midnight, and the full moon cast a path of shimmering white light across the quiet sea. He watched, as it came to him in a perfect line. He reached in his mouth with his index finger and felt the place on the roof of his mouth that kept begging for his tongue, right where the palate went from hard to soft. It's sensitive all right. The tip of his tongue could reach it with a constant effort. What's holding it back? He felt underneath his tongue, finding the membrane taut there, holding his tongue at bay.

He went into the bathroom and flipped on the light. He leaned over the sink and opened his mouth, raising and pulling his tongue back as far as he could. There it was, the culprit, that membrane underneath. It was so thin, so insubstantial. *What purpose could it serve – to keep me from swallowing my tongue and choking to death? Nah.*

He pushed on it hard, trying to stretch it. Not much give. It could take years to get comfortable at the sensitive spot, even if I could stretch it a little at a time. *How about I help it a little?*

John opened the medicine cabinet and found his cuticle nippers, the little clippers that came in so handy for efficient and precise removal of every kind of unwelcome small piece of skin from the body. *Now let's see*

He looked back under his tongue. *It's so thin, such a tiny little edge to it, not much thicker than a hair. And it looks like there's a sail behind it, just a thin layer of skin. Maybe I'll cut just that tiny edge, not even enough to bleed much.*

Snip...

I'm still here. I didn't die. It didn't even hurt. He looked at it in the mirror. A miniscule bit of red appeared where he had cut. He closed his mouth and reached down with the tip of his tongue, feeling the small laceration he'd made. Then he pulled his tongue back to see how much extra reach this would give him.

He felt something tear and let go inside his mouth. His tongue went back easily to the place he could barely reach before. *Now that's better.* Then a wave of fear swept over him. *But what happened in there?*

He opened his mouth and it was all gone: the edge and the sail. When the edge was cut and the tongue went back the whole membrane just went. There was maybe a drop of blood where the membrane had been. He licked it away with the tip of his tongue and swallowed. It was smooth underneath where the membrane had been. Now he was looking at the narrow edge of more tendon that went all the way back under his tongue. He pulled his tongue back and tickled the sensitive spot on the roof of his mouth. He could easily let it rest there now. *Well, that wasn't so bad.*

He went and sat in root seat on the bed and began to meditate again, with his tongue comfortably resting on the point where his hard and soft palates met. The energy rose up and circulated blissfully. He was happy to have the problem solved.

After letting go into to the radiant silence of *i am* a few times, he was surprised to find his tongue pulling further back, beyond the sensitive spot, reaching back along the soft part of his palate. And then it was stuck again, just short of his uvula, still straining for more.

This is ridiculous. Where's it going? Determined to get to the end of it, he reached in with his index finger. He was shaking, nervously following the energy that was calling him from every quivering nerve. He pushed his tongue back, back, back...

Something slipped, and suddenly his tongue disappeared behind his soft palate and slid straight up into the center of his head.

Chapter 12 – The Secret Chamber

The secret chamber is cavernous. There is a tall slender altar in the center going from the floor to the ceiling. It is the altar of bliss, opening the doorways to heaven. The altar stands between two dark tunnels. Great trumpets guard the tunnels, one on each side.

It was 3:00 AM. John put down the ballpoint pen. The words stared back at him from the blue-lined paper in the three-ring notebook. He could barely believe what he had just written. He closed the big bulging notebook that recorded every step of this journey and set it on the night table, balanced precariously on top of his *Bible* and dog-eared copy of *Gray's Anatomy*.

He'd spent the last several hours exploring his nasal pharynx with his tongue. It went up behind his soft palate, a large cavity that his tongue wanted to fit into naturally. It had been a strain the first few times. He pulled out immediately after the first penetration. It was so shocking. The firm elastic tendon hiding behind the back edge his soft palate had stretched suddenly around the bottom of his tongue like a snare, and he was in. His eyes and nose watered profusely. He sneezed. He became intensely aroused. His emotions ran wild, and his heart palpitated like he imagined a bride's would at the moment of first entry on her wedding night. He had just lost his virginity, sort of.

After the first time, he got up and huddled on the windowsill in the moonlight, quivering inside. He tried it again while sitting there. It was a little easier. The snare began to stretch and it slid under his tongue invitingly, but he retreated quickly. Then he went in again, and he began to feel the glimmer of a homecoming. He started to explore with his tongue that third time going in. He could feel the back edge of his septum, the slender altar in the center, going from bottom to top. It was so sensitive, especially the small protrusion about half way up. He realized it was directly above the point on the roof of his mouth that had been the previous place of attraction. He realized the point in his mouth was a less sensitive part of the main nerve connection above in the septum. The small bump on his septum was as sensitive as his sex organ, only in a different way. It drew everything up out of his loins in a great fountain of luminous pleasure, an ecstatic vacuum cleaner, adding greatly to the previous level of inner stimulation achieved by all the other means he used. The bliss party just got much bigger.

On either side of the septum were the inner openings of his nostrils, the tunnels. Within them, there was highly sensitive erectile tissue that he could not touch with his tongue. Not yet. It made him water and sneeze. It was too much. On the outer edges of the nostrils were curious horn-like structures, one on each side, the trumpets, with small holes in the middle, his eustachian tubes. The septum and nostrils met at the top of the pharynx, and from there a soft wall of flesh curved down the back, becoming the back of his throat. The whole cavity was soft and moist. It was stimulated to more slippery moistness by the explorations of his tongue. *It's like a female organ in the middle of my head!*

John found that it was impossible to breathe through his mouth when his tongue was up in the pharynx, but easy to breathe through his nose, so he could stay up there as long as he liked. He tried a meditation at the end of his new explorations, in the wee hours of the morning. It was uncomfortable at first. His mouth kept filling with saliva, and he had to come out to swallow it. Also, there was some drying and slight stinging in the pharynx at the end, causing him to withdraw for the night.

His sleep was filled with a delightful sense of well-being, and visions of flying with ease through great expanses of inner space.

The next morning, when John woke up, he began again. He managed to stay in the secret chamber for about half of his practices. The stimulation was almost more than he could bear. Like when he learned the root seat, acclimation to the onslaught of new levels of energy took some time.

He had to come out from time to time during his practices to swallow more saliva that accumulated in his mouth while his tongue was up. The secretions became less as his mouth got used to the new configuration. The saliva had a sweetness he had not noticed before. The moisture coming down into his pharynx from somewhere above was sweet as well. It trickled down his throat, joining with the alchemy in his GI tract in small bursts of light, and then spread out inside him. There was a strange aroma of flowers, like gardenias. He didn't know where it came from. He thought it might be a fragrance coming in the open window on the morning air. Later, he realized it was on his breath, coming from somewhere inside him. The fragrance was nearly gone by the end of the morning. *Or maybe I got used to it?*

In the weeks that followed, John worked toward keeping his tongue on the most sensitive part of his septum throughout his practices. His tongue slowly made love with the altar in instinctive ways. It ballooned his experiences of the amorous silence of *i am* dancing through his body. He felt drunk as he went about his daily activities, bathing in a constant smoldering inner orgasm. He was overflowing with molten silk.

He didn't tell anyone about the new discovery, not even Devi. *Later, when I know what I'm doing. When I know what it's doing.*

As the weeks went by, John took more tiny snips of the tendon under his tongue to make his entry into the pharynx easier. The hymen-tendon exposed a callous-like edge each time it healed and stretched, which made it fairly easy, bloodless and painless to slowly liberate the tongue to its greater purpose. The healing of each small snip was quick, a few days, and he was able to forward the project a little each week. In time, he could enter the pharynx without the help of his finger. He found the left side of the soft palate was the easiest way in, the shortest route to the altar of bliss. He went there often and stayed for longer periods, stimulating himself there to powerful states of ecstatic bliss. It was the kind of thing he could do anywhere and no one could tell as long as he kept his mouth shut. If someone spoke to him, he could slip out of it unnoticed and reply. He even did it while he was running, which made the fastest man alive run even faster. He never timed himself though. He'd had enough of world records. The God quest was all that mattered. He saw everything and everyone in that way.

Devi took a job in customer service with a health insurance company in Jacksonville. She'd wear a telephone headset all day and help sick people lament their chronically unpaid medical claims. She signed up for a class at the community college two nights a week. She was diligent with her practices. Silent bliss settled into her like a concrete foundation, a rock that could withstand any shock. Hadn't she experienced the greatest shock of her life already? As the months rolled by, she'd patiently wait for each time she'd see John again. Her life revolved around her anticipation of being in his presence. The constant intense longing for him made her grow, drawing expansive energies from deep within her, tearing her heart open in a constant poignant pain. Even being away from him a day made it happen. It was like suspending her breath in practices. The restraint of breath drew the essences up from her loins. Not being with John engorged her with the spirit of *i am*. She moaned for John, knowing that it was *i am* she moaned for. They were the same, and she was constantly stretched inside. Her longing was the filling. Every emotion has its greater purpose.

As Devi drove through the sky over the high Intracoastal Waterway bridge on her way home from work, she opened the windows wide and breathed the fresh Coquina Island air. The salty marshes disappeared into the lush forested ambiance of the island. The sea welled up beyond, like a joyous mother welcoming home her children. Many of the cars streaming over the bridge with Devi had opened windows too. They were all fugitives from the work-a-day world, at least until tomorrow morning.

When she came around the corner, she saw Papa's Bronco in the front yard askew, off to the side, not in the driveway.

Oh no, not again. Papa's been doing so well. He'd gone to Alcoholics Anonymous and joined the ranks of perpetual recovering alcoholics. He'd acknowledged his *Higher Power* and mentioned how he'd felt a connection. He'd gotten some hope. She told him about *i am* meditation, placing her small hand on his big barrel chest as she imparted it. He said he'd try it. Now here he was, probably drunk again. As she came in the driveway, she noticed the front door was ajar. *Oh great, mosquitoes in the house too.*

"Papa, I'm home," she called as she came in, closing the front door behind her and throwing her purse on the table.

She went into the hall and saw his bedroom door was shut. *Maybe he's asleep.* She kicked her shoes off, flopped on her back on the couch, and closed her eyes. *I'll go and meditate in a few minutes.*

Then her eyes were pulled halfway open by an eerie feeling. They darted around the room, coming to rest on the mantel, on the glass case John had made containing Joe's model of the George Washington Bridge. On top was a piece of paper. *What's that?* She got up, went over, and reached up to get it. The scrawl was barely legible. It was Papa's handwriting:

> *Im sorry Darling*
> > *I cant do it anymore*
> *I love you*
> > *Papa*

Devi froze. Terror grabbed her by the throat, like the night they came and told her Mama and Joe had been killed.

"Papa ... Papa!" She ran to his door. "Papa, please come out. Oh, please come out."

There was no answer. She turned the knob and slowly opened the door. The shades were drawn. It was dark inside. She reached in and lifted the light switch on the wall next to the door.

The chair lay on its side on the floor. Charles Duran's form hung above her on a rope tied to the stem of the ceiling fan.

She fell on her knees and hunched over in front of her father's slightly swinging corpse, her face buried in her hands.

"Ohhh..." She couldn't move. She couldn't feel or think. She couldn't cry.

After a few minutes, she got up and went into the kitchen. She picked up the phone and dialed *911*.

"My father's hung himself in the bedroom," she said.

"Don't touch anything," a woman's voice said. "Is this 216 Waterway Lane?"

Devi sank to the floor, leaning against the kitchen cupboard. The coiled phone wire lay strewn across her tangled legs.

"Is this 216 Waterway Lane?"

"Yes…" Devi's voice trailed off.

"The police and ambulance are on the way." The voice took on a compassionate tone. "Will you be alright till they get there?"

"I … I … don't know." Devi pushed the hang-up button on the phone. It was too late for Papa. The only emergency was hers, and it hadn't hit her yet.

She let go of the button. The dial tone filled the house that was hollow with death. She dialed the Wilders.

"Hello?"

"Mrs. Wilder? Is John there?" Devi's voice was quivering.

"He's up in his room. Are you all right? You don't sound well."

"My father ... my father ... he's dead. Will you get John, please." Her voice was breaking now.

"Oh my God. Oh dear, I'm so sorry. I'll get him."

"Please send him over. I don't know what to do. I don't know what to do…" The tears started to run down Devi's cheeks.

"Of course, dear. I'll get him right now."

Devi pushed the hang-up button on the phone again and lay down on the shiny linoleum floor. There would be no dancing today.

John screeched to a halt in front of Devi's house and jumped out. The medical technicians were sliding the gurney with the covered body on it into the ambulance. Two police cars with lights flashing littered the yard. A small cluster of neighbors stood on the other side of the street.

Devi was with three policemen in the living room. One was filling out a form. When she saw him, she ran into his arms.

"Oh, John. He did it. Papa killed himself." She burst into tears.

He held her close. He didn't know what to say, so he just held her close. That was all he could do. She drew strength from him. He let go into *i am* and it flowed into her.

The policeman in charge spoke: "Ms. Duran, we'll be going now. If there's anything else you think of, please call. We're sorry for your loss." And they went out.

Devi and John sat on the couch. She stayed in his healing arms for a long time.

"Why would he do such a thing?" she sobbed. "Why would anyone? We are divine beings for God's sake. There's so much to live for."

"Not all can see it," he said. "How else can it be explained? How else can we explain the abuse and misery in the world?"

"How can we make them see, John?" She lifted her tear-filled eyes to him. "How? I don't want another life to go to waste. I want everyone to know what we know."

"People have to choose, just seeing a little," he said. "Then they must keep choosing until they see more. We can show them a little, but they have to choose to see more. We can't choose for anyone else, though we wish we could."

"Papa said he chose at Alcoholics Anonymous," she said. "It didn't save him."

"Saying and doing are not the same. There has to be inner light, some awakened *i am*. One day it will be much stronger in everyone. It is up to us to cultivate it in ourselves. In doing that, we cultivate it in others. There will be more *i am*, more hope. Then people can choose the light. They will see it as we do now."

"I choose the light," she said, rocking in his arms. "Now, and always."

In that moment John knew the die was cast. What they wanted would come to pass. Every blind act on earth would spur new recognition of *i am*. In time, all would see.

John Wilder would be sacrificed for this awakening.

Chapter 13 – Consumed by Fire

The death of Devi's father lit a fire under John. He had to break through, for everyone's sake. In the months that followed, he practiced his disciplines with mounting fervor, determined to peel the steel onion of his body and permanently reveal the inner light. The energy swirling up around the center of his spine grew stronger and more aggressive. It took on a life of its own, sunburning him from the inside. His entry into the secret chamber multiplied the inferno. The stem of his brain ached for weeks, like it would explode. A raging column of energy filled his body. The currents howled through him. It went from white, to blue, to yellow, to dark red as it marauded everywhere through his insides. A crown-shaped cone of intense energy flared out the top of his head, threatening to suck him out into oblivion. The energy cone on top of his head was excruciatingly pleasurable, and he was attracted to put his attention on it. When he did, it grew stronger. He indulged it recklessly. He was obsessed. He was being cracked open from the inside. Something had to give.

When we wasn't meditating or being an errand boy at Wilder Corp, he ran on the beach like a madman, a streak flying across the shoreline, desperate to dissipate the excesses roaring up through him. It was all going up. It was out of control.

It was late afternoon. Stella came up the driveway on her way back from the supermarket with a load of groceries. She came in the back door of the kitchen with a bag in each arm. She put them down on the counter and was going back to the car for more when she heard a moan from the other side of the peninsula counter that separated the cooking area from the eating area. She walked around.

"John? What are you doing there?"

He was huddled on the floor in the corner where the counter met the wall. He had on a pair of running shorts and a T-shirt. His was soaked in perspiration and all drawn up in a ball.

"John? Are you all right?"

He winced at the sound of her voice. His face turned up to her. It was swollen and red. His eyes were slits. He could barely open them. "Mom, I think I'm sick."

She pulled a chair out from the table. "Get up, dear. Come sit here where I can see you."

He struggled up, fell in the chair and hunched over.

Then she saw. She gasped. "John, you're all swollen!"

His breathing was strained. "I'm breaking out everywhere. Inside too." His arms and legs were as red as his face, and just as distended. His hands and feet were puffed up and festering.

"Let's get you in bed," she said. "I'll call the doctor."

"No doctor! Let me get a good night's sleep. I'll be okay. I just need rest."

"Are you sure?" she said. Can you make it upstairs? Would you rather use the guest room down here?"

"Guest room," he groaned.

He got up and staggered out of the kitchen. She followed. The corridor leading to the guestroom was off the living room. The room had an ornate mahogany four poster bed, a large matching bureau, a light pink sofa under the window, and an elaborate red Persian rug. It was a dark room. John fell on the bed and rolled on his side, now shaking.

Stella tucked a pillow under his head and put a comforter on him. She felt his head. "No fever. I'll be right back."

John lay on the bed exploding out from the inside. Red fire licked angrily through every nerve in his body. *Now I've done it. I pushed too hard, and this is what I get.*

That afternoon he had a long breath retention and meditation session and got extremely hot and antsy inside. He ran after that, and started to swell up about halfway back. He barely made it home. His whole body itched like crazy now. Not only were his legs, arms and head on fire, but his torso was breaking out too. He shook violently with the fire fighting its way out of him.

Stella came back with cold packs she'd made with ice cubes from the freezer, and a large glass of ice water. She brought an antihistamine tablet.

"Here, take this," she said.

John took the pill. The cold water felt good going down. Even his insides were inflamed.

"Let's put this ice wherever it helps," she said. "Are you sure you don't want the doctor?"

"No doctor." *How could a doctor understand this?* He put one ice pack between his thighs where the itching was most acute and the others around his hands and feet. The one in his hands he hugged to his exploding chest. "Th-Th-Thanks, Mom. I want to sleep."

"You call if you feel worse," she said. "I'll check every so often. Your father is in Mobile. I'll call him. If it gets worse, he'll fly home."

As she left, he could see she was nearly panicked, but she had risen to the occasion, and he was thankful for it. She did not draw energy from him as she so often did. He needed all his energy right now. He'd get through this. Even when he was sick, he was tenacious.

John's sleep was fitful and nightmarish. He was being chased by red demons that grew out of his body. They held him down all night. He couldn't overpower them. The next morning they were still there. Through the fading delirium he watched as the demons devoured his flesh. Yet, strangely, his essence was not touched. Behind it all he remained whole in his silence.

Later, he got up to go to the bathroom and saw that his swelling remained and had erupted into blisters all over his body – the insides of his legs and arms, up and down his stomach and back, and on both sides of his neck and face. It all looked and itched like the worst case of poison ivy imaginable. The blisters were rupturing and clear fluid was oozing down his body. The smell was putrid. He looked and smelled like a corpse. But he was alive. When his mother came in, she nearly fainted.

"Oh my God, John, you're dying."

"No, no," he said through his agony. "It's just a bad rash. It will pass."

"Just a rash? Just a rash?" she said. "What is that awful smell?"

"I don't know," he said. "I just need to lie still. It itches to move."

So he lay there all day, half-sleeping, half-rotting. The room was filled with the stench of death. His mother kept bringing cool compresses for his rupturing skin. It seemed like days later when he opened his eyes, but it was only that evening.

"John, it's me," Devi said softly.

"And me, brother John," Luke said.

"Hey, it's my two most favorite people in the world," John said weakly. "Welcome to the morgue."

Devi kissed him softly on the forehead, and Luke laid a giant healing hand on top of his head.

"I'm glad you haven't lost your sense of humor," Devi said. "What happened?"

"Too much of a good thing, I think ... it got away from me."

"Something sure did," Luke said.

"This itch, this itch is killing me. If there's a part of me that isn't itching, I haven't found it. I even itch on the inside. All my cells are exploding."

"Is it getting worse?" Devi said. "Shouldn't you be in the hospital?"

"I don't know. It's the inner energy. Fire is coming out. No more practices for now. It'll heal, I think, I hope. I want to tough it out here. No doctors."

"Tough guy, huh?" Devi said.

"You aren't going to die on us are you?" Luke said.

"I hope not," John murmured. "There's still lots to –" He was fading off. He was exhausted and the antihistamines his mother gave him were making him drowsy.

He woke up in the middle of the night. Luke was gone. Devi sat in root seat on the sofa meditating. He could see her rocking slightly in the dim light. The ocean purred in the background.

Then she stopped. He could feel her eyes open to him. Her legs came out from under her and she came over and gently laid her hand on his. "Hi, handsome. How you doing?"

His mouth and throat were dry. He couldn't speak. She cradled his head in her arm and gave him some water. She went and got more cold compresses and put them on his raw skin. She stayed with him all night, all the next day, all the next night and for the weeks that followed. She never left his side for more than a few hours.

From time to time visitors came to see John. Luke was there several times a week all the way through.

Everyone was busy going to work or school, keeping up with the daily routine of life. The Thursday night meditation meetings petered out without John's presence. Most kept up their practices at home, but not all. Those who relied on others for spiritual motivation, rather than on their own hunger for the living presence of *i am* within, fell off their practices completely. More inner energy was needed for everyone, and John knew it, even in his diminished condition. He considered it his responsibility to do something about it. He knew that his spiritual progress and that of everyone else were one and the same. So he pressed on inside as best he could, though it would be months before he would be able to undertake significant structured practices again.

Weeks went by. John woke up and thought to scooch himself up against the pillow to meditate. But he could hardly move. The huge scabs that fought to contain his running sores were slowly beginning to come loose. There was the hope of fresh sensitive skin forming underneath. He was in cotton briefs and a white T-shirt. A crumpled white sheet covered him to the waist. He watched barefoot Devi straightening her pink couch-bed. She had on a wrinkled blue blouse with the bottom tied around her bare midriff, and beltless light muslin pants that hung low on her hips. The crystal cross dangled out of her blouse as she leaned over the couch. Her breasts swayed freely inside. The morning sunlight coming in the window was scattered by the cross into a multitude of small rainbows dancing on the walls and ceiling. She had dark circles under her eyes and no makeup. Her hair hung loose and tangled.

"You're beautiful when you're exhausted," he said.

She stood up. "Well, good morning," she said. "Flattery will get you everywhere."

She lifted her hair on top of her head, threw her chest out and wagged her breasts at him, pouting her lips as she did.

"God, where's my heel?" he said weakly.

"It's alive," she said watching him grow under the sheet. She smiled tenderly and dropped her hair.

"Barely. The last time someone told me flattery would get me everywhere, I ended up diving into *i am* for the first time."

"Don't know if I can outdo that one," she said.

"You did," he said as he forced himself up against the pillow. "You are *i am* in the flesh. You are pure love, and I love you."

She sat on the bed, and hugged him. Then she kissed him on his lips. She softly rubbed her nose back and forth on his. "I'm so glad you're back with us. Shall we meditate, darling?"

His world was in her eyes. "Yes, I have to start building back up."

She leaned back. "I hope not to where you went over the edge last time."

"No. Don't want to do that again."

"What then?"

"I'll put it all back," he said. "And be more careful, stay on this side of too much."

"Doesn't sound like you," she said.

"It has to be. I have to work smarter if I'm going to get this done."

"Yep," she said as she went into root seat on the foot of the bed, facing him.

They dove into the bliss of *i am* together.

In the months that followed, John healed and resumed his disciplines, step by step, taking time to adjust to the energy flows that resulted. Ironically, his brush with whole body cellular destruction left him a purer vehicle for the living light of *i am*, so he could sustain more ecstasy than before with less resistance in his nervous system. But he no longer pushed beyond the capacities of his body as he once did. He slowed down his routine to accommodate his energies and exercised his body in ways that balanced rather than aggravated the flows. He changed his diet, reducing his intake of acidic and spicy heat-producing foods, and ate heavier foods when necessary to help quell flare-ups of the tongues of fire that still arose in him from time to time. John became a devoted servant of the power that surged in him. He realized that what he had been pursuing could now chase him right out of his body. His disregard for balancing between the needs of his body and the needs of the fiery currents is what had gotten him in trouble. His relationship with God proceeded along more measured lines.

Because his energy currents tended to run on their own in many directions, some uncomfortable, he developed methods for dealing more directly with them. Breath suspension and meditation tended to aggravate them, but there was no way he'd quit his practices. He would not stop all spiritual progress just to live a normal physical life. He'd rather be dead.

One day as he sat at the blueprint table at Wilder Corp, he was feeling the energies surging through him. With his arm propped on the table like an arm wrestler he started waving his forearm and hand slowly back and forth. To his surprise, when he made his arm move very slowly the energy flows in his arm slowed down too. When he got home that night he stood in the center of his room and did some very slow movements with his arms, and torso, pivoting on his legs. First he put all his weight on one leg, and then all his weight on the other as he shifted and rotated slowly, moving his arms in a way that soothed the energy moving in him. It turned into a slow motion energy dance. As his eyes slowly panned his bedroom with his movements, the boundaries in his line of sight became blurred, blending with the settling energies within him, spreading him out in a stabilizing way. After ten minutes of it he felt relaxed, settled. The slow rhythmic motions calmed the inner currents, providing balance, something he really needed. He'd take it wherever he could find it. He added the slow energy dance to his routine, right before spiritual stretching.

He showed Devi the energy dance and they did it together in a free form way. Sometimes they'd do a slow motion dirty dance, lose their balance on purpose, and end up wrapped around each other on the floor laughing and kissing. But the balancing of John's wayward inner energies was serious business, and they both did their best to calm the finicky, fiery currents in him. The slow energy dancing helped a lot, combined with the other conservative measures he applied. Taken together it all helped ground the wayward fires.

It frustrated him having to be so careful. He felt he was at an impasse, though his bliss states were considerable. It wasn't his style to stay at a fixed level of experience, no matter how pleasurable it might be. He had to progress. He pined for faster growth, and was always looking for a way through. He believed that sooner or later he'd discover knowledge that would enable him to get on the fast track again.

He longed for Devi and the others to have all his secrets, but he could not share his knowledge of the secret chamber and the altar of bliss with anyone until he could open the door to unlimited energy flow. It was too dangerous.

If only I could find a way to both stimulate and quench this ravenous energy without consuming the flesh of this body in the process. The answer is in here somewhere...

Chapter 14 – The Sacred Tunnel

"Yeah, yeah, yeah, Horace," Mable Butkus chirped into the phone. "Come on, you know it's never too late. You need to meet with Darren and Kurt today."

She covered the mouthpiece of the phone with her hand and winked at Kurt. "He's in the bag."

Her jaws chewed obsessively. Then she was admiring her long red nails. "Remember that party last Christmas, Horace? ... Oh yeah, what a hoot. I thought we'd never get home. How's the Mrs., anyway? I ran into her at Penney's last week. Nice dress she – Oh? When? Three O'clock? Great, they'll be there. Bye, hon..."

Kurt gave her the high-five. "Way to go, Mable! Chairman of the State Senate appropriations committee in our pocket."

"Anytime, cutie," she said. "So, who else over there you wanna twist on this Interstate project?"

"I think we got them all. A few more tweaks by Darren with the deep pockets in D.C., and we ought to have it. Biggest contract yet out of here. A hundred million for Wilder Corp."

"Whewee, that mean I get a raise?" she said.

"You stick with me, and I'll be raisin' you all over the place."

"Well, light my fire, baby!" Mable popped a bubble and dove back into her spreadsheets.

Kurt admired her backside as he went into Darren McKenzie's office. Darren had on a rumpled suit. He had a mussed up gray mop, and was peering over his glasses as Kurt came in. He threw the newspaper he was reading in the round trashcan in the corner with a clatter.

"You hear that?' Kurt said. "Three o'clock at Wallace's office. Between Mable and his accounting screwups we got him by the old yin-yang. You think that'll do it?"

"We're close," Darren said. "But it isn't done till it's done. A couple more calls to the Feds, and, well, I give it eighty percent right now."

"Pretty good odds," Kurt said.

"It's all about the odds, kid."

"Speaking of odds," Kurt said. "How're we doing on Glades?"

"Still stroking," Darren said. "There's much more to do in D.C. I'm leaving tonight. Senator Weatherhold needs more ass kissing, plus the unmentionable thing we talked about."

"You let me know when he's ready," Kurt said. "I'll take care of it."

"I thought you wanted me to work in Florida. Why the hell am I going back to that human cesspool for the third time this month?"

"For a billion dollars," Kurt said, "that's why. We get the new Glades Air Force Base project, and you can buy a nice chunk of Florida and never leave again."

"I could retire right now. This is more than I signed on for. The wife's fuming while I'm up there doing for you what I did for everybody else in this stinking business for the last thirty-five years. I live here now."

Kurt paced in front of Darren's olive green metal desk. "We get this one, and I promise you'll never have to go to D.C. again. I'll move there. If we get Glades we'll have to expand our Fort Myers office and put staff in D.C. too. It'll be my ticket to the big time."

"Better you than me, kid," Darren said. "This'll be the last big one I cook up there. Got it?"

"Yes, sir," Kurt said. "Absolutely. After this one, all you do is point me at where the big bones are in that cesspool, and I'll dive in and fish 'em out myself."

Darren leaned back in his swivel chair and ran both hands back through his gray hair. "Well son, Washington may represent the glorious high ideals of our country, but it is also where the biggest thieves live."

Kurt stopped pacing and looked Darren square in the eye. "I have no problem with that." He would say or do anything to get a mammoth slice of the Glades project. It would be the biggest river of Federal money flowing into Florida since the heydays of the space program. And Kurt knew it would lead to more, much more.

They ended up bending the rules pretty far – and, besides the Interstate highway work, Wilder Corp got a leading role on the Glades project.

"I miss Papa," Devi said as she turned the Bronco on to A1A. They drove past the shops and strip malls.

John had his elbow resting out the open the window. She saw the warm night air rippling through his hair. His serene face told her he was alive again. He seemed to appreciate the simple things, like riding with her on balmy summer evenings. "There's so much we all have to live for," he said.

"Papa could have made it if he'd have given it a little more time," she said. "Now I've got the house, the savings, the cars and no family."

"You've got me. What's left of me anyway." He reached over and put his hand on her shoulder. She nuzzled it with her cheek.

They drove north toward his house.

"Here it comes," she said. "The place where it happened."

As they went by the convenience store, she peered toward it. "And that's where the rest of my family left this world. In that alley."

"Wait!" John yelled. "Stop! Quick!"

She screeched to a stop on the side of A1A three quarters of a block past the store. "What?"

John jumped out and started running back.

What the...? Devi turned off the truck, got out, and began to walk in the direction he went. He'd run in the very alley where Mama and Joe had been stabbed and strangled five years before. *This is not where I wanted to go tonight. Where'd he go?* "John! John!" She started running toward the alley. When she got to the entrance, she stopped and looked in. A cluster of metal trash cans blocked part of her view and empty boxes were piled along the side of the store. "John?"

"Here … I'm over here," he called from behind the trash cans.

She waded in. When she came around the trash cans, she saw John on his knees over a man lying on the ground. The man was moving in pain. She came up behind John. "What happened?"

"I saw someone beating him as we drove by," he said. "The guy took off out the back when he saw me coming."

John held his hand up in the light streaming into the alley from the street. It was covered with blood. "He's been stabbed. Tell the clerk in the store to call for help."

Devi ran around the corner. When she was coming out of the store, she realized the man must be only a few feet from where it had happened to Mama and Joe. Her imagination painted the grisly scene she'd woken up sweating with so many nights as teenager. *But maybe this man can be saved.* She ran to John and the bleeding man. When she got closer, she could see he was a homeless man. He was unshaven, dirty and tattered. There was a small scruffy bedroll and a plastic bag full of aluminum cans on the ground next to him.

His head turned from side to side, and he was moaning. "Oh God. Oh God. God have mercy on me."

She saw the blood coming around John's hand pressed flat over the man's heart. The old blue shirt was soaked red. She was on her knees. She put the bedroll under the man's head and cleared the long gray hair out of his sweaty bearded face.

"Please rest easy, Sir. Help will be here soon," John said.

"I can't, I ... Oh, oh, it's so beautiful."

John looked up. "Yes, I see it. It is beautiful. But are you sure?"

"I want to..."

"But help is coming," John said.

"No. I see Jesus. I'm saved. Let me go. Please let me go."

John lifted his bloody hand off the man and looked up. Both he and the man were looking up for a minute, transfixed. Devi didn't see anything except the two of them looking upward. She felt a peaceful presence.

Finally, the man let out a long breath and was gone. John kept looking up, even as the ambulance screamed into the parking lot, bathing them in flashing red light.

Devi put her hand on John's shoulder. "Are they too late?"

"No. He is okay," he said. "His name was Mathew and he is okay. I still see him. They have him now." John reached his bloody hand up into the alley air.

Devi looked up past John's hand where his gaze went. She saw a faint opening. A tiny point of light that was somehow very big. *What?*

"There they go – Now they're gone." He went off his knees and sat on the ground next to the body as the medics rushed up. He looked up at them. "He's gone, but he's okay."

They looked at him strangely as they began to try and resuscitate the body.

They were in the Bronco on A1A again with Devi driving. They didn't speak for a while.

"What happened back there," she said.

"I saw him go," John said. "It was beautiful. There was a tunnel of light leading out of his head. It started at the base of his spine. He went out through it. He chose it. It was so bright at the end, and someone was there. They came for him. He was happy to go. Life was so hard for him here. He tried. He really wanted to do better. He was an accountant. Had a wife and three kids. He lost his job. It wrecked his confidence. They went broke. Finally, she left with the kids. He never got over it. He's been on the street for seven years."

"How do you know all that?"

"I saw it in myself."

John's lips quivered. He began to cry. "I was in him. I was him. Oh, what burdens we carry in this earth life," he sobbed. "There's so much work to do."

"Do you have to do it all?"

"Yes."

"Why?"

"Because I can. We all have to do what we can." John stared out the window into the summer night, with the tears still running down his cheeks.

They didn't speak until they were in the driveway in front of his house.

"I'm going back to work tomorrow," she said. "Will you be all right?"

"Yes, I will be meditating," He was silent for what seemed a minute. "You know what?"

"What?"

"I think tonight wasn't an accident. Mathew gave me something, a gift. Now I have to figure out what to do with it."

"When you figure it out, will you let me know?"

"You'll be the first." He leaned over and kissed her. She put her arms around his neck. He still had the smell of Mathew's blood on him, but she didn't care. They were kissing for ten minutes before they finally tore themselves away from each other for the night.

As Devi drove away, she was puzzled. *How did John see all that? How is he able to recognize all this sacred knowledge? I am in love with a spiritual genius, and he loves me. How can this be happening?* She was overcome with emotion. She pulled off on the shoulder of Beach Road a few blocks from the Wilder house and wept with her head down and arms draped over the steering wheel. The silent strength of *i am* overflowed from her in upward surges as she cried on the quiet road. A soft glow of white light emanated from her as she wept, filling the Bronco and illuminating the warm night air around the truck. She didn't notice it. But from that moment on she knew she was on a sacred mission that would change the world, and that there was no turning back.

Months went by. John continued working at Wilder Corp in the design and drafting department. He was in a stable routine. Compromise had never been a prominent aspect of his personality. While his spiritual experiences were more than pleasant, he found himself becoming impatient. His strategy of moderation and careful regulation of his lifestyle was working to prevent a disaster like the one he had experienced the year before, he wondered if it had been inevitable. *How can the human race progress without risk?* How can we move to the next level without some failures?

Everyone seemed to want a sanitary, risk free, existence. And yet, we all ultimately end up staring into the same great chasm called *death*. He'd looked into it with a homeless man named Mathew. It wasn't so bad. In fact, it looked more friendly than earth life.

He was realizing that avoiding risk altogether, sacrificing the vision that was always creeping up in him, was a life of mediocrity. He was in that mode now, like so many who had fallen and gotten up scared. He was filled with radiant vistas, and was seeing things that others apparently couldn't. *So what? Where is the next step?* He was coming to the conclusion that being on a plateau of experience could be as bad as being stuck in the limits of bodily illness. Yes, hiding from the quest, the all-consuming vision, was a kind of illness too. It was time to move on. Time to walk through fear again. *How will I do it? I'm not stupid. Jumping into the fire didn't work, not completely anyway. There must be another way for me to get through, a smarter way.*

As he sat on his bed in root, his heart cried inwardly for God. His tongue caressed his altar of bliss in his secret chamber, filling him with ecstatic energy. He let go and dove into the silent depths of *i am*, carrying the faintest feeling of his longing with him. Again and again, he let go of the seed of his desire as he let go of the seed of *i am* into infinite inner expansion. In his letting go, something began to emerge.

Breath suspension had been the practice John cut back the most, because it had the greatest simulative effect on his inner energies. In concert with all the other means, breath suspension was the engine that let the fiery genie out of the bottle. Without suspension of breath, everything thing else went slower. Breath suspension was the gas pedal that opened the nerves and released the fuel of sexual essences up into his body where the biological alchemies occurred. He realized if he was to get going again, breath suspension would have to come back in some form. He began to experiment with it before each meditation. As soon as he suspended breath inside for any length of time, the fires would flare up, so he tried breathing slow instead of suspending. It helped, but the fires still rose. They roared up through the silver thread, the tiny nerve that went up the center of his spine, spilling out in all directions, whirling, desperately seeking something.

Mentally, he went into the spinal nerve with his breathing, imagining it as a tunnel. A tunnel! Like dying Mathew had shown him. He inhaled his breath slowly up the tunnel – up, up, up ... all the way up, and out to where he imagined the bright light would be at the end of his tunnel, out the front of his forehead through the point between his eyebrows and above to a bright rising inner star. That's where Mathew's had been. There he was full with air. Then John came back down the tunnel, back through his forehead to the center of his brain and down his spine with a long slow exhale – down, down, down ... all the way back to his pulsating root at his perineum. Then up again slowly on inhalation, and down again slowly on exhalation. It felt good, smooth, and a strange thing happened. The fires subsided and a serene blissful spaciousness filled his nerve tunnel. The walls of the tunnel disappeared, and he was in a vast space.

John found himself sustained inside the silver thread for the first time. The rising fires gave way to a celestial vision. *But why?* He watched as he continued. He saw his rising breath dissolving into his falling breath and his falling breath dissolving into his rising breath. The duality of up and down in his spine dissolved into a new singularity that immediately cleared the storms of inner imbalance. He had always assumed the journey was up.

Now he found that up and down was the secret. There was a polarity of energies in him that must be balanced in the spinal nerve, the sacred tunnel that connects earth and heaven. It was far more stable than the undirected, and sometimes dangerous, path he had followed in the past. Going out the front through the point between his eyebrows also had an instant calming effect on his hungry raised crown that had been a central cause of the chaos. Going slowly up an down inside the spinal nerve with the breath between root and brow yielded balance and opening combined. *Balance! Oh, how I've longed for that. Have I finally found the secret of breath?*

In the months that followed, John refined spinal breathing in the sacred tunnel between his root and brow, together with his other practices, to a fine art that was rapidly opening his nervous system wide to the glories of God, *i am*.

He found the way to transform his surging energies at last. There were no more limits. He embraced his vision fully again, and it embraced him.

Chapter 15 – Sharing the Good

Kurt drove up the Georgetown hill to the long row of connected townhouses. He leaned forward over the wheel looking up through the windshield of his Mercedes at the large upstairs apartment he'd rented in the triplex. *So, here begins the big time.*

He looked forward to pursuing the introductions Darren McKenzie had set up for him with Washington power brokers, connections that would enable him to build on the growing success Wilder Corp was having with the Glades project. They'd opened a liaison office in D.C., and spin-off engineering work quickly flowed into it. They took on more space in Crystal City, and were at seventy-five employees already, and growing.

The tendrils of power in Washington were a morass. Kurt knew he would thrive in it, the confusion and the trading of favors to reach the desired ends. *Let me in that briar patch.*

An athletic young woman in shorts and a T-shirt came bounding down the stairs of the triplex and nearly knocked Kurt over. She had her arms full of loose laundry. He was hugging a large garment bag, on the way up. She stopped next to him on the same step. She was breathing hard like she'd been up and down the stairs more than once, and he could feel her vitality beaming though her laundry and his garment bag like X-rays.

"Sorry, I'm trying to get these stragglers in before the wash cycle ends. You moving in?"

"Yeah, I just rented the third-floor apartment. I'm Kurt Wilder." He extended a free hand.

Her blue eyes caught his like she knew him as she reached out through her dirty laundry. "Nadine Grant. I'm on the second floor. Welcome to this humble abode."

"Where can I get a bite to eat around here?" he said.

"A little café a block up the street. I'm going as soon as this pile is in. Want to join me?"

"Sure." He liked her already. There was no nonsense about her, and she was beautiful.

A half-hour later, they sat across from each other in the café having a sandwich at a small table by the window.

"So what brings you to Washington?" she said.

"Lobbyist," he said while chewing.

"Any particular flavor?"

"Engineering and construction. Big Federal projects. What about you?" Kurt eyed her playful look.

"I'm in Senator Weatherhold's office," she said. "Administrative assistant. Jill of all trades, master of none. She threw out her hands and cocked her head in a gesture of helplessness. Helpless like a lioness. "By any chance are you with Wilder Corp, Mr. Wilder?"

"How'd you guess?" He smiled, concealing his surprise at the coincidence of their meeting. He'd rather she thought it was planned. "I haven't met the good Senator, yet. Would you like to be the one to introduce me?"

"So you're the invisible man behind Darren McKenzie," she said. "What moves you made. I love to watch hungry men competing. Congratulations, you won." She laughed, shaking her short brown hair in a way that turned him on.

"Will you join me for dinner tonight?" he said.

"You don't waste time, do you?"

Kurt shrugged. "Not asking is not getting. And not offering something good isn't getting either."

She smiled. "And just what have you got to offer?"

"Say yes, and you'll find out."

He looked into her probing blue eyes, and knew they'd both be on either his or her floor of the Georgetown triplex that night.

It went much further than that.

"You ready?" John said.

"Ready for what?" Devi said.

"For the good stuff."

"Uh oh, I smell trouble," she said.

"That's my middle name."

"I know. I was there, remember?"

John lifted his head from her lap and got up off the couch. He slowly paced Devi's living room with his hands clasped behind him, cricking his head slightly from side to side a few times, like he was clearing something inside his spine. She waited expectantly. She knew he'd built back to intense practices in the year since his illness, and he hadn't exploded again yet, thank goodness. He didn't tell her what new things he was doing. He said he didn't want her to have to go through what he did. That had sounded more than fair, so she did not push him. Her experiences were plenty blissful. So she bided her time and watched him gradually melt into a radiant puddle of pleasure. But now he had a serious look on his face, standing in the middle of the living room with his arms folded in front of him like a drill sergeant.

"Okay, you've got the meditation, right?" he said.

"That's for sure."

"Every day, twice, right?"

"Like clockwork," she said. "Only a fool would miss."

"The root seat?"

"Yep." She slipped her foot under her cotton pants. "See?"

"The abdominal lift?"

"Roger," she said. "What, are we getting ready to blast off to outer space here?"

"Blasting off to inner space. All aboard," he said. "Got the chin lock?"

"Check." She dropped her chin into the hollow of her throat. Then she lifted her head back up. It felt good all over.

"The breath suspension? You've been going easy on that one, like I said, right?"

"Absolutely," she said. "I don't want to fry like you did."

"Good. We're going to fix that," he said. "Okay, what else?"

"How about the anal squeeze, the root lift. I really love that part."

"Yeah, me too," he said. "Good. Anything else?"

"How about the eyes?" she asked. "Do they count? Raising them together is getting as good as the anal squeeze. In fact, I can't do one without stimulating the other. It's like they are connected electrically."

"That's perfect," he said. "Yeah, the eye lift is important. If your eyes are lifted and single at the point between the eyebrows, your body will be filled with light."

"Oh yes," she said. She pulled her eyes up and her belly and pelvic muscles got visibly sucked up with them. She was squeezing gently, rhythmically underneath, and *i am* started to hum radiantly inside her. It was all working together like a single organic function. Her face went into a silent moan.

"Okay, okay," he said. "You pass. Did we miss anything?"

"I think that's it, captain," she purred as her teary eyes came back down from heavenly bliss. "Isn't that enough? I just want to meditate with you now."

"It's never enough."

"Oh my," she said.

"Spinal breathing," he said.

"Don't think I have that one."

"The secret chamber," he said.

"Not that either," she said. "Unless you're talking about the secret chamber I've been saving for you since high school."

"Nope, not that one," he said. "We've both got the secret chamber I'm talking about."

"Really?"

"Yep."

"Intriguing," she said.

He smiled widely for the first time in the drill, and she knew something wonderful was about to happen.

"Remember Mathew, the homeless man who died?" John said.

"How could I forget?"

"He showed me that the spinal nerve is more than a nerve. It's a sacred spiritual tunnel. A tunnel we can travel through up and down the spine, and out into the full light of heaven, the place we go when we die. When we do this up and down, we blend two kinds of energy inside us in a special kind of lovemaking."

"You know I'm always up for lovemaking," she said.

"We are the matchmakers," he said. God the Father comes down from heaven. God the Mother comes up from the earth, our root. When we breathe them up and down intentionally, they merge in us, and, voila, new life is born."

"I hope it's friendlier than the life you had running around in you last year," she said.

"That wasn't the new life. That was the Mother aroused from below, lacking her husband. She was looking for him in every cell in me, and raising hell."

"I can relate to that." Occasionally, Devi felt like raping John where he stood. His holding back for the God quest drove her bananas sometimes, making her feel like raising a little hell of her own. *Argh!*

"Spinal breathing resolves it," he said, "bringing the male energy down the spine, blending it with the female energy coming up – new life."

"So what kind of breathing is it?" she said.

"Slooow breathing, inhale up from the root through the tiny tunnel to the head and out through the forehead to the bright star of heaven about this high." He gestured to where their eyes went naturally in ecstasy. "Where the bliss is, that's where we go. It's where they came and got Mathew. It's where God the Father comes down into us. After the in-breath going up, then take the out-breath slowly back down through the tunnel from the star to the root again, following the same root. Do that round trip over and over again."

"And Jesus is in the star?" she said.

"Yes, Jesus, *i am*, the Father, all the same," he said. "I haven't met him personally there yet. But there is huge energy coming down, and that's what has quelled the fire of the rising feminine energy."

"What's it like?" She put her feet down on the floor and came to the edge of the couch, her elbows on her knees. She brought the crystal cross Mama had given her out of her shirt and held it in her hand, caressing it with her thumb.

"It's expansive lightness. The outer world disappears. The walls of the tunnel disappear. It's someplace else inside us. All the senses work there, but it isn't physical. It is like the other end of our senses in there, the most refined sensing you can imagine. Well, it is unimaginable. Out here it's all pretty coarse. In there, lights, sounds, the feelings of it are, well, *celestial* is the best way I can describe it. You have to try it yourself."

" I want to," she said.

"Let's do it now," he said.

They sat on the couch side by side, and he took her through it. They did the slow spinal breathing for ten minutes in root seat. She labored with it at first, but it got smoother toward the end.

"How was it?" he asked.

"Clunky, but I got pretty spread out inside near the end. It's not exactly like meditation, is it?"

"No, it's different, and it will get easier," he said. "Do it for ten minutes before meditation. Don't try and mix spinal breathing and meditation."

"Don't know if I could if I wanted to," she said. "What's the difference between the two?"

"The breathing plows the ground of the inner body, the nervous system. That helps make meditation much broader and deeper. The seed of *i am* in meditation goes through the plowed earth of the nervous system like you wouldn't believe. All of inner space vibrates with *i am*."

"Oh God," she said. "You're giving me goosebumps." A thrill of vibrating *i am* went through her. "Can we meditate now?"

"Let's do five more minutes of spinal breathing, just to make sure you are plowed good, and then twenty minutes of meditation."

First she did the spinal breathing, which opened her up inside, and then she meditated with *i am* and she was filled with a multitude of inner sensory experiences. What had been blissful silence before came alive as a vast inner space filled with celestial sights and sounds of *i am*. All of her inner senses were titillated with ecstasy.

At the end, she slowly came out of the inner dimension she was in. It took a few minutes before she could speak. "That's unbelievable."

"Amazing, isn't it?" he said. "There is no limit to how far we can go with it. You can make spinal breathing more powerful in several ways. It's your option."

"So tell me already," she said.

"First, keep your anal squeeze going. That makes a big difference. Squeezing it on the up breath and letting it go on the down breath is a good rhythm. Or you can do it the other way – letting it go upward and squeezing it on the way down."

"That'll be easy for me," she said, smiling. She started again blissfully underneath as she spoke the words.

"Another thing you can do is restrain and lengthen the out-breath with your epiglottis."

"My what?"

"That's what we hold our breath in with," he said. "The door to our windpipe. If you make like you are holding your breath, only let it seep out the top at a comfortable rate. It makes a high-pitched hiss like a snake in your throat. Remember, that's on the way back down the spinal tunnel. When you breathe back in, on the way up the tunnel, open your throat deep down as wide as you can. Go slow in both directions. Don't restrict it coming in. The lungs don't like that. I know, I tried it."

She tried making the hiss in her throat with her out-breath, taking it down the tunnel as she did. "Okay, I see. Does that force more air somewhere."

"Yeah, it puts more oxygen in the cells," he said. "When I do it that way, my breathing practically stops during meditation afterwards. Everything in the body stops, even the heart rate goes to near nothing, and then the inside really opens up."

"Whew, what a way to go," she said. "I think I can handle all this. It'll take a while to get used to it, but it shouldn't be a problem, especially if the experience is going to be like this."

"Oh, it'll get better," he said.

"Good grief, what are we into here?"

He smiled and gave her a poke in the ribs. "God quest."

She jumped on him and wrestled him to his back on the couch. She sat straddling him, pinning his arms over his head.

"Ya got me again," he said.

"Yep." She leaned over and kissed him. Then she pulled up. "You've been saving the best for last, haven't you?"

"How'd you guess?"

"I know you, John Wilder. Now let's have it. Where's the secret chamber?"

Chapter 16 – Flood of Knowledge

Devi's bathroom door was closed for a long time. She was in there doing something courageous.

Suddenly there was a scream. Her sound pierced the closed door, filled the empty house, and penetrated out to the street.

No one heard.

The bathroom door flew open, and Devi ran out in nothing but her panties, still screaming. She dove onto the bed and writhed around madly on the thick comforter. Her screams turned into hysterical laughter as she writhed.

"I can't believe it!" she cried, shaking her head, her hair flying everywhere. "I can't believe it! It's another clitoris!"

She sat up in the middle of the billowing comforter and went into root seat. She put her index finger in her mouth and pushed under her tongue slowly back and to the left side. Her tongue slid smoothly up into her secret chamber, finding its home on her sensitive altar of bliss.

I can't believe it ... I can't ... i ... she let go, her eyes ascended, she disappeared into the deep delicious vibrations of *i am*.

All that remained of the uproar was the look of ecstatic bliss on her face.

The Thursday night meditation gatherings had resumed. John told everyone in the group about the expanded practices – the secret chamber and the spinal breathing. Most were in root seat and doing breath suspension already.

Luke, Carol, Melony, George, Coach Johnson, and Mr. Culpepper all took on the new practices enthusiastically.

By the end of the summer, a dozen secret chambers were entered for the first time. With that, and as more *i am* meditators undertook spinal breathing, new dimensions of inner ecstasy were added to the beauty of Coquina Island. The palms, oaks, dunes, and surging sea all sang with the ecstatic vibrations of *i am*. Word spread, and the Thursday night gatherings grew.

John continued his research on spiritual practices in the quiet of his room, recording each step in the big three-ring notebook which had long since overflowed to a second one, and now a third. The pace quickened. Every day brought new discoveries. Since beginning spinal breathing, his energies became much more stable, and blissfully luminous most of the time. After the raging hurricane in him was quelled, he could see and feel the energy byways inside more clearly. The spinal nerve was no longer a searing silver thread. He was inside it, and it took on changing qualities of vibration as he passed up and down through its wide open spaces during spinal breathing. The root was the denser, earthy realm. As he went up, the vibrations became progressively more refined until reaching the bright white star above and beyond the place between his eyebrows. He felt like he was looking out a spiritual eye extending from the center of his head through the point between his eyebrows. The realms between the root and the star had their signature colors, following the spectrum of the rainbow. It began with dense red at the root, and went through orange, yellow, green, blue, indigo, violet, going up the spinal tunnel. Then, at the top, the pure white light of the star.

All of the senses were involved in the up and down journey. The root had a characteristic buzzing sound. He heard mystical flutes and harps echoing inside him as he went higher. Lovely creatures were touching him with their gentle breath. *Are they angels?* In his heart there was a mystical gong sound that filled the vast space inside him. He felt everyone around him could hear it. No one seemed to, though sometimes he heard it in others. Each person had their own distinct gong sound. When he tapped them on the breast, he was tuning their gong with *i am*, enabling the energies to quicken throughout them. Higher up, in his throat, he heard roaring sounds. They called for him to do something there. But what? And finally there was the ecstatic hum of *i am* in his head as it pulsated in and out of the blazing white star. Often *i am* encompassed his whole spine, his whole body. It's home was in the center of his head, in the space beginning in the stem of his brain and coming out through the point between his eyebrows and up into the rising star. From there it commanded all the lower regions in him with its unspeakable bliss.

He also could see thousands of illuminated nerves interpenetrating his body. He couldn't count them all. Three stood out. The spinal nerve, and two others that were like snakes weaving their way back and forth up his spine. They met with themselves and the spinal nerve at points on the way up. Where they met he saw flaming intersections of light, almost as bright as the inner star above him. There were flaming intersections in his loins, near his solar plexus, near his heart, deep in the hollow of his throat, in the center of his brain where it went upward brightly into his crown of a thousand beams, and at the point between his eyebrows where it dissolved out and up into the bright inner star. He could feel the lights as well as see them – all different grades of pleasure ... so many kinds of ecstasy. He couldn't describe them all. He found his body to be a bliss machine. He understood why Jesus considered the human body to be the temple of God.

When he did his spiritual stretching before spinal breathing, the nerves would become more illuminated. Spinal breathing took him inside, opened the nerves up, and filled them with sexual essence rising from his loins.

With the smoothness that spinal breathing brought, he found he could go back to long suspensions of breath next without energy imbalances. The marriage of his masculine and feminine energies was far reaching in its stabilizing effects. When he finished his regular slow spinal breathing session, he'd go into a mode of staying full a while after an in-breath up the spine. In root seat he'd do the root lift, abdominal lift, chin lock, and have his tongue moving slowly on his altar of bliss, as he did during spinal breathing. He would suspend his breath as long as he could.

When he was full on the in-breath, his head began to move with the energy. This was not completely new. For years his neck often automatically jerked to one side or the other as the energy moved through him. It was an automatic movement with an apparent inner purpose. But now the movement became more pronounced.

As he sat on the bed with a full in-breath, finished with spinal breathing, his chin began to move back and forth in chin lock on his chest. It was pleasurable. Then he let it rotate in a small circle. Also pleasurable. Then it went into to a big circle, all the way up, to one side, to the back, to the other side, and then falling quickly back down like a rock to his breastbone, making a *thump* inside his chest. His chin didn't stop there. It swept across his breastbone on its way to the next circle, creating friction in his chest, like a nerve slipping across cartilage. It sent a current up his neck and into his head. This was the most pleasurable of all. He went clockwise, then counterclockwise with each successive suspended breath. This whirling, alternating one way and then the other with each suspended in-breath, lasted ten minutes, sometimes longer. Afterwards, his chest and head were filled with a profusion of light and bliss. As the practice evolved over weeks and months, the increased intensity of light and bliss became constant in his life.

He called the practice the "chin pump," because it literally pumped ecstatic energy into his chest and head.

Another practice that came up was after his meditation, at the end of each session. His eyes were giving so much pleasure that he put his index fingers in the outside corners, on the lower lids, and pushed his eyeballs firmly up toward the point between his eyebrows through the lower lids. This created a surge of energy coming up from his root. He found that it could be accentuated by furrowing his brow in the center between the eyebrows. The furrowing pulled on the stem in the center of his brain (the medulla oblongata, according to his *Gray's Anatomy*) and could be felt pleasurably all the way down his spine into his loins. He'd do this while holding an in-breath and trap the air, under pressure from his lungs, in his upper sinuses by pinching his nostrils with his middle fingers and by having his tongue up in the secret chamber so no air could escape his mouth. He'd keep his brow furrowed in the "medulla pull," as he called it, during this practice, and his attention on the bright inner star which was a vision that filled his body with a palpable pleasure. So, he'd be holding his breath with index fingers in the outer corners of his eyes and center fingers closing his nose from each side. In this way he could expand his nasal passages and sinuses with air pressure, which filled his head with more light. He did several of these at the end of each meditation. He called this practice the "spiritual eye purge," because it acted directly on the pleasurable currents coursing between the point between his eyebrows and the center of his brain, and down the medulla oblongata into the spine. The medulla was emerging as a central organ in the metamorphosis, like a sex organ in his head, forever pulsating, quivering, and sometimes spasming as ecstatic energy gushed up into his head and out to the inner star. His medulla was alive with *i am*. The faintest thought of the sacred name of God sent him into ecstasy. His meditations had become orgies.

Sometimes during ecstasy episodes, his breathing would accelerate rapidly into a bellows-like panting mode. When it did, it stimulated his insides greatly. This rapid panting would often continue automatically for five or ten minutes, taking John's experience much deeper. Breathing in general became an ecstatic activity. Conscious breathing was like having sex.

What did he know about having sex? Not much. But he knew a lot about whole body ecstasy. He was filled with pleasure, listening to the love moving in him. His delight was in the law of the Lord. The law of *i am* vibrated in his human form, and in it he meditated day and night.

All of these practices evolved organically simply by following the deep pleasure coursing through his body. But one development stood out above all others in terms of the drama. That was when his tongue went up and far beyond his altar of bliss. It happened quite suddenly.

In the two and a half years since he first went into the secret chamber, John kept taking tiny snips from the hymen under his tongue, usually not much bigger than a hair. It was an ongoing thing. They'd heal up in a day or two and he'd take a little snip every week or two. Each time after healing, a calloused edge would appear that was painless to snip. The only time he wasn't doing it was when he was too sick to get out of bed after the inner energy explosions and subsequent rash that covered most of his body.

Over time, the snipping gave his tongue more latitude in the secret chamber. He experimented with the inner nostril openings, trying to enter them, without much success. The nostrils were too narrow to go straight in with his tongue lying horizontal. It had to be turned on its side. The natural way seemed to be to turn his tongue outward away from the septum on whichever side he was entering. This exposed the sensitive erectile tissues, also on the outside, to the textured top of his tongue, which was quite irritating. Plus, the angle was wrong to go in very far.

One day, as he sat in root seat on his bed experimenting, he was tracing with the tip of his tongue over the top of the flared horn of one of his eustachian tubes. There was a channel up over the horn that went inward toward the nostril. He was sliding down the channel with the tip of his tongue, trying to feel how it went into the side of the nostril. Then he realized the channel was guiding his tongue inward, twisting the top of his tongue toward the center of the secret chamber, toward the wall of the septum. A twist to the center like this would not be easy without the guidance of the channel he was tracing.

Then his tongue entered the nostril with the top against the central wall of the septum, and it slid quickly all the way up inside toward the place between his eyebrows. The ease and eroticism of the entry to a new level of ecstasy shocked him. It was incredibly stimulating. His eyes watered and he shivered all over the first few times he did it. He was being stretched inside like a new bride again. The smoother underside of his tongue passed over the erectile tissues with no irritation. He went past his altar of bliss to a new level of stimulation much higher up. His tongue slid over the sensitive protrusion on the edge of his septum as he went up, and again when he came back down. The tip of his tongue kissed the sensitive place between his eyebrows from the inside. *This is astounding!*

He found he could do this in either nostril, the twisting to the center and sliding up to the inner brow along the sensitive wall of the septum, using the channel above the eustachian horn on either side to guide him in. Whichever nostril he was in would be blocked. He began to practice his spinal breathing being always up in one nostril or the other, alternating sides with each breath. It brought his spinal breathing to a much higher level of ecstatic effectiveness, and his inner experiences were enhanced multifold again. His ecstatic conductivity went deeper than ever before. He marveled at the fantastic discovery. He began to see everyone as glorious bliss temples just waiting to be discovered. *How will I tell them all?*

He called the new practice the entry into the "upper passages" of the secret chamber. It was a huge breakthrough.

With all the methods of practice, which seemed to be increasing in depth each week, he still found the greatest peace and bliss in the radiant silence of the simple *i am* meditation that comprised the second half of his practices. He did it in root seat with his tongue on his altar of bliss. That was all. Meditation was his center, and he was well aware that *i am* was the source of it all. Everything else was plowing the earth to prepare him for the seed of *i am*. Plow he did, and *i am* continued to grow in remarkable ways.

A few months later, John was coming out of meditation on his bed and was leaning back on his pillow resting. He noticed a dirty sock draped over the back of the chair at his desk across the room, and thought it should be in the pile of clothes on the floor. Whimsically, he waved his hand, thinking:

...move...

He picked up the thought faintly, deep inside, and let it go into the abyss of his resonating silence. Something jerked inside him – an energy. He caught his breath as his lungs lurched slightly in a strange reflexive motion.

The sock flipped off the back of the chair and dropped to the floor.

What the?

He sat up straight and looked at the sock lying on the floor. *Wait a minute.* He picked up the thought again, this time with the intention to move the sock to the pile three feet away:

...move...

Again, he picked it up faintly and let it go. This time, no wave of the hand. His lungs reflexed inwardly again in an invisible pant and energy through him.

The sock slid three feet across the floor and ran into the pile of dirty laundry in front of the bookcase.

John got goose bumps all over. But part of him wasn't impressed. *Is it just another world record kind of thing? I really don't need it. Well, if I'm going to do this...*

He did it again, this time adding the intention to throw the pile of laundry all over the room:

...move...

Socks, pants, shirts, underwear; everything in the pile flew up and everywhere like a hurricane had just blown through the room. But there was no wind. Just John Wilder's faint intention boomeranging as pure energy out of the infinite silent depths of *i am*...

Oh, man, this is too much! I don't want it.

He pulled on the dirty shorts that landed on the bed in front of him, went out of his disheveled room and bounded down the back stairs.

A few minutes later he was running down the beach at world record speed. He felt the energy streaming up through him. It was ecstatic, smooth, and clear. He realized he could do anything with it he wished. It scared him. He fought it. He ran faster, resisting the urge to take to the air.

An elderly couple walking on the beach watched him streak by. They looked with amazement at the dark wet sand lighting up under his bare churning feet, and the white sparks coming off his fast-flicking hands.

Chapter 17 – Miracle Worker

John did not feel like a miracle worker. He did not want to be a miracle worker. He knew it came with awesome responsibilities. He didn't want to be distracted from his practices. He stood in front of his bathroom mirror lecturing himself on the subject:

"You think you are so special, huh? Well good for you. Moses parted the sea. Jesus walked on the water and fed the multitude. And you, what did you do? You threw the laundry all over your room, smart ass."

He clung to his ordinary humanity as long as he could, but it was too late. The butterfly had to come out of its cocoon and fly.

Nat Cleveland died about the same time John was flinging his laundry around his room. Nat was the richest man in Jacksonville. His grandparents had owned most of the undeveloped land east of downtown. As Jacksonville grew toward the ocean, the Clevelands grew ever richer. Nat was the current patriarch. He died on his treadmill behind the big picture window overlooking the panoramic St. Johns River. The funeral would be at the prestigious First Church of Christ downtown. Nat's extended family would be there. The Mayor and local political figures would be there. The Governor would be there, as well as assorted State and Federal officials.

Prominent business leaders from the community would be there. The Wilders would be there. More than five hundred people were expected.

As John walked into the church in his dark suit, red tie, and shiny black shoes, he was struck by the profusion of white marble. The ornate columns holding up the huge church were marble. The altar was marble. The pulpit was marble. He suspected the floor was marble too under the lush red carpet they shuffled in on to the polished wooden pew about halfway toward the front.

Over the altar on the white marble wall hung a huge golden cross with a full-sized suffering Jesus on it, painted to look real.

Nat Cleveland's mahogany coffin with its white skirt sat at the foot of the red-carpeted steps leading up to the altar.

"Isn't it beautiful?" Stella whispered as the four of them sat down on the soft red velvet cushion that went the length of the pew.

Kurt looked around the church. "Yeah, look at all these deal makers." He had flown down from Washington for the opportunity to mingle with the Florida elite.

"Yes, they are all here," Harry said. "There's the Governor up front, with the Cleveland family, next to the Mayor, and..." Harry and Kurt fell into a whispered conversation planning who they would bump into after the service.

John put an assuring hand on Stella's arm. "Yes, it's beautiful, Mom." He closed his eyes and was meditating as more people came in.

His eyes opened slowly when the organ music boomed, heralding the a procession of white robed acolytes, climaxed by the Minister striding down the aisle in a deliberately reserved fashion. He had on an elaborate white vestment with a large golden cross embroidered on his front, and then another one on his back after he passed by. He was a man about sixty, with glasses and white hair, a well-rehearsed fixture of this Christian institution.

The funeral service followed Protestant protocol. John got restless with the getting up-and-down and parroting of scripture, hymns and prayers, and the platitudes about dying into the arms of eternal life with Jesus. *Well, what about dying into the arms of Jesus, i am, when you were alive, Mr. Cleveland? It's a little late now, isn't it? It is getting late for all of us.*

Something was surging up inside John. He didn't know what. Something was very wrong with all this. It welled up in him like a horse pulling hard on its bridle. He took his hand off his mother's arm where it had lightly rested and grabbed the edge of the pew under him on both sides, just as something in him began to lurch upward. He held on, knowing if he let go he would fly out of the pew. The pressure was building inside.

The Minister was into his homily, praising Nat Cleveland's accomplishments in the community, painting the picture everyone wanted to see.

And then the Minister said it: "...And I know Nat Cleveland is in heaven with Jesus today, because he has been a solid supporter of our great church. His place in heaven has been assured –"

John exploded. "Nooooo!"

The Minister, startled, stopped and looked out over the crowd, spotting the young man in the dark suit and red tie standing up, yelling.

"You hypocrite! How dare you use this house of God as a tollbooth to heaven!"

Stella grabbed the tail of John's jacket desperately. "Sit down, John. Oh God, sit down!" She was shouting in a whisper.

"No!" He pulled away from her and jumped up on the velvet seat, yelling, "No one here needs people like you to find God! You are an obstacle to God!"

People all around John, including his family, were beginning to try and grab him and bring him down. A loud murmur went up in the crowded church. The Governor's two bodyguards started up the aisle toward the pew where the Wilders were sitting.

John jumped up on the backrest of the pew in front of him and leapt from backrest to backrest going forward toward the front of the church, waving an arm angrily at the Minister as he went. He looked like he was running with giant steps. The murmur in the church increased to a roar. Many began shouting obscenities at him. The bodyguards followed in the center aisle. They'd grab him when he got to the front. He got there first and leapt down into the open area between the front pew and the steps. He ran past the coffin, halfway up the steps, and turned.

The bodyguards were right behind him, followed by half a dozen other men. They were about to engulf him. He swung his arm in a broad sweeping gesture toward them. They were thrown back like bowling pins onto the red carpet.

John paused, looking with disbelief for a second at the men strewn on the floor. He glanced at his hand curiously and shrugged. The bodyguards recovered and were drawing their guns.

John held his open palms out to his sides and closed his eyes. A hush came over the crowd. No one moved. Though it never occurred to him, the similarity of John's pose to the perpetual life-sized crucifixion on the wall behind him subdued the crowd. The church became silent. Was this going to be a shooting or an epiphany? Or both?

After half a minute, no one fired. Neither could they speak. And it was obvious they dared not rush him again. John slowly let his arms down, turned and walked serenely up the remaining steps to where the Minister was standing nervously by the pulpit. He stopped in front of the Minister. John's demeanor had shifted from outright anger to a radiant calmness. The barrels of the guns were still on him.

The Minister had his notes in his hands. They were shaking. John reached out slowly with his right hand and placed it on the chest of the Minister, over the gold cross that was sewn there.

"*i am*," he said softly. "Can you say it, sir?"

"I, I, I AM," said the Minister.

John's gaze penetrated deep into him.

"*i am*," the Minister said, his voice still shaking.

John pulled his hand away. The Minister dropped his notes as the vibration of *i am* surged through him. They fluttered down and littered the red carpet. The minister's head bowed slightly.

John continued to speak softly. "Please, sir, from now on preach only the inner word of God, Jesus, *i am*. This is the Lord's house of prayer. I beg of you." John went down on his knees and placed his forehead on the Minister's shiny black shoes protruding from under his white robe. The

Minister was transfixed as divine energy surged up through him from his feet. He began to weep as the congregation looked on in amazement.

John didn't move for a minute. Except for the Minister's broken sobs and a nearly visible white light emanating from him, the big marble church was silent.

Finally, John got up and started back down the steps. The Minister turned benignly, watching him go, not moving from the place where he stood. The men with the guns lowered them. They and the crowd that had gathered in the front of the church stepped back with a muffled rustling sound as John came down. He stopped at Nat Cleveland's coffin and placed both his hands on it, and then his forehead. Those who were close to the front could see him quiver as an unseen energy came out of him. Then he straightened up and went toward the center aisle.

When John came near the first pew, he turned toward a little girl in a dark blue dress sitting in a wheelchair right in front of the pew between the Mayor and his wife. He went to her. Her gaze was fixed on him and she was smiling. He knelt in front of her, and looked into her eyes.

He placed his hand on her chest and said, "*i am.*"

She was silent. Her body shook slightly. John nodded slowly, and the little girl said, "*i am*" into his eyes.

He got up and took her hands, helping her up. She stood there holding his hands. He backed up a little, and she took a step, and then another. The Mayor's wife began to shake and broke down in tears. Then another step, and another. John let go of her and she turned to her parents, smiling at them on her wobbly new legs. She walked back to them, into their arms and their tears.

A murmur went up in the crowd.

The Mayor stood up. "Who are you, young man?"

"Just a man," John said. "A person like everyone here."

"I don't think so," the Mayor said, his hand steadying his daughter as she stood close next to him. He looked at her beaming face and back to John. "What you have done here today – thank you."

John nodded and smiled widely at the little girl, who was now giggling at him. Then he turned toward the aisle to go. The crowd that had shrunk from him earlier now surged toward him. Many people flowed noisily out of the pews into the aisle, blocking his way, streaming closer, touching him, drawing all they could of what he had. He sensed their pain, their desperation, and the cramped inner condition from which they craved relief. He instinctively put out his hands, giving freely of his inner energies. They grabbed him, pressing closer in an increasing frenzy, taking all they could. The congregation had become a mob, and they swallowed him.

Then he went down.

"He's fainted!" a voice cried out. "Somebody get help!"

Chapter 18 – Heavenly Healing

"We don't know, Mr. and Mrs. Wilder," Dr. Chu said. "He's in some sort of coma, though none like we've ever seen. His body is shut down, he won't breathe, his heart rate is thirty-six, but his EEG is active. It means his brain is functioning normally, which is highly unusual."

"Oh, God," Stella said. "What's happened to our John? It's so bizarre. All of a sudden he starts performing outrageous tricks, and now this."

"Is there anything else that can be done?" Harry said.

"Nothing for now. Let's give him a few days. If he hasn't come around by then, we'll try a neural stimulator."

"What's that?" Harry said.

"It's a class of drug that sometimes helps coma patients," Dr. Chu said. "But it can have serious side effects. It is a high risk approach, so we hope that he'll come out of it on his own."

John lay comatose in the hospital bed. He had an I.V. needle in the back of his hand and he was on a breathing device that went down his windpipe. It made grotesque sucking noises as the piston pumped up and down on the small steel table on wheels next to his bed. His breathing stopped at the church and hadn't resumed. No one thought to do CPR in the chaos of the hungry mob. The doctors didn't know how he survived until the ambulance got there.

Inside he was awake, nourished by the vital essences rising continuously in his body.

John was in a vast region of pure white light. There were tunnels of light going off in all directions, more than he could count, becoming blue, gold, and, finally, red, as they went further away from the white realm he was in. It was a tapestry of pure white light and millions of tiny tunnels. Many other beings were in the white realm with him, endless waves of beings floating all around him. Some were moving into tunnels, others were moving out of tunnels, but most were floating joyously like he was. He stayed there drinking the profound peace and bliss. He had no desire to leave. The landscape of light beings seemed to be doing the same, going on forever in waves beyond his sight in every direction.

After some time of floating in bliss, he didn't know how long, he noticed one of the beings coming in his direction. As it came closer, he could see a human-like figure surrounded in a radiant cloak of energy. It spoke to him:

"*i am.*"

It was the faintest feeling of the vibration he had surrendered himself to so many times before. *"i am,"* he replied as though he were deep in meditation.

"i am Jesus," the light being said.

John, in his light body, quivered in humility. He bowed before the light being, saying, *"i am your servant, Jesus, Lord, i am."*

Jesus turned and gestured toward a particular region of the vast array of tunnels. They began to move in that direction.

"I must go back?"

Jesus affirmed with an invisible nod. *"You will rejoin us when you have completed your earth work. Many have done so."* He gestured to the innumerable beings floating around them.

"Who are they?"

"The saviors of innumerable creeds on innumerable worlds. We are i am. All is i am. All is of the One. The knowledge you have been given has been shared in every time and in every place. The truth of God the Father of all is timeless and boundless."

Another light being was drawing close, and came next to Jesus. It had a unique bluish inner glow and faint greenish outer aura. The vibration was familiar. *"Christi? Is that you, Christi?"*

The light being bowed slightly, and John felt waves of love coming from her. Before he could react, he was drawn into one of the tunnels in the region Jesus had brought him to. The two divine figures floating side by side faded quickly as he was sucked in. He accelerated as he went through the tunnel. There were many flashes of colored light as he zoomed through. It seemed like minutes passed as he went careening deep into the earth realm again. And then, suddenly, he was gagging on the respirator that was in his windpipe.

"He's coming around," a voice said. "The neural stimulator is working." Then there was a long beeping sound, and John faded back up into the tunnel toward the white light. He was happy to be going back.

"Drug reaction. Cardiac arrest. We're losing him! Paddles ready ... Clear!"

Ka-thunk! ...

"No pulse ... Again ... Clear!"

Ka-thunk! ...

"Still nothing ... Again ... Clear!"

Ka-thunk! ...

"Okay, we have a pulse. We got him back..."

John was gagging again. His chest hurt terribly. Everything was a blur. Nothing was clear. He didn't know where he was, or who he was. He only knew he was in great discomfort ... definitely not in the heavenly realm anymore. Yet, his inner silence remained, so the deepest part of him was at peace, as always. Only now, something had been added – a new connection and a new depth.

People kept coming. Flowers were piled up in the room everywhere. Finally, there was a break in the stream of visitors.

"John ... John, can you hear me?"

John had a glazed look. Devi looked at Luke.

"He's out of it," she said. "It's been a week since he came out, but he's so drugged, he doesn't know anything."

"They did that to me too, when I was busted up in Atlanta," Luke said. "They'd rather have you drugged than well. My parents finally got me out of the hospital, so I could recover from what the drugs did."

Devi folded her arms in disgust. "You think they'd figure out by now that treating side effects with drugs that have more side effects doesn't work. He's on six drugs, each one worse than the last. Neural stimulator, tranquilizer, anti-psychotic, anti-biotic, anti-nausea ... anti-you name it, he's on it, all through that needle in his vein. "

"Did you meet the speech therapist?" Luke said.

"Speech therapist?"

"Yeah, they want to teach him to talk, now that he's so drugged he can't talk."

"You're kidding," she said.

"Nope."

"Deeevvvi..."

"I'm here, John," she said, getting close to him.

"Woo dat ova der?" John was reaching for the empty space by the window.

"No one. There's no one there."

"I wan gooooo ter." He was reaching into space, into nowhere.

"Can't we get him off this stuff?" she said.

"The Wilders have to decide," Luke said. "And they won't question the four doctors giving it to him. Every time a doctor comes he gets another drug added on. And Kurt went back to Washington. Not that he would help. We can't do nothin'."

"Is he sick, Luke?"

"I don't know. They say he did some powerful stuff at that funeral. It made the paper. You know the Mayor's wife has been here twice with her cute little girl. She was skipping down the hall. They said she was paralyzed before he touched her. Is he sick? I dunno."

Devi pushed her hair back over her shoulder. "We need to get him away from here, someplace where he can recover. Too many people know about him now. They're all after him."

Luke stroked his chin. "How 'bout Blue Ridge Hollow? Nobody knows where that is."

"Where?" she said.

"Blue Ridge Hollow. It's where my Daddy grew up, way up in the North Carolina mountains. I got kin up there. It's real remote. We can go there."

Devi's eyes lit up. "Tonight ... let's take him tonight."

Luke straightened up to his near seven-foot height. The gentle giant towered over tiny Devi. "He's your man. If you want to take him, we will take him."

"Deeevvvi! Deeevvvi!"

She leaned close to him. "I'm here, John."

"Hello, I'm Prissy Flailing, John's speech therapist."

Devi and Luke looked up from the chairs they were slouched in, half asleep. Devi eyed Prissy. She was a short trim blond, very neat, very controlled, and very uptight.

"You're going to teach this druggy how to talk?" Devi said.

"Oh, it isn't the drugs. He has neurological damage, and we can help him compensate. In time he will be able to converse again."

Devi rolled her eyes. "I'm really glad to hear that."

"Deeevvvi!"

"Can you teach him to say 'Devi?'" Luke said.

"Let's see," Prissy sat in a chair close to the bed. "John, it is Prissy. I'm your speech therapist. Can you hear me?"

"Prifffie!"

"It's 'Prissy.' Can you say 'Prissy,' John? Let your tongue come forward and make the "Sss" sound."

"Prifffie!"

"With the tongue, John – 'Prisssssy,'" Prissy said. "Can you use your tongue?"

"Prifffie!"

"Can you show me your tongue, John? Let me see it. Stick it out."

John did a move in his mouth, and then opened it wide.

"That's it ... where's your tongue? There's no tongue. My God, he's got no –"

Suddenly, John slipped his tongue out of his secret chamber and shot it way out of his mouth at Prissy, opening his eyes wide, almost hitting her in the nose as she leaned over him. As he did it, he added a loud "Ahhhhhhh!"

Prissy jumped up off the chair in shock. "God, what was that?"

John pulled his tongue back in and opened his mouth wide at her. No tongue. Then he shot it out at her again. "Ahhhhhhh!"

Prissy let out a shriek and bolted toward the hospital room door.

John gave her one more "Ahhhhhhh!" as she ran out and down the stairwell across the hall. They could hear her screams echoing up from three flights down.

Devi and Luke grinned at each other.

"He must be okay under all those chemicals," she said. "He can still find his secret chamber, and hasn't lost his sense of humor either."

"They've got a couple of wheelchairs in the closet down the hall," Luke said.

"Tonight," she said.

Just then, six people showed up at the door with flowers. A stocky woman said, "Is this the John Wilder from First Church of Christ? We need a healing."

"So does he, Ma'am," Luke said. "So does he."

They all shrank at the sight of the huge black man with the dark angelic eyes.

It was the dead of night, and all was quiet in the hospital. Devi pulled out the I.V. The colorless chemicals dripped slowly out onto the floor. She and Luke got John dressed in his suit pants, white shirt and shiny black shoes left over from the funeral. Soon they were walking out as casually as they could with John in the wheelchair. His head was bobbing on his chest and he was mumbling incoherently. They made it past the nurse's station, down the elevator, and were on the home stretch through the main lobby. On the wall was a big Caduceus, the symbol of the medical profession, a staff with two snakes spiraling up it, biting the wings of an orb on top.

John's head bobbed up. A look of recognition lit him up.

"Thaaaat's meeeeee!" he yelled, pointing at the Caduceus. "Thaaaat's meeeeee!"

"Shhhh," Devi said as they hurried for the front door. Luke led the way, looking a little nervous, as Devi pushed the wheelchair behind him.

"Thaaaat's meeeeee!" John yelled. His arms were reaching back over his shoulder for the Caduceus as they went out.

"Yeah, right," Devi said. "These people around here wouldn't know a real Caduceus if it came up and bit them in the ass."

Only a night janitor saw the huge black man and feisty little Indian beauty wheeling the raving lunatic out the front door of the hospital. He watched until they went around the corner of the building, off into the night. He shrugged and went back to his mopping.

Chapter 19 – Wheeler Dealer

"Will you marry me?"

"Are you sure it's time?"

"I know what I want."

"That was clear the first time we met."

"Then the answer is yes?"

"Oh, why not? I always wanted to marry a millionaire."

Kurt pulled the two-carat ring out of his pocket and slipped it on Nadine's finger.

"It fits," she said.

He smiled. "If it fits, wear it."

"Don't mind if I do." She held the sparkling rock up to the light. "Not bad. So when's the happy day?"

"As soon as I finish the new Navy deal and close on that little place on the Potomac."

"You mean the Woodmere estate?" she said. "That little place?"

"Yeah, all two hundred acres of it," he said. "They threw in the stone mansion and boathouse as a bonus."

"How nice of them."

"I thought so. It was that or no deal."

"Tough negotiator. When do we move in?"

"Next month."

"I guess we'll have to slum it until then," she said, admiring the diamond again.

"We'll manage somehow," he said.

The drab, government-green meeting room was strewn with men in suits, brief cases and computer printouts.

"Ten percent," Kurt said. "Take it or leave it."

"We did all the leg work," Clive Naegle said. "Minority business status is worth more than ten percent."

"Not in this market. I can go to any of you hustlers for the same thing. It's the deep pockets like us behind you the Feds want. Not you. Ask Mahoney at the procurement office. He'll tell you. Why do you think it's called 'minority business?' "

"Brother, you'll fry in hell for this," Clive said. "You came in talkin' fifty-fifty, and now when you got us, it's ninety-ten."

"Live with it," Kurt said. "Welcome to the jungle. You in or out?"

"What do you think?"

"Good. Carl, give them the contract. You guys sign and we'll be in business. I gotta go." And he left the meeting, another fifty million ahead.

Kurt congratulated himself as he went down the elevator. *There's a way around every rule. The deals keep falling like rain out of this D.C. cesspool. I love this shit!*

The center of gravity of Wilder Corp had shifted from Jacksonville to Washington, and Kurt insisted that D.C. would now be corporate headquarters, with him in charge. Harry acquiesced, retaining his Chairman of the Board role, and directorship over projects in the Southeast. He couldn't argue with Kurt's steamroller approach, let alone the thousands he had working for him in Washington and dozens of other offices across the country, many obtained through acquisitions. He only hoped that the meteoric rise of the company wouldn't be followed by a catastrophic collapse. It all seemed too good to be true.

They were having one of those feel good personnel training sessions at Wilder Corp's Washington office. Kurt showed up halfway through.

Dave Smart, the director of Human Resources, was doing an informal survey of psychological test profiles that the nearly one hundred participants generated earlier in the day. Each person ended up with a four-letter profile representing their main personality traits, indicating their way of approaching life and work. It also indicated compatibility or incompatibility with other profiles, which could aid in improving employee relations and productivity.

"So how many INTJs do we have here today?" Dave said.

About fifteen people raised their hands.

"And how many ENFPs?"

Twenty raised their hands.

"And how many –"

"CEOs ... how many CEOs?" Kurt was on his feet and walking to the front of the large meeting room. "Only one, and that's me. Now everybody get back to work. Out!" He waved his arm toward the double doors in back the large meeting room as he walked toward the front.

The large group of people started milling their way out, murmuring.

Dave Smart put his notebook on the podium as Kurt approached. "Mr. Wilder, I –"

"Listen Dave, if you want to stay around here, I suggest you focus on skills training, not this crap."

"Well, this is important for morale and productivity –"

"Skills training," Kurt said. "We've got three hundred people who can't run the new CAD machines, and you're screwing around with this touchy-feelie bullshit. If we don't put out the designs, we don't get paid. If we don't get paid, you are out of a job. Understand?"

"Yes, I —"

"Good, so get on the stick, man," Kurt said. "And no more proposals to ratchet up the pay grades. We gotta squeeze these bastards or they'll steal us blind." He gestured to the last of the group going out at the other end of the room. "Capiche?"

"Yes, sir," Dave said.

It was a sunny day at the Woodmere Estate. Kurt was out on the patio in his bathrobe.

"Never use my name on these deals," Kurt said, pacing the flagstones. "Not on anything, not one memo or email. Got that?"

The voice on the other end of the phone was hesitant. "What about —"

"None of them. Not on any of these split-pie deals. I am not to be mentioned. You just do them. On those contracts, whoever wins, we divvy it up, understand? We're all big boys. No sense fighting over the business."

"Okay," the voice said. "It's not legal, you know."

"I didn't hear that," Kurt said. "You just get the deals done. Do whatever it takes. If we're going to hit two billion in revenue next year, you have to do whatever it takes. What about the acquisitions? How many going?"

"Six."

"That's all?" Kurt said. "You need at least ten to get to the revenue mark. That's if you get the pie deals. Find at least four more to buy."

"What about cash flow?"

"Cash flow, smash flow! Do the god-damn deals, Scott, or I'll find another COO who can. Let me worry about the money."

"Okay, Kurt. That all?"

"What, you want more? Well, how about sending Mable down here with the division reports I should have had yesterday."

"Okay."

Kurt threw the portable phone on the table and flopped on the chaise. The cool Virginia air went through his hair. There was a yacht passing lazily on the river. *That's where I should be right now.* He gazed at the forty-foot cabin cruiser tied up at the dock along side the boathouse. *Maybe Sid and I'll go out. Mable can come too. Can always count on Mable for a good time, not to mention the scoop on what's going on behind my back at the office.*

He lay there a while, dozing off. When he woke up he found *i am* creeping into his thoughts. He pushed it out. *No, not that. Wonder what's happening with my fool brother? Jeez, what a screwball.* The phone rang again...

"Yeah? ... Oh, hi, honey. You comin' home? No? Tomorrow? Okay. Really? Sure ... have fun in New York. I'll hold down the fort here ... fine, everything's fine. Same old corporate wars, you know ... love you too ... bye."

The phone bounced on the patio table again. *Yeah, definitely taking good old oral Mable on a boat ride today.*

Kurt got up and went in the house. As he came into the cavernous front foyer, he heard a car pulling up in the front driveway. He opened the big oak front door in time to see a long sleek leg swing out of the Jaguar and a three-inch heel crunch into the gravel. The other leg stayed behind long enough to reveal too much.

Mable Butkus popped a bubble. "Hi, baby."

"Sid!" Kurt yelled over his shoulder, never taking his eyes off her. His voice echoed through the massive foyer.

An answer came ricocheting out from the kitchen way in the back. "Yes, sir, Mr. Wilder."

"Go down and get the boat ready. We're going for a ride."

Chapter 20 – God in the Hollow

The back room of the two-room shack was dim, lit by a single lamp hanging from the rafters. The inside of the tin roof nailed to the beams was visible above. John lay on the bed, coming to his senses for the first time. Devi sat at his side.

"Where are we?"

"Blue Ridge Hollow," she said. "Do you remember what happened?"

"The last thing I remember is a mob grabbing me ... at the funeral."

"That's it?" she said. "You were in the hospital for two weeks. First, you were in a coma. You came out of it. Then you were drugged beyond belief. We took you away. We've been here three days."

"I remember being with Jesus. I remember that. It was so real. Christi Jensen was there too."

"Really?" she said, looking into his eyes. "Did they say anything?"

"Not a lot, but I felt their presence in me. I feel it now. They are *i am*. We are all *i am*. Everything is *i am*. It's so clear. I'm to continue here with the work. I have to go back home."

"It will take some time for you to recover. This will be home for a while, I'm afraid," she said, looking around the small dark room.

John tried to get up and fell back on the bed, exhausted.

"See? Mama knows best."

"What about my family?"

"We called them from the little church down the road. They know you're okay," she said. "But no one knows where we are. Just Luke. He brought us. You're a celebrity now. There will be more mobs."

John sighed. "I had to do it. I couldn't stand it anymore."

"You did it all right," she said. "What's with the miracles?"

"I don't know. It just happened. It started with a sock in my room."

"A sock?"

"Yeah, I didn't want it to move again, but it did."

"You healed a little girl. Remember that?"

"Yeah, I had to go to her. She had so much courage. When we believe, *i am* is drawn. She drew me. The mob didn't believe. They just wanted to take and take."

"They nearly killed you."

"I don't know," he said. "It needed to happen. It threw me into the light realm, out of my body into the arms of Jesus."

"Your breathing stopped. Your heart stopped."

"I wasn't dead. I was alive inside. If the doctors had left me alone, I would have come back anyway. Jesus sent me back. I know he did."

Devi put her hand on his forehead. "You like to live on the edge, don't you?"

"What else is there?" he said. "We're all dangling on this little ball spinning through space, one breath away from not being here – always on the edge."

"Hmmm," she said.

"Yeah." He took her hand. "Or so it seems. The edge is an illusion. Death is an illusion. We never die."

"So why not just walk through it, huh?" she said.

"Yeah, why not?" he said. "For the right reason –" His voice got weaker. He was fading off to sleep. "I promise to come back to you. Will you be here?"

"I'll try," she said. "But no guarantees. I could fall off this spinning ball any second."

She leaned over and kissed him softly on the lips. Bright energy flowed back and forth between them. Then he slept.

Weeks went by. John slowly recovered his strength. He and Devi took short walks on the dirt road that led to the church, and along the path that went into the woods behind the shack. It led to a waterfall with a pond in front of it. It was called Gem Pond Falls. The shack belonged to Luke's family. Luke came up every other weekend. He was working in his father's machine shop in Jacksonville, preparing to take over the business when his father retired. While Luke's football career had been a promising possibility, he ended up taking a less high-profile route in his life, much for the reasons John had. Less high-profile?

Blue Ridge Hollow was in a valley a few miles off the scenic Blue Ridge Parkway, not far from Mount Mitchell, the highest point east of the Rocky Mountains. The community was formed by a group of freed slaves after the Civil War. For over a hundred years it maintained an existence through farming and jewelry made with semiprecious stones that came from several small mines in the valley. Everyone in Blue Ridge Hollow slept with a sparkling sapphire, ruby or emerald under the mattress. It was said it helped lift their spirits closer to God. Social and spiritual life revolved around the Blue Ridge Hollow Church, which was started by the original leader of the community, a charismatic former cotton gin operator named Elijah. Luke's Grandfather, O'Pa Smith, a direct descendant of Elijah, had been pastor of the church for the past fifty years.

The old church was plain, unfinished, and alive with God. Sundays were a happening in Blue Ridge Hollow. Everyone came and jammed into the rows of worn out benches, or sat on the floor, and the valley shook with adoration for the divine presence.

Two Sundays in a row John shook in the bed, nearly lifting off it, as the waves came rolling up the valley.

Devi had to hold him down, thinking he was going into seizures.

"No," he said afterward. "It's the love that shakes me."

By the third Sunday, John was strong enough, and they walked down to the service. Luke was visiting from Jacksonville, and he went with them.

Old cars and pickups were scattered around the small field in front of the church. Many people came on foot.

"This is how it's always been," Luke said, as they walked toward the rickety steepled building.

They were joined by whole walking families, spruced up for this peak of the week.

Devi held John's hand, in awe of the eager flow of community streaming into the church that was dwarfed by the forested mountainside accelerating up behind it and away into the sky.

"There's something about this place," she said. "I'm tingling all over."

"Oh, you wait," Luke said.

John was quiet. He seemed strangely intent.

Inside the noisy church, they found a few empty feet of space at the outside end of a bench near the back and sat down. People were greeting each other loudly with exaggerated handshakes after a week away. Children were running up and down the aisles on both sides and in the middle. A baby was crying. With all this, there was noticeable expectancy in the crowd.

Devi sat quietly on the bench, slipping into *i am* with her eyes half open. She saw the cracked wooden pulpit gracing the front of the church, the small organ played by tiny old O'Ma in her polka-dot dress, and the choir of shy looking girls and boys in threadbare white robes. The altar was a wooden table with a cross hanging over it on the unfinished wall. It was made with two sticks lashed together.

"That's how Elijah had done it," Luke said, "and how he left it in 1900 when he passed on."

Jubilant vibrations from somewhere increasingly penetrated everything and everyone. They were in Devi too, and her eyes went up in bliss. But the scene in the church was disjointed and chaotic. Bliss and chaos – close bedfellows.

John sat quietly on the end of the bench with his eyes closed. He began swaying slightly against her. She began to sway with him. Then Luke next to her. Then the next person, a large woman with a fan. Then the family next to her. It jumped to the row in front and the row in back. The swaying was working its way around the church.

A side door opened and in walked a withered old man in a black suit – O'Pa. A hush came over everyone. The running children sat on the floor. The baby stopped crying. Only the migrating swaying continued. The organ began with low tones. O'Pa came to the center in front, observing the moving congregation.

"Praise the Lord," he said gently.

Devi thought he looked weak. The old black man's eyes were barely open and he was a bit hunched.

"Praise the Lord," the congregation replied quietly, relaxing into itself as it moved.

Devi heard John say it again in a whisper: "Praise the Lord."

Then it came from O'Pa, louder: "Praise the Lord."

The organ picked up a notch in tone and volume. The Choir began to hum quietly, melodically.

"Praise the Lord." the congregation chanted louder.

The organ stopped. The place was dead quiet for a few seconds.

Suddenly, the young Choir exploded into a three-part harmony, one single line:

"Praise the Lord!"

A young woman's voice, an angel's voice, rang out above all the rest. The entire church filled up with the divine sound for an instant.

Then there was silence again, except for the rustling of clean clothes and God-inspired breath ... ten seconds went by. Then the polka-dot O'Ma organ started up again, louder this time, and faster.

O'Pa stood up straight, the years disappearing out of his face.

"Praise the Lord!" He was dancing in place now, shifting from left to right, waving his hands in the air.

O'Ma cut loose into a cascading organ harmony. The congregation and choir broke out singing at the same time. Everyone followed the angel's voice that came from the center of the choir.

"Praise the Lord!"

"Praise the Lord!"

"Praise the Lord!"

"Praise the Lord!"

Everyone was on their feet, clapping, swaying, singing with all they had, as the musical mantra continued. Many had tears running down their cheeks. John and Devi did as they lost themselves in the reverie of singing spirit.

A woman in the front row waving a white handkerchief went down. Her husband picked her up, and she was waving the handkerchief again. Hands were in the air everywhere.

John was waving his hands in the air too. He was whirling them around in two separate spirals rhythmically towards each other over him.

He came out in the side aisle near at the back of the church singing, "Praise the Lord!" Still whirling. His whole body swayed forward toward the congregation as his hands came forward together over him.

And then it happened.

Bright white flecks came off his hands like a cloud of dust, and went over the singing crowd. Everyone turned, and saw John surrounded in the speckled white light, and it was coming out all over them. The congregation went into a frenzy:

"Praise the Lord!"

"Praise the Lord!"

Then it changed...

"Come on, Jesus!"

"Come on, Jesus!"

"Come on, Jesus!"

"Come on, Jesus!"

"Praise the Lord!"

"Praise the Lord!"

The room was filled with the divine light. John was moving. He seemed to float to the front of the church. He came in front of O'Pa and went down on his knees, never stopping his hands or the deluge of light. The light surrounded O'Pa as he danced. He was transfixed, singing and dancing all the while.

When they saw the moving light, some people stopped singing and went on their knees where they stood. Then more. Some wept. Some just stared. O'Pa never stopped singing. Nor did the choir. The words changed:

"Amen, Jesus!"

"Amen, Jesus!"

"Amen, Jesus!"

"Amen, Jesus!"

The congregation began to join back in. As they did, O'Pa came part way back to earth consciousness. John let his hands down and went prostrate on the floor before O'Pa, and did not move. The light reduced in its intensity, but remained as a faint whiteness in the air.

The singing gradually faded off, and everyone was watching John. Devi was standing on the bench in the back with her hand on Luke's shoulder. Tears were running down their cheeks. *What is this wonder? Who is this man I love?*

John finally began to move. He got up in front of O'Pa and bowed his head.

O'Pa placed his right hand on John's bowed head, and softly said, "Amen." He took it away and stood there.

John raised his head and looked into the old man's eyes. He slowly raised his right hand and tapped O'Pa's breastbone with his fingertips and said softly, "*i am*." O'Pa breathed in suddenly, as though catching his breath. All could see a light shoot up through him and out the top of his head. Then he said, "*iii ammm*."

The congregation was silent. John stepped to the side and sat down on the floor cross-legged next to four little boys who were close to the front of the church. He leaned to each of them, smiling, and taped their breastbones with the tips his fingers saying, "*i am*." As he nodded, they each said, "*i am*." And white light went up from them.

He got up and others came to him, their heads bowed. Then everyone was lined up in the center aisle. He tapped them all in the same way, and each said, "*i am*," as he did. Light went up from everyone who was touched. Ailments were cured at the Blue Ridge Hollow Church that day. Luke's Uncle Kemo left his crutches by the church bench and walked home.

"I haven't seen him walk like that since I was a kid." Luke said to Devi. "It was his place in Georgia where John gave me the *i am*."

"He gave it to me in my living room," she said. "Now he's giving it to everyone."

Devi and Luke stayed at the back of the church, watching as the people milled about in spiritual intoxication. They were slowly going outside. The silence of *i am* filled them. O'Pa came and kissed John on the cheek. John whispered in his ear for several minutes. O'Pa nodded and nodded. John kissed him on the cheek, and then O'Pa went out front to the congregation. John was weak again, and Devi went and got him. They sat on the first row bench.

"Are you all right?"

"Yes, I feel wonderful," he said. "Just a little tired."

"It's beautiful," she said.

"Hey, brother Luke," he said weakly as Luke approached.

"Brother John," he said. "I don't know what to say."

"Nothing to say," John said. "Just keep meditating. That's all."

The three of them were sitting on the bench, leaning against each other in a post-miracle collapse.

"Luke? Luke Smith? Is that you?"

They looked up, and it was the beautiful singing angel from the choir smiling in the lingering soft white light.

"Joy!" Luke said.

"Yep, it's me," she said. "I was wondering if you recognized me?"

"Oh, I did. Your voice sure has grown since we were kids running around here summers barefoot. So has the rest of you. Where'd you get all them curves?"

"Luke!" She gave him a sock in the arm.

"You haven't changed a bit." He smiled, rubbing his massive arm where she hit him.

"You sing like an angel," Devi said.

"Aw, thanks," Joy said. "My Mama taught me."

"Thank God for Mamas," Devi said.

"Amen to that," Joy said. She got a serious look and bowed her head to John. "Thank you for touching me. It feels so good inside, like I been singin' all day."

"*i am* is the one who sings," John said, "and is always singing in us. We only need to meditate on *i am*."

"Meditate?"

"Yes." And he told her how. The four of them meditated together on the bench in the empty church. When they came out, Joy was soaked in bliss.

"Oh, it's wonderful," she said. "How can I ever thank you?"

"Pass it on," John said, making a tapping motion in the air with his fingers.

"I will. I promise." And she burst out in song that filled the empty church to overflowing.

"Praise the Lord!..."

That night a soft rain pattered gently on the tin roof of the shack. Devi lay on her side on the bed against the opposite wall of the back room, her head on the pillow, watching John sleeping across the room. He'd have small lurches and moans now and then as the power of *i am* coursed through him, constantly rearranging the subtle realms of his body for its divine purpose. *He's becoming a God-man.*

She went on her back, pulled the wrinkled tail of his shirt flat under her lifted rear end, and dropped down on it. She undid the bottom button and rested the palm of her hand on her belly over her womb. Her little finger curled a tuft of her soft pubic hair around it.

John had been ambivalent about sex for years, always affectionate, but never lustful. She'd never bared her body to him completely, only tempted him, helping "raise his love," as he called it. She couldn't bring herself to seduce him. It was obvious now that his love went out to everyone in the form of pure white light, and that was most important.

His sexual energies are transforming to a higher purpose. I can understand that. It is what I want too. I can feel the essence of my womanhood drawn up as light in me.

She gently squeezed her perineum and felt the currents rising. Her belly was sucked in and up. Her eyes were pulled up by pleasure. Her tongue slipped into her secret chamber, and caressed her sensitive altar of bliss. Her eyes rose high in inner pleasure. After a moment, her thoughts returned.

I can understand. When his love flows out to others, it weakens him. He pays a price with his body for this divine loving. I will take care of him for the rest of my life. It is my destiny. But what about the child he predicted so long ago? Our child. My taunting isn't about a sexual romp anymore. It's beyond that. Oh, how I want his seed in my womb. How I long to feel our baby growing inside. My life is for him, and for our child to be. But how will it happen? Immaculate Conception?

Her longing for their union and their child went on through the night. Through her longing and practices, *i am* was transforming her body in a thousand ways, preparing her.

As he strengthened, John's practices worked their way back to full strength, and then some. A persistent hunger drew his tongue high up into his nasal passages. When he looked out the center of his forehead at the bright white realm rising in his spiritual sky, the hunger became intense. It grabbed all his energies inside, and his body had to follow. The tether under his tongue was nearly gone now. He could reach easily up to the top of his nasal passages from the inside to the soft spongy ceiling, deliciously stimulating the area between his eyebrows from the inside, and up and down the sensitive passages. His altar of bliss at the entrance-way to the upper passages also received constant stimulation as his tongue slid over it going in and out of his upper passages. It was a lovemaking that fueled his accelerating transformation.

When he did the spiritual eye purge, the pressure from his lungs filled the upper passages, going from the area between his eyebrows, back into the center of his brain, and down through his medulla into his spine. He regarded this air pressure maneuver as kind of backwash, a clearing of the channel. That's why he called it a purge. The normal direction of the flow of sweet substance was up the spine, through the medulla and forward through the center of the brain. As part of this process, John's brow would automatically furrow slightly in the center when his eyes went up, pulling ecstatically on his medulla inside. From the front of his brain the substance went down through the nasal passages to his GI tract. Then it would join in the alchemy in the GI tract and find its way back up into the spine again. It went in a circle like that. He marveled at the natural process unfolding inside him. He did all he could to promote it.

Sometimes when John was high in the upper passages, a surge of energy would shoot from his chest to his head and out to the bright star. His internal spiritual energy flows went into overtime. He naturally went into long breath suspensions with his tongue high up. His need for breath became less and less. With the constant source of vitality flowing up through him from his loins, breathing was gradually becoming less of a necessity. During his breath suspensions, his head naturally rotated in chin pump down and across his chest, first one way for a time, and then the other way. He would also be high in his upper passages during chin pump.

A dramatic new energy dynamic was spawned, catapulting John into a new realm of experience and power. It turned him into a spiritual dynamo that lifted everyone for miles around. It also sealed his fate as a modern-day savior of humankind. It was something he was not fully aware of yet – not something he would have chosen at the start. But as his sense of self crept out into the world around him, it became inevitable that he would do whatever was necessary to illuminate everyone on the planet – for it was becoming clear to him that all were expressions of his own sweet *i am*.

Chapter 21 – Union

"C'mon, lazy, get up. Let's go to the falls."

Devi opened one eye and saw John standing over her, dressed in rolled-up jeans and a flannel shirt hanging out. "Huh?" Her brain was in a fuzz.

"Let's go to the falls. There's something I want to show you."

She rubbed her eyes and propped herself up on her elbows. "You want to show me something?" she whispered, not completely awake.

"Yeah. Get dressed, okay? I'll make you some orange juice."

"Okaaay, I'm comin'." She hauled herself out of bed, holding the nightshirt around herself awkwardly in a half-sleep.

It had been six months since their arrival in Blue Ridge Hollow. She was happy that John was recovered. He spent hours more each day than she did in the back room meditating. He needed that time alone, and she honored it. He was running too, though not as aggressively as in his younger days. His body was strong again, but he had a certain delicacy about him, a sort of translucence. He seemed to wear his body like a loose set of clothes that could fall off him at any time. Devi sensed him to be more of an energy than a body. But he was still John: cheerful, humorous, loving, and deadly serious about his continuing spiritual transformation, regardless of the cost to his body.

She yawned widely. *Whatever he is, whatever he becomes, I love him. If he wants to go to the falls at sunrise, we'll go to he falls at sunrise.*

She pulled on her jeans, rolled them up, threw on a long sleeved flannel shirt, leaving it untucked, brushed her hair, and put it in a ponytail. She slipped on her flip-flops and went out.

The sun was rising through the woods as they walked arm in arm along the dirt path leading from the shack to the falls. It was a quarter-mile walk. The summer woods were alive with green and odors stimulated by the overnight dew. Birds were singing their morning greetings. They came upon a doe with her fawn grazing next to the trail. The two deer stopped their munching to feel the calmness of John and Devi walking by.

"So what are you going to show me?" she finally said.

"Oh, you'll see."

"A surprise?"

"Oh, maybe." He smiled mischievously.

They could hear the falls, the sound of constant cascading water coming down the rock ledges into Gem Pond. As they made the last turn in the path, the pond and the falls came into view. The sun came into the clearing, giving new life, making a soft rainbow in the mist that drifted across the pond from the falls at the other end.

"It's always so beautiful here," she said. "Thanks for getting me up."

"Over here," John pointed to the bench-like rock at the edge of the pond. They went and sat down, like they had so many times before. He put his arm around her and she snuggled her flannel up to his in the cool morning air.

After a few minutes of listening to the oration of the falls a hundred feet across the pond, John kicked off his flip-flops. He got up and walked to the edge of the water. He dipped his toe in.

"Brrr, it's cold," he said.

"What, are we going in?" she said.

"Too cold. Well maybe just a little."

He took a step forward into the pond and was standing with the soles of his feet barely in where it was six inches deep. He turned around and extended his hand to her, inviting her to join him.

"What?" she said with amazement.

"Don't worry, it's safe. C'mon." He took a few steps in place to assure her of his footing on the water. Small ripples went out around his feet.

She slowly got up. She put her hands on her hips. "You expect me to do that?"

"Just hold my hand," he said. "It'll be fine. Here, watch." He took a few steps back, then skipped in a circle that took him ten feet away from the bank and back to her. His feet splashed like he was in a quarter inch of water. "See? No problem."

"John Wilder, what will you think of next?"

He smiled. "God only knows."

She left her flip-flops by the rock bench and went to the edge of the bank, reached out, and took his outstretched hand. She took a cautious step forward into the water, fully expecting to sink six inches under him. She didn't. She was standing in front of him on the water. It felt cool and wet on the bottoms of her bare feet. She caught her breath as a strange new energy lurched up her spine. A luscious spaciousness filled her, and the surroundings took on a surrealistic hue.

"See? It works," he said. "Now, every now and then just easily pick up the faint vibration of *...inner space – lightness of air*. Very faint, deep in *i am,* and let it go." John was easing them both away from shore over deeper water.

With her spare hand she clutched his shirt, feeling a little unsteady. "Okay, I'll try."

"No trying allowed," he said. It's just like meditation, except you are picking up an intention deep inside and giving it time to come back out again with the power of God, *i am*."

"Okay, no trying then." She picked up the faint fuzzy vibration of *...inner space – lightness of air*, and let it go. She experienced the pleasurable lurching inside again and felt herself getting steadier on the water as she expanded inside. "Oh yeah, I see … Can I go back to shore now?" She turned toward the bank twenty feet away, wondering how'd she'd ever walk that far on the water.

"Let's take a spin around the pond first," he said. He pushed her away keeping one hand in his. She slid from him on the water like she was on ice. Then he started to walk with her in tow, and they went around the pond. She found she could get traction like he did if she had the intention in the vibration of *...inner space – lightness of air*. The second time around the pond she was walking shakily with him. The third time, she was getting the hang of it.

Then he took her to the center of the pond and stopped, backing away from her. He let his fingers slide to the ends of hers on the verge of letting her go. She went down in the water to her ankles, and was sinking.

"Not ready yet," she said, feeling the cold water starting to creep up her bare shins. *...inner space – lightness of air ... inner space – lightness of air ... inner space – lightness of air...*

"Nuh-uh, no trying. You will be ready," he said. "A few more doors to open inside, and then, voila..."

He took her hand again and she came back up. He bowed before her and said, "May I have the honor of this dance, Miss?"

She curtsied daintily in her rolled up jeans, holding out the loose tail of her flannel shirt with her free hand like a fine evening gown. "But, of course, fine sir."

And they danced ... around and around Gem Pond to the tune of the cascading waterfall. It sounded like a waltz to them as they stepped wetly in their love dance. John rolled her into and out of his arms again and again as they glided across the water, making little splashes and wakes on the surface as they went. When they came to the middle of the pond again, he had both her hands in his. She went up over his head, hanging horizontally in the air with her feet away from him as they went around. Then he rose up and was horizontal in the air too, his feet away from her as they went around slowly like a giant ceiling fan with two blades. They resumed their vertical position and they were close to each other, several feet above the water, turning slowly in the air. The dance got slower, and slower. They were embracing, rising up above the pond, above the falls, nearly to the top of the trees, turning gently in each other's arms. One of her legs wrapped around his, and they were as one. They came quietly spiraling back down and touched gently onto the water. John walked Devi gracefully back to the shore, and they kissed on the bank.

Then John gathered himself and stepped back. "Oh, I almost forgot."

Devi pulled herself out of her levitated love-trance. "Forgot?"

"Yeah, there's something I want to show you, remember?"

She gestured to the pond. "You mean that wasn't it?"

"Nah. This is going to be much better," he said. "Something I've been saving for you here for a while until I could get up the nerve..."

He went around the rock bench and reached down. He came up with something in his hand.

Devi was perplexed. "What's that?"

He opened his hand. It was a white stone the size of an egg. It had a few thin gold lines across its curved white surface.

She cocked her head. "What is it?"

He handed it to her shyly. "It's for you."

She looked at what John had put in her hand. "Um, it's ... beautiful. It's a rock, isn't it? A special rock?"

John scuffed around, looking a bit embarrassed. "Oh yes. Well, it's not quite ready yet. Here..." He took it back and cupped it between both his hands. "Wait a minute now. It's feldspar with gold running through it. There's something pretty inside. I'm getting it out for you."

A fine white dust came out of his closed hands. He kept moving the rock around in his hands out of her sight as she watched curiously.

"Almost done," he said. "There."

He held his hand out to her and opened it. Nestled in his palm was a smooth gold ring with a small sparkling light blue sapphire mounted on it.

John got down on his knees in front of her, looking up into her eyes.

"Dearest Devi, divine goddess of my life, I love you, will you marry me?"

Her eyes welled up with tears. Her voice broke, "Oh John ... Oh John ... Yes, I'll marry you. Of course, I'll marry you..." And she was on her knees in his arms sobbing into his soft shirt.

After a moment he said, "Try it on."

She gave him her left hand, and he slid the ring on her wedding finger. It fit perfectly. It sparkled brightly when one of her tears fell on it. She looked into his loving eyes. "I'll wear it till the day I die."

She reached under her hair behind her neck and undid the silver chain that held the crystal cross she always wore. She lifted it out of her shirt.

"Please accept this from me," she said. "It is all I am, and I want you to have it."

"I will wear it always," he said.

She reached around his neck and put it on him. It reflected bright beams of the morning sun before she let it go into his shirt.

Then John spoke:

"In the name of God, Lord Jesus, *i am*, we are declared husband and wife this day, in sacred union for all our life."

He touched her breastbone with the tips of the fingers of his right hand and said, "*i am*."

She touched his breastbone with the tips of the fingers of her right hand and said, "*i am*."

On their knees on the mossy bank of Gem Pond, they kissed, and John and Devi were married.

They walked quietly back to the shack. The doe and her fawn were still near the path eating leaves from the young saplings. She licked her offspring tenderly on the neck. Devi looked up at John as they walked, pulling him close against her hip with her arm around his waist, putting her other hand on his abdomen. He had his arm around her shoulders. He looked into her eyes and nodded. They stopped and kissed. The time had finally come.

By the time they were in the bedroom of the shack Devi was nervous. She didn't think she would be when this moment arrived. They were both twenty-five, and she had been anticipating this for seven years. Now, here they were. They were standing face to face.

"You know, I've never seen you naked," he said. "Except in my dreams, of course. A thousand times in my dreams."

She was flushed. "I've seen you when I was caring for you when you were sick, but that doesn't count, does it?" She could tell he was nervous too.

"I'm glad you were there," he said. "You saved me."

"You saved me the very first day we met." She came closer.

He unbuttoned her soft flannel shirt as she unbuttoned his. When their shirts fell to the floor, they came together, and she felt his body touching her sensitive breasts for the first time. She moved slowly back and forth, delighting in the feel of him against her.

He pulled her ponytail loose, and lost himself in her shining black hair. "You smell so good."

They separated slightly. His hands found her breasts and cupped them lovingly. He kissed her on the lips and their tongues did a slow love dance. Then he was kissing her neck. Their breathing became audible. Her head swooned back as he went gradually lower with his adoring kisses.

His hands slid down, and he undid her jeans, pulling them down along with her panties. She stepped out of them. He went down on his knees. He kissed her belly. His hands were on her slim waist.

"In here?" he said, kissing her over her womb.

"Ya huh," she said. "But the way in is lower."

She sat on the bed and leaned back on her elbows. She opened her legs to him. He was on his knees in front of her. He kissed her soft dark hair. Then he ran his hands lightly down from her waist on top of her thighs to her knees and slowly up the insides. He kissed her and began to caress her delicately with his fingers and untethered tongue.

"Ohhhhh ... ohh, Johhhn." Her hands were in his hair as she drank in his loving.

After a few minutes, she became anxious. "John, John, please come inside me. Oh, please, come inside..."

She sat up on the edge of the bed and he came up and kissed her deeply, stroking her moist softness with his hands as he did. She could taste her own love essence in his mouth.

He got up and she undid his jeans. When she pulled his briefs down, his manhood was fully revealed to her. She kissed and caressed him with tenderness. Then she looked up into his eyes as she lay back on the bed, calling him to her with her arms and her soul. He came to her, putting his head on her shoulder. They lay quietly. His leg was draped between hers. After a few minutes he began caressing her breasts softly. He kissed them slowly all over, sending thrills through her. Then his lips found hers again and they drank deeply from each other.

Oh, how long I have waited for my love to come to me. Now he is here.

"My precious husband," she moaned.

He came over her on his haunches with his knees under her spreading legs. She lifted them around his waist so he could come close. He supported himself on his elbows. As they gazed lovingly into each other's eyes, she reached down with her hands and guided him toward her womb. He came into her slightly, lingering in her entrance. They both shivered. His head went down on her shoulder.

"More," she whispered in his ear. "More."

"Oh Devi, I love you." He slid slowly into her, and they caught their breath. His radiant light merged with hers deep inside.

She began to move her hips rhythmically under him at the same time he started moving in and out. Her mound massaged him in the place above his pubic bone that hastened him. Her muscles were firmly pulling on him each time he withdrew, making him larger inside her. She enveloped his expanding love fully each time he came in. She was lost in the sacred love dance that filled her again and again. In a few minutes, she sensed he was on the edge of ejaculating his sacred seed into her. She was in a frenzy for it, gyrating her hips, panting and moaning. Then, suddenly, he withdrew from her completely, holding himself just outside her swollen flower. *What?*

"Is something wrong?" she gushed, fearing he was leaving.

"No, I want to last for you."

"But I want you to fill me now," she said desperately. She tried to take him in again, but he held just outside her.

"You will have everything, my darling. But sex for us will be different. It has to be."

"Ohhhh, please," she begged. Everything inside her was crying for his seed. *I can't wait anymore. I can't wait. I can't –*

Suddenly, when she was not expecting it, he plunged deep into her and slowly came all the way out again.

"Ahhhhh!" she cried out. *Oh God, what's he doing?*

Then he was teasing her opening, barely penetrating her and withdrawing.

"Ohhhhh, Johhhn ... Johhhn..."

Then he surprised her again, suddenly going all the way to her womb deep inside.

"Ahhhhh! Oh God!..."

John slid out slowly to a pause again, waiting as Devi opened wider and wider in her own anticipation. He continued unpredictably – thrusting once, twice or three times, and stopping. She didn't know what was next. He ravished her this way until she couldn't stand it any more. A huge ball of energy welled up in her loins. It got bigger and bigger. It was about to burst. He must have known, because he came out of her and stopped completely for a while.

"John! Pleeease!"

In his stillness, her ball of energy slowly subsided. He kissed her softly. Then, he started again, bringing her back to the edge of oblivion. And then he stopped again. The longer he went the more staying power he seemed to have. She was helpless. Everything was opening inside her. She was falling, falling, losing all sense of their bodies. She was beyond moaning. They were one ecstatic being. It went on and on like that. She did not know how long. Time had no meaning.

Finally, he went into a pattern of steady deep stroking and did not stop. Again and again he was deep inside her. The all-consuming ball of ecstatic energy came up in her, getting bigger and bigger. She was about to explode. He didn't stop this time. Something caused her to look into his loving eyes as he was coming into her again and again. "Oh, oh, oh, Johhhn, mmmmm, uh, uh uh, God, oh God..."

As she fell over the edge into orgasm, her eyes melted into his. She felt him let go completely. Then he was crying out with her. Together they were in spasms as he went over an edge she knew he hadn't crossed in many years.

"Ahhh! Ahhh! Ahhhhh!" they cried out as they climaxed together.

Tears burst from Devi's eyes as she felt his warm radiant seed rushing into her.

"Oh, John! Fill me, John! Fill me!"

They were lost in each other as his life essence flowed into her. She instinctively pulled her belly up, drawing every bit of his precious living seed toward her glowing golden womb.

Finally, he melted slowly onto her soft body. There was nothing but their mingled sweat between them, and they lay together in love.

Some time later, she began to caress his hair, his back, his buttocks, everywhere she could reach with him lying on her. She wanted to touch him, and touch him more. He was still inside her, and she caressed him there too. The crystal cross draping from his neck rested in the pool of their perspiration glowing in the hollow of her throat. She felt complete.

She wanted him to stay in her all day, but she knew he needed to rest. It pained her to feel him slip out. He kissed her softly as he went. They fell asleep in each other's arms and woke up a few hours later. They made love again. And then again later. Today was their day of reckless abandon – their honeymoon.

She knew it could not always be like this. His seed was too precious. His spiritual journey depended on it. So many others would depend on his life force as it conveyed the pure white light of God, *i am*. How many would he ultimately touch with his love? Spilling the sacred elixir endlessly in her could not be, especially with its purpose fulfilled when she became pregnant. Would they continue to make love? She finally knew completeness, and it was John's life essence inside her.

She hoped they could manage lovemaking while preserving the precious life energy. She wanted their lovemaking to stimulate ecstatic ascension in both of them. She thought of the blocking techniques he shared with her years before, and Mama's lessons. It was coming together at last. *I am the nurturer and guardian of my husband's precious seed. I am the goddess who raises the God-man's love. I am the mother who brings divine life into the world in all ways.*

It took a few days for John to recover his vitality. He knew his union with Devi would have an energy cost. It didn't matter. He wanted to fill her in every way. His love for her was unconditional, at the center of his God quest. Her fulfillment was the same as his own. The time had come for them, and they would go forward together as sacred wife and husband. Their love and joining would bring forth new life.

Chapter 22 – Dancing in Silence

In the months that followed, the world around John was changing its shape and its consistency, at least as he saw it.

Sometimes when he sat in practices he became absorbed for hours in the crown of light on top of his head. As he deliberately lifted it high into a bowl shape, it no longer sucked him inside-out in raging fire like it had in years past. Spinal breathing had given him the ability to regulate the opening of his crown without unleashing the prior extremes. And now there was practically no fiery resistance to the great energies that surged through him to his raised crown. He was like an infinite surging sea of ecstatic bliss inside. As the cosmic experience overflowed from within, the world around him was becoming part of this inner reality.

John sensed something more in his crown, something far greater. He was certain that his crown contained the ultimate secret of his mission. *What is it? And when will it be revealed?*

He took long walks in the woods alone, and on the rickety table in the front room of the shack he wrote regularly in his three-ring notebook about his ongoing discoveries and changing perceptions. What had been trees, animals, earth, water, and sky, now became emerging vistas of moving energy, moving light. What had been happening in his body for so many years seemed now to be happening all around him. Even gravity did not hold him. Sometimes it became confusing, and he would laugh. *Which way is up? Which way is down? Is this the edge of the tree, or is it here? Is this the ground, or is this it up around my ankles?* Physical reality would become fuzzy like that sometimes. He was good-natured about it and adjusted quickly to his emerging new reality.

It all had to do with the powerful energy transformations he had been going through since coming to Blue Ridge Hollow, and these were a direct result of the practices he had done, and continued doing. It all led to this inevitable state. *Sooner or later everyone will fulfill this same destiny. We are all built for it. There's no doubt about it.*

The people of Blue Ridge Hollow came to John for guidance on meditation, for healings and for advice. Often his touch was enough. The flow of *i am* he was able to hasten in them filled them with answers, healing, or whatever they needed. They were a beautiful people, and he loved them. They looked so different to him now, like angels. His view kept expanding, and so did theirs.

"Hello, John," Jo Smith said, coming up the path to the shack with three friends. Jo was Luke's cousin. She'd lived in Blue Ridge Hollow all her life. She was short and slim, the physical antithesis of Luke. But she had the warm kindly Smith heart.

John was lying on the porch, looking up at the sparkling texture of the mountain sky. It was full of tiny beings, and he could watch them for hours. Sometimes they came and sat on him, fanning him with their humming bird-like wings.

He sat up, squinting through the energy fields to see who was coming. "Hi, Jo. Who's that you have there?"

"These are my friends from Mitchell Valley, yonder." She was pointing over the mountain across from the shack toward the neighboring black community. "This is Henry, this is Mark, and Grace." They were all about John's age, shy, but with eagerness in their eyes. "Will you touch them like you did me?"

"Sure," John said. "But with one condition, okay?"

"O-O-Oh, shu-shu-shu-shu-sure," Henry said. "I Kn-kn-kn-kn-knew th-th-there w-w-was a ca-ca-ca-catch."

"No catch, Henry," John said, standing up and walking over to him. "Only a truth, that's all."

"W-w-w-what?"

"Well, I wouldn't want to mislead you. This spiritual stuff – I don't have a monopoly on it. It's not about me. It's about you. If you want it bad enough, you will have it. It's in us and all around us. Nobody owns it. I can give you a jump-start, but it's up to you. Someone once gave me a jump-start, and here I am. So the condition is, if you want this, you have to take it and do something with it. No free rides – no such thing. See?"

"W-w-w-well –"

"I see," said Grace. She was a tall slender woman with intense dark eyes. "Yes, I can do that. I want to know God. I can do it. Please touch me."

She came up to John and looked into his eyes with an uncertain boldness. She reminded him of how he was the day he went to the Island Christian Church all those years ago. He was filled with joy to be returning the favor that had come to him through Christi Jensen. With his right hand he tapped her breastbone with the tips of his fingers. She let out a cry as the air rushed out of her, nearly falling over forward. John and the others reached to catch her, but she caught her balance and stood up slowly, breathing in again. She had a look of disoriented bliss on her face.

"Here," John said, "come sit." They all went and sat on the edge of the porch.

Grace rocked there for a few minutes, then turned to John, and smiled. "I'm all right. Thank you." Then she closed her eyes into the waves of *i am* coursing through her.

"Touch me?" Mark said. He was a big fellow with glasses, quite overweight.

He had a sweet aura around him that drew John immediately. He touched him.

Whooosh... Mark's lungs collapsed. When he breathed back in, he began to laugh. He couldn't stop himself. He was shaking all over like jelly.

"It'll be all right," John said, patting Mark on the back. "It starts that way sometimes. We are all different. *i am* is the great purifier, you know. If your funny bone needs purifying, it will make you laugh."

They all laughed with Mark. After a few minutes they settled down.

"Ok-k-k-kay," Henry said nervously. "I'm-m-m r-r-r-ready."

John nodded, and Henry came and sat next to him, looking apprehensive. John reached over and touched Henry's breastbone. Nothing happened.

"I-I-I d-d-d-idn't fe-fe-feel any-any-anything!"

"It's okay Henry." John looked intently into his eyes. He saw fear, and, deeper down, terror. Henry was a short stocky man who carried himself tensely.

"It's okay, Henry," he said. "You are with friends. Do you want this?"

Tears were welling up in Henry's eyes. "Y-y-y-yesss."

John touched him on the chest again. Henry looked into John's eyes and fearfully showed him that something was melting, breaking loose, caving in.

"I-I-I ca-ca-can't —"

"Yes, you can, Henry," John said. "Let it go. Let it all go. Let the peace and bliss of *i am* in."

Henry doubled over as the air rushed out of him. He gasped an in-breath. Then he exploded in great sobs as the darkness gave way to the bright light coming from within him. They all could see it too. Henry fell into John's lap, crying like a baby. John held him and rocked him.

"It's all right, Henry. Everything is going to be all right."

They all sat there for ten minutes with arms wrapped around each other on the edge of the porch of the old shack.

Devi came walking up the path. They raised their heads and saw her.

"Hi, honey," John said. "Want to join us?"

"Definitely," she said. "I never pass up a group hug." She put her canvas bag filled with fruits and vegetables on the porch and knelt behind them, wrapping her arms as far around the five of them as she could. They rocked there in the inner light for a while.

"Thank you, John," Jo said, stirring for the first time. "It means so much to all of us."

The hug began to loosen up and come apart. Everyone sat on the edge of the porch looking around.

"Remember, this is a jump start," John said. "The rest is up to you. Here is what you can do every day..."

John told them how to do the *i am* meditation, and encouraged them to stay in touch with others who were advancing in their practices.

"There is so much you can do to hasten the work of *i am* inside you. It's up to you."

"I promise I w-will," Henry said. "I p-promise I will." He had a look of amazement hearing his own steadying voice.

"I promise I will!" Henry got up and started dancing around in front of the shack, singing the phrase over and over. They all got up and danced with him, holding hands, laughing, and singing together:

"I promise I will!"

"I promise I will!"

"I promise I will! ..."

Devi and John got a little carried away and floated off the ground a bit, dancing round and round in each other's arms. It didn't seem to matter. The air was full with miracles that day in Blue Ridge Hollow. So many of the days were like that.

Devi stayed close and cared for John as he adapted to his changing relationship with the world. Their lovemaking was measured; both stimulating and preserving the essences of *i am* flowing through them. When the fertile golden glow in her womb was strong they'd fill her with his seed, preparing the way. They knew their child would come when the time was right.

Devi was progressing rapidly in her experiences. She was in the upper passages of her secret chamber now, kissing her spiritual eye with the tip of her tongue, and filled with radiant white light. She could almost walk on Gem Pond by herself. Almost. Once she lost it out in the middle by herself and came home soaking wet. To him it looked like she was covered with dripping light. He laughed hysterically when she came in the shack looking like that. She pounced on him, mopping him with her wet hair, sharing as much of it with him as she could. They laughed and laughed as they peeled off their soggy clothes and started making love. Their laughter melted into moans as they went into their long ecstatic union.

As his relationship with the energies around him coalesced, John saw a pattern between his desires and the flow of *i am* everywhere. He saw that all things were his own *i am,* his own self. The separation between his sense of self and what was all around him was dissolving. His core desires became even more universal than before. He sought a way to formulate these universal desires in a way that people could benefit in practice, a way that could be applied to accelerate their progress. This was how the "nine prayers of *i am*" came to be.

"Hey, brother Luke," John said. "Good to see you back up here."

They were on the small front porch of the shack.

"Oh, you know," Luke said. "Since Joy came down to Jacksonville to work, I haven't had much chance to come up here." He put his arm around Joy sitting next to him. "How's the married life treating you two? We're thinking the same way, right, Joy?"

"More than thinkin'," Joy said with a big smile. "Time for Luke to put up or shut up."

"You gonna start singin' again?" Luke said. "She sings whenever we're –"

"Only if you want me to, honey," she said.

"How are the folks on Coquina Island?" John said.

"Oh, it's pretty dry, brother John," Luke said. "Thursday meditations are down to nothin'. We miss you both something awful."

"One day we'll be back," Devi said. "This is a time for growing up here. You've done so much for us, Luke." She put her hand on his massive arm.

"Yeah, we've been through a lot together," Luke said. "A lot."

"There's more," John said. "You interested in the latest?"

"Well, why do you think we came all the way up here?" Luke said. "To sit around and twiddle our thumbs? Spill the beans, brother John."

So John told them all that was happening. Luke and Joy's eyes went wide with each new puncturing of earth-reality, as John told them of how he was seeing the world now.

"You mean we are all just the same energy?" Joy said.

"You knew it already, didn't you?" John gazed into their eyes.

"I guess we all kind of know it." Luke looked away for a second. "But Lord Almighty, the kind of knowing and seeing you do sounds like another world."

"It is this world all right. We just haven't noticed till now." John paused for what seemed like a whole minute... "Well, here's some seeing for you." He floated up off the porch and hovered six inches above it. "Devi?"

She closed her eyes came up a few inches off the porch, not as smoothly or as high as John.

"What?" Luke and Joy were getting up nervously.

"Now don't go all spooky on us," Devi opened her eyes and came back down on the porch with a *thump*. "We can all do this. It's just a matter of cleaning out inside, and knowing where the controls are."

Joy's eyes were wide. "Why do these things? People won't understand."

"I suppose you're right," John came down softly to rest on the wood plank porch. "But where would we be if people didn't get on those small ships and sail across the great ocean, or get in those rockets and blast off into space? We human beings just have to find out what's out there, and in here." He had his hand on his chest. "We have this need to find out what's true."

"That's all it is," Devi said. "Just the truth. Truth is always surrounded by superstition until it becomes known. After it's known, it's just normal, right?"

"But you gotta admit, this isn't quite normal," Luke's voice was extra deep.

"Not today," John said. "But years from now, it will be. This is just the beginning."

There was a long pause... the four dear friends savored the inner silence they shared.

Finally, Joy smiled. "Well, I guess you better sign us up. We don't want to be the last ones floating in the air.

"Yeah," Luke said. "Does this mean we can leave the car here and fly home?"

"You don't want to fly the way I do." Devi grinned. "It takes some learning ... or some serious inner opening is a better way to put it." Then she sang the all-important word: "Prrractices!..."

"Sorry," Devi said. "My voice is garbage next to yours, Joy."

"Not bad, honey," Joy said.

Then they both sang it: "Prrractices!..."

John got up and brushed the toe of his sneaker through the dirt in front of the porch. "Listen, there is something you can do that will help *i am* move out through you to wake up everything and everyone around you. The floating is only part of it. A small part, really. There is more to it. It is something you can add on right after your meditation. I call it the nine prayers of *i am*."

"Nine prayers?" Luke said.

"Yeah," John said. "You use each one the same way in a series after meditation. The first one is *...love*. You just pick it up real faintly like you do *i am*, and you leave it alone for about fifteen seconds. Then you pick it up again the same way, only fainter. If you do that a few times with each prayer, you will be amazed at what happens."

"What are the other prayers?" Joy said, leaning forward on the edge of the porch.

John kicked the dust again with the outside toe of his sneaker. "The nine are: love, radiance, unity, health, strength, abundance, wisdom, inner sensuality, and, last but not least, inner space – lightness of air. That last one makes the body very light. Now let's repeat them out loud a few times together."

They did.

John paced slowly in front of the porch. "Not so hard to remember, are they? Each one is used in the same way I told you. Pick it up lightly and let it go in silence for fifteen seconds. Do each one twice. That's a half minute of each prayer with the fifteen second incubations in silence in-between, about five minutes in all. You can do any of them more if there is a need, up to five minutes extra."

"I do the lightness prayer for the extra time," Devi smiled.

John continued. "So that is up to ten minutes in all as a starting practice. If you do them all together after meditation like that, there is a huge effect."

"Like what?" Joy asked.

"Well, let's sit and meditate together for ten minutes and then do the nine prayers, and you can see what it is like, okay?"

"Sounds good. Let's do it," Luke said.

They all leaned up against the shack and meditated. Ten minutes later, they went into the prayers, repeating each prayer twice faintly and fuzzily inside, with about fifteen seconds of incubating silence between repetitions:

...love...
...radiance...
...unity...
...health...
...strength...
...abundance...
...wisdom...
...inner sensuality...
...inner space – lightness of air...

When they got done, everyone was quiet. Finally Luke spoke:
"I feel like I'm glued inside everything."

"Me too," Joy said. She waved her hand slowly in front of her face. "It's like when I'm moving here I'm moving everywhere."

"You got it," John said. "That's what the nine prayers do. They bring out *i am* everywhere, and that is none other than you. You are bringing it out into your awareness. When you first start to see yourself everywhere, it feels like everything is glued together. It is like that. All the senses get involved."

"Wait'll you try singing again," Devi said, smiling. "The things we love become even lovelier." She took John's hand and brought it up to her lips, kissing it softly. "All loving becomes so soft, so sweet, a part of our intimate self."

"Don't expect any miracles, though," John said. "It's not about that. It's about hastening your openings all around. It is most effective when done as part of the routine of meditation, root seat, secret chamber, spinal breathing, breath retention, and the rest. It's best to do all the prayers right after *i am* meditation. The prayers work together as a whole to create the broad result."

"What about sensuality?" Joy said. "Isn't that going the other way from God?"

"It might seem so," John said. "But we have it going on in *i am*. It is *inner sensuality*, so it is not about physical sensuality, or lusting. It is about the inner spectrum of sensuality, developing perception of our inner reality with the subtle senses in spirit. It is opening the inner beauty behind the physical."

"So, when we use the words, *inner sensuality*, that intent should be there," Joy said, "rather than physical sensuality?"

"Yes," John said. "Intent will paint the prayers. In fact, the prayers strengthen all intentions, so be careful what you wish for. Your desires will become much more powerful."

"Can this be used for evil?" Luke said.

"No," John said. "Because it can only spring from *i am*. There is no evil in *i am*, only the pure light of God. Someone might try and use them for bad things, but they won't get far. These are not that kind of formula; darkness cannot exist in the light. These are God prayers. Remember outer I AM has little power. Inner *i am* has all the power. Saying the prayers from the level of outer I AM is weak, ego-based. Not much can come of it. Saying them in the depths of inner *i am* brings all the power of God out."

"Jesus," Luke said, "what a discovery."

"It is what we are, brother Luke," John said. "We are the children of God, all of us. When we are fully soaked in *i am,* then our outer words become the words of *i am* too.

Luke ran his hand over the top of his head. "Brother John, you have done it again."

"You're going to do it too, dear friend. Pass all you've heard here on to the folks on Coquina Island. Tell them to keep practicing. Tell them we'll be back. Coquina Island will rise again."

A week later, John and Devi were sitting at the rickety table in the shack having dinner. They were eating their salads as the soup she had just taken off the wood stove cooled. She was eyeing him as he munched his salad, which to him looked like sacred luminous life. He felt her watching him intently.

"It's pretty primitive isn't it?" he said.

"What's primitive?"

"Me assimilating this lettuce and tomato. I'd much rather just draw energy straight from the sunlight and the air. I'm working on it."

"Oh well," she said, drumming her fingers on the table and looking up into the dark rafters. "Everything's got a purpose, you know."

"Yeah?" he said, feeling her curious vibrations. "And?..."

She got up and came and sat on his lap.

"This is much better than eating." He wrapped his arms around her and snuggled with her. He looked down into her. He was gently feeling the currents of *i am* inside her womb.

"Ooh, you know how I love it when you do that," she said, burying her face in his neck. "What do you feel there, darling?"

Deep in the life-giving tissues of her golden pear John saw a tiny bright flame of energy. Her life currents were congealing around the light, whirling in the creation of something new in his beloved Devi. "My God, you're pregnant."

"Yes! Yes! Yes!" she cried, hugging him around the neck and kicking her bare feet in the air as they floated off the chair into the middle of the room.

"Oh, that's incredible," he said. "Fantastic! That's a real miracle."

He pulled up her shirt and slid his hand down her smooth brown belly, coming to rest over the sacred new life in her.

She looked into his eyes as only an expectant mother could. "Our baby, my love. Two weeks, with eight and a half months to go."

He kissed her tenderly on the lips. They embraced for a long time, floating in the middle of the front room of the rickety old shack, turning slowly in the air.

Chapter 23 – Love Waves

The runway was short at Key West Airport. Harry Wilder pulled back on the control yoke of the corporate jet and he and Stella went up with a roar, clearing the barbed wire fence at the end of the runway by a wide margin.

"I love Key West," Harry said. "We'll have to come back soon."

"Can we drive next time?" Stella said nervously. "You know how I hate to fly."

"It's safer than driving, dear. You know that, especially with the jet, we can go right over most of the weather."

"I still prefer to drive."

Later, when they reached cruising altitude, Harry put on the auto-pilot. "Now we can go in back for an hour and take a nap. Next stop Jacksonville. Let's go, dear." He pretended to get up to go in the back.

"Harry!"

He sat back down. "Only kidding."

They rode a while looking out the window at the bright blue sky, and the Florida coastline as it passed beneath them.

"What do you think John's up to these days?" he said. "It's been months since he's called."

"I've been so worried about him," she said. "No address, no number. All we get are these once-in-a-blue-moon calls. And he doesn't sound normal. Distant, you know."

"I know where he's at," he said. "The number he calls from is a church up in the North Carolina mountains. A black church. But I think we ought to leave him be. He was right to get out of Jacksonville."

"After that ... that mayhem at the funeral two years ago?"

"That's right," Harry said. "It was bizarre. It had to stop. He's probably better off out in the woods somewhere. You know Devi is with him. She's quite a gal. He'll be all right."

Stella looked over at Harry. "I just wish we could see –"

Suddenly there was a loud *Bang* and *Whoosh* under where they sat.

"What was that?" she said. "My ears..."

"I don't know –"

An alarm was beeping. Harry looked at the control panel at red flashing lights. His vision was blurring.

"Cabin pressure –"

The oxygen masks were there next to them. But it was too late. They were both unconscious at thirty-five thousand feet. The cabin temperature gauge was dropping fast – forty degrees ... twenty ... zero ... minus ten ...

John was meditating on the bed in the shack, in blissful silence. He heard a loud *Bang* in the depths of *i am* that gave him a start. Inside himself he went to the place where it came from. He saw two familiar beings there on the verge of ascending into the bright white light above them.

I must go to them ... *i am* ...

Harry felt something tapping on his chest, and then the mask going on his face.

"*Bring the plane down*," a voice said inside him. It was John's voice.

It was freezing cold. Harry turned off the auto-pilot and pushed the control yoke forward. The plane went down. He knew what had happened. They'd suddenly lost cabin pressure and they had to get down to ten thousand feet fast. As they went screaming downward in a controlled descent, he looked over and saw John with Stella, reviving her. She had on the oxygen mask and was slowly coming around.

"John, what are you doing here?" Harry said.

John turned to his father. "*You needed me. It's all right now...*"

"But, how –"

Harry watched as the figure of John faded away, and he was left staring at Stella, groggily opening her eyes.

"Oh, Harry. Thank God you got our masks on," she said weakly. "What happened? It's so cold –"

"It wasn't me," he said. "Hang on, we're going down to where there's air and it's not so cold. We lost cabin pressure."

"It wasn't you?" she said. "I don't understand."

Harry was silent. When he completed piloting the plane down to a safe altitude, he turned to Stella. "It was John, it was John. John saved us." The tears were running down his cheeks.

"John? But how?" she said.

"I don't know how. But he was here. He revived us. He told me to bring the plane down. He's the one who put that mask on you."

"My God," she gasped. "Oh my God." And she began to cry.

They didn't say much in the hour it took to get to Jacksonville. Harry reported the problem with the jet on the radio and a crew was waiting for them when they touched down. Everyone assumed that Harry and Stella were lucky, getting to the oxygen in time after the sudden loss of cabin pressure at thirty-five thousand feet. Harry didn't tell them what really happened. No one would understand.

That day, Harry and Stella became believers in John's God quest, and ached all the more for his return.

Devi was deep in meditation. The blissful vibrations of *i am* were coursing naturally inside her. Each time she picked up faintest trace of *iiii* ... the energy rose through her until it resonated in the bright white star way out and above the center of her brow. Her eyes were high up, and she reflexively coaxed the ecstatic energy with a slight furrow between her eyebrows, pulling on her medulla. Her whole body hummed inside with pleasure.

iiii melted into *ammmm* ... quivering in deep silence down through the stem of her brain and continuing down her spine to her root. Bliss radiated out in all directions as the two subtle sounds merged into one in her again and again. *iiii ... ammmm, iiii ... ammmm, iiii ... ammmm* ... The long, sleek '*i*' with its seed-star dot; it was the loving male-God in her, and also her spinal nerve, reaching beyond her eyebrows to the bright inner star. The all-absorbing '*am*' with its openness, delicious curves and unending ecstatic vibration; it was the loving female-God in her, and also her own deep ecstasy.

She knew that God, *i am*, is the essence of both male and female, and to let go and meditate deeply in *i am* is divine lovemaking within the human form. What divine child would be conceived in this sacred union that filled her with silent moving bliss? The offspring of God, *i am*, in the human form: the Christ child. The human form was created for this sacred purpose. This is the greatest secret of *i am* manifesting in the human form, the greatest of the many secrets. These subtle thoughts played in her as she dove again and again into her inner silence.

While Devi meditated, her tongue slowly caressed her altar of bliss in her secret chamber. With each stroke, her pelvic muscles responded reflexively, coaxing rapture within her. She saw the bright white flame expanding in her radiant womb as their baby took form. The forming of each new cell profoundly fulfilled her. *Ahhh*...

Then she leaned forward and went up, sliding up on John's firmness part way. Her arms were resting on his shoulders, her fingers nestled in the hair on the back of his head. She floated slightly above his lap, her legs around him as he meditated in root seat under her. His hands gently held her waist. She felt a luminous thrill as her breasts brushed lightly through the hair on his chest, touching the coolness of the crystal cross he always wore. And then she was thrilled again as her lips grazed his. She hovered there a minute, and then sank down slowly on him again. As his fullness went up into her, they both moaned quietly in their deep lovemaking meditation. They had been like this for an hour, two divine beings joined as one, lost in the undulating bliss of *i am*, worshipping the new life they were creating together.

After they were married, John and Devi had quickly mastered the art of long preorgasmic sexual unions, and took full advantage of the spiritual benefits. They were hardly strangers to intelligent regenerative relations. They had been doing clothed versions for years before they were married. The vision of the God quest had served them well. Now they were producing divine offspring for both the world and the cosmos.

When they finished meditating they remained sitting in union, gazing into each other's eyes. They were in a cocoon of silent sensual light, and did not want to leave it. It was beyond physical touch, beyond their bodies that were joined there.

"I never want to leave this place," Devi said. "I never want to leave this bed, or your lap."

"I don't want you to," John said.

Her hips floated in a slow circle on him, in the dance that never wanted to end.

"But we are called," he said with a deep sigh.

"I know."

"We will leave here soon ... for Coquina Island."

"Yes," she said with a soft moan in his neck.

"There is much to be done, the transmission of *i am* expands."

"It begins here on this bed," she said, "and goes out to all the world."

"It's true," he said. "When *i am* makes love, all the world is changed."

"Then let us stay like this a while longer," she said.

And so they stayed in union another hour, taking a long slow journey through the prayers of *i am*, picking up the faintest vibration of each one many times, letting each incubate in the deep silence of *i am*. Huge waves of healing went out from them to all the world.

... *love* ... radiance ... unity ...

Chapter 24 – The Return

A few months later, John and Devi quietly moved into Devi's house on Coquina Island. No one but Luke and Joy knew they were back. Devi was at five months, and showing her maternity. It melted John's heart to look at her. The first thing he wanted to do was take her to the Duval County tax collector's office on the island to obtain a marriage license for them.

They were in the old Bronco, riding down A1A.

"Why are we doing this?" Devi said. "Our vows are good enough for me."

"By the law of God we are married," John said. "By the law of society, we are not."

"So what's the difference?"

"It is so you and our child will be provided for, no matter what happens to me. I want you to be a legal Wilder."

"Oh, what could happen to you?" A chill came over her as she realized John might not be telling her something.

She looked at him as he drove.

"Honey, is there something I should know?"

"Only that you will never lack for material support," he said firmly.

"That's not good enough," she said. "It's you I want. To hell with material support."

John's face softened. "Some things are beyond our control. I only want to make sure you and our divine flame there will never go hungry. All families need a plan, just in case."

"Well, it doesn't sit easy with me," she said.

The tax collector's local branch office was in a storefront in a strip mall on A1A. They stood in line inside for fifteen minutes while people paid their electric bills, car registrations and title transfers. When they finally stood at the counter and said, "I do" to the notary public, Devi broke down in tears.

The fat lady behind the counter said, "Now don't you worry, dear. You really look like you need to be married today."

Devi turned to John. "It's the reason we are doing this that upsets me." She threw her arms around him and sobbed. He held her close as people in the line behind them marveled at the soft white light that surrounded them.

"Awww, isn't that sweet," the fat lady said. "Congratulations, Mr. and Mrs. Wilder."

Everyone in the tax collector's office broke out in smiles and applause.

"John! John!" Stella cried as she ran up and embraced him at the front door of the Wilder house. "Two and a half years is too long. I've missed you so. And Devi. Devi, it's so nice to – why, why, you're pregnant." A look of dismay started creeping into her face.

"It's all right, Mom," John said. "We're married. We were married last year."

Stella's dismay turned to a glow. "Oh my. You mean I'm going to be a grandmother? Oh, Devi, I'm so proud of you." She gave Devi a big stiff hug.

"Thank you, Mrs. Wilder," Devi said.

"Call me 'Mom,' dear."

"I'd like that," Devi said.

Harry was standing quietly behind Stella, taking it all in. He wasn't sure how he would react to seeing John again. He had so many mixed feelings.

"Hi, Dad." John came and hugged him.

Harry felt a wave of love going through him, and he held John close. "Son, I'm so glad you came back."

"Me too," John said.

After dinner, Harry and John went and sat in the den while Stella and Devi were visiting in the kitchen.

"So, it looks like we are here to stay for a while," John said.

"Do you have any plans?" Harry said. "Not that you need to. No plans are fine with me. I'm off that kick." He put up his hands as though pleading innocence.

"It's okay, Dad. I'd be asking if I were you. I never told you much because I didn't know. I appreciate you sticking by me while I figured it out."

"So what now?"

"I'm going to teach," John said. "I guess that's what it will be. It won't be traditional."

"Listen if there is any help you need, anything at all, let me know. I mean that."

"Thanks, Dad."

"And I'd like to sign up for your first class. I think your mother would too."

"That's wonderful," John said. He got up and went over to where his father sat. He tapped the fingertips of his right hand on Harry's breastbone and softly said, "*i am.*" The air rushed out of Harry. He breathed in deeply and felt a pleasurable current rising up through the center of him.

"What was that?"

"That was the first class," John said, grinning. "The second class is even better."

"Um, okay, I'm game," Harry said. He was feeling a little disoriented, and giddy.

"Shall we go help the wives?"

"Sure," Harry said, getting up. "But before we go, can I ask you a personal question?"

"Anything."

"Umm, do you know anything about jet planes, son?"

John smiled. "Not much, Dad. Only that you shouldn't be flying one at thirty-five thousand feet with the windows open."

"Oh, okay, okay," Harry said. "That's enough for me. Let's go find the girls."

As they went out of the den, John put his arm around his father's shoulders. "It's going to be a wild ride, Dad, so hang on."

"Even wilder than Wilder Corp?"

"Definitely, and much more fun."

"I could use some fun. Your brother has been driving us all crazy."

John and Devi weren't home two days before people started showing up at their house. Luke and Joy were there for meditations almost every night, as were some people from the original Thursday night group. New people were not in short supply either. Within a couple of weeks, the house couldn't hold all the people who were coming, so they moved it out into the back yard overlooking the waterway. It was like a carnival.

A reporter, Herman Welsch, came from the Jacksonville Union Newspaper to interview John. His performance at the First Church of Christ several years before had not been forgotten. Also, his lingering celebrity as *the fastest man alive who wouldn't run* added a mystique to the story.

John and Devi sat with Herman on the back porch of their house looking out over the yard, and marshland and waterway beyond. Herman had his recorder running.

"Mr. Wilder –"

"Call me 'John,' okay?"

"John, where have you been the last few years?" Herman said.

"In retreat up in the North Carolina mountains, meditating, being with the one I love, just living," John said as he held Devi's hand.

"Are you still doing miracles?"

"Miracles?"

"Yes, you healed the former Mayor's daughter, you threw the Governor's bodyguards on the floor without touching them. And before that, running a three and a half minute mile in front of a few thousand people. Things like that."

"Oh, those things. Not if I can avoid it."

"You mean you still can?"

"You are looking at the greatest miracle I've ever seen. It's a joint effort." He smiled and put his hand gently on Devi's plump belly. "Now that's a miracle."

"With all due respect," Herman said, "we can all do that."

"We can all do the other so-called miracles too."

"Really?"

"Absolutely," John said. "We are all spun from the same infinite vibration of God, *i am*. We all have the same potential. The only difference between some other people and us is that we have made an effort to rejoin with the inner source. So we have some access to that. So can you. Want me to show you?"

"Well, I –"

John reached across and tapped Herman on the chest with his fingers. *Whoosh* ... Herman was out of breath.

"There, how does it feel?" John said.

Herman gasped his first deep breath. As he did, he floated off the pillow in the wicker chair an inch and then fell back into it.

"See? It's not hard," John said. "You can do it."

"Mr. Wilder, I –"

"Call me 'John.'"

"John, I, I don't know what to ask next. I, I feel a little strange." Suddenly, Herman burst out laughing uncontrollably. He nearly fell out of his chair.

Devi giggled.

"Don't worry, Herman," John said. "It'll be all right. It just takes a little getting used to. It happens to all of us."

Herman was regaining his composure, barely. "Well, other than a tap from you, how do people get in touch with this infinite vibration you talk about?"

"Simple," John said. "Practices. Every single day, practices."

"Practices?" Herman said.

"Yep, practices. Redirecting desire to do this great thing we all can do, meditation, breathing exercises, postures, and, pardon me, management of sexual energy."

"Management of sexual energy? Do you mean celibacy?" Herman was getting a long face.

"Oh, no, nothing like that," John said, "though some may be inclined that way at times. Do we look like celibates? Just management of sexual energy, that's all. Like safe sex. Only this is intelligent sex. There's actually more sex, not less, but it's managed to illuminate the body with the spirit."

"Illuminate the body with the spirit?" Herman said.

"Yeah, it's a figure of speech. The silent inner vibration, *i am*, enlivened in meditation, travels on the nerves. It travels best when sexual energy is circulating upward in the body instead of downward and out of the body. The more sexual energy is circulating, the more divine light is circulating. So stimulating a lot of sexual energy upward is good. Hence, more sex, but in a different direction than most people think about, and using some special tricks to do it. Does that make sense?"

"Um, well, I think I see what you mean," Herman said. "Pretty unconventional, isn't it?"

"Well, it works." John said. "It just worked in you."

"You mean –"

"Yeah, that surge of pleasure you felt going up, the one that lifted you off the chair, it was your sexual energy going up, and *i am* with it."

Herman was wiping his mouth with his hand nervously. "I'll have to take your word for it."

"Never do that," John said. "Always verify things for yourself. We are not offering a canned approach here. No dogma. There are principles operating in us, laws of nature, and there are practices that use those principles. Like using a lever to move a big rock, you know. I don't claim to have the last word on any of it. It is a new science. I encourage interested people to verify what we have learned and make it better if they can. So don't take my word for it. Find out the truth for yourself. If any of what I have done helps, great."

"Mr.– Uh, John, a lot of food for thought here. I –"

"Good," John said. "That's what we're here for. Listen, we have to go now. There's a crowd waiting inside. Thanks for coming. Come back and learn to meditate. We are getting some classes organized..."

John and Devi got up and walked silently into the house. Herman thought he saw them both leave the floor as they went across the porch. And there was that pleasant soft light around them. The light followed Herman home that night.

Herman's article brought people to John and Devi by the hundreds, from as far away as Miami and Atlanta. There were constant lines of cars and people in front of their house. The neighbors, while sympathetic to what was happening, needed a break. So did John and Devi. John went to his father, and they decided to buy the grand old Coquina Dame Hotel on the south end of the island. It was a massive relic of times past, with two hundred rooms and a huge ballroom. It had been deserted and decaying for decades. Under pressure from developers, the Coquina Island City Commission had moved to condemn the Dame. Nostalgia was yielding to commercial interests. No one felt they could make a going concern out of the Dame, though most people didn't want to see her torn down, particularly the Hudson family who had owned her for generations. When the property was condemned, they were close to throwing in the towel and selling the valuable ocean front land to Sly Grossman, a hungry high-rise condo builder. When the Wilders made an offer, with a promise to restore the grand old place, the Hudsons jumped at it. Harry would provide the money for purchasing the hotel and the materials for renovation.

John felt pretty sure he could come up with the labor. He would invite everyone who was showing up over to the hotel and let them work on it in exchange for a place to stay and training in the practices. When any heavy construction work needed to be done, Wilder Corp would do it.

John and Devi ventured into the master suite of the Dame for the first time. The ceiling was hanging down in water-stained sheets. The carpets were rolled up in musty masses on the sides of the room. A faded picture of the Coquina Dame in her grand days hung cockeyed on the wall. The kitchen was in shambles. They went in one of the two bedrooms. A canopy bed lay collapsed and decaying on the floor. A sea breeze blew the stringy drapes through a broken oceanfront window.

"So what do you think?" he said.

"Well, you know I always wanted to live in a luxury hotel, sweetie," she said, coming to him through the scattered trash. "It's just so ... romantic." She gave him a passionate kiss over her protruding belly.

Devi went into the bathroom. She came out in a few seconds with a deadpan look. "Now the bathroom I really like. We shouldn't change anything in there."

John walked inside. The walls were horizontal puttied slats of wood where the elegant tile once hung. It lay in shattered heaps all around the bathroom where it had fallen many years before, including generous piles in the toilet and bathtub. The ceiling had come down too, leaving a layer of smashed plaster over everything. There was a big hole in the wall where the sink had been. The room reeked of mildew.

He burst out laughing and staggered out. "Yeah, we shouldn't change a thing in there. It's ... it's perfect."

"Okay," she said. "Now that we're settled on the bathroom, what minor renovations should we do on the rest of the place?"

They went back in the living room and pulled on the salt-covered sliding glass door to the balcony. It opened reluctantly with a *screech*.

They went out into the sun, ocean air and the panorama of the restless sea. The surf hugged the beach. The spine of dunes stretched up and down the coast.

John put his arm around Devi. "It started right down there, you know." He pointed to the large dune in front of the Dame. "That's where I made my commitment."

She turned and looked deep into his eyes. "I'm so glad you did. It's made all the difference."

They stood embracing, gazing out to sea over the fragile rail of the balcony.

The biggest difference was yet to come.

Chapter 25 – A Mother's Giving

John was in the huge dilapidated grand ballroom of the Coquina Dame Hotel with a hundred people. The ceiling was drooping seriously near the back from roof leaks. The chandeliers were clothed in cobwebs with only a few of the hundreds of small flame-shaped bulbs working. The walls were peeling. The once elegant drapes on the tall oceanfront windows were a dreary purple. He was in root seat on an old water-stained sofa at the front of the room. Everyone was haphazardly gathered around in that end of the huge room on worn-out easy chairs, moldy folding chairs, and on floor pillows they'd brought. Some sat on the soggy carpet.

John raised his hands majestically in the air. "Welcome to paradise. It needs a little work."

Everyone laughed.

"And so do we."

More laughter...

"We are divine beings," he said. "All of us, each appearing as a ray of the living God, *i am*, here on earth. We can trace our individual rays back to the source by multiple means and reclaim our birthright, the eternal silent bliss of *i am*. This is who we are. We don't have to wait for salvation. It's already here. We only have to uncover it. Just as the grand old Coquina Dame is here ready to be uncovered, so too are we the word of God, *i am* ready to be uncovered. Through our own desire for God we can act today, and every day, to fulfill our destiny. This is the place we can do it. This is the time we can do it. Can we do it some other place and some other time? Sure. But if that's what you want, you don't belong here in these luxurious surroundings."

Just then, a soggy acoustic tile came sailing down from the high ceiling, landing with a splat on the stained carpet six feet in front of John. He looked at the tile, and then around at the falling down ballroom. "The Dame calls us."

The crowd roared with laughter. John sat silently until they settled down. Then he spoke with an energy that vibrated deep within every heart.

"And so too does *i am* call us."

Boxes were packed and ready at John and Devi's house. They would soon move to the Coquina Dame. Stella and Devi, the next Wilder mother-to-be, sat on the couch. They did not hear the old battered ford pull in next to the house, the sound of the rusty door creaking shut, or the heavy footsteps coming toward the front door.

"So what do you think?" Devi said, holding the catalogue on her lap. "Brown or white?"

"I've always been partial to white," Stella said. "But it's up to you."

"White'll be good. Much easier to see the dirt and keep clean."

"That's the reason I went that way. You can't keep a crib too clean."

Devi shifted herself on the couch toward Stella. "I feel like I'm carrying a watermelon around, eight months and counting." She laid her hands on her belly in a nurturing way.

Stella's eyes were teary as she looked at Devi. "I envy you. It's so special to have a baby, the most sacred thing a woman can do. I'm vicariously living through you." She put her hands on Devi's, leaned over her huge belly, and kissed her tenderly on the cheek. "You're so dear. John is a lucky man. Thank you for inviting me over."

"I'm really counting on you, Mom" Devi said. "You've done all this before and –"

Suddenly, the front door crashed open and a big black boot stomped into the living room. Then a second sickening thud, and he was in. There stood big Jake Lasher in greasy jeans, his huge tattooed arms folded under his menacing hairy chest. Long sweaty hair matted the sides of his face. He smiled, showing a few rotten teeth. His stench reached out and engulfed Devi and Stella where they sat.

"Well, hello bitches. Mind if I join the party?"

He kicked the door again and it slammed shut.

"Everyone here knows the *i am* meditation, right?" John said to the crowd in the ballroom. "Anyone not?"

No one raised a hand.

"Good, let's do one now for about twenty minutes, and then we can see what's on everyone's mind after that."

John closed his eyes with the hundred eager seekers.

Devi watched Jake as he paced back and forth in front of the fireplace. She and Stella were still on the couch.

"You know, I spent two years at Stark Prison after we last was together," he said. "My daddy was on death row on the opposite wing. The mornin' they fried him, the lights went dim. Somethin' went wrong. They told me it took three jolts to waste him."

"I'm sorry, Jake," Devi said, "for all that –"

"Shut up, whore!" With a grotesque grimace Jake pounded his fist against his thigh uncontrollably. "Since that day, I been waitin' fer this one. The day I'd get to come get even."

"Even for what?" Devi said. "For your daddy killing my mother and brother? For my father's suicide? What, Jake? What do you want?"

Jake looked away, as though his mind was already made up. He leaned on the mantel, admiring the glass case with the matchstick model of the George Washington Bridge in it. He ran a dirty finger along the smooth wood frame that John had carefully shaped in love many years before. "This is nice? Who made it?"

"My brother."

"Your brother?" Jake's fist came down hard, smashing the case and the bridge inside. He licked the blood off his hand. "May he rest in peace in half-breed heaven."

Devi and Stella were on their feet, moving for the front door. Jake stepped in front of them and came closer. Devi could smell the alcohol on his breath. His vibrations were thick and dark. *i am* was extremely cloaked in him.

"Jake, we are two helpless women. You don't want to hurt us do you? Look, I'm eight months pregnant."

For a second, Jake's eyes softened. There was a faint glimmer of compassion on his face. Then he turned dark again and reached for the tight front pocket of his jeans. A long thick bulge was there. He gripped the end of it with his fingers and pulled out a long folded knife. With a flip of his wrist it snapped open. Its sharp serrated blade was pointed at Devi. Stella was right behind Devi, her eyes wide with fear. She gasped as the knife came out. "No ... no."

"I love to hurt women," he sneered. "And besides, you ... you look like you need an abortion, Hindu whore. This baby's not to see the light of day." He swiped the blade across at Devi. She stepped back, just as it grazed her maternity dress, opening a slit in the loose fabric between her breasts and belly. She raised her right hand toward him. Stella was right behind her. He took a step toward them, meeting an invisible resistance that emanated from Devi. He paused a second with a puzzled look. And then he strained against it, getting closer.

Devi closed her eyes and the field became a visible white energy between her and Jake. He was startled for a second, and then was leaning into the white energy hard, not moving. Sparks appeared where his mass pressed against the white energy.

"Bitch! You can't stop me!"

He worked his way closer, swinging the knife through the energy field like a machete. It made blood red flashes of light through the white energy with each pass, and sounds like static electricity. Soon he was close enough to reach Devi. She had her eyes closed with her hand extended toward Jake, who towered over her. He grabbed her arm and leaned against the energy she emitted. He pulled the knife way back behind him underhanded one last time, and began to swing his arm forward and up toward her. The long sharp blade was coming straight at Devi's beautiful unborn baby.

"Nooooo!" Stella screamed.

John sat meditating with the large group in the grand ballroom. A hundred minds were inside him. Some were quietly resting in the deep silent bliss of *i am*. Others were being drawn there through their own letting go into *i am*, and the settling influence of the group. Some were struggling, trying to force the quieting of *i am*, having many other thoughts. Some were having angry thoughts:

"What the hell am I doing here?"

"This place sucks, what a disgusting mess."

"Gotta go, gotta pick up the new car..."

"These people are idiots. I'm outta here when this is over..."

All of it was normal. John knew they'd come out of meditation feeling better, having unloaded some inner baggage. He was there to help smooth the process. They were all there for that, to help each other. While it was going on, he was full of everyone else's baggage. That was the price he paid for finding himself everywhere. The world was filled with infinite joys and infinite sorrows, and everything in-between.

Suddenly, John felt something stab into his spirit, a long sharp serrated energy plunged deeply into his stomach. Then it twisted. He screamed in pain and fell forward off the couch onto the floor. Everyone opened their eyes and gasped to see John writhing in agony on the floor in front of the couch, clenching his stomach. A few ran to him. Inside, he went to the pain, seeking its source. Something terrible had happened. He went there.

John appeared next to Devi in the living room. His mother had her arms around Jake's thick neck, clinging to him, as he staggered backward. He pushed her off and she fell, the long bloody knife came out of her belly as she fell to the floor moaning, "No ... don't hurt them. No..."

Jake looked down at her. He was taken aback, wiping his sweaty face with his forearm. He turned to swing the bloody knife at Devi again. Then he saw John.

His dull angry eyes opened wide, part in surprise, part in fear.

"What ... what the hell are you doing here?" he grunted.

John stepped in front of Devi and faced Jake. "*Stand down.*"

The sound echoed in Jake's head like it was coming from the inside. He lashed out at John, slicing across his body with the knife. It passed through John's chest, leaving no mark. Jake looked confused. Then he came straight down with the knife on John, penetrating deep into him from above the collarbone.

John raised his hand, and Jake was flung back on the floor in front of the fireplace, taking the knife with him. John showed no ill effect from the deep stab down into his torso. A white aura moved out from him in Jake's direction.

"*Stand down now, Jake,*" John said inside Jake's head. "*Your hate will destroy you if you don't stop now.*"

Jake got up slowly with the knife dangling in his hand.

He let out a strained hopeless laugh. "Stand down? Jake Lasher, stand down? Never."

He lunged toward John with the knife, slicing it through the air. His hate-saturated energy hit John's white aura. Angry red and orange lightning-like bolts were reflected back into him. Jake lurched and burned in his reflected rage, as though a strong electric current was going through him. He fell back against the mantel, his elbow hitting the remainder of the glass case there. Glass shards tinkled down on the brick hearth. Jake hung on the mantel, the knife swinging in his hand. He looked at John standing quietly in the white light. He could see Devi behind him, her eyes looking at him with dispassion, and then shifting with compassion to Stella lying motionless on the floor. He took a deep breath and went at them again with the knife in front. It hit the white energy and the fire of his hatred flashed back into him again, jolting his body chaotically, and throwing him back against the fireplace hard. He came down in a heap on the shattered glass. The knife clattered loose on the hearth.

Jake's face revealed his final agony, and then he was gone. All that was left was the self-annihilated corpse that had housed a dark, deluded life for twenty-nine years. Where would he go now?

John knelt by his mother lying on the floor, resting his hand on her breastbone. Devi called 911. In a minute she was with John and Stella.

John, in luminescent form, looked into Devi's eyes and shook his head. His voice was in her head. "*She is going. I can't keep her here.*"

Devi began to cry, speaking to him inside. "*She got in front of me. She took the knife into herself to save our baby and me.*"

Stella opened her eyes weakly. "Are you all right, dear?"

"Yes, I'm fine. The baby is fine," Devi said through her tears.

"I see your baby now," Stella said. "She is strong and good, a bright light like you..." Her voice was otherworldly. "John, is that you?"

"*I'm here, Mom. I'm here.*"

"You feel like you are inside me," Stella said.

"*We are in each other, always,*" he said. "*I love you, Mom.*" He was crying radiant tears.

"Oh, I … I have to go. I see someone. It's ... it's Jesus..." Her breath went out slowly and she went up. John and Devi saw her go into the bright light above her head. In a moment she was fully embraced by it and was gone.

Devi hunched over, sobbing, enveloping the precious child she carried, the child Stella had saved by sacrificing her life. John put a comforting hand on Devi. A siren came close. Then John's form faded away.

In the ballroom, the crowd that gathered around John where he lay on the floor sighed with relief as he began to regain consciousness. He slowly sat up and looked into all the concerned faces around him. Then he wrapped his arms around his knees, pulling them to his chest. He began to rock forward and back. He looked off into space high above his forehead. Everyone was close and quiet, sitting on the floor with him.

"My mother has died," he said softly. His head dropped and he began to cry into his knees.

Others began to weep. Some put their hands on him, trying to console him. Soon, everyone was weeping with John. It was a time of broken-hearted intimacy that opened more inner doors in all who were present.

Chapter 26 – The Teacher

The last of the guests had left the Wilder house after Stella's funeral. There were two platters of half eaten food on the coffee table in the living room. Harry was slumped in a chair. John and Kurt were sitting on the sofa. Devi and Nadine were on the love seat on the other side.

"This house sure is empty without her," Harry said. "I don't know if I can stay here."

"Why did this happen?" Kurt said. "What was she doing over there where everyone has gotten murdered?"

"We were looking at cribs," Devi said. "Jake broke in. She saved the baby's life, and my life."

"She shouldn't have been there," Kurt said angrily. "It's a damn slum over there."

"It was our home —"

"Your home, not our home," Kurt said. "She never should have been there."

"Kurt," John said, "this isn't doing anyone any good."

"Yeah, well, it never would have happened if I'd been here. You should have stayed in the mountains."

There was silence.

"Why did she do that?" Kurt said. "She was such a coward, scared of her own shadow."

"She'd have died for either of you boys," Harry said. "She was scared of the world, but not of anything that threatened either of you, or John and Devi's baby. Not anything. She was very brave that way. A mother's instinct. We can be thankful for that, or Devi might not be sitting here today."

Devi started to cry. John went to her. He sat between Devi and Nadine and held Devi. Nadine glared at Kurt.

"Shit," said Kurt. He got up and walked out toward the veranda.

The next morning Kurt was packing up to go back to Washington.

"I think I'll stay here a while," Nadine said. "Your father could use some support."

"What about the President's reception on Friday?" he said.

"Your father needs support."

"So does the business."

"I'm sure you'll do fine without me," she said. "Take Mable."

"What's that supposed to mean?"

"She's your right hand man at the company, isn't she? So take her. She'd love to meet the President."

Kurt sighed. "Maybe I will. But she's not my type, you know. Too old for me."

"I'll call you," she said.

It was six weeks before Nadine went back to Washington.

A few weeks later, the Coquina Dame Hotel was full with several hundred enthusiastic worker-meditators. Each day brought a few more wanting to take up residence and join the restoration project – the hotel's restoration, and their own spiritual restoration.

The day after Stella's funeral, John came back, doing manual labor in the daytime, and sitting at the head of the slowly improving ballroom at night. He and Devi moved into the restored master suite. Devi sometimes sat at John's side during the evening meetings. She looked like she could deliver any minute.

Luke took charge of most of the renovation projects. Joy had many talents, including midwifery, which John and Devi planned on using. Joy ran the hotel kitchen, which was barely functioning. Whenever she was cooking, she sang. Her helpers joined in, so the kitchen became known for its huge pots of hot food and beautiful echoing melodies. Getting the kitchen fully operational was a priority, and Joy pulled it together fabulously. There was always enough to feed the growing population. The roof was another high priority. Together, the kitchen and the roof added up to food and shelter. But even before these, came daily *i am* meditations, and the dissemination of knowledge by John, who provided anyone the opportunity to learn additional practices if they felt ready.

The Dame was bustling like a beehive. At meditation time, everyone disappeared. Then the swarm resumed immediately after.

Harry took time off from work, and he and Nadine started coming to the hotel every day.

Harry was instrumental in helping Luke organize and manage the dozens of projects that had to be done. He arranged for Wilder Corp to come in and install new air conditioning units, plumbing, wiring, and other utilities that were needed. Wilder Corp also repaired the roof, the broken sea wall, the crumbling concrete decks, and refurbished the swimming pool.

The day she walked in, Nadine got involved in the burgeoning financial and administrative challenges that came with the growing project. She was an able administrator, setting everything up systematically.

Nadine took to meditation like she was born for it. One tap on the breastbone from John a few days after she started coming to the hotel and she went deep into the silence of *i am* and was filled with bliss.

"John, I've never experienced anything like this," she told him the day she started *i am* meditation. "I want to spend the rest of my life meditating."

"You're a natural," he said. "You will take your gift wherever you go. If you want, I can help you with further developments in your practice. Just call from home."

"I don't want to go anywhere," she said. "I want to stay here and do this sacred work."

"You're welcome to stay as long as you like," he said. "I'm sorry things aren't working out with Kurt."

"Me too," she said. "I hope we can find some common ground again. He is so obsessed with the business. It is destroying him and everyone around him."

Nadine found two things on Coquina Island that she wanted desperately, a useful purpose, and inner peace. Both had been hard to come by in Washington. She had resigned from Senator Weatherhold's office years before. Her marriage to Kurt raised potential conflict of interest concerns. She tried working at Wilder Corp, but it was untenable because Kurt was so feared and hated by everyone there. She could not walk the halls of Wilder Corp without receiving suspicious stares. Retreating into a Washington society lifestyle and spending Kurt's money by the truckload redecorating the Woodmere mansion didn't do anything for her either. There wasn't much else for her in Washington. Kurt was emotionally unavailable, and openly hostile toward anything that was not completely for the business. As his life narrowed into a singular focus on the expansion of the company, he expressed himself more frequently in expeditious outbursts. Nadine knew that her staying on Coquina Island would anger him. She hoped his wrath would not spill over onto John.

There were a lot of new faces in the huge grand ballroom of the Coquina Dame.

"Welcome everyone. You all know I am pretty new at this public speaking thing," John shifted into root seat on the old sofa. "Not long ago we were practically hermits living in the mountains." He glanced over at Devi, sitting in a well-worn easy chair a few feet on the side. She smiled encouragingly. Her hands caressed her swollen belly.

John paused and touched the small black clip on the front of his shirt. "This microphone is new tonight. Hello in the back. Can you hear me?"

He heard a few muffled voices calling, "Yes!" from the back of the packed ballroom.

"Great. So here we are. Maybe the best thing to do is see if anyone has any questions." A few hands shot up. John was always happy to have real life situations in practices to respond to. "Yes, sir, you in the blue shirt."

"John, by what authority do you teach?" the young man said.

"By what authority do I teach? None really. I am only sharing what I've learned about natural human spiritual capabilities, and how to activate them. The real teacher is within each of us. The only difference between other people and me is the work I've done. It's allowed me to make discoveries that I think everyone is entitled to know about. It's everyone's business. I hope others will add to the knowledge. That is what science is, evolving knowledge, tested over and over again on the anvil of experience. I consider this to be spiritual science.

"If you think some authority is needed to sit here and talk, then I would say it comes to me from God, *i am*, from inside me, just as divine authority comes from within you. My advice is, get in touch with your own inner divine authority, the *i am* in you. Don't rely on anyone else's authority too much."

John pointed to his chest.

"Ten years ago my hunger for God led to me being touched here by a great lady named Christi Jensen. She died that very night. She told me to pass it on. So I touch people in the same way she touched me and tell what I can about it. I've had some visions that instructed me along the way. Is that authority? God lives in you as your own hunger and that is ultimately the only authority. If you hunger for God, you will be touched by the divine inside and outside. For those who unceasingly hunger and thirst for God, all of life becomes God's authority in action. That is the greatest of all secrets. I hope it answers your question. Yes, in the back."

A pretty woman in a red dress got up. "You have spoken about our natural abilities underlying the practices of *i am*. What are they?"

"Yes. Certain inherent natural abilities exist in us enabling us to attune with *i am*. First and foremost, as just mentioned, is the ability of desire in our heart to be redirected and intensified to bring out a response from *i am* both in us and around us. Second is the ability of the mind to become silent in *i am*, giving us great peace, stability, and blissful resonance in God. Third is the ability of the body to be cultivated through the breath and other means to become a superconductor of *i am*, expanding bliss and our view of the inner and outer realms through refined sensory perception. Fourth is the ability of the sexual energy to permeate the body, enabling *i am* to illuminate us. Fifth is the ability of the quieted mind to stimulate *i am* beyond the boundaries of the body, resulting in the direct experience that others are our own self. All of these are natural abilities. We all have them in us. The practices capitalize on these natural abilities. With or without the practices, the abilities exist. They are inherent, and can be used to our advantage."

"How is that," the woman asked.

"Just as a big boulder sitting on a ledge way up on a mountain has the ability to roll all the way down, so too do we have many boulders ready to roll in us. If we push a boulder, it may be hard to move it. So we find a board and a rock to make a lever to pry it over the edge. Then, down it goes with ease. That's what spiritual practices are. They are levers, tools that enable us to initiate the natural abilities in us to do their thing. We are *i am* machines waiting to be turned on. Yes, you, sir."

"How many practices are there?" a man in the front row asked.

"Lots. I was thinking about it the other day. It took me all these years to put them together. How could I ever convey it in a few hours? I can only give you a flavor right now. There are basic categories of practice relating to the abilities just mentioned. First is the desire, the wanting. If we aren't continuously wanting God, nothing will happen. This is the prerequisite for everything else. It doesn't have to be as specific as G-O-D. It can be an intense desire to know the truth, or grow, or advance, or just move forward. The intensity of desire is extremely important. Cultivating that intensity of desire is by far the most important practice. All desires are a cry for God. This is a great truth. If you develop the habit of intensely infusing all your desires with this recognition, everything will be easy. This habit is called devotion. With strong devotion, God, *i am*, will shower you with knowledge of all the ways to move inward in awareness. With strong devotion, a small touch from someone who has been meditating will be enough. If your devotion is strong enough, you won't even need that. As Jesus said, 'Blessed are those that hunger and thirst after righteousness, for they shall be filled.

"Second is meditation. You all know how to do that. Systematically and daily bringing the mind to the deep silence of *i am* is the greatest practice after devotion. It infuses the mind and body with the divine essence of *i am*.

"Third is restraint of breath in certain ways and at certain times. Not at all times. There are several ways to do this, and the effect is to open the body and nervous system, making it a much better conductor of the bliss currents of *i am*.

"Fourth are various postures inside and outside the body that are used during breathing practices and meditation enabling the body to become a superconductor for the bliss of *i am*. Breathing practices and postures raise sexual energy in the body. The rise of ecstatic spiritual conductivity in the nervous system throughout the body is a result of opening the nerves, infusing them with sexual essences, and diving deep into *i am* meditation.

The most important nerve in the body is one that runs up the center of the spine from the perineum at the root, through the center of the head, and out between the eyebrows to the bright rising star. It is very important to ecstatically awaken this nerve. From this nerve, *i am* goes out, awakening the entire nervous system of the temple-body, and beyond. Also, through this nerve we enter the white light of heaven above. Many of the practices are aimed at awakening the spinal nerve.

"Fifth are the nine prayers of *i am*. These are not prayers as most people think of them – weak ego-based petitions for worldly favors. No. The nine prayers are specific thought impulses we initiate deep in the silent depths of *i am*, which are magnified and go out with great power. The nine prayers of *i am*, practiced together, expand every aspect of *i am* in us and everywhere. They lead to so-called miraculous powers, which really aren't miraculous at all, just normal human evolution. Yes, ma'am?"

An elderly lady spoke: "In what order are these practices done, and which are most important, assuming we have a time limit and can only do a few?"

"Devotion is all the time. The clock should never stop on that. It is our spiritual hunger that matters most ... we must become devotion to succeed. Of course, devotion works only if we act on it. We must act. Whether we are doing daily practices or not is the acid test of devotion. Devotion is wasted if we are not acting on it. It's like having a jet plane sitting on the runway with the engines blasting and the brakes on. Not much happens. Just a lot of noise. Wanting without acting is waiting. So, we do some practices. If time is short we focus on the practices that will do the most for us in the shortest time.

"In a given session sequence, breathing is first, meditation is second, and the prayers of *i am* are third. There are some other things, but that is the basic sequence. The reason breathing is first is because it prepares the nervous system for the flow of *i am*. It cultivates the body for the seed of *i am*. Meditation soaks us in the blissful silence of *i am*, and that is the preparation for starting deep with the nine prayers of *i am*. So each element of practice leads logically to the next. As for which is most important, if you have fifteen minutes to spend, spend it on the *i am* meditation. *i am* meditation covers everything. Breathing practices help meditation go much broader and deeper. The prayers of *i am* manifest from meditation outward.

"If you have twenty or thirty minute for practice, do five minutes of spinal breathing, fifteen minutes of meditation, and five minutes of the nine prayers – that's two repetitions of each one. Make sure to rest for about five minutes before getting up. While sitting in practices, get into root seat and your secret chamber, if you have learned them. These two make a huge difference. Neither adds any time. They are concurrent practices. Do the cycle of practices twice a day for half an hour and you will progress handily. You can progress with less. It's up to you. There's no fixed formula. But remember, being established in the silent bliss of *i am* is the master key, so meditation is the most important core practice. That's why we teach *i am* meditation first, after a person's desire brings them to us.

"Make sure your devotion has gotten you in the habit of regular daily practice. Without regular practice, all bets are off. How many people do you know who are good at something who don't focus on it daily?

"If you approach the God quest like you would any serious endeavor, you will do well. If you approach it haphazardly, you will have the haphazard results that go with that effort. The God quest is like doing anything else. That's why devotion is first. Devotion to do something yields a constant effort. It's that simple. So many people have the belief that success in an endeavor can be had with a little lip service, that it will somehow rub off someone else who has done the work. The truth is we achieve according to our own effort in all things. Spiritual endeavor is no exception. 'As you sow, so shall you reap.' The God quest is not a spectator sport. If you really want it, you have to roll up your sleeves and do practices every day. Yes, over on the side there?"

An attractive black woman, who had her hand up, got up. "How important are the spiritual stretching exercises?"

"They are important, but not as important as meditation or breathing exercises. In other words, if you are doing a full routine, it is good to start with the stretches. They help settle and open the body for spinal breathing and meditation. Being limber is a plus going into practices, just as an empty stomach is. So we try and do the practices before meals and do the stretching. That is ideal. And if time is very short, just meditate.

"While we are talking about the body, it is also important to keep the body in good physical tone. This means exercise. Not too excessive, unless you are a competing athlete, of course. That's different. For most people it is good to do a short routine of calisthenics and isometrics on all the major muscle groups every other day, plus fifteen minutes or more of aerobic exercise, like brisk walking. Don't do it right before spiritual practices though. Right after is okay, as long as you take adequate rest time after meditation and the nine prayers.

"Well, thank you everyone. Let's continue tomorrow night."

John and Devi were holding hands, slowly walking up the long corridor back to the master suite. A soft white light emanated from them as they went, illuminating the dim passageway.

"How do you think that went?" he said.

"Not bad," she said. "If they were listening, they got a lot."

"You think they weren't listening?"

"Well, some were. Others were drifting. Everyone is different. All you can do is put it out there. Some will get it now. Others will get it later. When they are ready is the right time, right?"

"That's for sure. I hope this will make it easier for those who are seeking a way in. It is something I could have used. It would have saved me a few lumps."

"You're a pioneer." She said. "Pioneers always take the most lumps."

"Yeah, I guess."

"Speaking of being pioneers and taking lumps, do you feel like helping me have this baby tonight?"

"What?"

"You heard me. I've been having contractions for the past hour while you've been jabbering."

"Oh my God, why didn't you say anything?" he said.

"Didn't want to spoil your fun. Besides, I knew our baby didn't want to be born on the floor of the ballroom anyway. Oh, here comes another one." She leaned against the corridor wall and began to pant, focusing on John's eyes, running her fingers in large circles on her huge belly.

John got her into the master suite and called Joy. Soon she came with Luke and a few others. The time had finally arrived.

Chapter 27 – Pearls and Swine

Bliss ... *nunga-nunga* ... warmth ... softness ... floating ... movement ... shadows ... rumbling ... sucking ... *nunga-nunga* ... sucking ... *nunga-nunga* ... pressure ... owww ... pushing ... turning ... *nunga-nunga-nunga* ... pressure ... sliding ... owww ... pushing ... pushing ... owww ... *nunga* –

"You can do it, sweetheart," John said, "Push again. Just a few more. Her crown is coming."

"Ahhhhhhh!" Devi gave it everything she had. "Ohhh, I'm so tired."

"Okay, rest a minute," John said.

"I can't. Here comes another one ... Uuuhhhhhhhhh!"

Devi lay naked and opened on the king-sized bed. She was on a white sheet over plastic. Her knees were up and her feet were on the bed outside John's thighs where he knelt in front of her. She was propped up with pillows, clutching the brass rail of the bed frame over her head. Joy was softly wiping Devi's perspiring face, neck, and breasts with a cool damp cloth.

"Way to go, girl," Joy said. "It'll just be a few minutes."

"Uuuhhhhh!"

"Here comes her head," John said. "Oh, she's beautiful ... one shoulder ... two..." And then she was out in John's loving hands. "We have her."

Devi let out a long cry of completion as a flood of pink fluid gushed out of her. The chord remained, connecting her with the beautiful girl her husband held up where she could see.

"nughh ... nughh ... nughh..." the baby girl uttered softly, taking her first breaths. John lay the baby on Devi's belly, into her waiting arms, and went to Devi's side. He kissed her and then kissed the baby's forehead. The baby opened her eyes and calmly looked straight into his.

"She's so beautiful," Devi said. "Oh, those eyes. Those beautiful eyes."

"Oh, yes," John said. "Such beautiful green-rimmed blue eyes."

The radiance of the baby filled John with a familiar light. There was silence as the three of them lay together on the bed floating in the eternal *i am*. Finally, Devi spoke:

"She is Christi."

The tears were running down John's cheeks.

"Yes, she is Christi ... the one who has saved us all."

A bright white light filled the room, and burst beyond.

Joy wept silently, overwhelmed, sitting on the floor next to the bed.

Two days later, John was back on the old sofa with the hungry crowd of seekers. "It's good to be back here in the ballroom. Many of you know what we've been up to."

Applause and cheers went up from the large audience. Though Devi and the baby were not present, nearly everyone in the room knew about the birth.

John smiled. "Why don't we continue with the questions and answers. Yes, here in front."

"Do you believe in reincarnation?" The pretty young woman had multiple ear piercing and wore a brown leather vest.

"Funny you should ask that," John said. "Three days ago Devi and I had our first child, a lovely girl we named Christi. She is named after Christi Jensen, the wise old woman who first touched me with *i am* ten years ago. I think she is Christi. So yes, I do believe. But is she really? Does it matter? How much time should I spend to find out for sure? Could I ever prove it? That is the reincarnation issue in a nutshell. We can easily become obsessed with what has happened or what will happen. We can sit and watch the world turn, record its every movement, measure the comings and goings of billions of lives. What does it mean? Not much. Why? Because it does not directly change our experience of spirit. If past events or premonitions about the future inspire us to take action to change, to do our daily practices, great. But if pursuing these things is at the expense of direct practices we can be doing to advance ourselves in the here and now, then it is a waste of time. My advice is do your practices and grow. There are so many diversions that can distract us. An excessive fascination with reincarnation is one of them. Yes, sir."

A man in a dark gray suit got up. "Are meditation and business compatible?"

"Well, since I have not been in business, I may not be the best person to ask. But my family is, so I can give you a few thoughts. Business definitely can help meditation. We would not be sitting here now were it not for the generosity of my family's business. Can meditation help business? It can help make it friendlier, more caring, less greedy. Is that good for business? In the long run it is. Empires built on greed and exploitation inevitably collapse. Business based on a plundering mentality is a wild ride to nowhere. History sends us this message over and over again. Meditation tempers the competitive drive with growing compassion and empathy for other people and all of nature. Maybe business leaders will not like to hear that. But that's how it is. On the practical side, it can be a challenge to fit practices into days that are dominated with the business of making a living. It can be done, though. Many of you here have regular jobs. You do your practices before and after work. It's not always easy, but you do it because you have the hunger for God. You meditate in taxis, on trains and in airplanes. But hopefully not in business meetings."

A snicker went up in the crowd.

"Well maybe a little ecstatic fiddling in the secret chamber." John held his index finger up to his lips. "Shhhhh..."

Laughter broke out, and slowly subsided...

"So, yes, it can work between business and meditation. It has to. Spiritual science is here to stay."

Cheers erupted in the crowd.

"Is it true that people who do these practices need less sleep?" a middle-aged woman said.

"Yes, it's true. But it also depends on the progress of purification going on inside us. Sometimes we need more rest while a lot of purification is happening, and it can be like that for some time. Then, when we are open inside, less sleep will be needed. Overall, the body becomes much less inclined to take in or store physical impurities and emotional stress. One becomes generally less vulnerable to sickness for the same reasons. Yes, in the center aisle, you with both hands waving."

A young enthusiastic man who had made his way to the center aisle spoke up loudly. "Are you a guru?"

"Am I a guru?" John said. "I don't know. What do you mean by guru?"

"A messiah, a prophet, a spiritual master," the young man said.

"Oh, that." John got up and walked toward the young man. As he walked, he pointed around into the audience. "Well, if I am, I'm one just like you, and you, and you." His arms embraced the crowd. " All of you."

He came to the young man and continued. "The silent bliss of *i am* is present everywhere, and is the beginning and end of everything. *i am* is the master, the guru, the messiah in all of us. When we are devoted and longing to be changed, *i am* moves to fill that longing. The filling may come from inside us, or in the form of an experience, or a person. But don't make the mistake of thinking that someone we bump into is our spiritual master. You will find the master first in your heart. Everything else is a reflection of the fire of devotion in your heart. Some reflections are stronger than others."

John paced the aisle slowly as he spoke. "Maybe I am a stronger than average reflection of the hunger for God you have in your heart. If I am, then it is your strong hunger that has created me. Don't get hung up on me. Get hung up on your inner hunger, and do practices. I cannot enlighten you. You must dive repeatedly into *i am*, and, in doing so, enlighten yourself. I'm just a helper, a spiritual scientist who is sharing knowledge that belongs to everyone."

"But what about Jesus?" the young man called as John was pacing away toward the back of the audience.

John turned and headed back toward the young man. "Jesus is a bright beacon of *i am*. He is *i am* moving in us every minute of every day. If you are attracted to him, hunger and thirst for his help, he will help you, as will any of the many saviors in heaven who people around the world worship. There is no shortage of saints and saviors. They are all available to us within, longing for our advancement. There is a great shortage of people who hunger and thirst for God, and an even greater shortage of people who are committed to do the practices that will lift humankind out of darkness. Finding saviors is easy. Finding people ready to dive into *i am* within is not so easy. It is a matter of vision, you know. Whatever we humans can visualize, we can attain. We can't want it until we can imagine it. That is the power of Jesus, or any iconic figure. The power is in our ability to see what is possible, desire it, and take steps to achieve it. The secret of Jesus is the same as the secret of humanity's ability to manifest whatever it desires. The power comes from within us, always. It is not somewhere else. When it seems to be coming from somewhere else, it is still coming from in us."

"But didn't Jesus say 'I am the way?'" the young man asked. "My church tells me that Jesus is God's only begotten son, the only door to heaven. Anyone who doesn't accept him as that goes to hell."

"Jesus is *i am, and i am* is the way. *i am* in all of us is the only way to heaven. *i am* is heaven, and *i am* has many sons and daughters. *i am* has many outward names in the many religions. They all lead to the same opening of truth in us. All sitting here today are the sons and daughters of God. *i am* is the kingdom of heaven within you. You are that. The church has its reasons for saying the things it says. And it is not entirely the church's fault that some externalized falsehoods are spread. You see, we the people have needed to have an external structure to worship at, a physical church, an imposing altar, a hierarchy of authority to bow before, a golden calf, a sacred cow, an esoteric wisdom, a watertight philosophical system, a magic bullet, you name it. We don't ask our churches for AN answer, we ask them for THE answer. So they have to give it to us – God's only begotten son. The clergy needs the structure as much as we do. We all need something to believe in, a rallying post. These are all man-made things, born out of fear of mortality and material loss. They all lead eventually to *i am* within."

John stood in front of the young man. "You see, it is often the institution against anything and anyone that is perceived as a threat in this physical realm. Does that sound like a good approach to God? All this posturing is going to be old history in the new era of spiritual science, when people can simply cultivate God in themselves every day at home, or wherever they happen to be. Who will care about the self-serving needs of the institution then? What we get is according to our desire, our belief. Narrowly defined spiritual doctrines that divide us here on earth are the product of narrow worldly desires. We are now waking up and realizing that the structure, any structure, is a manmade illusion. Look within yourself. Use your God-given abilities. Do the practices that open you to the divine experience of *i am* within you. Then everything changes. It's as simple as that. All the rest is human posturing that gets in the way of the hunger and thirst that is *i am* calling us home from within. Don't worry about God's only begotten son. It is an imaginary territory, a manmade structure that will only delay you. Dive into the bliss of God, *i am,* that is vibrating in you right now. If it is Jesus you seek, seek him by doing *i am* meditation, for he is that. And so are you."

John extended his hand and touched the young man on his chest. A barely discernable energy entered him. The young man was taken aback, appearing to be out of breath. He was suddenly dazed.

John withdrew his touch. "It will be all right. Jesus is with you."

A faint smile came on the young man's face as he turned and made his way unsteadily back to his seat. As soon as he sat down he closed his eyes, and he fell deep into *i am.*

John went slowly back to the front, turned and sat down. "Yes, sir?" he said to a man in round steel-rimmed glasses with long hair and a beard who came into the center aisle.

"Most spiritual traditions are very secretive about the practices they teach, giving them out only to a deserving few. Some say you are a renegade, and that you are wrong to be teaching these practices to the public. They say you are throwing pearls before swine."

John lifted his leg up under him on the sofa, shifting into root seat. He looked out into the air. "Well, I don't know about most spiritual traditions. I only know about the journey I have taken. If putting the truth out in the open for everyone to see is being a renegade, then maybe I am one. It is about time, isn't it?

"Knowledge cannot advance as long as people are preoccupied with protecting what they think is their turf. Modern science does not accept that narrow-minded approach. If there is a better way, we should uncover it and not be hoarding secret teachings, trying to protect them. Protect them from what? By keeping such secrets, the whole of knowledge cannot be known, because all these secretive people are hiding fragments of the whole from each other and everyone else. The practices shared here are called *The Secrets of Wilder*. Well, they are open secrets. Anyone can test them and see what is true. These principles and methods belong to everyone. They are your natural abilities. Who has the right to keep you from using what is yours? Where would we be today if Newton's laws of motion were locked up in a vault all this time? What if mathematics was a proprietary esoteric language reserved for the few? We'd still be living in caves, wouldn't we? The way spiritual knowledge is processed and distributed must change, or we will continue to live in the caves of spiritual ignorance. Isn't it obvious?

"As for throwing pearls before swine, people who say that in these modern times must have a low regard for humanity. Such pessimism about human spiritual potential can accomplish little. That attitude casts doubt over everything they do. Since when is one person more deserving of spiritual practices than another – less of a pig than another?"

John hesitated and looked around the room at all the eager faces. So many hungering to have a chance to open to God within themselves. He knew there were millions more around the world. He wanted to reach them all.

He looked at the long-haired bearded man standing in the aisle. "Sir, all I can say is, our time has come ... Oink! Oink!"

The packed ballroom roared with laughter, including the bearded man who had asked the question. He was so undone that he doubled over. After a few minutes everyone was settling down.

Then someone yelled, "Oink! Oink!"

Then another. "Oink! Oink!"

Then nearly everyone was crying, "Oink! Oink! Oink! Oink! Oink! Oink! Oink! Oink!..."

John oinked along with them, waving his arms as though conducting an oinking orchestra. Then it went back to laughter again, and finally settled down.

"Okay, are we all oinked out?" John got a look of trying to contain himself inside. He couldn't. He burst out laughing, and everyone started again, and it went on infectiously for another few minutes.

He had tears running down his cheeks. "Whewee, all right ... Listen, I'm not knocking the need for the esoteric secrecy of the past. The transmission of spiritual knowledge has been a dangerous business for thousands of years, as we know well from history. Presenting any new knowledge has always been risky. There was a time when people were burned at the stake for suggesting that the sun might be at the center of the solar system instead of the earth. We have come a long way since those days of bloodthirsty ignorance. America is a free country, ruled by the people. That's us. Spiritual information does not have to be hidden anymore. It is essential that it not be. Too many need it. Ordinary people like you and me. The materialistic times we live in must give way to a kinder, gentler era where people will have full access to their own divinity, their own inner *i am*. It's time to replace the word 'esoteric' with the word 'open.' It's time for everyone to have equal access to spiritual tools."

Everyone applauded. A few cheered....

"Also, it is time for all of us to go direct to the divine within, rather than relying on so many intermediaries. That's how it happened for me. It can be like that for anyone. This is what open practices are about. Take them and go inside. You have the ability in yourself already. You live in an *i am* machine. It is time for a new approach based on the journey happening within each person.

"Outer teachings have ebbed and flowed over the centuries with the tides of humanity, and the sacrifices of great teachers. Impure biases have crept in. That is certainly true of Christianity, where the original teachings of Jesus have been distorted. It is no one's fault. It was the times. Spiritual endeavors have not had the advantage of a scientific approach. Now it will change. I encourage all people with practical spiritual knowledge to bring what they have to the table of science. Not pseudo-science that uses a so-called scientific approach to justify inflexible ideas. Let's check our dogmas at the door. I mean real science that puts it all there for everyone to see, and makes objective assessments of causes and effects. Such examinations will lead to productive research and an integration of knowledge that will benefit everyone.

"We need open systems of practice that cross the artificial boundaries people have drawn, integrating all knowledge about human spiritual transformation. The processes of science will test and gradually mold systems of practice to a much higher level than previously seen. If given the opportunity, science will do for spiritual practice what it has done so successfully in other areas of human knowledge. There are no boundaries in true knowledge. We can no longer afford to keep spiritual knowledge fixed in the past. We must move forward, expanding our knowledge through constant inquiry.

"Neither are there real boundaries in matter. Our perceptions and abilities will change as the era of spiritual science takes hold. It is all beautiful radiant energy moving in empty space. It is how we all will see the world. I'll show you."

John got up off the sofa and held his hand up over the crowd. A wave of radiant white light particles went out over everyone and slowly settled down on them like dust. The crowd gasped. Many saw the room as John saw it, as streams of living light animating the translucent borders of matter. Every person was a being of light, surging with ecstatic bliss.

"See?" he said. "It is all energy. It is all *i am*. It is what we are. Do your practices and you will see this truth in every moment of every day."

He walked slowly out of the ballroom.

Kurt lay reading the newspaper in the chaise on the deck overlooking the Potomac River. The expansive lawn hugged the river's edge and faded into the woods upstream and downstream. Large boulders rested at the water's edge on either side of the boathouse. The yacht was tied up along the dock.

He turned his head when he heard Nadine come out of the house, heading toward him across the deck. He lay the newspaper down in his lap. She had been home a few days, and had been acting strange. She had gone away for weeks at a time before, always scurrying back to the luxury of the Woodmere estate, but this time she didn't seem to be happy to be home.

"It's good to have you back," he said. "I missed you."

"I want to talk to you," she said. "Have you got a minute?"

"Sure," he said. *Maybe now I'll find out what's bugging her.*

"I've decided I want to stay at the hotel on Coquina Island," she said. "I am useful there and I love the meditation and the lifestyle. There are incredible things happening there, I want to be part of it."

Kurt felt his temper begin to flare inside. He restrained himself from exploding in a fit of anger and said, "Oh, and when did you decide this?"

"While I was down there taking care of your father. It is good for me being in that environment."

Kurt looked away toward the river, and the woods on the other side. He sighed. "Well, I suppose it was to be expected. Damn that brother of mine."

"It's not John's fault," she said. "It's been good for me. Life is too stressful here. I want the inner peace that meditation and the community there give."

"So, you want to join John's cult, do you?" Kurt said. A hiss was creeping into his voice. John's constant pointing to some nebulous abstract inner life irritated Kurt to no end. *Now Nadine wants to join. Shit!*

Kurt turned and got up off the other side of the chaise, continuing to gaze out over the river.

"Do what you have to," he said. "I think you know my feelings about it."

"Yes," she said. "I'm sorry but it is something I must do. The more financial success we have had here, the emptier I have felt. I just want to have some inner happiness. Is that so bad?"

"Well, if you could have a baby, it might help." Kurt's words, thrown over his shoulder like a hand grenade, were designed to inflict pain on her.

There was silence.

Finally she said, "I'm sorry that I can't give you children. Do you have to use it to hurt me?"

He turned and looked into her eyes that were welling up with tears. "I'm sorry," he said. "I'm sorry." He felt he was losing control of the things most important to him: his wife, a future family to leave all this to. Even the business was becoming unwieldy, getting harder and harder to control. And now the investigations starting in the Justice Department. *Christ!*

"So much has gone right for us for so long," he said, "And now I seem to be out of things going right."

"You could come back to Florida and we could adopt," she said. "You need a change as much as I do. I love you. I always will."

"Florida?" Kurt said, bristling. "Are you kidding? That backwater? And any child I rear will be by my own blood. My own blood! You hear me?"

"Yes, I know. I'm sorry." She turned to go.

"Nadine."

She stopped and turned. "Yes?"

"If you go down there again to the Coquina Dame Hotel, don't come back to this house."

"Do you really mean that?"

He shrugged. "I'm afraid so." He hadn't intended to say it, but it came out naturally, a logical response to the course of events. It was the way he always did things. And now it was done, because he knew she would be gone.

A tear ran down her cheek. "All right, if that's what you want." She went back into the stone mansion.

Kurt flopped on the chaise and opened his newspaper. He hurt all over inside.

The next time he saw her was three months later at the first meeting with the divorce lawyers.

Chapter 28 – Openings

A year later, John stood on the ocean terrace in front of the Coquina Dame Hotel with one foot propped up on the seawall. The breeze coming in off the ocean caught his hair and flapped the bottoms of the light cotton pants hanging loosely above his bare feet. The collar of his muslin shirt blew against his cheek. He gazed out at the surf roaring beyond the wide beach. It was liquid light.

"We've come along way," he said to the sea.

He turned and surveyed the sprawling building behind him. The renovation work was nearly done. The grand old Coquina Dame stood proudly again.

He walked slowly across the new concrete toward the building. His feet shot fountains of energy upward with each step. He was in a kaleidoscope of inner light, maneuvering his way carefully through it, avoiding floating up into the thin textured energy of the air. He went through the side entrance. Luke met him and walked with him down the corridor to the ballroom.

"You doing all right, brother Luke?" John said.

The deep divine voice came back. "Oh, yeah, the world's a-shining today. And you, brother John?"

"Like always, dear friend." In a gesture of spiritual giving, he put his hand on Luke's broad back as they went through the door into the packed ballroom.

There were several hundred people sitting on padded folding chairs in neat rows on the endless beige carpet. The old chandeliers sparkled above. New golden drapes graced the tall ocean view windows. The murmur of the crowd subsided when John and Luke walked in. They went to the modest sofa up on the stage in the front of the room. John sat down in root seat. Luke put the microphone on John, flipped on the belt unit, patted him on the shoulder and walked off to the side.

John surveyed the audience. There were many familiar faces, and some new ones. A few people were queuing up at the microphone standing in the center aisle. There was a middle-aged lady hunched over in a wheelchair at the end of the front row. Several others with serious ailments were sitting nearby, hoping for a healing. He could read it in their energy. He would help them if he could. It depended on their desire as much as his ability to provide healing energy.

Over the months, John had grown familiar with this daily event, and he had long since stopped being uneasy about it. It had become an extension of his practices. The openings of the people had become his openings. The dynamics of *i am* went far beyond his small body now. His sense of self was expanding to encompass the world.

He knew that many in the audience saw him as an energy source. He had what they instinctively wanted, just like that day many years ago when the crowd charged him at the First Church of Christ. He constantly encouraged the people that came to look to themselves, and open from within. It was a running skirmish between them. They wanted his help, and he wanted them to help themselves.

He sat quietly surveying them, much as he had surveyed his own clogged nervous system years before, forever trying strategies to purify and open himself. Nothing had changed. Only the playing field was different. It had expanded. And he knew more about the game than he did before.

"Today is a good day to talk about practices," he said to the gathering of light beings he saw in front of him. These were the words he usually opened with. "Does anyone have questions about practices?"

A young lady with frazzled energy was standing at the microphone. "I can't seem to meditate. No matter what I do, I am on the surface."

"Being on the surface is okay," John said. "It means that is where the work is being done. Let it happen. Don't try and fight your way in. The trying is an impediment. If you are not trying and you are picking up the thought of *i am* comfortably at any level of clarity, you are meditating, no matter what the experience is. Expectations are not part of meditation."

"But sometimes I feel like jumping out of my skin," the young lady said.

"Do you feel that way after meditation?"

"Yes, often I do."

"Then take more time to come out of meditation," John said. "Lie down for a while. If the uneasiness continues, try shortening your meditation time by five or ten minutes until things smooth out. Then go back up in time when you think you are ready. Find where your balance is."

"How long should I be meditating?"

"Twenty minutes once before breakfast and once before dinner is good for most people, but not everyone. Some are comfortable with more, some with less. Find what works for you. Finding your balance is very important. Also, spinal breathing before meditation does much to settle the body and mind down. It smoothes out energy imbalances and cultivates the body for *i am* meditation. Are you doing spinal breathing?"

"No, I haven't learned that."

"Get with Luke after the meeting and he will make sure you get help with that. Anyone who is meditating and is inclined to do more practice, please see Luke after the meeting. If you are not meditating yet, and would like to learn, he can help you with that too."

An overweight man came to the microphone. "I can't get into the root seat. My leg won't bend that far."

"You should never give up gently nudging yourself in that direction, but don't force it. The body was designed for the heel to eventually find the perineum. Either leg will do. Alternating now and then will give one leg a rest. Until you can get there, or if you never can for some reason, you can use a substitute of your choosing – a ball, a rolled up sock, whatever works to produce the same effect that the heel does. It doesn't have to be the heel. The key is to have pressure in the soft area of the perineum between the pubic bone and anus."

"Do you offer diet recommendations?" the overweight man said.

"My recommendation is not to be obsessed with diet. It can be a distraction. Doing meditation and the other practices will naturally change your appetites and preferences. Go with those. Everyone is different. Meditation eventually leads to a diet that is light and nutritious. This means not too light to be nutritious, and not too nutritious to be light. A balance, you know. If you want to help it along in that direction, that's fine. Most of us have had that urge. The practices are interconnected. Doing one brings on the others. A naturally rising desire for a purer diet is one example of how practices change our life."

An attractive woman took the microphone. "I can get in root seat, but it is so, um, distracting that I can't meditate. What should I do?"

"How long have you been using it?" John said.

"About a month," she said.

"The distraction is normal. Give it some time. It will become manageable. It is a very important concurrent practice underlying meditation, and all of the practices. If the sexual tension is too much, impossible to bear, try using something softer than your heel, like a pillow. Then try and move to your heel over time. Remind yourself that your sexual energy can and will be tamed to a higher purpose. Once it evolves to smooth blissful cultivation, root seat will become one of your best spiritual friends. Many have made the journey. You will get there."

A middle-aged man in a suit, with gray hair and glasses was next.

"My name is Dr. Keith Stonemeyer, with the Fraternity of American Physicians. I am here to protest your recommendation that people cut the frenum under their tongue in order to put the tongue in the nasal pharynx. This a foolish and dangerous thing to do."

"Foolish and dangerous?" John said. "Have you tried it, sir?"

"Why would I do something stupid like that?" the doctor said.

"If you haven't experienced it, then you are hardly in a position to judge. Important natural spiritual connections are achieved in the nasal pharynx. To get there in most people, something must be broken, much the way a hymen is broken so reproduction can occur. At the appropriate time, it is a natural spiritual change in a person's life, one of great importance. Humankind has always reached out beyond its boundaries to new vistas of experience. Removing the hymen under the tongue and going up is one of the greatest experiences a person can have. You would deprive us all because you have no experience with it?"

"It is unnatural —"

"So are body piercing and tattooing ... even surgery could be viewed as unnatural. Does that mean we should abandon all these things? Is circumcision natural? It robs males of a part of their anatomy while they are babies. A person who feels ready and chooses to go up into the nasal pharynx robs no one, least of all themselves. It is *i am* that calls us to the secret chamber and the altar of bliss, and then it is a personal choice, an act of unfolding divine ecstasy. If it is done prudently, at the appropriate time on the journey, it will add immeasurably to the quality of our life, and to the quality of our surroundings."

"The doctor was noticeably agitated. "Young man, you don't know what you are talking about. You are outside the boundaries of modern medicine and our society."

"Maybe so, but I'm in good company. Nearly everyone in history who has called for breakthroughs in human progress has been outside the boundaries. Some were murdered for it. It seems progress always comes at a high price to those who are promoting it. But how else can we advance except by taking the next steps, regardless of cost? We have to keep going forward. The information is there. People will choose for themselves."

"We are going to file a complaint with the board of public health, Mr. Wilder." Dr. Stonemeyer turned and walked out, working his way through the people crowded in the back of the ballroom.

John shrugged. "Well, everyone is entitled to their opinion. It will be all right as long as people like the good doctor there are never put in charge of what we may or may not choose for ourselves."

A smiling woman came up to the microphone. "I have a question about *i am* and the nine prayers."

"Oh, good," John said. "A couple of my favorite subjects."

"When we think '*i am*' in meditation, who is the *i am* we are letting go into? Is it me, or is it God *i am*? When we let go in the nine prayers, who, or what, are we letting go into? "

"Both you and your inner silence are aspects of what we call *God*. Both are manifestations of the reality of *i am*. In most people the individual ego self is a weak and narrow reflection of *i am*, like a light shining through a dense dark fog. You can always spot the small one, because it is spelled with the big 'I.' The weaker the light beam, the more it tries to compensate by puffing itself up."

Laughter...

"Meditation and the nine prayers of *i am* are going to change that. The nine prayers of *i am* are close cousins of meditation, with one important difference. Meditation takes us into the silent depths of *i am*, while the prayers are for starting in those awakened silent depths and coming back out with particular intentions. Because we are starting deep inside with the prayers, the intentions have the infinite power of *i am* behind them. A mind in repose is the most powerful mind. It is God-mind. Regular practice of the nine prayers gradually strengthens our ability to initiate all desires in *i am*. As this evolves, the miraculous becomes commonplace. And the big 'I' becomes the small '*i,*' which is infinitely big."

John smiled. "See? Before our surface consciousness becomes the same as the depths of *i am*, there will not be much power on the surface or in spoken words. So to think or say 'LOVE' on the surface of the mind with the personal 'I' will not do much. If we pick up ...*love*... faintly in the silent depths of *i am*, the effect is much greater, infinitely greater. This cultivates our awareness in *i am* everywhere, while at the same time projecting the power of ...*love*... outward in all directions. When we get to the stage of development where *i am* is as much on the surface of our mind as it is in the depths, then the effect on the surface will be the same as picking up the prayer in the depths.

"Then it works like this..." John closed his eyes and quietly said, "...*love*..." A wave of visible white light went out from him in all directions, penetrating everyone in the ballroom. A reflection of the energy rose from the audience in many different colors. Some started laughing. Some were putting their hands over their faces in tears. Some dissolved into meditation.

After a few minutes, everyone settled down. The smiling woman shyly put the microphone up to her mouth again. "Should everyone be doing the nine prayers of *i am*, or only advanced meditators?"

"Anyone who wants to," John said. "But recognize that some inner silence is necessary. That comes from weeks, months, or years of daily *i am* meditation. Also recognize that using the prayers daily has a cumulative effect, like meditation. You are building up a permanent conscious presence in *i am* for great distances around you. You are becoming that. It is a process of evolution that happens as a result of daily practices. While your influence in your surroundings grows, so too do you realize that you are your surroundings. There is only one of us here – *i am*. Open to *i am* and you will realize that you are everything."

The smiling lady yielded the microphone to an energetic young man. "I've been using the spinal breathing and the breath suspension and they really take me to another dimension. I'm hooked. How do these work?"

"That's wonderful," John said. "These are essential practices to break beyond the boundaries of the body, and the grip of the material senses especially.

"Make sure you meditate right after breathing practices. Breathing practices plow the soil of the nervous system and fertilize the tilled soil with sexual essences drawn up from below. Meditation plants the seed of *i am* deep in the fertilized soil of the nervous system. The crop is the pure light of God. If you don't plant the seed of God, anything could grow there. This is why breathing practices are a support to meditation and not vise versa. You can usually spot someone who is hooked on breathing practices without meditation. They can be rigid, argumentative, intolerant, insecure, or narrow in their views. These are all signs of limited meditation. Any kind of weed can be growing there. But with meditation, breathing practices are the gateway to heaven.

"As for how they work, a few things are going on. First, restraint of breath causes sexual essences to rise up in the body to replace the temporary shortage of life force created by the restraint of breath. The body draws on its vast storehouse of life force in the loins to compensate. It more than compensates. The sexual energy is much more dynamic and multi-purposed than what comes from simple oxygenation of the blood from the lungs. The sexual essences open and flow on every nerve, transforming the nervous system into a superconductor of spiritual energy. Once the energy rises above the pelvic region, we don't consider it sexual anymore. It is divine ecstasy rising up. Same energy – different purpose in the body. The human nervous system's capacity for ecstasy far exceeds what is generally understood. It's wonderful. Second, by directing the life force up and down the spine during slow breathing, a union of the polarities in the human being is achieved. The masculine energy comes down from the bright realm beyond the spiritual eye, and the feminine energy comes up from the root. They join, and new spiritual life is created in us. The mind has the ability to create these movements in the spine through mental energy induction. Breath and mind together can move energy through the body very effectively. Anyone who does spinal breathing knows this.

"Spinal breathing also has a deepening effect on sensory perception. Our senses exist on a spectrum, like thoughts do, beginning in the depths of *i am*, and ending up on the physical level of experience. Most of us operate sensually mostly on the physical level, thinking that is all there is. This is like thinking the world is flat, when it is really round. All you have to do is sail over the horizon to find out the truth. With spinal breathing, meditation and the nine prayers, our sensory experience expands into the light realms, over the horizon into the celestial realms of God, *i am*. What we see inside is that life is an endless kaleidoscope of ecstatic energy constantly dancing with itself. Opening the sensory spectrum shows us that the extraordinary is the ordinary. It is all around us, and in us. You will recall that one of the prayers of *i am* is *...inner sensuality...* This is not to enhance physical sensuality, but to expand the experience of the senses inward on the sensory spectrum.

"The breath suspension practice is an add-on, beyond spinal breathing. It should only be done after spinal breathing, because spinal breathing sets up a stable balance of the polar energies in the body. Without this balance, breath retention can lead to unstable energy flows. This is why I recommended spinal breathing to the young lady having restless meditations. Advanced breath suspension practice involves manipulating the ecstatic flows in the body with rotating motions of the head that greatly magnify the amount of energy going into the chest and brain. Ultimately, it is the awakening of *i am* in the head that brings us beyond body consciousness. Breath suspension is a key part of this process."

The young man spoke again. "What about the spiritual eye purge? That is breath suspension too. How is it different?"

"Yes, good question. The spiritual eye purge is a specialized practice focused on opening the spiritual eye located between the center of the brow and the center of the brain, above the nasal passages and nasal pharynx. We suspend the in-breath during that and apply pressure in the nasal passages, combined with other physical means to exert pressure back through the eye, and back through the brain. The spiritual eye purge clears the nerves all the way back and down through the brain stem, the medulla oblongata. It is a very good practice that helps the flow of energy through the brain and out to the bright white rising star. It should be done at the very end of practices, after the nine prayers and before rest. Detailed instructions on any of the practices we have discussed are available here at the Coquina Dame. You can sign up for them at the desk in the main lobby.

"Well, shall we meditate for a while before we call it a night?"

Everyone stirred in their seats for a few seconds, closed their eyes, and went into the silence of *i am*.

During the course of the meditation, a few moans of pleasure could be heard here and there around the ballroom. Twice, voices cried out in ecstasy as they were pierced by the hungry penetrations of *i am* into their human form. John felt all of their openings occurring within himself. He sat silently, weightless on the sofa, deep in *i am*, his eyes raised into the brightness.

Chapter 29 – Northern Clouds

Kurt took the call from his attorney in the study at Woodmere.

"It's final," Carl Steiner said. "Nadine signed the papers. Now she's your wealthy ex-wife. We managed to keep it under ten million like you wanted, barely. Her attorney held out for the last dollar. He must be getting a percentage."

"Thanks a lot," Kurt said. "I don't know what I'd do without you guys." He slammed the phone down on the receiver.

It wasn't the deal that bothered him. It was a fleabite in his net worth. It was losing that made him burn inside. Losing Nadine, losing the life they had, losing her to his whacko brother's cult. And the rest of his family too. His father had drifted into the la-la land of meditation since his mother died, wasting company money on John's foolish mission. He placed blame for his mother's death squarely on John and his Indian wife. None of it should have ever happened.

In an effort to soothe his ego, Kurt hosted several large parties at Woodmere. These events began in the afternoon, ran throughout the night, and into the next day. The attendees included Washington notables, corporate moguls, and Hollywood celebrities. They all came to rub shoulders with each other, eat, drink, dance, mingle, and engage in mischief.

Kurt was rarely seen at the parties, only showing his face occasionally when it suited him. More often he would invite certain guests into his study or to other back rooms for private liaisons that met his needs.

Senator Weatherhold walked into the cavernous study. Kurt rose from the couch by the fireplace to greet him.

"Senator, thanks for coming. Would you like some brandy?"

"Don't mind if I do," the Senator said. "Wonderful party. You should come out and join the fun."

Kurt poured brandy into large snifters and they sat on the two couches facing each other in front of the huge barren fireplace. The Senator could only see the edges of the large low chessboard parquet table between them. The middle of the table was piled with weeks' worth of rumpled magazines and newspapers. Several had overflowed onto the floor.

Kurt slouched back on the couch with his snifter.

"Are you all right?"

"I've been better," Kurt said. He took a gulp of the brandy.

"Sorry to hear about Nadine. You two were quite a couple."

"Yeah," Kurt said absently.

"We sure missed her when she left our office. Where is she now?"

"Florida."

"Oh, yes, that brother of yours with his cult."

"Can't we do anything to put him out of business?"

"That's the second time you've asked me that. We looked into it. They are breaking no laws. It looks harmless enough. A bunch of people sitting around meditating –"

"Harmless as a snake," Kurt said. "They're ruining my life."

"Sorry to hear that," the Senator said. "But it is your problem, isn't it? Why make it mine?"

"Because you owe me, Senator."

"Sorry, nothing I can do there, Kurt." The Senator took his last swallow, got up, and started out. "Thanks for the brandy."

"There's one more thing."

The Senator stopped and turned back toward Kurt. "Yes?"

"The company," Kurt said. "The Justice Department investigation. We are cooperating, but I'm concerned about how things are going."

"Is there any reason to be concerned?" the Senator said.

"Come on, Senator, you know how we run our business. You are part of it."

"I don't think so, Kurt. You did this all by yourself. Those business sharing deals have nothing to do with me."

"Remember Glades?" Kurt said.

"You know I'm clean," the Senator said.

"But the Feds don't. You sure there isn't anything you can do to call off the dogs?"

The Senator didn't want to incite Kurt. "I don't know ... I don't know. It's gone pretty far. Let me think about it. Maybe there's something –"

"You do that, Senator."

Senator Weatherhold's gaze shifted from Kurt to the opulent decor of the huge study.

"This is quite a place you've got here, Kurt, quite a place." He turned and went toward the door.

As Senator Weatherhold went out, Kurt could hear loud music and raucous laughter drifting across the foyer from the huge living room on the other side of the house. It was a playroom for the rich and famous this weekend. He slumped back into the couch.

"Hi, baby, you call me?"

Mable Butkus slipped through the crack in the tall door of the study and closed it behind her.

"Yeah," Kurt said.

A Story of Inner Silence, Ecstasy and Enlightenment – 201

"You look positively shitty," she said with her hand on her slung out hip. "Somethin' wrong?"

"Only everything."

"Oooh, baby ... you need some therapy..."

"Yeah."

She popped a bubble, kicked off her shoes, and came over. She stepped between the low table and the couch, straddling Kurt's legs that were drooping down. She knelt on the soft pillows, coming down on his crotch. Her red gown split open like a banana peel, revealing her legs and hot pink panties. With her hands on the back of the couch on both sides of his head, she leaned over and kissed him on the mouth.

"Everything's gonna be okay," she said. "I'm gonna take good care of you."

Then she kissed his nose, his forehead, and higher and higher up until his face was in her dangling cleavage.

He was coming to life. He put his hands on her waist and began to kiss the insides of her breasts. She swiveled on him. He felt her zeroing in on his erection under her.

"Oh, I like that," she moaned as she squirmed with passion on him.

She lifted up and put a leg between his, and then the other. She slid on the floor with her cleavage resting on the edge of the couch between his legs, and her hands and face close to his crotch. She stroked him through his slacks with one hand while she undid him with the other. Soon, Kurt was exposed and ready. He was filled with anticipation.

"Mable?" he said.

She pulled up her head just as she was about to come down on him. "Yeah, baby?

"How about losing the gum."

"Oh yeah..." She spit it over his head. The pink wad landed on the antique Oriental rug behind the couch. Then her head came down, and he let out a long sigh.

Mable was eager on him, making constant hungry noises.

In a few minutes Kurt was over the edge. She milked him for every drop. She came up slowly the last time, finally letting him go with a *flop*. She looked into his glazed eyes, smiling. "You feelin' better, baby?"

"A little," he mumbled, sinking into a post-orgasmic stupor.

"You know what?" she said, licking her lips.

"Huh?"

"You always taste much better than gum."

Chapter 30 – A Day in Court

"Mr. Wilder, you are under arrest," the Federal agent said as he turned Kurt around and put the handcuffs on him.

The same thing was happening to Harry Wilder in Jacksonville, and to dozens of Wilder Corp executives across the country. It was occurring at several other large engineering and construction firms as well. The charges were voluminous. Most were related to bid rigging and collusion on Federal contracts. Some of Wilder Corp's lower echelon executives arrested were also charged with bribery of government officials, and a few with extortion.

On all the TV news networks, dozens of men in expensive suits were shown being led off in handcuffs. Voiceovers trumpeted, "Corporate predators are meeting their fate," "Massive government contractor scandals erupted nationwide today," and, "Now Wilder is getting tamed – the upstart mega-company is at the center of the contractor scandals."

After two days behind bars, Kurt, his father, and most of the other executives were out on bail. From the records that had been seized by Federal agents, it was determined that the wrongdoing had mainly been in the Washington area offices of the firms involved. This was certainly the case with Wilder Corp.

Though Harry would have to face a judge, it was unlikely that he'd receive punishment beyond probation. There was no evidence to tie him to the company's illegal activities. If he was guilty of anything, it was of not keeping closer tabs on his wayward son. Though he still held the position of chairman of the board, he hadn't been active in the company for the past two years, and never in the Washington, D.C. business dealings, all which worked in his favor legally.

Kurt was the one they wanted, but he was coming up clean. The meticulous ways that he concealed his corruption seemed impenetrable. It appeared he would get off with a slap on the wrist. But others in the organization had little choice in their conduct. They either had to do whatever was necessary to get the business, or not have a job. The corporate culture demanded it. Now, many of them would go to jail, including Mable Butkus, who was a leading lobbyist for Wilder Corp in Washington and Florida. Her fingers had been in many pies. She loved her work.

Several large Federal contracts that were pending were pulled back, and other contracts Wilder Corp was working on were in jeopardy. The company would survive, however. Tens of thousands of jobs depended on it, so the government wouldn't let it fold. But Wilder Corp would not be run by Kurt anymore. At Harry's direction, Kurt was removed as CEO. His henchmen were purged. A new management team with impeccable credentials was brought in to clean up the company. The new management would steer Wilder Corp steadily toward the realms of respectable conduct. It would take time. In spite of the serious legal difficulties and change to a less aggressive and more honest management, the unfathomable force of corporate momentum would keep Wilder Corp growing for decades to come.

Kurt sat confidently with his lawyers in the packed courtroom. *They can't touch me. All bases are covered. I'm soon out of this mess.*

"All rise for Her Honor, Judge Maggie Jones," trumpeted the Clerk for the District of Columbia Federal Court.

The courtroom rustled to its feet as the stout black Federal judge came in.

"Please be seated," Judge Jones said. The courtroom rustled back down. "Today we are continuing with the U.S. Department of Justice versus Kurt Wilder, formerly of Wilder Corp. "Does the prosecution wish to call a witness?"

"We do, Your Honor. The Prosecution calls Ms. Mable Butkus."

Her hips came bumping down the aisle. She had on a thin white blouse and a tight dark skirt. The blouse was open an extra button. Her high heels pecked the shiny wood floor as she walked, and she was chewing confidently. Kurt's jaw dropped. *What's she doing here?*

As she came through the gate near Kurt, she winked at him. She took her oath and mounted the witness stand.

"Ms. Butkus, is it true that you had a close, ahhh, business relationship with the defendant?"

"Oh, yes sir, very close. So close that –"

"Thank you, Ms. Butkus. Just answer the questions, please."

"Yes, sir." She smacked her gum and crossed her legs conspicuously. All the men in the courtroom pretended not to look through the railing in front of her.

"And during the time of your business relationship with Mr. Wilder, did he at any time mention or imply to you anything about collusive dealings with other large engineering and construction companies?"

"Collusive dealings? Oh, no sir, nothing like that. He never said anything collusive."

Kurt breathed a sigh of relief. *She's trying to help me. Poor bitch, she is going to jail for her lobbying hanky panky, and taking a few senators with her.*

The prosecutor held up a black notebook. "Ms. Butkus, do you recognize this?"

"Why sure," she said. "That's my insurance book."

"Would you care to elaborate?"

"Oh, it's nothing really." She slid her crossed thighs against each other under her skirt. Her face pouted with pleasure...

"Ms. Butkus? Ms. Butkus?" the prosecutor said, as he pulled on his snug white collar with his finger.

"Oh, oh, just little scraps of paper I keep for insurance."

"Insur ... insurance against what?" the prosecutor said, looking at her legs through the rail.

"Oh, you know," she said. "In case I get in trouble."

"You mean like you have been lately?"

"Yeah, like lately." Mable looked at Kurt. The blood started to drain out of his head.

"So what's in this notebook, Ms. Butkus?"

"A few papers signed by Mr. Wilder over there. Papers I was supposed to put in the shredder. I was a bad girl. I kept them for my insurance book. Good thing too, huh?"

"I think so, ma'am. Your Honor, ahhh, we'd like to enter into evidence Ms. Butkus's ... notebook ... The court will find that it contains memos signed by the defendant authorizing collusive arrangements on Federal contracts involving at least three competing companies. There are also documents in the notebook directly implicating Mr. Wilder in securities fraud relating to the financing of acquisitions of nine companies by Wilder Corp over the past five years."

"The notebook will be so entered into evidence as exhibit twenty-seven," Judge Jones said.

"Your witness," the prosecutor said, gesturing to Kurt's lead attorney.

"Does the defense wish to cross examine the witness?" Judge Jones said.

Kurt's lead attorney gave him a helpless look. "No, Your Honor."

"Then the witness is released," Judge Jones said.

"Thank you, Ms. Butkus," the prosecutor said. "You may step down now." He went to the witness stand and offered his hand to her. "You are free to go, ma'am."

"Oh, that's terrific," she said as she took his hand and stepped down daintily.

On the way out, she went up to the defense's table. She leaned way over to Kurt, giving him one last look down into her cleavage. Her cheek was next to his. He could smell her perfume. He could feel her energy tugging on him inside.

"So sorry, baby," she whispered. "I just can't stand the thought of jail. No men, ya know."

As he stared into her lush curvaceous canyon, he wondered for the first time if he had missed something vitally important in his life.

She stood up straight and popped a pink bubble. He jumped in his chair as it exploded like a cherry bomb inside him. She turned and swiveled through the gate. Kurt watched limply as the tight dark skirt undulated back up the aisle. All eyes were on her as she passed through the double doors and into the light.

After much grappling between the lawyers and the judge, a deal was struck. Kurt's sentence was set at five years in a minimum-security prison, with a chance for parole in two. He'd pay nearly fifty million in fines to the Federal Government. No one ever admitted that the money saved him from a much longer sentence.

He had ten days to report.

That night, Kurt sat at the big desk in the dimly lit study at Woodmere. His mood was whimsical. He floated somewhere between hate and love, somewhere between insanity and clarity. He doggedly pushed out the resonance of *i am* that was slowly creeping into his mind and body.

"Well, John, who's it gonna be, you or me?"

He spun the shiny chrome revolver on top of his desk like he was playing spin the bottle. He watched it going around and around, hard cold metal on the fine antique walnut. It stopped, pointing to the side. He looked at the empty chair on the other side of his desk.

"Looks like we both lucked out on that one, little brother. Wanna play again? Me too."

He spun the gun again. It went around like a top on the desk, finally stopping, pointing at the chair Kurt was talking to.

"Oops, you lose, John." He picked up the revolver, pointed it at the chair, and said, "Bang."

Then he threw it in the open briefcase next to him and shut the lid. He picked up the phone and poked three digits. Someone picked up. "Sid, call the airport and tell them to have the plane ready tomorrow morning. I'm going to Florida."

He hung up the phone. He was going to Coquina Island for the first time since his mother's funeral. *Why not? I've got ten days of freedom left. I may as well go see my family.*

He picked up the briefcase and sauntered toward the door of the study, straightening a few of the Royal Doulton figures on the end tables on the way.

Chapter 31 – Road Map

Christi was no ordinary toddler. There was a serenity about her – and a joy that defied description. She was inherently happy, and nothing seemed to distract her from that. John and Devi watched her play happily with her rag doll on the floor as they sat on the couch. John was seeing her as a play of his own consciousness, which amused him greatly. Each time she hugged her doll and giggled, he giggled with her. Devi saw Christi that way too, but was more connected to the world than John. Her motherly instincts were in full swing.

The close friends and leaders at the Coquina Dame who were gathered in John and Devi's living room were enjoying the radiant child too. A dozen people were packed into the main room of the master suite, filling the living room furniture and some chairs brought from the kitchen.

John finally turned his attention from Christi. "We asked you all here to see what you think about presenting the teachings in a more organized way."

"Do you mean putting restrictions on who can learn what, and when," Luke said. "A lot of people wouldn't like that."

"No," John said. "This is an open system of practices, to be used however people choose. But we can give recommendations to the people on the what and the when, and also in what order the practices work best. Then it's up to them."

"Isn't that what your talks are about?" Joy said.

"Yes, but I won't always be around for that."

"But we recorded them all," she said. "I hope you aren't going anywhere soon."

"The information is scattered among many talks," John said. "It's not easy to decipher it all. There are five different core practices and about a dozen concurrent practices, all interacting differently at the various levels of advancement. That is a lot to summarize for beginners, or for anyone. So we made a chart."

"A chart?" Harry said. "Now you are talking my language. Let's see it."

Devi slipped off the couch and went to a large poster board leaning face-in against the wall. She turned it face-out for all to see.

"*Wilder Open System of Spiritual Practices*," Harry read, squinting across the room. He came closer. "Okay, let's see, core practices: spinal breathing, breath suspensions, *i am* meditation, nine prayers, spiritual eye purges."

"Yes," Devi said, "across the top in the order done, and it's got all the concurrent practices going down the left side, like root seat, eye lift, secret chamber, and so on. The asterisks show what concurrent practices are performed with the core practices at different levels of advancement. It's got suggested practice times at the bottom for each of the five core practices at three levels of aggressiveness."

She looked up and grinned at everyone. "Any diehards here?" John's hand shot up.

Everyone laughed. "Now that's the understatement of the year," Devi rolled her eyes. "The chart's got everything on it but how to do the practices. They're all listed, showing how they relate to each other. That is what we are trying to make clear, the relationships of practices at different levels."

"Very cool," Melony said. "I could have used this five years ago."

"I could have used it ten years ago," John said. "That's why we are putting this together now, so no one will be lacking the overall framework."

"It appeals to my need for organization," Nadine said. "I'm not as far along as the rest of you, and I have sometimes wondered what to tackle next. I want to tackle it all, but I get overexposed sometimes. This is a great road map. Maybe I can relax a little, knowing better what comes next."

"Don't relax too much," John said. "Devotion drives everything, and real devotion never relaxes. But don't throw caution to the wind either." He pointed to the chart. "I hope this will help people build their practices, reduce some of the trial and error that we all have to go through sometimes. It shows how you can start with *i am* meditation twenty minutes twice each day. Very simple, very powerful, and then go on from there into spinal breathing, adding root seat along the way, and so on. Nothing is cast in stone, of course, but this is a guideline, an open system. All paths lead home."

"Those aggressive and diehard practice times look pretty intense," Henry said.

"They are just general guidelines. Times can be mixed and matched," Devi said. "The standard time for spinal breathing can go with the aggressive time for meditation, or vise versa, or any other time, for that matter. Some people may end up doing less than standard times if they are

Wilder Open System of Spiritual Practices

Core Practices Sequence* >	Spinal Breathing			Breath Suspensions			*i am* Meditation			Nine Prayers of *i am*			Spiritual Eye Purges		
Learning Sequence >	2nd			5th			1st			4th			3rd		
Level** >	B	I	A	B	I	A	B	I	A	B	I	A	B	I	A
Concurrent Practices															
Root Seat		*	*		*	*		*	*		*	*		*	*
Root Lift	*	*	*	*	*	*			*				*	*	*
Abdominal Lift		*	*	*	*	*			*				*	*	*
Eye Lift	*	*	*	*	*	*		*	*				*	*	*
Medulla Pull		*	*		*	*			*				*	*	*
Chin Lock				*											*
Chin Pump					*	*									
Palate Lift	*			*			*			*			*		
Secret Chamber Altar of Bliss		*			*			*	*		*	*		*	*
Secret Chamber Upper Passages			*			*									
i am's Embrace		*	*		*	*		*	*		*	*		*	*
Practice Times*															
Standard	5 min			5 min			20 min			10 min			3 min		
Aggressive	10 min			10 min			25 min			15 min			5 min		
Diehard	15 min			15 min			30 min			20 min			10 min		

Notes:
* Each cycle of core practices is preceded by spiritual stretching exercises, and followed by rest.
** Levels: **B** = Basic, **I** = Intermediate, **A** = Advanced
*** Practice times are twice per day. Periods of intense practice may include more cycles per day.

sensitive. Others may do more than the diehard times. Everyone has different inclinations.

"On going for less time in practices, just make sure not to leave out meditation completely after spinal breathing," John said. "That is weeds growing in a plowed and fertilized field, remember? Always do meditation, with or without spinal breathing, even if it is only a little."

"Yes, sir," Luke saluted with a giant hand.

"Ay ay, brother Luke." John picked up the rag doll lying across his foot and handed it tenderly to Christi, who sat peacefully on the floor in front of him. She seemed to be taking in all that was being said.

"Annie!" Christi chirped. Her bright green-rimmed blue eyes radiated love as her father placed the soft doll in her hands. She hugged it with both arms, rocking back and forth in her energy.

John looked up again. "As for intensity, everyone will know how much or how little they should be doing. Devotion drives us forward, and the body tells us how much we can handle, the never-ending balancing act. We have to press the vehicle forward according to our devotion, but *i am* is not best served by burning up the vehicle before we get there."

"Amen to that," Nadine said. "Sometimes when I'm going at it with practices I feel like my head is blowing off. Is it possible to have too much ecstasy?"

"Oh, yeah," John said. "Definitely, but that's no reason to abandon the journey. The energy can be regulated up or down by adjusting our practice times. That's how it is. That is how we play the game – always moving forward at a rate according to what we can handle."

"I'm hooked," Nadine said. "No way I'm backing off this."

Luke was examining the chart. "What's '*i am's* embrace,' brother John? Did you ever tell us about that one?"

"It's a new name for something we all are experiencing. It isn't a structured and timed practice like the others on the list. It is allowing the natural embrace of *i am* that comes during practices, and during the day too. You know, when everything is working together by itself automatically."

"Oh, I know what you mean," Luke said. "I didn't know what to call it when the spirit comes up and everything is lifting and squeezing quietly all by itself inside. And my eyes go up and I feel all hugged by God. *i am's* embrace. Oh yeah, what a great name."

"We put it on the chart, so people can recognize it as something that is happening, and allow it to happen. Most people would anyway. Right?"

"We'd be fools not to," Joy said. It's better than sex – 'cept of course with you, honey." She rubbed her bare foot up Luke's leg.

Everyone laughed.

"Now comes the hard part," John said. "The proverbial good news and bad news."

Everyone let out a collective, "Huh?"

John gave Devi a look of resigned commitment to what must happen. She nodded with her eyes.

"We've been invited to go on national television – *Herb Hyatt's Night Time Live Show*."

"Oh God," Ted said. "Millions watch that show."

"Yeah," Devi said. "Isn't it wonderful? We are making a difference here, and they noticed us out there in Hollywood."

"That's the good news," John said. "The bad news is we are not prepared to handle the response this show could produce. We have to send people out to all the major cities to teach the practices. Do we have enough knowledgeable people to do this?"

"We have enough to teach *i am* meditation and spinal breathing, if we have people traveling from city to city," Luke said. "We will have to make plans. We will have to train more. That's a tall order you got there."

"Yeah," John said. "I know. You'll have to gear up to whatever the demand ends up being. And will you have someone organize all the tapes by subject and get them copied so they can be distributed? They can be used to help train more teachers and also used by the teachers when they are with new students."

"Sure," Luke said. "We'll get it all together. What about you? After *Night Time Live*, everybody is gonna want you even more than now."

"Yes," said John. "I will have to go into a completely different mode to cover it all. It's all going to change." He paused... "You are all so precious to me. Many challenges lie ahead. I will always be with you. Always."

Devi turned and looked over at John with concern on her face. There was silence in the room.

John glanced around a little uneasily. "There's one more thing. I'd like Devi and Luke to take charge of publishing all my notes. That is a complete record of all I have gone through since the beginning."

Luke turned on the kitchen chair barely visible beneath him. "You mean all those three-ring notebooks you've been keeping since high school?"

"Yes, all those. I think it is time for everyone to have them."

Luke rested his chin on his hand like the great thinker statue. "You plannin' on goin' somewhere, brother John? This all sure looks like a road map you are leaving us for after you're gone."

There was a moment of silence. John's eyes filled with tears. "I love you, Luke … I love all of you." He turned his head slowly, looking at each of them as though they were the only one in the room with him. "A big change is coming. Please carry on the work, no matter what, okay?"

Everyone gave their unwavering unspoken promise with their eyes. John nodded and got up. He walked unsteadily out of the room. All eyes followed him. No one said anything, but they all were thinking the same thing: *What is going to happen to John?*

Everyone had gone back to their rooms in the Coquina Dame. John and Devi tucked Christi in, and she was soon sleeping blissfully in her crib. They cleaned up the kitchen and went in the bedroom.

He was still unsteady. He shed his clothes and fell on the bed lightly. She could see he was in one of those states where he was barely in his body. She pulled her shirt over her head and then let her muslin pants drop to the floor. She threw her bra on the chair in the corner. She lay on the bed next to him on her back and pulled her panties off, flinging them off the end of the bed with her foot. She felt the air from the ceiling fan caressing her body. It made her inner lights swirl in beautiful patterns. She turned her head to John. He was lying on his back with his eyes way up. He was somewhere else. She rolled over halfway on him, putting her leg over his thighs, and kissed his chest. She laid her head on his shoulder, gazing into his face. He brought his eyes down and looked into her inquiring eyes.

"Oh, those eyes," he said. "I love you, my darling. I always will."

"You're making me a little nervous with this 'It's all going to change' talk."

"I'm sorry," he said. "I know it isn't easy for you. It isn't for me either."

"What isn't easy?"

"What's happening," he said.

"Oh yeah, we're going to be huge celebrities. I can't wait." She grimaced. "You know, this means the paparazzi will be hounding us all the time."

"I don't mean that."

"No? What then?"

"The outer stuff is just a reflection of the inner changes."

"Yeah?"

"I am neither here nor there right now," he said. "Neither fish nor fowl."

"What are you becoming?"

"Spirit, the spirit of *i am* in all. This body will dissolve soon."

"No!" She sat up. "John, you are a husband and a father. We need you."

"I can't help it. I will be here in a different way. It is best for everyone. It is the only way *i am* can continue to expand in the world. I have no control over it. It is where I must go. It is where the world must go."

She was welling up with tears. "But how will I hold you in my arms? How will your daughter know your touch?"

"Christi knows my touch in every moment, and you know I am with you always, my love."

"Oh God, when?"

"Soon," he said.

His body appeared transparent to her then. She could see through him like he was dissolving into light before her eyes. She ran her hand softly over the hair on his chest, brushing the crystal cross. It cast rainbows on the ceiling as the light shimmered out from him. It felt like her hand could go through him.

"It's all right, sweetheart," he said. "It is for the best." He caressed her hair softly with his luminous fingers.

She lay with him for hours, trembling in his light and in her fear of losing him, until she finally fell asleep.

Early in the morning they joined in corporal lovemaking for the last time, tearfully embraced in each other's arms until dawn.

Chapter 32 – Transition

The jet touched down in Jacksonville and made its way to the corporate hanger. The crew pulled down the door and Kurt came down the steps.

"Good morning, Mr. Wilder," the manager of airport corporate relations said. "We, ahh…"

"Didn't expect to see me here today? Well, surprise. But don't worry, this will be the last time for a while."

He got behind the wheel of the Wilder Corp Mercedes that was waiting for him and screeched across the tarmac heading for Coquina Island.

John was on the beach, alone. It had been years since he'd wandered the beach by himself. He meandered slowly along the shore for some distance south of the Wilder house. The water felt good between his toes as it lapped gently up on the beach. The coquinas were on their journey up as the tide came in.

John, Devi and Christi were visiting Harry for lunch. Nadine came over too. He left everyone inside. He wanted some time alone on the beach. He wanted to savor years long gone one last time. Harry said Kurt was coming to visit before going off to prison. John hadn't seen or spoken with him for two years. He wondered if Kurt had been changed by his recent experiences. What would it take to break *i am* loose in him? John hoped the hard times might help Kurt focus on things of lasting value. *i am has its mysterious ways of bringing everyone home – it is inevitable. It's never easy for anyone. The human journey is often a painful one, but ultimately a fruitful one.*

John jogged the last mile north up the beach toward the house. It was effortless. He glided quickly across the wet sand. He was no longer in a hurry. All was as it should be. His legs skimmed across the shallow water coming up with the rising tide. It splashed up around his white trunks. The sun felt good on his bare back.

He came up the walkway leading through the dunes to the house. He started up the stairs leading to the veranda.

"Hey, dreamer, where you been?"

The voice sounded the same as it did so many times all those years ago. He looked up at the figure dressed in black standing halfway up the stairs, with one arm on each rail.

"Hi, Kurt."

"It'll cost you a buck to get through."

John sat down on the step in front of Kurt and looked back out to the surf. "I'm broke, you know. I'm at your mercy again."

John heard a click. He turned and looked up. Kurt had the shiny pistol cocked and was pointing it at John's head, less than two feet away.

"I never thought it would come to this," Kurt said.

John looked out to the shimmering sea again. "Oh, Kurt, it's been a tough ride, hasn't it? We've both struggled for the things we love, and here we are, right back where we started."

John was silent for a few seconds, deep in *i am*. Then he looked back up at Kurt, who was about to pull the trigger.

"I have to go, you know," John said. "But not like this. Not at your expense." He lifted his hand up toward the gun, briefly touching the tip of it with his index finger. A visible light went up the barrel, up Kurt's arm and into his chest. The air went out of Kurt and the gun wavered. He breathed in deeply, holding his aim on John. His hand began to tremble. John touched the tip of the gun again and another wave when up into Kurt. The gun came down with Kurt's shaking arm. It fell out of his hand, clattering onto the wooden step John was sitting on. John glanced at it, and it disappeared.

John got up and went up onto Kurt's step. Kurt was undone, quivering, confused. John took Kurt in his arms and held him close. Kurt began to shake uncontrollably, slowly lifting his shaking arms around John. Then he was sobbing with his head bowed down on John's bare shoulder.

"Oh John, Oh John, I'm so sorry..." His voice went in great heaves of breath, as he was being purged of a huge burden.

"It's all right," John gently hugged Kurt. "Everything is going to be all right now."

They stood there for a few minutes, sharing what never could be shared before. Their paths as brothers in spirit finally crossed for the first time. The dysfunctions of flesh and blood were transcended.

"Come on," John said, "Let's go see the family."

"I'm so ashamed."

"Come on." John led him up the stairs. "I know everyone wants to see you. Nadine's here too."

Chapter 33 – For the World

John dozed in the back of the limousine. His consciousness surged far beyond his body, across seas and galaxies. His body was a trembling, fading shell of who he had been.

"Look, dear, it's Tinsel Town," Devi's sweet voice echoed through his infinite spaces. She put her hand on his arm gently. "Are you all right, John? We don't have to do this, you know."

He reached up and touched her hand. He opened his eyes, seeing her concerned gaze. He smiled into her eyes, and then looked beyond her out the car window. Sleek mirrored high-rise buildings went up all around them into the hot, hazy late afternoon Los Angeles sky. He turned back to Devi. "Yes, we have to do this. It has all been leading here. So this is Hollywood?"

"Yeah, welcome to the big time, tiger."

"Just help me carry this body to the stage, and it will be all right."

"Anything, my dear. Anything for you." She looked away and bit her lip. Then she turned back to him with large moistened eyes, her voice cracking a little. "Well, honey, you know, it's too late to chicken out now. Here's Hyatt Studios."

He looked out just as they drove into the dark parking tunnel leading under the tall shiny building.

"Swallowed by the beast," he sighed.

"Yeah," she said. "God help us."

"Now, just be yourself," Nancy Harmon said. "Follow Herb's lead. I'll be up in the control booth."

John was looking around the backstage area and up in the air in front of him.

"Are you all right, John?" Nancy said.

"For the moment," he said, turning to gaze into her eyes.

She caught her breath as ecstatic energy shot up through her. She patted her brown curly hair nervously. "Well, um, that's good, John. Listen… Oh, here comes Herb – Herb! Herb!"

Herb Hyatt came striding up. He was a buoyant intense man who had turned his gift for ironic comedy and a flare for live drama into a highly successful live night time talk show, beamed simultaneously across four time zones to the nation five nights a week. Other than sporting events and news, *Herb Hyatt's Night Time Live* was the only truly live show left on television. All the competition was pre-taped. Live broadcasting was a risky business. Anything could go wrong, and often it did, which added to the show's appeal. Audiences loved the unpredictability of *Night Time Live*.

"John! Devi! How nice to meet you. Are you ready to drop in and visit all of America?"

"Why not?" Devi bobbed up and down with Herb's fast enthusiastic handshake.

"That's the spirit," Herb said. "I'll tell you a little secret" He was pressing down on the Band-Aid on the back of his right hand. "I get nervous every time I do this. It's normal. I mean, who does live TV these days? Once we're on, you'll feel right at home. I guarantee it. Just follow my lead."

"Nice to meet you, Mr. Hyatt," John said as Herb grabbed his hand and tried to shake it.

No matter how Herb tried to make it go fast, the handshake was slow and relaxed. When Herb finally got loose from John, his hand had a glow on it that was creeping up his arm. He tried to shake it off, but it went into him. His eyes went quiet and he became noticeably less frantic.

Devi grinned in a knowing way at wide-eyed Nancy.

Herb shook himself. "Ahhh, well, I guess I better go get made up. Looking forward to seeing you both on stage in a while – Live!" He pointed both hands at them like pistols as he retreated.

Herb sat in front of the dressing room mirror combing his mustache. He looked in the mirror at Nancy standing behind him with her clipboard.

"Who the hell are these people," he said into the glass. "That John Wilder is a sorcerer or something. Do you see what he did to my arm? It's still tingling." He pulled the Band-Aid off the back of his hand. "Remember the cut I got here yesterday? Now it's gone. My chest is all – goosey. Where did you find this pair?"

Nancy looked at his hand, nodding. "They're healers, Herbie. Spiritual teachers from Florida. Very popular down there. If you'd read the script ahead of time like you're supposed to, you'd know that. John Wilder is a miracle worker. I think the audience will like them. I'm the producer. It's my job to find interesting guests, remember?"

"Yeah, well, I hope it turns out better than the damn cockfighters you brought in here from Georgia last year. I've still got the scars on the back of my legs from being chased around the stage by that lunatic rooster."

"I don't think you'll be disappointed, Herbie. You remember that stir about ten years ago about the so-called fastest man alive? The kid who ran a three and a half minute mile at a high school track meet and then disappeared?"

"Yeah?"

"And no one could ever get near him, and he never ran again?"

"Yeah. So what?"

"It was John Wilder."

"You're shitting me."

"And now he's on *Night Time Live*."

"Why didn't you tell me?"

"We are live and spontaneous, remember? You just don't know who's going to walk out on that stage, do you, Herbie? Of course, if you'd read the damn script ahead of time, you would."

"I love you, Nancy."

Herb straightened his toupee and went out, happily rubbing his hands together. He shook the hand John had healed and a few flecks of sparkling light shot from it. "Jesus Christ! What are we in for tonight?" He hustled down the hall toward the stage entrance like a big runaway scarecrow, shaking his arm all the way.

The cameras were trained on the stage and the audience. The music came up. Nancy sat in anticipation at the console in the control booth with two technicians, as she had hundreds of times before. Herb came prancing out on the stage and the music climaxed. The audience cheered enthusiastically on command. Herb waited patiently, rubbing his hands together, until their scripted outburst was spent.

"Hello, ladies and gentlemen. Welcome to *Night Time Live*, direct from Hollywood!" Herb checked the cue screen, expertly concealing it from the cameras with his panning glances and body movements. "We have special guests here for you tonight all the way from exotic Coquina Island, Florida."

Applause...

Cheers erupted inside the Coquina Dame Hotel. It was eleven PM, and a few hundred people were up to see John and Devi on national television. A projection TV was set up in the ballroom, and it was happening live on the big screen in front where John and Devi usually sat.

At the Wilder house, Harry sat watching on the couch, with Christi asleep in his lap. Kurt was there with Nadine. He'd decided to spend his last few days of freedom at his father's house, hoping to heal as many old wounds as he could before leaving for white-collar prison.

Across the continent, millions in an overworked nation tuned in for a little relief. *Herb Hyatt's Night Time Live* offered an escape into the spontaneous and unusual. Anything to break the monotony. *Coquina Island, Florida? Where's that?*

There was excitement in the studio. In the control room, Nancy was watching the monitor closely.

"Yes, ladies and gentlemen," Herb bellowed enthusiastically. "We are going to hear some secrets tonight. John and Devi Wilder are here to share a few of *The Secrets of Wilder*. I have a few secrets too, but you won't hear any of them here."

Laughter...

"Some say the Wilders are on the leading edge of a second coming in America, a new age. My wife will be glad to hear it. She has been asking me about a second coming every night for years. I tell her, 'What's the matter, the first coming isn't good enough for you?'"

The audience roared ... Nancy rolled her eyes up in the control booth. *That wasn't in the script! Nice one, Herbie ... Liz'll love it. Anything for ratings.*

"So, let's see what Coquina Island, Florida is bringing us tonight, folks. Let's welcome John and Devi Wilder!"

The audience cheered on cue, and John and Devi walked out on the stage hand in hand. Devi was leading, smiling, and John was trailing behind her, looking distracted. She was in light blue slacks with a pretty flowered blouse. Her shiny black hair hung over her shoulders. He was wearing beige pants with a dark blue silk shirt, open at the collar. The silver chain hanging inside his shirt glinted into the camera when the lights hit it. They both had on sandals.

Herb gave Devi a big hug, like he had known her all her life. He almost went to shake John's hand, but thought better of it. John and Devi sat on the broad sofa next to Herb's desk. Herb sat behind the desk and propped his elbows on it. He smiled. Devi smiled. John, in the middle, seemed to be looking up toward the control booth. That's what it looked like to Nancy. She got shivers up her spine seeing him looking toward her from way down there, and again seeing him up close on the monitor in front of her with his eyes raised up. She adjusted her headset. *Who is this John Wilder?*

The audience settled down.

"First," Herb said, "I wonder if we could cover some old business. Ten years ago a young man ran a three and a half minute mile at a Florida high school State championship track meet. He never ran again, and no one has ever been able to ask him on the record how he did it. Is it true you are the mysterious so-called fastest man alive?"

John slowly turned his head to Herb. "Yes, that was me."

"How did you do it? And why didn't you ever run again? It would have been a sure gold medal at the Olympics."

John looked up again. He seemed to be having trouble concentrating.

"John?" Herb said.

Devi softly touched his arm. His eyes came down again. "It was an aberration. I was doing research on spiritual practices at the time, putting the pieces together, and I was out of balance. The energies coming up through me had no place to go, so I ran. That's how it happened."

"Could you do it again?"

"Probably," John said. "But why?"

"Well the Olympics for one – "

"We've got much bigger fish to fry," John said. "We all do. Physical athletics are great, but there is a much bigger kind of athletics."

"Really?" Herb said. "What kind of athletics?"

"Spiritual athletics," John said. "In spiritual athletics everyone wins no matter who's running. No losers."

"Hmmm, well, I see you've gotten us over to the subject we all want to hear about – your secrets. We'll take a short break and be right back." Herb looked straight into the camera with the red light on top. "Don't go away all you wonderful folks. *The Secrets of Wilder* are next up."

The audience applauded on cue, the music came up, and they were off the air for few minutes. Herb slumped back in his chair. Nancy was buzzing in his ear-piece. "Get to the miracles, Herbie. Get to the miracles!"

He nodded up toward the booth. "Way to go, John," he said. "You handled that like a pro."

John was distracted again. It was as though he was looking at something in the air above him. Devi glanced up occasionally with a concerned look. Nancy was watching them closely on the monitor in the control booth. She could tell they both could see it, whatever it was. It was overwhelming John, and making Devi concerned.

Lights started flashing. A voice rang out, "Coming back on the air! And five, four, three, two..."

"Welcome back ladies and gentlemen," Herb said with his arms spread wide open over his desk. "We're here with John and Devi Wilder. So, what are *The Secrets of Wilder,* John?"

John was still distracted. He didn't say anything. Herb waited, sensing the moment. A strange hush hung over the set. Fifteen seconds went by. It seemed like an eternity.

Come on ... Nancy was squirming in the booth. Then Devi moved. She turned and softly put her hand on John's thigh.

He came to life, swinging his gaze around onto Herb. "The secrets of you, Herb." He turned and pointed at a young couple in the front row of the audience, "And you..." And then at a group of teenagers in the top row, "And you up there..." He waved his arm across the entire audience, sending out a luminescence that could barely be seen and easily felt. "All of you..." Then he looked straight into the camera in front of the stage with the red light lit on top, piercing through the lens with his eyes. "And all of you watching here tonight. These are your secrets, your truths." Then he stopped and put his hand on Devi's, still resting on his thigh.

Nancy was breathless. She could see a soft white light lingering in the studio. *Jesus.*

"Um, John, but what are the secrets?" Herb said. He could see the glow. He knew that John had grabbed the audience. Now he just had to keep him going, and this show would run itself, maybe right into the history books.

John took Devi's hand in both of his and looked into the camera. "You see, we are all born of a vibration in the silence within us. This vibrating silence is the infinite One, and it is our consciousness. Each of us is like a window with different patterns painted on it. We each have natural abilities to clean off our windows, enabling us to recognize ourselves inside as blissfully vibrating silence, and enabling the divine vibration to come out into the world."

"Is it God you are talking about?" Herb asked.

"Yes, the sacred vibration in silence is the oneness of God. The vibration is *i am*. If we meditate on *i am* in a particular way deep within, our window gets cleaned. This is one of the secrets. It is a practice. Another great secret is hidden in our desire."

"Desire?" Herb rested the side of his head on his hand with his elbow on the desk.

"Yes, it is our wanting that opens the way to all the secrets. Without wanting, there is no practice, and no opening. Ultimately, all desires are desires for God. All actions seek God. It is a matter of focusing desires and actions directly into practices. Blessed are those that hunger and thirst."

"Oh, we've all heard that one," Herb said. "Listen, is it true you can do miracles? And you, Devi?"

John ignored the question. "Hunger for God is the greatest secret. *i am* meditation is next. There are many more methods that can help open each of us to our divine destiny. Taken together, all the practices are *The Secrets of Wilder*. They are also referred to as an open system of practices, freely available for anyone to investigate and use. We are in the beginning stages of a new science, spiritual science. Great things will be happening on the earth."

"But the miracles," Herb said. "John? Devi? Can you help me out, we are running out of time."

John shrugged, and patted Devi's hand. "Would you like to show them something, sweetheart?"

"Oh, you're making me go first?"

A few people in the front row of the audience snickered. Devi smiled at them. "Thanks a lot. The whole world wants me to do a miracle and you gotta snicker at me. Hey, I'm nervous up here."

The audience roared...

She looked at Herb, and then out into the audience. "He's the miracle man. I'm just the sorcerer's apprentice."

More laughter...

"Okay, okay..." Devi sat back on the couch. She opened her mouth slightly and something moved deep inside. Her eyes went up. After a few seconds, she floated up off the sofa a few inches.

The audience gasped.

John swung her out in front of him by the hand he held and he floated up off the sofa too. He took her other hand like he did when they had danced in the air so many times before. They came together in an embrace floating a few feet above the stage and then went up slowly, up between the beams and lights above the stage. The camera lost them. Herb was left alone on the stage gazing upward while the camera went looking around in the steel rafters for the departed couple.

The audience broke out in pandemonium, standing and cheering wildly. A few were running out of the studio, while others looked up in silent awe at the couple floating high above the set.

Herb looked straight up in disbelief as John and Devi hung there. Nancy was frantic in the booth. "Get camera three pointed up there!" she barked. *Holy Christ, what's going on here? This is out of control. We need a commercial.* "We need a commercial, Herbie! Commercial! Commercial!" she yelled into his ear-piece. He shook his head.

John and Devi were coming back down slowly in their graceful turning dance. She had one leg gracefully wrapped around him like a ballet dancer. She leaned her head back as they came circling down. Her shining black hair floated in the air behind her. They landed softly in front of Herb's desk and went and sat down.

Devi looked quietly at the audience and the camera. "Was that okay?"

Cheers erupted again ... it took more than a minute for everyone to finally settle down, even with Herb giving the palms down signal.

"It was more than adequate for me," Herb said, clearing his throat. "But some of our viewers will think we are playing tricks on them."

"Oh, I see," Devi said. "Well, I'm sure those who are interested will follow up. There are many possibilities in all of us."

"Yes, they are everyone's secrets," John said. He leaned over toward Herb and tapped him on the chest.

Herb wheezed as the air rushed out of him. Then he gasped in air and went up in the air, arms and legs flailing. He floated down and landed softly in the middle of his desk, where he sat in a trace-like state for a few seconds.

"See?" John said. "You can do it."

The audience was cheering and laughing uncontrollably again, off cue. They were cheering and laughing on Coquina Island uncontrollably too, and in living rooms across the nation.

"My God, I can't believe this," Herb yelled over the crowd, floundering down from the top of his desk. He looked disoriented. He looked into the camera. "Honest, folks, I don't know how this is being done. We'll be back after a commercial break..."

The set was in chaos. Nancy broke down crying in the control booth. The spiritual energy was increasing dramatically in the studio and everyone could feel it. Viewers were tuning in across the nation as people were calling their friends and relatives during the commercial break, telling them to turn on *Night Time Live* right now!

John and Devi sat quietly on the sofa during the break. John was falling into one of his translucent light episodes. He kicked off his sandals and went into root seat. Devi held his hand attentively. The studio audience murmured as they watched John beginning to glow on the stage. Nancy, recovering herself, could see it on the monitor. She tapped the screen. She looked out the window of the control booth and could see white light emanating from John down on the stage. In addition to the light radiating in all directions from John, a much brighter white cup-shaped light had formed on top of his head, like a brilliant crown. It was the size of a salad bowl, and was growing.

"What's happening?" Herb said. "We're back on the air in thirty seconds."

"He's having a spell," Devi said. "They usually pass."

John was nearly incoherent.

"John, John, can you hear me," she said.

"Uh, yes, dear," His voice was distant. "I am with you always, my love." His eyes were way up high.

"John? John?" she said. He didn't reply. Her tears welled up.

"We're coming back on the air," Herb said. "Is that okay?"

Devi nodded tearfully. "He wants this. We're here for this."

"Okay, we're back," Herb said. "Well, we've regrouped here ladies and gentlemen, and I honestly can't tell you what's next. John is not feeling well right now."

The camera revealed the light, now radiating profusely from John. And it kept increasing. The brilliant crown on top of his head filled the stage over them. Herb retreated to the other end of his desk. As everyone watched, the light emanating from John became brighter than a spotlight, shining in all directions. It seemed to be fed by an intense beam coming down through the center of the expanding crown. The whole studio was illuminated and the light was beginning to penetrate out through the walls of the building. From high above, the Hyatt Studios building bloomed like a giant flower on the Los Angeles landscape. The bright white light filled the night sky, expanding upward and outward.

Inside, most in the audience were shielding their eyes. Nancy could still see John close-up in the monitor with the profuse white light going out all around him. He was looking up into the intense white beam of white light coming down into him from directly above, through the center of the vast blazing crown. It illuminated his spine, which was visible as a pillar of blinding white light. Nancy could see Devi buried in the light with her hands on John's knee, her head bowed in surrender to what was happening. Viewers on Coquina Island, and everywhere, gasped at what they were seeing on television.

Then it happened.

A huge flash like an atomic explosion burst where John sat. A shock wave of blinding white light went out in all directions faster than lightning. It engulfed the State of California, the West, the Rocky Mountains, the Midwest and the East in seconds. The people at the Dame on Coquina Island felt it flash through them and shoot out to sea. It went across the Atlantic, Europe, Africa and the Middle East. At the same time, it went west from California across the Pacific, flashing over the Pacific islands and through Asia, Indonesia and Australia. It went north through Canada and south through Central and South America to the poles of the earth, and around the other side. The living white light met itself on the other side of the earth in the middle of the Indian Ocean, and its journey was complete. In less than ten seconds, the world was swallowed by the great spiritual explosion. Everyone on the earth could see it. Everyone on the earth could feel it. After a few minutes, the intensity of the light began to fade, leaving a residual glow in everything. *i am* became permanently perceptible in all of humanity as omnipresent silent bliss and a perennial hunger for truth. It was John's gift to the world.

In the studio, at ground zero, everyone was in a state of shock. The great white light that had come from John was slowly fading to a faint glow. Nancy got up off the floor of the control booth. The cameras were still running. Somehow they were still on the air. She looked at the monitor and could see Devi hunched over on the sofa where John had been sitting. Herb was stirring on the floor where he lay at the other end of the desk.

There was no sign of John. Nancy watched with the nation as Devi slowly sat up. She was crying. In her hands were John's clothes – his blue silk shirt and beige pants.

Something fell out of the clothes onto the sofa. It sent a flash of light into the camera. The camera zoomed in. It was a crystal cross on a silver chain. Devi picked it up and held it tenderly to her breast. The camera zoomed out slowly on the cross and focused on the beautiful Indian woman weeping alone on the sofa. The picture gradually faded to black.

Chapter 34 – Ascending

No one fully grasped the consequences of what had happened on *Herb Hyatt's Night Time Live*. All that Devi and everyone on Coquina Island knew was that John was gone, apparently by divine ascension, and that a delicate blissful presence remained with them. They did not know yet that the divine presence was being felt throughout the world as inner bliss and a rising hunger in millions to take up their own God quest.

Though Devi felt John as the greatly strengthened *i am* within her, she missed his physical presence intensely. She would not find herself fully at peace in his arms again until her own ascension many years later. Until then, she settled deeply into the silent bliss of him within her, always radiating peace and love to all. She devoted herself to raising their beautiful Christi and to the work that John started, becoming the leading exponent of the knowledge he discovered and gave freely to everyone he encountered. She and Luke oversaw the publication of all of John's writings in five thick volumes under the title John had written on the first blue-lined page in his three-ring notebook all those years ago: *The Secrets of Wilder.*

Harry Wilder stayed active in the work, supervising the restoration of numerous facilities across the nation and overseas. Many were like the Coquina Dame Hotel, grand old resorts that had been lost in time, and reborn to a divine purpose.

Nadine visited Kurt regularly at the Miami Lakes Minimum Security Federal Prison. They remarried when he was released. Though the doctors had said she could never have children, Nadine gave birth to twin boys a few years later. They devoted their lives to their practices, to raising their boys and to the work John started.

Luke and Joy continued full time in leadership positions in the work. Their first child, a lovely girl, was born a year after John's ascension. A few years later they had a boy.

Others from the original Coquina Island meditation group, Blue Ridge Hollow, and the early days at the Coquina Dame Hotel went on supporting the work all their lives. John's wish came true, as thousands were given the means to teach the spiritual practices to anyone who wished to learn them. The teachers fanned out across the globe. Tens of millions of people around the world benefited directly from the practices in the decades that followed, and no one on the earth was without the uplifting effects.

Spiritual science advanced rapidly through the ongoing cooperative efforts of dedicated pioneers, practitioners, researchers and educators everywhere. The rigid boundaries that had divided the sacred knowledge of human spiritual transformation for centuries gradually dissolved.

It was a sunny autumn morning on Coquina Island. Devi was in root seat on the wicker sofa on the balcony of the Coquina Dame master suite. She had her arms gently around Christi who sat lightly in her lap. The warm ocean wind caressed their faces.

The prominent dunes below guarded the coastline. The tall sea oats blew like soft hair over the great mounds. The surf roared beyond, as huge waves thundered in from the outer break. A light sparkling mist hung over the white foam. A hurricane was passing by two hundred miles out, whirling northward toward the Carolina Outer Banks.

Devi's tongue slid up. Her eyes went high to her inner brightness. Her inner star blazed in the shape of a brilliant cross. Her chin made a few rotations down toward the hollow of her throat. She was permeated with a profound presence. *Oh, my darling husband...*

Minutes passed.

"Mama, look," Christi said.

Devi slowly opened her eyes. Every cell in her was soaked in the silent love of tender vibrating *i am.*

"There..." Christi waved her small hand north along the line of dunes. "And there..." She extended her hand to the south.

They were going up, a vast surge of new life rising from the pregnant dunes as far as Christi and Devi could see. Thousands of butterflies filled the sparkling spirit sky up and down the Florida coast, each one fluttering away on great golden wings.

As they ascended, Christi began to glow with a soft white light and floated a little off her mother's lap ... Her eyes were wide with joy…

Also by the Author

Yogani is an American spiritual scientist who, for more than thirty years, has been integrating ancient techniques from around the world which cultivate human spiritual transformation. The approach he has developed is non-sectarian, and open to all. He has also written:

Advanced Yoga Practices – Easy Lessons for Ecstatic Living

This large book provides detailed instructions on all the practices in *The Secrets of Wilder*, including many enhancements and additions.

For more information on the writings of Yogani, please visit:

www.advancedyogapractices.com

Printed in the United States
31587LVS00004B/220